A Stranger in the Third Reich

Ruth Bohle

Copyright © 2001 by Ruth Bohle.

Library of Congress Number:		2001118439
ISBN #:	Hardcover	1-4010-2748-2
	Softcover	1-4010-2747-4

All rights reserved. No part of this book may be reproduced or transmitted in any form or by any means, electronic or mechanical, including photocopying, recording, or by any information storage and retrieval system, without permission in writing from the copyright owner.

This book was printed in the United States of America.

To order additional copies of this book, contact:
Xlibris Corporation
1-888-7-XLIBRIS
www.Xlibris.com
Orders@Xlibris.com

CONTENTS

CHAPTER 1
Beginnings 9
CHAPTER 2
The Girl Who Never Grew Up 15
CHAPTER 3
A Dream Realized 19
CHAPTER 4
To Germany and My Future 27
CHAPTER 5
Married at Last 37
CHAPTER 6
Newlyweds 45
CHAPTER 7
And Baby Makes Three 53
CHAPTER 8
Birth, Death and the Growing 60
CHAPTER 9
A Home in Berlin 74
CHAPTER 10
A Last Interlude 84
CHAPTER 11
Premonitions of War 99
CHAPTER 12
The War Begins 109
CHAPTER 13
The "Blitzkrieg" Becomes the "Sitzkrieg" 122
CHAPTER 14
Terror from Above 130
CHAPTER 15
The Struggle to Stay Warm 133
CHAPTER 16
Assignment: Poland 141

CHAPTER 17
  Together in Enemy Territory 148
CHAPTER 18
  A Refuge in the Black Forest 162
CHAPTER 19
  A Brief Family Reunion 169
CHAPTER 20
  Posen Again 178
CHAPTER 21
  A Respite from War Worries 184
CHAPTER 22
  Shuttling Between Posen and the Black Forest 192
CHAPTER 23
  An Aborted Return to Berlin 206
CHAPTER 24
  Together Again in Berlin 216
CHAPTER 25
  The Family Moves to Posen 223
CHAPTER 26
  An Interlude in the Country 237
CHAPTER 27
  Hans Becomes a Soldier 252
CHAPTER 28
  Destination: The Russian Front 261
CHAPTER 29
  My Wounded Soldier Fights for Life 272
CHAPTER 30
  Allied Bombs Blast Posen 295
CHAPTER 31
  A Slow But Steady Recovery 303
CHAPTER 32
  Hans Comes Home 320
CHAPTER 33
  We Flee Approaching Russian Tanks 325

CHAPTER 34
　Our Final Farewell to Berlin 338
CHAPTER 35
　A Refuge with Family in Hamburg 346
CHAPTER 36
　An Improvised Home in Rahlstedt 366
CHAPTER 37
　An End to Hitler and the War! 383
CHAPTER 38
　Living Under Allied Occupation 389
CHAPTER 39
　The Journey to Bremen 400
CHAPTER 40
　An Adventurous Return to Hamburg 413
CHAPTER 41
　A Message from Home 433
CHAPTER 42
　Searching for Lost Loves 446
CHAPTER 43
　Charges Against Hans 455
CHAPTER 44
　Vindication and Reinstatement 461
CHAPTER 45
　A Hazardous Trip and Poignant Farewells 465
CHAPTER 46
　The Lady with the Torch 491
CHAPTER 47
　Home Again in Chicago 496
CHAPTER 48
　Westward Ho 502
CHAPTER 49
　Together in California 510

CHAPTER 1

Beginnings

"What are you doing with that book?" my father questioned, taking the volume from my hands. "It's not fit for the eyes or mind of a 10-year-old."

I've long since forgotten the title and author of that small volume, but not the feelings it created in me. It was a wonderful story of tender and gentle love between a man and his lady.

My innate romanticism awakened, I reflected for days on the book's vivid images. Finally, my emotions crystallized into a secret resolution. I, too, would know that kind of love one day. Through the years I held unequivocally to that vow.

My mind held no thoughts of the future, however, as I stood in silence, stunned by the anger of my beloved father. Since earliest childhood, I had adored and obeyed him without question. Why did my innocent exploration trigger such a reaction, when his own relationship with my mother exemplified just such a love?

Unknowingly, I had broken my father's strict moral code. Deep religious faith had become the central focus of my parents' lives, and my father believed it his duty to protect his only daughter from the corrupting influences of a sinful world.

Church first brought my parents together. In 1890, at the age of 18, my father had journeyed from Hamburg, Germany to the U.S.A. to represent his employer at the Chicago World's Fair. Unusually devout, he and his family belonged to a small Baptist sect.

On arriving in Chicago, father naturally sought out a similar congregation—the only one in the city—on Paulina Street, the pastor, Rev. Jacob Meier, also from Germany.

Father was soon an active, enthusiastic member of the congregation. He also met and fell in love with the pastor's daughter, Mary, a young widow with a small daughter named Maria. He often said with great amusement that it took three proposals before she consented to marry him.

He became a sales representative for a wholesale coal company and the new couple settled into married life in Chicago. Two years later, I arrived in the Kuechler household.

My first childhood memory stems from the death of Maria, who contracted tuberculosis. I remember the great sadness I felt at not finding my sister and playmate one morning. I sat in a swing my father had erected in the kitchen, calling for Maria in plaintive tones while my mother stood nearby, ironing, the tears streaming down her face. Perhaps the loss of his stepdaughter at such an early age helped make my father overprotective of me in later years.

* * *

And so until my two brothers arrived some years later, I was an only child, accustomed to prompt obedience and eating what was set before me. Each night found me in bed exactly at 8 p.m., hoping to hear my mother practice. The piano music lofted from the living room to my bedroom.

Regardless of wind or weather, Sunday meant church for most of the day. We lived some distance away, and walked to church since we owned no car. Father, always a little late, hurried too quickly for my young legs to follow. How I dreaded the long walk—frigid in winter and sweltering in summer—that left me breathless for the entire morning.

Father led the singing in Sunday School, which was followed by the church service. Mother was the official organist and played the great pipe organ. Many of her preludes to the morning service were by Bach, her favorite composer. The large sanctuary seated 1,000 worshippers, who crowded into the benches. When they all rose to join heartily in the opening hymn, with the mighty organ in full throttle, the sound fairly shook the rafters and brought tears to my eyes. It overwhelmed me, and I anticipated that moment as the greatest of every Sunday. Next to it came the moment when, after squirming in my seat through an hour-long sermon, I heard my grandfather's words, "And now in closing, in summary . . ." Then I knew that a small girl's agony of sitting quietly and understanding little soon would end for one more week.

Mother used to tell us how hard it was for her to practice the organ during the week, when the church in winter was unheated and unbearably hot in summer. Sometimes little mice ran over her feet as she played. They loved the music, she said, but she did not like being alone in that large church.

Grandfather, as pastor, was a man of pioneer spirit, tirelessly busy in any cause concerning the church, religion and humanity, and he accomplished an enormous amount of good. However, it often came at the expense of his family. When he needed them, he used them and felt he had the right. They grumbled a bit, but they helped.

My father joined in with fervor, and his devotion extended to the point of contributing a tenth of his income monthly, regardless of what remained to nurture his family. When he assured us "The Lord will provide," he really was relying on the efficiency and frugality of my mother to save the day. She was indeed a very proficient organizer, and besides being a highly gifted musician, possessed a surprising understanding of nutrition and excelled as a seamstress.

* * *

I was a fidgety child, so Mother introduced activities to keep me busy, such as coloring with crayons and stitchery. We once stitched a pillow with silken pansies of lavender blue, purple and yellow. I liked the purple ones best, and purple still is my favorite color. Later, she also sent me to the Saturday sewing class at the church. Still, all of that failed to cure my restlessness.

My parents decided I needed a more structured environment for my boundless energies, so they enrolled me in the first grade at the age of five and one half years. School demanded the highest discipline and attention, and all too well I recall the torture of trying to sit quietly and listen for five hours daily. But I also recall the joy I felt when I learned to write and could spell "Philadelphia."

Extremely shy and naturally reticent, I shrank from any attention directed to me personally. The beautiful clothes that Mother made for me from silks and other fine fabrics separated me from my peers who dressed in cotton play togs. Although I wanted to learn everything my teachers introduced, Friday always brought freedom and relief. My nervous apprehension returned Sunday afternoons as I faced the beginning of another school week.

My dear mother taught me many useful skills, but she never taught me how to play. Our time together, although interesting and enjoyable, always focused on practical matters. Neither she nor my father spent much time having fun, nor did they encourage their children in that direction.

Genial and outgoing, my handsome father was called "the Count" by his business associates for his German accent and regal manner. His love for my mother was readily apparent, but it was clear to me from the beginning that he was "the head of the house." He set the rules and the pace, and Mother cooperated. She was plainly not a liberated person. I believe it never occurred to her to assert herself against her husband's way of life. If she had any thought of it, she hid those feelings well. Willingly, she relinquished the right to any success that could have been hers had she not married a man with so little ambition.

Most of our free time on week-ends we spent in the company of close relatives, aunts and uncles. I learned much from listening to their discussions about people, about church, and even politics and business in our country. They fascinated me and I comprehended far more than they could have imagined or even liked. With great reluctance I responded to Mother's call from the kitchen, when she needed my help.

Mother could have used my assistance much more also on weekdays, after school, but my interests had turned roller-skating, skipping rope and playing jacks. Then, little by little, my tomboy days seemed to flitter away, and all of my attention turned to a passion for reading. Neither my mother nor my father had reckoned with or noticed that gradual transition, and by the time they caught up with the development, I had read every book in their quite adequate library. Most were classics, but one was not. Father was horrified that I should have read a book "not for the eyes or mind of a 10-year old girl." It was too late.

His discovery precipitated a flood of new rules and regulations to govern my conduct. No more uncensored reading. No sinful movies. No dancing—too immoral. No theater or operas, with their sordid stories.. Above all, no newspapers filled with stories of man's sin and depravity. To his credit, Father adhered religiously to those rules in his own life—with one exception, his daily newspaper.

For the first time in my life I rebelled against my father's authority, eagerly reading everything I could lay my hands on. I stored books and magazines under my bed or my pillow and read at night by lamplight, under cover of my thick blanket. My nocturnal reading ended, however, when Mother discovered the scorched imprint of the light bulb on a pillowslip.

As I grew, I rejected my parent's narrow view of religion and life and resented the restrictions imposed upon me. Yet I kept my doubts to myself, knowing that discussion would not alter their beliefs or actions, and resolved to make my own evaluations and decisions from then on, despite any feelings of guilt my rebellion engendered.

* * *

I do not remember playing with my two brothers, Carl and George, during my childhood. They attended different grammar schools than I, and they spent their high school years in trade schools. Occasionally we found points of mutual interest, but true friendship never blossomed until many years later when I returned with my husband and children from Germany.

My high school years intensified my feelings of separation, both from my classmates and my family. A good student, I applied myself to my studies and achieved a four-year academic average that put me on the honor roll. Socially, however, I remained a "wall flower," escorted to and from proms and similar events by my father.

For four long years I made the daily one-hour trek to and from Tuley High School, crossing lonely Humboldt Park in every kind of weather. Sometimes in early spring I detoured through high snow drifts to follow a bird call before continuing on to school. Car sickness prevented me from taking the trolley, and the 50 cents car fare saved each day eventually paid for my graduation dress. I graduated in the spring of 1917, at the age of 16, unsure of everything except my desire for adventure, for something new. Then, most unexpectedly, just such an opportunity appeared

CHAPTER 2

The Girl Who Never Grew Up

Hour after hour, the train rolled west from Chicago. Most of the other passengers slept, read or stared vacantly out the window at the never-ending fields of corn. But I did not. Oblivious of the tedium, I reflected on my good fortune and thought excitedly about the adventure that lay ahead. I would spend the summer in the glorious isolation of a log cabin high up in the Rocky Mountains, immersed in the study of music with two family friends, Prof. and Mrs. Scheve.

The professor who headed the music department at Grinnell College in Iowa had previously served as music director at my grandfather's church in Chicago. Prof. Scheve, a former member of the Berlin Opera Company with a gorgeous voice, noted my intense love of music and said I had natural but unformed talent. He offered me a course of study under his instruction as a sort of proving ground for a possible career. Lois Rogers, another student at Grinnell College, joined us for the summer.

Called Scheve Volmar Stone, the cabin was perched on a mountain at 9,100 ft, near Estes Park, Colorado, the gateway to Rocky Mountain National Park. Nearby stood a cabin owned by the president of Grinnell, the only other dwelling within many miles. Students from the college had rolled huge stones from far away to build both cabins and fireplaces.

Music filled our days. The professor instructed us in both piano and organ, and Mrs. Scheve sang for us. Her voice and manner, like that of a Schumann-Heinck, went straight to my heart. Oh, to sing like that!

We also enjoyed the natural beauty around us. Groves of aspen interspersed the dense pine forest, and a few wild flowers grew around the rocks. Bird's nests were abundant and we saw eagles and other birds, as well as a badger and mountain lion.

Mount Meeker loomed in front of the cabin and behind us, the peak of Twin Sisters mountain soared 11,000 feet high. One day we hiked up past the timberline, through a boulder field to the very top. As we climbed, a little marmot whistled our approach, alerting the ranger that he soon would receive visitors. When we reached the summit, we signed the guest register, exhilarated by the climb and the breathtaking scenery.

I loved the wild country and primitive style of life, and could have stayed forever. I also enjoyed studying with Prof. and Mrs. Scheve, both fine musicians and wonderful people. As summer ended, they offered me a piano scholarship at Grinnell College and a place in their home.

After careful consideration, I declined their most gracious and tempting offer. The Scheves governed their lives by the same narrow religious precepts as my parents. I also decided that I preferred singing to piano. Thus, with some regret on my part, we all left Scheve Volniar Stone on September 1, just in time to avoid the first great snow of the season.

* * *

My life still lacked direction. Hoping to figure out my future course, and to learn a skill with which to earn my way, I enrolled in a secretarial course at Carl Schurz High School in Chicago, studying typing, shorthand, letter writing and other office skills. On completion, I took a job as a secretary. Music occupied nearly all of my free time. I studied voice with Antoinette Le Brun, a well-known teacher in Chicago, and attended many performances of the opera and symphony. My supper money often paid for tickets, rather than dinner.

How I loved listening to the many great artists of that era. Almost always alone, I heard the glorious Galli-Curci, my favorite, as well as the renowned Irish tenor John McCormack; Rosa Raisa; the famous Russian basso, Chaliapin, in the opera Boris Gudenoff; and the inimitable Mary Garden in Peleas Melissonda—a rare treat. At least once a week I climbed the steep staircase in Orchestra Hall that led to the topmost seats—the cheapest and, I thought, the best in the house—to listen to the Chicago Symphony.

As a member, I took part in the rehearsals of the Apollo Musical Club, which performed oratorios several times annually with the Chicago Symphony. I also sang in public recitals, receiving several excellent reviews.

In 1921, Grandfather Meier died and left me a small legacy for study at the Oberlin Conservatory of Music in Oberlin, Ohio. The curriculum stressed all aspects of music—voice, piano, theory, composition and history of music.

I did well in them all, but voice remained my chief love. Music theory I liked least. Incredibly, however, my theory professor eventually offered me a full scholarship, believing I might make an excellent teacher—possibly his assistant. But I declined, because I wanted to sing, sing, sing, not teach!

Still with no clear direction for my future, I returned to Chicago and continued my studies with Miss Le Brun, supporting myself with part-time jobs. Through her I met Mme. Luella Melius, of the Chicago Civic Opera, who made it possible for me to study with the acclaimed vocal professor Frantz Proschowsky, of New York, a guest teacher for the summer at the Chicago Musical College. My voice responded and grew under his teaching. At the end of his stay he suggested I consider relocating to New York so we could continue our studies, but I lacked the financial resources to make such a move. I regretted losing such a valuable teacher.

Instead, I toured for a year with a group called the Randall

Players, performing throughout the Eastern United States. Our group consisted of an actress; a violinist; and myself as vocal soloist. The first half of our program included selected classicals. The second half featured the last act of the opera Madame Butterfly, complete with scenery, special lighting and costuming. Throughout the program, I provided accompaniment on the piano.

Although I loved the enthusiastic audiences, the length of the tour and the rigors of travel left me exhausted. When the year ended, I returned eagerly to Chicago, with no special plans for the following year.

Unusual circumstances led to an offer to teach music in a private girls' school in South Chicago, something I had never dreamed of doing. Why not? I accepted for one semester, leaving open the possibility of continuing. The position required that I live at the school from Monday morning through Friday evening. Weekends I could enjoy with my parents, if I wished.

In the years following my graduation from high school, I had drifted from one situation to another with no clear goal or plan in mind. Several suitors appeared during that period, but none matched my mental picture of a prospective husband. I rejected them all, despite my mother's warning that I might some day find myself alone. My insistence on a romantic ideal led my brother Carl to dub me, "The girl who never grew up."

But I refused to settle for less than my dream. I would wait all my life, if necessary, for the man I could give myself to, wholeheartedly and without reservation. So I continued with my teaching and my music, until a Sunday dinner in my parents' home finally brought my destiny into focus.

CHAPTER 3

A Dream Realized

"Oh no, not another one of Father's Germans," I protested silently. No quiet Sunday with my family for me. Once again, my father had invited a foreign visitor home to enjoy some American hospitality at our dinner table. After suffering through many such meals, I dreaded the prospect of another.

Father often brought home any lonely young German he encountered, to feed and befriend him, talk religion and offer help finding a job or even a place to live. That habit no doubt stemmed from his experiences as a young man, when people helped him after his arrival in America.

On that day, our expected visitor was Hans Bohle, recently arrived from Mannheim, Germany. The door bell rang just as we returned from church, and Father went to greet our guest, a tall, slender and handsome young man with white blond hair, merry blue eyes and a friendly smile. He returned my father's greeting in elegant high German, his manner poised and aristocratic. I liked that!

After the introductions, Father suggested he and Hans adjourn to the porch for a chat, while Mother and I prepared dinner. Although Mother needed my help, I felt a terrible urge to go to my bedroom, with its curtained window through to the porch, and eavesdrop on their conversation. Already I knew that Sunday held unprecedented promise. The young man spoke elegant German and seemed well educated, from a fine family.

During an enjoyable, hour-long dinner, I observed Hans' continental table manners—certainly not like ours, but no doubt the custom there. Mother served peas and carrots—his two least- favorite vegetables, I later learned. I also noticed that his elegant, graceful hands were marred by one crooked finger, a defect passed down through many generations of his family, he explained.

After dinner and the clean-up in the kitchen, Mother and I joined the two men in conversation. Filled with curiosity about that young man, I peppered him with questions. "Where did you learn such excellent English?" "Where did you go to school?" What does your father do?" And on and on.

Hans answered without hesitation, thinking it great fun. "We have wonderful schools in Germany," he said. "I attended one called the Humanistic Gymnasium that specialized in foreign languages. In addition to the regular curriculum of literature, history, etc., we studied many years of Latin, Greek, French and English as well as our native German."

"And can you read and write those languages as well as you speak them?"

"Oh yes." He smiled.

"Well, then, let's try you," I challenged, hauling Ivanhoe off the shelf and handing it to him. "Now take this, kind sir, and read."

Amused, he complied and read with ease, downplaying his accomplishment by reminding me that many of our words were derived from Latin or Greek. But I was impressed nonetheless.

"Now tell me, how did you meet my father?" I asked.

"I came to see Mr. Koeber," he explained, referring to my father's employer at the coal company. "On a visit to Germany, he looked up my father, who directs the southern branch of the Rheinisches Braunkohl Syndicate, owner of the largest coal strip mine in the world today. My father briefed him on the workings of the organization and gave him a tour of the mine.

"During their conversation, my father mentioned my upcoming trip to the United States. After Mr. Koeber returned home, he wrote my father a thank you letter and suggested I visit him during my trip. So I did, but Mr. Koeber was not in that day. Instead, I met your father and now I am here."

"What brought you to America?" I continued, probing.

"My desire to learn American business methods. My father is grooming me to take over for him when he retires. After my time here, I must return to finish my schooling. First I'll go to Geneva, to attend the university half days and work in the Syndicate offices half days. Then I'll go to Paris, under the same arrangement. All this before I can enter the Syndicate and begin working my way up.

"Already in my brief stay here, I love the U.S.A. so much I wish I could stay,' he added. "For the moment, I work to support myself and live in Cicero with a friend from Germany, Fritz Laun, a chemist whom I met while I worked in a chemical laboratory in Mannheim."

"Do you have any brothers or sisters?" I inquired.

"One brother, Walter. He's a musician now being trained by our mother to become a concert pianist. She is a concert pianist in her own right."

Noting our grand piano, Hans said that their music room in Mannheim held two such instruments, and that his mother and Walter often played duets. He then spoke of his own musical education and demonstrated broad knowledge of musical subjects, which thrilled me.

Soon my turn arrived to answer his questions. I talked about climbing the tall steps to the top of Orchestra Hall. "The seats are cheaper up there and the music sounds better," I explained. "I go not only for the symphonies, but also to hear the marvelous singers, particularly Galli-Curci, my favorite."

I also told him about my education, my summer in the Rockies, my time at Oberlin, and my studies with Mme. Le Brun and Prof. Proschowsky.

"And what are you doing now?" he asked.

"Relaxing after almost a year-long concert tour with the Randall Group," I explained. I told him about our program, the rigors of travel and the rewards of bringing music to smaller cities often bypassed by the great artists of the day.

Hans noted that in Germany, all large and small cities and even many towns offered cultural opportunities, with local talent offering excellent renditions of plays and operas.

"And now, I want to hear you sing. Will you?" he entreated.

"Sometime," I promised vaguely.

That evening after Hans left, Mother, Father and I sat together, reflecting on the day and our visitor. Mother was disturbed by my "teasing that young man so unmercifully," and voiced the opinion that "You will never see Hans again."

Ignoring her comment and hoping she was wrong, I mused aloud, "With those beautiful hands, I cannot understand why he wants to go into business instead of music. Perhaps the crooked finger?"

* * *

As time went on and we heard nothing more from Hans Bohle, my mother's prediction seemed accurate. Then one day I answered the phone.

"When can I hear you sing?" said a voice I recognized as Hans'.

"By coincidence, I have been asked to sing a few numbers during a student recital on Tuesday at the Chicago Musical College," I answered. "Would you like to attend with me?"

He did, and listened attentively. Afterward, his critique hit the mark. "Your voice is excellent, but your selections seemed rather unimportant. You must learn the German Lieder."

Hans then invited me to join him at a concert by a Spanish singer and the great German pianist Walter Gieseking, his favorite performer. During the concert, he sat oblivious of my presence, totally consumed by Gieseking's magical performance of compositions by Debussy and Ravel. I did not like that, but understood.

Hans and I left the concert hall very late, and decided to save time by taking a taxi home instead of the elevated train, or "el." We roved up one street and down the next in the pitch black night, but no taxis appeared. As we passed between the massive skyscrapers lining La Salle Street, hordes of beggars emerged from the dark, deep alley and surrounded us.

Hans reached for his purse, intending to secure our safety by paying them off. Totally without thinking of possible consequences, I shouted a good loud "No!" At the sound of my voice, the mob melted back into the alley as strangely and silently as they had emerged.

Somewhat shaken, we finally found a cab and sang to each other all the way home. I felt so sorry for him having to make the long trip to his apartment. The next day he told me he had fallen asleep in the "el" car.

"I woke up at the end of the line, and had to ride back to my stop," he laughed. "But the evening was worth it—the good music and even the beggar episode—because you were with me and enjoyed it too," he said.

From then on, we spent every weekend together, exploring all the sights and delights of Chicago. We explored the city's parks and neighborhoods, walked along the lake shore and went anywhere that offered a bit of culture. We visited museums, attended Shakespearean plays performed in Olde English and heard as many concerts as we could afford.

Occasionally, we dressed in evening clothes and took in the opera, courtesy of Aunt Cora, who had season tickets. We also enjoyed canoeing on the Fox and Des Plaines rivers, hiking in the Indiana Dunes, and picnicking and exploring the surrounding countryside. Occasionally overriding my admonition, he defied the rip tides and enjoyed a swim in Lake Michigan.

Much of our time we spent with friends, especially Fritz Laun and his new bride, Anne, and we seldom found ourselves alone.

Fritz and Hans chipped in to buy a car which they claimed had three speeds—slow, damn slow and stop.

*   *   *

I spent Monday through Friday at my school in South Chicago, and it was there that I received a letter from Hans one day. I wondered why he was writing to me, since we would see each other again in a few days. Opening the envelope, I read,

> "You will be surprised to receive a letter from me at your school, but I just had to write, to tell you how I feel. I suddenly realized how deeply I am in love with you. The emotion has hit me so strongly that I cannot eat or sleep and I cannot work. I am walking from one end of Michigan Avenue to the other, trying somehow to divert my mind until I can see you again on Sunday. Your Hans."

After all these years, all I can remember of my reaction is a tiny bit of surprise, then a feeling of emotion deep from the heart. Hans had poured out his heart so openly, so honestly, bringing out in me feelings I had suppressed. I wondered what he would feel if he knew I was five years his senior, and a letter reaching him by Saturday would tell him so.

I also wondered about his family's reaction. Cultured and wealthy, would they accept their son's choice of a girl of lesser means? My family certainly could point with pride to many accomplishments, but would they satisfy Hans' parents? And what about his program of learning, still with several years to go?

When Hans arrived on Sunday, he answered my questions without talking. He asked me to become his wife. He would go home, try to hurry his education and then bring me to join him in Germany.

How strange, I thought. After my years of considering and deciding against various suitors, a young man showed up from another country with every attribute I wanted in a husband. It felt perfect.

After Hans left that night, I told my parents of his proposal. I believe they had anticipated it, because their sole reaction was, "How wonderful.' They, too, recognized him as a fine person and loved him, and I appreciated their acceptance.

* * *

Hans' six month visa expired in January, and he had to leave the country. To circumvent the immigration laws, however, he crossed the border into Canada, by way of Niagara Falls, and advised the U.S. State Department of his departure. He waited a week, then returned to the U.S.A. for another six months.

We then began spending more time with my relatives, especially Aunt Emma and Uncle Will in Michigan and Aunt Cora and Uncle John in Oak Park, a Chicago suburb. Hans attended church with me each Sunday and, in general, we played as big a part as possible in each other's lives until his next six months ended.

Hans also wrote to notify his parents of our engagement. They responded immediately, horrified at the idea of his involvement with an American girl, considering me "a gold digger after your money and station in life." Fritz Laun vouched for me and helped calm their fears, but to see for themselves they invited me to visit them in Germany at Christmas.

All too soon, the time came for Hans' departure. The prospect of a reunion at Christmas provided some consolation, but not much. Once Hans boarded the train for New York, his hectic schedule kept him from missing me as much as I missed him. He spent a few days in Manhattan, taking photos, then sailed for Germany and a reunion with his mother and brother in Hamburg. Once at home, much discussion and planning kept him busy, although he found time to write to me often.

Meanwhile, I found myself thinking of him, needing him and missing both his lively spirit and his quiet, reflective strength.

With his arms about me, all my fears and questions had disappeared. But with him gone, I faced my apprehensions alone.

Several days after Hans left, I traveled with my mother to Mobile, Missouri, to attend brother Carl's wedding. Indeed, I played the wedding march for the small, intimate affair held at the bride's home. On our return trip I became very ill, and found myself in the hospital for an emergency appendectomy. The result was a bad case of adhesions, which still trouble me to this day.

When fall arrived, I returned to my teaching position at the girls' school near Chicago and spent my free time preparing for my departure for Germany. Father helped me secure my visa and purchase railroad and steamship tickets, while Mother and I gathered an appropriate wardrobe. With Mother's great talent in tailoring, she sent me off with the loveliest clothes, shoes, fur coat and hat, the equal of any wardrobe from the top fashion department at Marshall Field.

On December 8, I said good-bye to my family at Union Station in Chicago, headed for New York and the ship that would take me to Hans.

CHAPTER 4

To Germany and My Future

Close to midnight on the dark, dark night of Dec. 10, 1928, the S.S. Deutschland slipped quietly out of New York harbor and entered the placid, moonlit sea. The expanse of water ahead was frightening. How would our little vessel find its way, I wondered, as my first ocean voyage began. I felt a part of a great adventure.

After standing on the foremost deck for some time alone, breathing in the cold, crisp air, I left in search of my cabin and sleep.

Many of my fellow passengers were German immigrants returning to their homeland for Christmas, an annual ritual, and the ship quickly became known as "The Christmas Boat." A holiday mood pervaded both passengers and crew, lending a festive atmosphere to the trip.

I spent most of my time below deck in the company of a warm, friendly and interesting group, including a Viennese gentleman who sang very well. Another member of our group was a young Hungarian woman who had aspired to a career as a concert pianist. Her entire village in Hungary had raised money to send her to America, but the effort had failed, and so she was returning home, despondent.

One moonlight night as our group clustered around the piano in the lounge for a sing-along before dinner, the ship shuddered suddenly and sharply to a halt. Frightened, we all rushed out on deck. A fur coat hung on the rail, and searchlights probed the waves below in a futile effort to locate the Hungarian girl. Unable to face her townspeople after failing to meet their hopes and expectations, she had thrown herself overboard.

Stunned, we all stood around in our thin evening clothes and watched while the ship circled for several hours, as required by maritime law, then gave up the search and proceeded to our destination. Poor little girl. Her failure was no shame! We had tried to tell her that few ever accomplished what she had set out to do.

The trip to Cuxhaven, Germany took 10 days. During the voyage, the purser—one of our table group often admonished me to practice speaking German. Despite my heritage, we spoke only English at home and I had studied German for only two years in high school. I needed the practice, but found it hard to start and so ignored the purser's entreaties which I soon regretted.

Upon leaving the ship, I could not understand the question the agent in charge asked repeatedly. When all the passengers except me had departed, the purser happened by and translated for me, saying that the agent wanted my baggage checks! "I told you to practice your German," the purser said with a smile. The delay almost caused me to miss the small boat transporting passengers from the ship to shore.

* * *

I traveled from Cuxhaven on the "boat train" to Hamburg to meet my father's family, who had been contacted about my arrival. As the train sped through the beautiful countryside, I admired the picturesque houses with their thatched roofs, barns integrated into the house structure and storks nesting in the chimneys.

The train pulled into Hamburg station and stopped with a screech. I looked out the window, wondering if I would recognize my relatives. My worries proved groundless; I knew them on sight. All the women wore black cloth coats with velvet collars and clutched tiny posies in their gloved hands. Smiles of welcome beamed on their faces.

Each of them, in turn, took me into their arms and hugged me, then off we went to Aunt Emma's home, where Grandfather Kuechler waited. He too embraced me, crying, "My angel, my angel." A bit theatrical, perhaps, but I found him charming. He spent the rest of the afternoon telling me of his adventures during the Franco-Prussian war, speaking in low German, most of which, of course, I did not understand. Aunt Emma came to my rescue, explaining that Grandfather had been a soldier in that war. Wounded and left for dead on the French battlefield, he had crawled away gradually and wormed his way alone back into Germany.

The next night the entire family took me to the station and put me on the 9 p.m. train to complete my journey to Mannheim. Although I rode in a sleeper car, the many stops along the way kept me awake throughout the long night.

The train arrived on time at 7 a.m. the following morning. Filled with excitement, I took the porter's hand and he assisted me down the few steps with my baggage. I looked around for Hans and soon saw him at the opposite end of the platform, dashing toward me. Reaching my side, he swept me up into his arms and whirled me around, while the conductor and brakeman stood by enjoying our little drama. Then suddenly they awoke to their duties, and the train rolled on.

Hans and I departed arm in arm for a small cafe to wait until 9 o'clock, when his mother—a late riser—would be up. Almost delirious with happiness at the fulfillment of our hopes and plans, we sat over a hot coffee and vowed to enjoy each minute of our month together, after which Hans would leave for Paris to continue his studies.

At the appointed hour, Hans took me home and a maid answered our buzz at the gate. Hans' father greeted me at the door with a big smile and a quick "Welcome to Germany" before he left for work. Behind him, his wife descended the stairs from the second floor. She too greeted me pleasantly, but more formally than her husband, then asked us to join her and Walter for breakfast.

Although Mother Bohle seemed completely absorbed in herself during the meal, she noted my fatigue and suggested I rest until noon, and I agreed gratefully. Hans showed me to my room, and I marveled at the view. The garden below included a wide terrace and covered a square city block and contained a hothouse that supplied flowers and vegetables throughout the winter.

The family sat down for dinner promptly at 1 p.m. Refreshed by my nap; I joined them and felt most welcome. Later, I explored the house with Hans. The decor intrigued me—stylish overstuffed furniture and drapes of beautiful fabric displaying excellent taste, style, quality and color and yet practical in every way. Gorgeous oil paintings adorned the walls and exquisite oriental rugs covered the highly polished parquet floors. The lack of ornaments or other tabletop embellishments surprised me, but I liked that, too.

To my delight, music filled the air day and evening. Mother Bohle and Walter, at the piano, were sometimes joined by a family friend, a violinist with the Mannheim Orchestra. Hans had told his family about my singing, and they all looked forward to hearing me. At first, however, a cold I contracted onboard ship prevented me from performing.

* * *

On Christmas Eve, Father Bohle, Walter, Hans and I attended a special service at the Christus Kirche (Church of Christ). A gigantic tree, at least two and a half stories high, stood inside. Lighted beeswax candles decorated the tree and provided the dim light in the large sanctuary. The organ played continuously, one song after another.

Mother Bohle greeted us at the door on our return. "Welcome to the beginning of our Christmas Festival," she said, "and to the bescherung (giving of gifts)." Another huge Christmas tree graced the parlor, again complete with beeswax candles that gave off a wonderful aroma. Small tables were placed around the room at random, one for each member of the family, each laden with attractively arranged, unwrapped gifts. The maids came in for their monetary gift and to receive new uniforms for the coming year. They also were given Christmas Day off work. I found all those customs different and lovely.

As the candles on the tree burned low, we adjourned to the music room. Immediately Dad Bohle opened the doors to the terrace, which overlooked the Christus Kirche tower, and we stepped outside into the snow. Suddenly, searchlights cut through the dark, starry night, illuminating the church steeple. Four trumpeters, dressed in medieval costumes, appeared on the tower, one on each facade.

Responding as if to a heavenly cue, the trumpeters began playing Christmas carols. How wonderfully the sounds floated out into the beautiful, still heavens. Oh, what a glorious way to celebrate the birth of Christ, I thought. "Ich Bete on die Macht der Liebe (I Worship the Power of Love)," completed the program and brought tears to my eyes as Hans and I stood together with joined hands, profoundly moved.

By then I had recovered fully from my cold, and happily concluded the evening's festivities by singing for the family for the first time; Mother Bohle accompanied me. The family was delighted, and despite my more modest appraisal of my performance, I found their enthusiastic response very gratifying.

With Christmas over and only eight more days before Hans would return to work, there was so much for him to show me. But foremost, he wanted to teach me to ski. So he took me to a sporting goods store, bought me a complete ski outfit, and the next day my lessons began. We drove to Heidelberg, then took a rail car up a mountain to "the Koenigstuhl," the very top of the mountain. Halfway up, I saw the ruin of the ancient castle of Heidelberg, the site of summertime performances of Medieval plays such as "Goetz von Berlichingen," recalling the glory of bygone days.

We reached the summit and strapped on our skis. My first venture, walking, was amusing—two steps forward, then one step back. Slipping and sliding, we reached the spot to begin our descent on the other side. Hans gave instructions and some demonstration, and I managed to make it to the bottom of the hill, crossing a small creek, only to fall on the other side. In a flash, Hans appeared beside me to help me up. It became quite a day—boasting only a good bump on my head.

Mannheim, Heidelberg, the Neckar Valley—all new and fascinating. Exploring kept us occupied until New Year's. The cold weather occasioned frequent stops in a conditorei (cafe) for a warming sip of an aperitif called "gold wasser." But neither of Hans' parents yet had acknowledged our intention to marry. That concerned me, but not Hans, who remained cheerfully confident as always and reminded me that my visit was not yet over.

On New Year's Eve, Father Bohle suggested I drive with him to Heidelberg to enjoy a private walk while Hans remained in Mannheim for other purposes. The family chauffeur, Herr Schwarz, drove us to a spot in the hills where steps ascended to the Koenigstuhl.

Father Bohle challenged me to climb with him, and promised to deliver an important announcement when we reached the top. It was a long, hard climb, but we arrived eventually at the summit, puffing and out of breath.

Then the important announcement: "We all have come to love you very much and want you here with us," he said. "You and Hans can marry, with our blessing, once he completes his program of studies." They assumed, of course, we would live in Germany after the wedding.

Relieved that his parents finally acknowledged our engagement, Hans and I still found the prospect of waiting another year and a half daunting. But we understood why Hans had to complete his preparation for a career with the Syndicate, so we agreed—albeit with some misgivings—to Father Bohle's plan.

That night, New Year's Eve, Bohle family members arrived from all parts of Germany for a celebration. By 6 p.m. they were gathered in the music room, waiting, all excited about meeting "Hans' girl from America."

I entered on Hans' arm, which gave me, in his words, "the grand entrance." He led me immediately across the large room to his grandmother. Etiquette demanded that the introductions begin with her. The kindly old lady greeted me with a sweet smile. She then took my hands in hers. "Tell me, Ruth, can you cook and do you love children?" she asked.

The evening continued with further introductions—aunts, uncles, and cousins—and with laughter, good food, drink and music. Midnight brought the big moment, the announcement of our engagement by Hans' father, to bursts of cheers, cries of approval and best wishes so very heartwarming. On impulse Hans grabbed me to him and we started the dancing, which lasted the rest of the night.

* * *

A few days later Hans left me for his studies in Paris, and shortly thereafter the Bohles closed their house for a few weeks and took me with them for a ski vacation in Switzerland. We traveled to St. Moritz by way of Chur, where we took the Albula Balin, a train of one coach no wider than a single seat with a narrow aisle.

Slowly we passed over a long, narrow trestle spanning a horribly deep gorge. For a moment I was afraid! But in scanning the faces of Father and Mother Bohle, I saw that they were totally composed. The little twinkle in their eyes amused me—they were watching to see my reaction to that new experience.

At St. Moritz, wrapped in fur robes and packed tightly into a horse-drawn sled, we rode through the heavy snow to our destination for the next two weeks, The Waldhaus, an elegant hotel in Sils

Maria. Residents of that quaint and picturesque little village spoke Romanisch, a language that existed nowhere in Europe outside the Engadin Valley.

Either Father or Mother Bohle walked with me each morning. One day we stopped a group of schoolboys skiing past on their way to classes. They chatted briefly with us, and we examined their schoolbooks, explaining that we found their unusual language intriguing.

Eventually the rich food served at the grand old Waldhaus caused me distress, so Mother Bohle and I returned to Mannheim sooner than planned to consult a physician. He attributed the problem to the adhesions from my appendectomy.

I overheard Mother Bohle say she hoped the condition would not hinder our marriage. "On the contrary," the doctor replied. "The first child's birth will loosen the adhesions and relieve the problem." She liked that. The thought of a grandchild pleased her.

At their insistence, I stayed with the Bohles for three months, visiting museums and galleries, attending the symphony and opera, and dining with them and their friends. There also was the unique experience of watching thousands of people walking on the totally frozen Neckar River. Unheard of! I came to love the life of Germany and the German people, and grew close to both Father and Mother Bohle, despite her reserve.

Kind, considerate, and generous, Father Bohle was a consummate gentleman. Hans' mother, more distant than her husband and sometimes autocratic, also treated me kindly. She loved to play the grand dame, a role that suited her well, and kept her feelings well guarded. Although they never considered themselves rich, the Bohles lacked for nothing and their standard of living differed sharply from that of my family. They dressed in the finest fashions, attended the theater, opera and the symphony regularly and took frequent vacations at chic locations across Europe.

* * *

It was enough! I had been in Germany for a long time and missed my family I had promised them I would return home, so I decided to do so while awaiting my marriage to Hans. On my own, I arranged for passage back to America. When they saw my resolve, the Bohles grudgingly accepted my decision. We packed my trunks and sent them ahead, then drove to Cologne for a brief visit with some of Mother Bohle's relatives. Walter accompanied us there, then went on to Leipzig to continue his studies. From Cologne, I traveled alone to Cuxhaven, where I boarded the S.S. Deutschland again for the return voyage.

Of course, I looked for a letter from Hans before departure, but there was none What a bitter disappointment! Had he changed his mind? I would not believe it. I remembered the Hungarian girl who had thrown herself overboard on my voyage to Germany. For the first time, I felt her devastation. Could I do something like that? A few anxious days followed.

How happy and relieved I was to find a letter waiting for me at Cherbourg, our final stop in the Channel. Nothing could change his mind about our marriage, Hans wrote. If the arrangements did not come about as planned, he vowed to come to the U.S.A. to be married there. That news made the crossing much more pleasant, despite the rough seas and a scary near collision with a huge iceberg.

The remaining eight days of the voyage gave me much time for reflection on my experiences. More than ever, I wanted to marry Hans. I had come to love his parents and brother. The atmosphere of music and refinement in which they lived held great appeal. I also felt an attachment to Hans homeland, and saw that life there would be very interesting. In my heart, I knew that I belonged with Hans, and that he belonged in Germany.

It was true that I knew a political situation was developing there, but it meant little to me. During my stay I had heard Hans' family and friends express concern about widespread unemployment, a government in chaos and the rise of a group called the Nazis, headed by a charismatic young leader named Adolph Hitler. These concerns seemed no more relevant to my life than did the deepening recession in the United States. So I put them out of my mind, and looked forward to the beginning of a new life in a new land.

CHAPTER 5

Married at Last

Home again, for the big wait. I returned to the girls' school and stayed busy earning money and preparing for my wedding. Hans and I exchanged long letters that helped establish the foundation for an excellent relationship in our future marriage.

Christmas brought a sizable gift and a beautiful letter from Hans' parents, promising that our wait soon would end. Another note from them at Easter told of a visit to Hans in Paris. Mother Bohle said they found him completely captivated by the fine French cuisine, oblivious to its impact on his personal appearance.

Finally, in May, 1930, the word came that I had awaited so eagerly. "Book the next ship to Germany," Hans said, to arrive in time for a late July wedding.

Once again my father took on the task of putting my visa and other papers in order, visiting the German consulate repeatedly to secure the necessary stamps, seals and approvals. Arranging passage to Germany at that late date proved difficult, but eventually we secured space in a shared cabin aboard the original S.S.Bremen, which had been captured by the British during World War I. Later they sold it back to the Germans, unaware of the fortune in iron ore secreted between the hull and the ship's false bottom.

Mother and I focused our attentions on my trousseau. Off we went to St. Joseph, Mich., where my Uncle Will Benning owned a shop of fine women's apparel. Choosing a wedding dress was exciting also the several wonderful suits, dresses, evening clothes, and many other necessary items. Mother, too, felt the thrill of the lovely new clothes.

As the departure date approached, my family and friends scheduled what seemed like an endless round of farewell parties and showers, which kept me busy sending thank you notes. More than 300 guests attended a beautiful farewell luncheon held in the recreation hall of our Oak Park Baptist Church. It was followed by the program I had promised, accompanied by Raymond Allen Smith, my friend and accompanist of many concerts and recitals. Mother fought back tears as I sang "auf wiedersehen" to my many friends and family members.

The attention everyone was paying to me soon generated more excitement than I could manage. For the first time, I began to realize the implications of my decision to join Hans in Germany, and the pain of the coming separation from my family slowly sank in.

On June 15, Mother and Aunt Cora took me to the train station. We said our farewells, and Mother bore up splendidly. All tried to give that good-bye a less-final feeling. I heard from Aunt Cora that Mother's tears came later—out of my sight and hearing.

I boarded the old S.S. Bremen two days later in New York and found my cabin filled to the brim with gifts and flowers—including two dozen long stemmed roses from a former admirer. With no room left for my cabin mate, she graciously sought other quarters.

It was my time to fight tears, and I ignored the first bell for lunch. But then, being in better control, I went to the dining room. I arrived late, hoping for an anonymous entry, but no such luck. As I approached my assigned place, I realized to my dismay that it was at a table in the very center of the room. My table Mates—six young American engineers on their way to Russia for an important and secret project—all stood until I took my seat.

Obviously, I was embarrassed, but they teased me gently about my perfect theatrical entrance and we all became fast friends. One of them looked forward with special eagerness to our arrival at our first stop in Galway, Ireland. Coming to meet him on another ship was his wife, for a happy reunion after a long separation.

During the 10-day voyage the clocks aboard ship remained unchanged, so night magically became day as we landed, this time in Bremerhaven. There on the dock below stood Hans' father and brother, Walter, quite as excited to see me as I was to see them. To avoid delay, I sent my luggage through to Mannheim to clear customs—a regrettable decision.

The reunion proved emotional and I was sorry when Walter soon left by train for Leipzig to continue his studies, while Father Bohle and I drove to Mannheim in his chauffeured limousine. Father Bohle explained that our three-day trip would acquaint me with the lovely countryside I had not seen before. He added that we would make several stops to visit family members unable to attend the wedding, many of them I never saw again. En route, I spoke to Hans by telephone in Munich, but neither of us could think of a thing to say.

* * *

We arrived at the Bohle home in Mannheim on June 27, 1930, and Mother Bohle greeted me with a happy welcome. "Well, the time finally has arrived," she said. We spent the afternoon discussing wedding plans, and I looked forward eagerly to Hans' arrival the following day.

I retired that night filled with excitement and anticipation, and awakened at 4 a.m. to the sound of Hans entering his room next to mine. I drifted back to sleep, then awoke again at 8, hearing him in discussion with his father on the terrace below. Walking to my window, I glanced down at him. How different he looked. Was that my future husband? I stared hard and long trying to match the man with the image I had carried in my memory for the last year and a half.

Finally pushing aside my doubts, I dressed and joined Hans.

The long absence made us shy with each other. He, too, struggled with the contrast between recollection and reality. Before long, however, our old rapport and closeness returned as we sensed each other's feelings and communicated without effort. We enjoyed a good breakfast together, then left to retrieve my trunks and obtain a permit and date for the wedding.

But our joy turned to consternation when we learned that one of my many papers lacked a necessary stamp or seal, preventing us from obtaining a wedding permit. And without that permit, customs would not turn over my trunks filled with clothes and wedding gifts from my family and friends in the United States. "Those items might well wind up on the black market," the city official explained. "You must return to the United States to get the appropriate seal." I stared at him in disbelief.

Unsure of our next step, we asked Father Bohle for advice. He suggested we go to Munich to get the wedding permit, since we planned to live there.

Hans returned to Munich on Monday by himself. I followed with his father a few days later and presented my case to the officials there myself. Unfortunately, I could not understand their Bavarian dialect and once more I needed Father Bohle's help.

Eventually, the officials agreed to overlook the missing document and give us a wedding permit—provided we established residence in Munich and paid them 800 Reichsmark (RM) for issuing a marriage permit on such short notice, without adhering to the usual German custom called the "posting of the bans." That meant that the wedding notice and date were published three weeks in advance, to give anyone opposed to the marriage time to state their objection.

How could we find an apartment immediately? One official suggested we contact moving van companies to see if they knew of any vacancies. We did, and eventually found and leased a very nice, modern apartment.

The entire transaction proved costly. In addition to the apartment rental, we now paid 800 RM for the certificate documenting our residence, as well as 800 RM to the moving van Company for their referral.

How simple all that would have been in the U.S.A., I thought, when, with marriage permit in hand, we next went to the courthouse to settle the date: July 19 for the civil ceremony in Munich and July 23 for the church wedding in Mannheim. Hans stayed in Munich to work, while his father and I left for Mannheim. With the paperwork completed, Mother Bohle could begin arranging for the caterer, minister, flowers, music and other details attendant to a large church wedding, and I could finally reclaim my trunks.

* * *

As we drove, Father Bohle asked how Hans and I planned to furnish our new home. In Germany, he explained, the bride provided furniture, linens, dishes, silverware and all other necessary household items—to last a lifetime. I could only respond that no such custom existed in America.

With a twinkle in his eye, Father Bohle smiled and said not to worry, that he would buy our furniture for us at a wholesaler in Stuttgart, on the way home to Mannheim—yes, that very day.

I worried that the sudden arrangement might displease Hans, since it gave him no choice in the selection. Also, would the furniture Father Bohle selected reflect our taste? We knew what we wanted, but did we have the right to appeal?

In great spirits and oblivious to my doubts, Father Bohle drove with me to his friend's factory in Stuttgart. He was greeted like an old acquaintance and he introduced me as his new daughter. We toured the entire warehouse before making decisions. He left me no choice: it was his day.

Father Bohle selected the bedroom furniture first, saying it was most important since one spent a third of one's life there. What a happy surprise! He chose a set made of Siberian burled acorn, absolutely stunning. Then, surprised at the price of his first selection, he bought the dining room set, of very quality mahogany but not quite as impressive as the bedroom furniture. Finally he selected the furnishings for the front room. His generosity overwhelmed me, but Father Bohle clearly enjoyed every minute of our shopping spree, like a small boy with his first toy.

Then, turning to me, he said, "The only remaining essential item—a piano—is your responsibility." So, I bought a piano—although not immediately.

* * *

Saturday, July 19, 1930, at 11 am. Hans and I arrived at the courthouse in Munich to meet his father and mother and our witnesses, Mr. and Mrs. Schwedhelm, from the Munich office of Father Bohle's company. It took just 10 minutes time to change my life forever.

After the brief ceremony, the judge said, "Mrs. Bohle, please sign here." When my mother-in-law did not respond, I turned to her and said, "The judge wants you to sign."

"Not me," she answered. "You are now also Mrs. Bohle."

I returned to Mannheim without Hans to help with final preparations for our church wedding the following week. Mother Bohle arranged for a very formal dinner after the ceremony, followed by photos and cognacs in the garden. For the evening, she scheduled music and dancing indoors.

At 2 o'clock on Wednesday, July 23, the bells of the beautiful Christus Kirche rang to tell all Mannheim of our wedding. Hans and I arrived last, and in keeping with German custom, we preceded our attendants and guests down the long center aisle to seats near the altar. Women sat on one side of the aisle and men on the other, separating Hans and me momentarily.

My dress was of ivory satin crepe with a long silk tulle veil and a cap caught by a narrow band of pearl-studded old lace and myrtle. Hans looked handsome and regal in his black tuxedo.

Glorious music emanated from the grand organ, and Otto Spamer, a family friend and member of the Mannheim Symphony, played the violin. The minister, Geheimrat Dr. Klein, invited Hans and me to the altar. He spoke, I understand, in both English and German. But I heard nothing of what he said, as I concentrated desperately on not sliding off the slippery satin pillow on which I kneeled!

In a daze, I soon found myself walking out of the lovely church clutching Hans' arm, husband and wife at last.

At the Bohle home, we found the stage set for a marvelous formal dinner for 40, served in the large music room. A string trio provided music, and between courses Mother Bohle and Hans' aunt read poems they composed in honor of the occasion.

The menu was splendid. A separate wine was served with each course, and according to German custom, the server whispered in each guest's ear the name and vintage of each wine. It was a beautiful wedding day, over much too swiftly.

The evening program included several selections by Mother Bohle and Walter, and I sang, accompanied by my new mother-in-law.

Only one cloud darkened that delightful occasion: the absence of my family. They received a full report on the day's activities from Mrs. Larson, a friend from Oak Park who generously took time from her travels in Europe to attend our wedding.

In the midst of the festivities, Hans and I slipped away, leaving the guests to remain for more music. Herr Schwarz, the family chauffeur, drove us to a darling chalet in Baden Baden, where we found our room filled with flowers, compliments of the hotel. The next morning, in lovely sunshine, we enjoyed a quiet and private breakfast on our balcony, which overlooked a manicured green lawn sloping down to the distant forest.

Our solitude did not last long, however. The following day the answer to a knock at our door brought unexpected guests. There in the hall stood Hans' parents and brother, Walter, eager to join us for the rest of our week-long honeymoon! Astonished, I said nothing, and neither did Hans.

To this day I wonder why they did not consider their visit

insensitive. Strangely enough, Hans and I never discussed our feelings about their intrusion, but I do not believe it was customary. Although we all enjoyed our time together, it fell far short of the romantic getaway Hans and I had envisioned for our honeymoon. At the end of the week, they returned to Mannheim and we headed for Munich and our new home, and the real beginning of our life together.

CHAPTER 6

Newlyweds

Hans and I stood in front of a door that looked like all the others in the apartment complex. This door was different, however, because it bore a small brass plate engraved with Hans' name.

Hans inserted the key in the lock. Opening the door he announced happily and proudly, "Welcome to the Hans Bohle residence. This is our first home; at last we can be alone." Quickly, he lifted me in his arms and carried me over the threshold.

Inside we found evidence of "elves" at work: furnishings in place, barrels of dishes ready to unpack in the kitchen and the refrigerator stocked with cold cuts, bread, butter, eggs, milk and other essentials. On the table lay a welcoming message from Mother and Dad Bohle.

Although unimaginative in design, our apartment was modern, spacious and light, with a full private bath—certainly not always the case in Germany. I would add touches of color and texture to make it a comfortable home we both could enjoy. The complex faced the Munich airport on one side and a garden on the other. The city's main thoroughfare passed the complex, and the streetcar that Hans took to work each day stopped right in front.

Mornings I spent in the nearby food markets and in my kitchen preparing lunch. I found less variety in the shops than at home in the United States. Some items—flank steak, for example were known by different names in Mannheim than in Bavaria. And my requests for pink or blue toilet paper called forth huge laughs from the shopkeepers, who of course quickly labeled me as a foreigner.

In the afternoons, I often shopped in the charming little boutiques lining the narrow streets that wound around the cathedral called "The Frauenkirche." The shopkeepers always greeted me warmly even though I seldom purchased anything. If I admired an object, they urged me to take it home for a few days and then bring it back if I didn't like it. What perfect trust—and what a contrast to American business methods!

Hans almost immediately established the habit of reading to me in German after our evening meal. His choice: *The Magic Mountain* or Buddenbrooks by Thomas Mann. His objective: to train my ear and tongue to hear and speak only the very best German, and not be confounded by the dialects that inevitably I would hear. I loved these times together and appreciated his effort.

Sometimes during the day, feeling a wisp of homesickness, I visited the Frauenkirche Cathedral near the Rathaus to pray for strength and courage. Marriage, with all its happiness, still placed many new demands on me and taxed my strength. The adhesions resulting from the earlier operation for appendicitis were also still causing me considerable discomfort. Did Hans know that? No! Why add to his burdens while he struggled to begin a career and support a family?

Not long after we arrived in Munich, I answered the door one morning and found a lady who introduced herself as Gertrude Harrington. Newly arrived from America, she and her husband Bill, an art student, lived across the street. Gert had seen the announcement of our marriage in an U.S. newspaper and had written to her mother, who lived just a few blocks from my parents in Oak Park, Ill. to obtain our address. We talked a long time that morning, and soon we saw Gert and Bill nearly every day.

Occasionally on Sundays, Hans and I attended church. First we tried a German Lutheran church, but the solemn service made me homesick and I choked back tears throughout. Not usually a church-goer but to please me, Hans suggested we try an Anglo-

Saxon church he had heard mentioned. We did, and found the small congregation comprised mostly of American art students. Rev. Fred Wissenbach, the minister, was an American who had also come to Germany to study art. Much better at painting than preaching, Rev. Wissenbach gave generously of his meager resources to aid many of his impoverished parishioners/art students whose parents forgot to send their allowance. We became very good friends with Fred and his wife Billie and their two daughters, and maintained contact with them long after we left Munich. In fact, Hans assisted them financially to return to the U.S.A. when their home church failed to support them.

* * *

As an apprentice with the Syndicate, Hans received a very modest salary of 400 marks per month. He would assume his father's position one day, but meanwhile Dad Bohle insisted that Hans begin at the bottom and rise on merit, to avoid charges of favoritism from others within the organization. We understood and accepted that reasoning, although we struggled sometimes to subdue our impatience. To supplement Hans' meager salary, however, Dad Bohle generously paid our rent for the first year of our marriage.

Hans' father demonstrated his generosity in other ways, as well. He loved to visit us, bearing a huge basket overflowing with the most delicious treats. Once he brought us a Bodensee Felchen (a special trout from Lake Constance), which I cooked immediately. My culinary skills impressed him since his own wife laughingly admitted she could not even boil an egg. In jest, after an especially good meal, Dad Bohle would comment, "We always can tell when Mother has been in the kitchen." We all laughed when he said it, Mother Bohle, too.

Living on a limited budget, a new experience for Hans, led to our first argument as newlyweds. When Mardi Gras time arrived,

Hans and I enjoyed an evening of dancing and celebration and spent our "fun money" for the month in the process. The next day, friends invited us to join them for another night of revelry, and Hans agreed readily. "We can't go," I objected. "We've already spent our fun money."

Hans insisted. "We can just scrimp on food the rest of the month." Equally determined, I appealed to him. "We can't spend money we don't have. Your father already pays the rent, and we do not dare ask him for more. If you go, you'll go alone."

Angrily, he stormed out of the house and did not return until after dinner. But neither did he go to Mardi Gras, and to my knowledge he never again tried to spend money we didn't have. Most times, however, we managed to enjoy ourselves despite our limited budget. We visited galleries and museums and browsed (without buying) in charming little shops. Weekends often found us touring the open country near Munich in the company car, and once I accompanied Hans on a business trip to Mittenwald, in South Bavaria.

Oberammergau, the site of the world famous Passion Play, was on our agenda, and we stopped there for the night. In the morning, Hans continued on to Mittenwald, a town best known for its master violin makers, to conduct his business while I stayed behind to explore.

My wandering from shop to shop brought me to one of a wood carver. When I plied the proprietor with questions about the Passion Play, he promptly closed his shop doors and escorted me to the theater where performances had just ended for another ten years. We toured the backstage area, the prop room and even the wardrobe rooms, all of which I found fascinating. During our walk back to his shop, a bearded native of the village roared by on a motorcycle, his long hair flying behind him in the wind. "That's John the Baptist," my tour guide said.

Winter finally arrived, and with it the skiing season. As often as possible, we headed for the nearby mountains on weekends, usually in the company of the Harringtons. Fourth- class rail coaches provided an inexpensive means of traveling the two hours from Munich to the slopes, where we enjoyed two days of fun in the snow before returning home for the start of another week. My skiing and Hans' instruction both fell short of perfection. A lifelong skier, Hans found traversing the slopes as easy as breathing, and failed to understand my difficulties. "Just do as I do," he insisted, forgetting the many hours of practice that produced his skill.

I soon insisted he go off by himself and "schuss" to his heart's content, leaving me on the simpler slopes to work on my technique. Gert and Bill, also amateurs, often kept me company. Despite our limited ability, the three of us enjoyed the snow, the sun and the exercise in the beautiful countryside.

* * *

At Mother Bohle's urging, and with her financial assistance, I resumed my music education. Hans traveled often for business, and my lessons and practice provided a welcome diversion during those lonely hours. Mother Bohle suggested that the Munich opera company might refer me to a suitable instructor, so off I went one morning.

I explained my wishes to the opera director, and he suggested I return that afternoon to sing for him on the stage, so he could suggest an instructor appropriate for my needs. I agreed and decided to fill the hours until my audition at 2 p.m. with lunch and shopping.

I walked the nearby streets, reminding myself repeatedly of the director's formal title, Herr Intendant. I knew the importance of referring to Germans by their title—or titles, if they owned more than one. Determined not to forget, I kept repeating, over and over to myself, "Herr Intendant, Herr Intendant . . ."

Unfortunately, as I wandered my eye caught a sign over the door of a fabric shop, advertising a new type of dye called "colorfast." The German word for that process, "indantrain," somehow replaced "intendant" in my mind.

I returned to the opera company and sang an aria from "Aida" for the intendant. He complimented me repeatedly, and referred me to Frau Mihaseek, his lead lyric soprano, as a teacher.

"Thank you, Herr Indantrain," I said gratefully. The resulting snickers from those in the room offended me at first, but then I realized my mistake and retreated quickly, in remorseful embarrassment. Smiling, he waved in acknowledgment of my thanks, as I left.

Frau Mihascek, a lovely tall lady, graciously accepted me as her student, and I took up my music again in earnest. I practiced daily at home, and once a week I traveled by train to her house in the suburbs of Munich for further instruction in the German Lieder.

"How wonderful that you still have so much to learn," she often said, recalling the joy of discovery she knew as a student. Occasionally she gave me complementary tickets to theatre performances where she sang the leading role.

My still-imperfect German and my American ways caused me other embarrassing but humorous moments. Shopping one rainy day with Billy Wissenbach, I searched unsuccessfully through several stores for shoes to fit my American foot. My rain-soaked hose soon made it difficult to try on the shoes, and in disgust I explained to the clerk.

"Meine hose sind zu nass," I said. His astonished expression told me I had erred once again, and too late I realized the actual translation of my comment: "My pants are too wet."

Another incident, in Munich, ended more happily. Late for a luncheon appointment with Hans, I saw him standing on the opposite side of a very busy eight-lane thoroughfare. A tall, handsome, white-clad policeman directed traffic from the center of the avenue.

With only an hour for lunch, I felt Hans mentally chiding me for my tardiness. So, true to my Chicago upbringing, I started into the traffic without waiting for a signal. Cars screeched to a halt in all eight lanes as I attempted to cross, and I could just hear the drivers exclaiming, "Crazy American tourist." No German would ignore the signal "verboten (forbidden)." I reached the middle of the intersection, where the policeman stood. Anticipating a lecture from him, I was surprised by his warm smile.

"Little lady, where do you come from and where are you going?" he asked.

"I come from America and am going to my husband, standing over there."

"Let me escort you," he said most graciously, offering me his arm. The cars remained motionless as we walked leisurely across the intersection and he handed me over to Hans with a smile. I knew then that I loved German policemen—at least that one.

* * *

After a Christmas visit with Hans' family in Mannheim, we returned to Munich to prepare for Mother and Dad Bohle's first joint visit to our new home. I fretted about the menu, finally deciding on pork loin roast with roasted potatoes, creamed onions (not knowing Mother Bohle detested them), and a Jello dessert. They told us they both enjoyed the meal very much and also complimented us on the appearance of the apartment.

The next day, Mother Bohle and I left for a hotel in the Bavarian Alps, to enjoy a week-long vacation together while the men went back to work. Each day when it wasn't snowing we visited a charming little coffee shop in Gartenkirchen, a half hour's walk from the hotel. Garmisch, another nearby town, featured many artists' studios.

On one visit, Mother Bohle tried to purchase a beautiful painting by a local artist, but it was sold. After returning to Mannheim, she mentioned the painting and her disappointment to Dad Bohle. Secretly, he asked me to return to Garmisch and locate Mr. Ketteman, the artist.

I found him living in Tegernsee and commissioned him to paint another like the original. He asked me to return the next day, when he promised it would be ready. True to his word, he painted the whole night through and finished it the following day. She received the framed painting for her birthday, and it hangs in our home today. Hans and I remained in contact with Mr. Ketteman and his family for years, even after the war. It still fascinates me that the artist needed to paint that beautiful masterpiece in only one session, no matter how long, so as not to lose his inspiration.

CHAPTER 7

And Baby Makes Three

After nearly six months of marriage, Hans and I learned of the impending birth of our first child. My early pregnancy proved difficult, and for awhile we feared we might lose the baby. The doctor put me in the hospital for a week, then prescribed total rest at home. Grandmother Bohle came from Essen to care for me. Sick to my stomach, I lived on orange juice and cognac for four months, then rallied and life became bearable again.

On Sept. 27, 1931, Robert John Bohle came into the world, a feisty little guy from the very beginning. Visiting the hospital nursery one day, I heard a baby crying at the top of his lungs. "Is that my child?" I asked the nurse, and she nodded—a sign of things to come.

Although I loved Bobby, I knew nothing about caring for an infant. I had never held a newborn, and I had not the slightest idea how to feed him or care for him.

Instinctively, and with some help, I soon learned the basics of baby care—feeding, diapering, bathing. But his habit of waking each night at 3 a.m., screaming and defying our every attempt to console him, left me tired and mystified.

At Mother Bohle's urging, Hans soon hired a nurse who specialized in caring for infants. She immediately moved Bobby's crib to the front room and set up a cot for herself.

That night Bobby began wailing right on schedule, whereupon the nurse firmly ordered, "Shush! Stop that!" As if by magic, he quieted and never again repeated his night-time tantrum. During her month with us the nurse instructed me well in infant care and gave me the confidence to carry on alone.

Hans now insisted that with a baby in the house, we needed a full time servant. For me, supervising a servant was a new—and not entirely comfortable—experience. Hans had grown up with servants and knew instinctively how to treat them well while also maintaining a proper distance and reserve. He explained that they derived satisfaction and status from the gentleman and lady they served. I noticed that the servants responded immediately to his slightest wish always eager to please. On the other hand, my attempts to befriend them, and even help sometimes with the work, embarrassed them. Once, I decided to clear the walkway to the entry to our home after a heavy snow. My maid came running out and took away the shovel.

"No, no!" she said. "A lady does not do that!" Too bad, when all I wanted was to get a little outdoor exercise. And so, I guessed, a lady doesn't!

My first maid proved a disaster—uneducated, unpolished and unable to cook. A friend urged me to find a "haustochter," or house daughter. Educated and from good families, those young women often were placed in other people's homes to learn housekeeping, rather than be taught at home. They filled a valuable role in running the home—taking care of the children, supervising servants, and doing shopping. They were considered part of the family they served, also eating with them—something no servant did.

I took my friend's advice and found a haustochter, a lovely girl, refined and well educated. We got along well, and she took very good care of Bobby. But I noticed that although she seemed happy with us, her eyes often betrayed a suppressed sadness.

One Sunday, after a day away together, Hans and I returned home to find our haustochter talking quietly with a fine-looking young man. Eyes glowing with happiness, she introduced him as her former fiancée'. He had ended their engagement after Army doctors gave him only six months to live. But the report was another man's, not his, and immediately he began searching for his lost love. He had found her at last, and we rejoiced with them and their new chance for a life together. We let her go and wished them well.

* * *

Not long after, we received another surprise, and a welcome one—a transfer to Mannheim, so Hans could work directly with his father. I found a nice airy three bedroom apartment on the Rhine River side of the city, and we moved in. The Neckar River side, where Mother and Dad Bohle lived, contained only single family homes beyond our budget—and we decided a little distance might benefit us all anyway.

Life soon settled into a comfortable routine. Hans continued to advance in his career with the Syndicate and earned a comfortable salary that allowed us more of the luxuries of life. We particularly enjoyed the cultural opportunities available in Mannheim. I resumed my musical education, studying with the conductor of the Mannheim Symphony, a good friend of Hans' parents. He often joined Mother Bohle, Walter and me in grand programs we put on at home for friends. What wonderful music we made together!

Hans and I also enjoyed weekends in the beautiful Neckar River countryside, where mountains, rivers and forests seemed a virtual fairyland. Hans' business also took him often to Switzerland, and it was not unusual for him to ask me to accompany him, especially when we could combine pleasure with business. When we visited friends in their homes, they often placed funds at our disposal, to counteract the government's strict limits on the amount of money we could take out of the country. We returned the favor when friends visited us.

* * *

Our move to Mannheim in 1933 meant we also saw more of Hans' brother, Walter, whose career as a professional pianist was progressing very well. The most wonderful news was that the violin virtuoso Yehudi Menuhin had chosen Walter as his accompanist for a worldwide concert tour, beginning in Paris a few weeks later.

Graciously the Menuhin family, with whom Walter was staying, sent invitations to Mother Bohle, Hans and me to spend a few days with them in their family villa outside Paris, essentially to attend Yehudi's and Walter's opening concert. We accepted happily and decided to go by car. Therefore we had to leave immediately.

The trip to Paris took us through Verdun, site of a famous battle during World War I. The French had lost that battle to the Germans when a change in wind direction blew the poison gas they planned to use on the enemy back over their own soldiers.

We stopped for the night and were surprised to find that the French people we encountered in the hotel and restaurant were far from friendly. We assumed that lingering hostility toward Germans prompted their reactions, but gave it little thought and retired for the night.

At 5 a.m. we awoke to shouts outside our doors of "Kill the Boche (Germans), to hell with the Boche." Frightened, we considered leaving immediately but decided to wait until morning, although we slept no more that night.

Hans informed the hotel manager of the incident, but he made no apology. Leaving town, we saw remnants of the great battle lying rusting in the fields, a continuing reminder of the tragedy. We decided to walk into a field where several tanks lay rusting out. There on the side of one was "Heinriche Bohle." Hans' father had ridden in a tank in World War I. Could it be that same one? With few Bohles anywhere in the world, we decided it likely was.

The battlefield reminders raised questions that bombarded

my mind as we drove. Could the hate kindle another conflict? Should we consider leaving Germany and returning to my homeland? It seemed impossible that war might again rage across Europe, and I pushed my doubts and fears aside.

The Menuhin family were delightful hosts. During the days, Mother Bohle remained at the villa, while Hans and I roamed Paris, visiting favorite haunts he discovered during his year there as a student. By 4 o'clock each afternoon, we returned to join Mother Bohle and Mrs. Menuhin listening as Yehudi and Walter practiced in the adjacent room. In the evenings, we enjoyed wonderful dinners and fascinating conversations conducted by the Menuhins in four languages, including Russian.

On the night of the concert, Mother Bohle, Hans and I joined Mrs. Menuhin and her two daughters in their box at the concert hall. Mrs. Menuhin introduced us to the occupant of the adjacent box, the Prince of Monaco, whose son later married Grace Kelly.

Yehudi and Walter's beautiful renditions brought great audience response. The two Menuhin daughters with us in the box were thrilled more by the enthusiasm of the audience than by the music, which they heard every day.

The next morning we left for Mannheim, stopping first in Paris to shop for a gift. Mother Bohle and I found beautiful linen set and sent it to the Menuhin family as a token of thanks and appreciation for their hospitality.

We stopped in the afternoon at a charming teahouse. Again we encountered French hostility, as the waiter gave Hans improper change and allowed no chance for argument. Therefore, we decided to drive through the night rather than stay at another hotel in France. Already it was 5 p.m.

Night fell, cold and clear. With not another soul on the road, we made good time but nearly froze in the icy cold of the unheated car. Even our fur blankets provided little warmth.

Only once did we need to cross a railroad, and there we found the barrier down. Hans awakened the guard, who lived in a shack nearby. It took some coaxing, and a generous gift from Hans, but the guard finally agreed to dress and raise the barrier, and we proceeded on our way.

We reached the French-German border later that morning, and our troubles continued. My passport said, "For Travel in France" but lacked the words "and return," and an overzealous border guard refused me reentry to Germany. Eventually our explanations prevailed and we completed our journey home.

* * *

We all enjoyed our visit to Paris and the concert, but the aftermath of that trip led to the only significant disagreement Mother Bohle and I ever experienced. A week after our return, I received a short but very pleasant letter from Mrs. Menuhin. She thanked me for the lovely gift and said she and her family enjoyed entertaining us as their guests. She added that she had written to thank my mother-in-law as well.

Thrilled, I phoned Mother Bohle and told her of my letter. To my astonishment, she became furious.

"I received no letter," she exclaimed. "How dare you receive acknowledgment first. Am I not the matriarch of this family?"

Listening in stunned silence as her fury increased, I agreed immediately when she insisted I come to her house to discuss the matter further. First, however, I phoned Hans, who promised to join me if things became too heated.

Mother Bohle appeared in control of her emotions once again by the time I arrived, but her anger simmered just beneath the surface. She began with ultimatums, notably that henceforth she intended to review all my mail before I saw it. If I objected, she would have Hans fired! Without responding, I called Hans, who came immediately and we left without further comment.

On his return home that evening, Hans' father learned of the confrontation and phoned immediately. Hans answered the phone. Minutes later, Dad Bohle came bursting into our apartment, brushing Hans aside. He apologized for intruding but wanted to listen to my story, seemingly consternated. He then left without giving any opinion.

No word came from Hans' parents for about a week. Then, a family friend called as an emissary and said that Mother and Dad Bohle wanted us to spend Sunday afternoon with them. We went, and Dad received us warmly. Mother Bohle, a bit distant toward me but still cordial, said nothing about her blow-up, and we never spoke of it again.

The incident produced one positive result. Fearful that we might decide to leave Germany and move back to the United States, Dad Bohle sought to soothe the waters. "I have sent your parents travel money to come for a visit," he told me. "The guest rooms of the Syndicate will be theirs as long as they wish to stay."

* * *

Mom and Dad Kuechler arrived that summer. Hans used his vacation to take them with us on a tour of Germany and Bavaria, and we spent two weeks discovering places of history and heredity. We also had the good fortune to attend the famous Passion Play in Oberammergau. My parents loved their handsome young grandson and became good friends with Hans' parents. Dad Bohle wanted them to stay permanently, offering as an inducement a position for my father in his oil firm if they remained. But on Sept. 1, Mom and Dad left for the U.S.A. They had been with us four weeks.

I grieved at their departure, knowing that the great distance and the expense of travel made another reunion in the near future unlikely. Had I known then all that would transpire in the years until next we saw them, would I have insisted that we, also, return to America? Most likely, yes—but no one could read the future. Germany was our home, and so we stayed.

CHAPTER 8

Birth, Death and the Growing
Nazi Menace

From the earliest days of our marriage, the Nazi cloud had hung heavy over Germany. It grew from a minor disturbance on the horizon, ignored by most Germans, to engulf the nation and become an all-pervasive force that dictated every aspect of life.

Hitler had risen to power, without the support of the majority of Germans. During 1932, a year in which five national elections were held, the Nazis' best showing was 37 percent. Germany's middle and upper classes considered Hitler nothing more than a demagogue—if they considered him at all. The prospect of him as the leader of Germany seemed unthinkable

On January 30, 1933, however, a stunned nation faced the reality that Hitler had been named chancellor of Germany. His ascent had come not through the ballot box but by back-room scheming, intrigue and betrayal—and the threat (sometimes realized) of terrorism from the S.A. His private army of thugs and hoodlums, also known as Storm Troopers or Brown Shirts, for the uniforms they wore, provided the threat of physical violence that enabled Hitler to bludgeon his way to power.

Once in control, Hitler wasted no time in strengthening his hand. On March 23, 1933, just weeks after a national election in which the Nazi Party received only 44 percent of the vote, he managed to force through the Reichstag a law that gave all legislative power to his cabinet for four years. Thus, by legal means and with no bloodshed, Hitler became dictator—or Fuehrer (leader), as he called himself—and the German Republic died.

Hitler wasted no time in demonstrating what he had in mind for the nation. By the end of 1933 he had dissolved all political parties except the Nazis, abolished the separate powers of the German states, banned labor unions, abolished freedom of speech and of the press, stifled the independence of the courts and put all aspects of the political, economic, cultural and social life of Germany under Nazi rule. He also withdrew Germany from the League of Nations and declared that Germany once again would become a world power.

* * *

Hitler's devastating blows to the personal freedom of the German people did little to erode his public support. For the masses, who were working once again, Hitler provided the tonic Germany needed to emerge from its economic doldrums. A popular catch phrase of the day was "We're no longer free to starve."

Even the intellectuals, who recognized Hitler as an unscrupulous despot surrounded by criminals and thugs, acknowledged his successes and the self-respect he had instilled once again in a proud people. Germans of all classes were eager to shed the shackles of Versailles. If Hitler was the price they had to pay, they seemed willing.

In June 1934, Hitler provided a compelling object lesson of the consequences of opposing him. Hundreds of political opponents—including Ernst Roehm, the head of the S.A. and once Hitler's closest personal friend—were rounded up and executed for conspiring to assassinate Hitler, or so the Nazis claimed. In reality, he simply was eliminating anyone who might stand in his way.

Hitler underscored the message of that massacre the following month in a speech. "If anyone reproaches me and asks why I did not resort to the regular courts of justice, then all I can say is this: in this hour I was responsible for the fate of the German people, and thereby I became the supreme judge of the German people."

Then he added a further threat. "Everyone must know for all future time that if he raises his hand to strike the State, then certain death is his lot." And by then Hitler was the state.

Each year under the Nazis the atmosphere became more oppressive, and too late people began to wake up to the reality of Hitler's intentions for Germany. He ruled with an iron fist and enforced his edicts with intimidation and terror. The Nazis encouraged citizens to inform on anyone suspected of disloyalty. Offenses—either real or imagined—were punished swiftly and ruthlessly. Concentration camps and even graveyards filled with "enemies of the Party."

Soon suspicion and secrecy replaced the trust and openness that formerly had characterized the German people. Long-time friends and even family became suspect, requiring one to stay on guard against a careless remark that might be misunderstood, and reported.

Understandably, that dampened political discussions of all kinds, in the Bohle family as in all others. Hans' parents never discussed their feelings about political developments and Hans and I kept our views private from everyone except each other.

Once in early 1935, however, Dad Bohle raised his veil of secrecy and took me into his confidence. I happened to visit him one evening when Mother Bohle attended a concert alone. At 10 p.m., Dad Bohle answered a knock at the door and found a former Army comrade standing there, nearly paralyzed with fear. He belonged to a group suspected of plotting against Hitler and was fleeing for his life. In his desperation, he had recalled that Dad lived nearby, so he came seeking help.

Dad let me know that he would be gone for a few hours and said not to worry. Then, summoning his chauffeur and car, he drove the man to the safety of the Swiss border. He returned the following morning and explained the situation to me, asking for my discretionary silence which, of course, he could depend upon. Dad Bohle had risked much for his friend.

* * *

The growing strength of the Nazis also affected Hans' professional life. Some time earlier, the Syndicate had purchased 500 one-tank gasoline stations along the Rhine River and had established the Pennsylvania Oil Company as a separate subsidiary. However, the government prohibited any company from running two businesses and often used that as a pretext to infiltrate a Party member into the senior management ranks. To preclude that, Hans was appointed head of the oil subsidiary at a secret meeting of the board of directors.

The company's main supplier was in Romania, and it became necessary for Hans to travel there to purchase oil. The oil then was shipped by barge to Frankfurt, where the Syndicate kept a bulk station. Hans proved a skilled administrator and shrewd bargainer, and the Pennsylvania Oil Company prospered under his leadership.

At the same meeting at which Hans was elected head of the oil company, the board accepted the resignation of one of its members, Mr. Silver, who as a man of considerable influence had opposed Hitler's rise to power. Since he was a Jew, he was convinced it would be best for the company and himself if he left Germany. Other than the board members, only a few top executives knew of Mr. Silver's official capacity with the Syndicate or of his financial interest in it. They reasoned, therefore, that his departure would cause little if any stir since no Nazi liaison had yet penetrated their ranks.

The only difficulty they anticipated was in transferring to another country the large sum due from the sale of his shares in the Syndicate. Taking money out of the country was strictly forbidden, other than the small sum allowed for travelers, which never went very far. Border inspections for currency were especially tight.

The timing of Mr. Silver's decision was perfect, since he still could leave the country at will. And so he did, evidently valuing his freedom foremost.

About 10 days after that extraordinary board meeting, Hans burst in at home with the news of his assignment as director of the oil division.

"What's more, until I can take over, you and I will enjoy a few days in Switzerland, a sort of vacation and business trip combined," he explained. "Friends of the Syndicate will cover our expenses, and we will go to Lugano, a lovely spot at any time of the year but especially now, when we are likely to have snow."

That seemed sudden, but not unusual. I was used to having Hans phone me with instructions to pack and be ready to leave for some destination on a few hours notice. With plenty of help in our home, I always was ready to go unless the children were sick or showed symptoms of illness. So, that news, coupled with Hans's new success, delighted me.

We arrived at a very fine old hotel in Lugano and were received like valued, long-time guests. I looked at Hans for an explanation of such lavish kindness, but he only smiled and made no comment.

In our rooms we found flowers and a basket of choice fruit, and a letter of invitation to dinner the following Sunday at the home of Mr. Silver. At that time I knew nothing of him, other than having heard Hans' father speak of him regarding business matters. I did not know that he had lived in Germany. How lovely, I thought. Hans' father must have told Mr. Silver that we were coming.

On the appointed day, we arrived at his elegant villa high above and facing Lake Lugano. A great fire burned in a huge fireplace, and the picture window in his living room afforded a view of nearby mountain peaks, which on that particular day were covered with heavy black snow clouds. It looked both ominous and beautiful.

Mr. Silver had other guests, and the men discussed work and politics. A woman in the group seemed openly hostile to both Hans and me, until she detected an American accent in my German. The day proved interesting and unforgettable. If Mr. Silver had chosen to leave Germany and live in Switzerland, the villa he had chosen seemed a most wonderful home.

Only after Hans and I had returned to Germany did I hear the story of Mr. Silver and his Syndicate affiliations and why he had left Germany. And it was then that I learned that Hans, at his own great personal risk, had brought to Mr. Silver negotiable papers terminating all interests with the Syndicate.

Hans explained that he deliberately had chosen Sunday to travel, to make the trip to Switzerland seem less likely for business. Also, he thought that taking along a chic wife would strengthen the illusion and, he hoped, avoid a more thorough inspection for money and papers. We were lucky, and I was glad I had not known.

* * *

Hitler never had made a secret of his intention to rebuild Germany's military might. From his earliest days as chancellor he had begun the rearmament process in secret. After he withdrew Germany from the League of Nations in 1934, that process accelerated openly. Although France, England and the United States issued formal objections, they did nothing to prevent Hitler's build-up.

Then, on March 16, 1935, Hitler announced in a radio address to the nation that he had decreed a law establishing universal military service and a peacetime army of nearly half a million men. Most Germans, even many who opposed Hitler, greeted the news with great celebration, since it brought to an end the last of the restrictions of Versailles, which had symbolized Germany's defeat and humiliation.

As a father and an executive employed in a strategic industry, Hans was exempt from conscription—at least for he moment. Still, I worried about what Hitler's decision might mean for Germany and for our family in the long run. I also wondered how the former Allies would respond. On that score I need not have concerned myself: once again they objected heatedly but did nothing.

* * *

Amid all the other changes in our lives, our family expanded once again with the birth of our daughter, Irmgard, on May 23, 1935. "It's a girl," the doctor announced in the delivery room.

"After only boys in the family, can you imagine how they will spoil her?" I said. Hans laughed. As I predicted, her grandparents and relatives loved fussing over our beautiful little princess.

But in less than two weeks, our joy at Irmgard's birth turned to sorrow due to the sudden death of Dad Bohle, who contracted sepsis while on vacation in Switzerland. It was his custom when he walked each day to twirl his cane as he strolled. The friction of the cane on his thumb caused a blister, which became infected. The mistake of a physician who lanced the boil caused the poison to enter Dad Bohle's bloodstream. Since there was no medication to counteract the infection, he was gone.

The family had gathered at the hospital in Baden-Baden the day preceding his death, and against the admonitions of my very concerned doctor, I had driven with them from Mannheim to see him.

I sat with that dear man whom I loved and respected like I did my own father, wiped his fevered brow and talked to him. He thanked me and in delirium pointed to the window. "Look, there comes Ruth. She is coming to see me," he said in his delirium. That night he left us.

In those days, German women did not take part in burial services, and it was good. I needed solitude and consented to a few days in a "rest home" near Heidelberg. Hans agreed to join me there for dinner each evening.

The night before my departure, I awoke to see the apparition of Dad Bohle entering our bedroom. He appeared in gray from top to toe, an expression of great sadness on his face. I cried out in surprise and fright, and he disappeared. To this day, I regret that my reaction ended the great moment. I wondered during my few days away from home if he would appear to me again, but he did not.

* * *

In addition to his work, Hans now faced the added responsibility of serving as executor of his father's estate. Reviewing papers, Hans found a small booklet. The last page bore the figure 90,000, along with the name of a business associate and friend of Dad Bohle's in Holland.

Hans suspected the entry might indicate some kind of funds transfer, so he left immediately to investigate. The Dutchman confirmed that he held British war bonds valued at 90,000 RM for Dad Bohle, pending further instructions. That arrangement demonstrated Dad Bohle's distrust of the Nazi regime.

What to do? Hans could not take the bonds back to Germany, and any German possessing money in a foreign land faced death. He asked the Dutchman to send the bonds to my parents in the U.S.A. and, eager to rid himself of the burden, the friend complied. Hans also decided to send me to visit my family in America and find a suitable place to invest the bonds.

I sailed for America, with Bobby in tow, aboard the German liner Europe on November 10, 1935. Mother Bohle delighted in the prospect of caring for Irmgard and Hans during my absence. Soon after leaving port we encountered an angry sea with winds of hurricane strength, and I wondered fearfully that the ship did not break in half. Eight such days were no great joy to me, even though luckily I did not get seasick.

Most of the passengers stayed out of sight all the time, but not Bobby he loved it all. He particularly enjoyed sitting on a chair in our stateroom, letting it slide from one side to the other with the roll of the ship.

Bobby became a favorite of the stewards, who spoiled him thoroughly. To help care for my lively young man part of the day, I hired a lovely lady, a permanent guest on the ship and the widow of a former ship's officer.

My parents loved the surprise of seeing me so much sooner than they had ever hoped. And all the family were anxious to see the little blond boy I had with me. With those soft blond curls, red lips and mischievous blue eyes, he captivated them all. They indulged him readily, and he became most difficult to manage.

Thanksgiving meant a big family gathering. Relatives from Michigan arrived for dinner, as did my brother Carl and his wife Esther, from St. Louis. It was a sort of get reacquainted visit, good for us all.

The bonds came from Holland in an unassuming bundle, wrapped in newspaper and tied with ordinary string. I carried them from one law office to another, seeking a safe way to sell or invest them. In each case, the point eventually arrived at which I needed to sign some documents to complete the transaction. I balked at that, however, fearing that it somehow might give us away to the German authorities.

Christmas came, and then New Year's, and still I found no solution. In desperation, I put the bonds in a safe deposit box at a bank in Oak Park until I could figure out what to do. An uncle and my brother, George, whom I took into my confidence, suggested I leave the bonds in the bank while they considered other options. George and I then devised a code to enable us to communicate in safety, if need be, after my return.

Meanwhile, thinking I had been gone long enough (six weeks), Hans phoned and asked me to come home. As we talked via the then-new transatlantic telephone service, our voices swelled up and down, sounding as though the ocean waves were washing against the cable buried at the bottom of the sea.

He asked me how much longer I intended to stay, and told me how much he missed me and Bobby. As an incentive for a quick return, he proposed a vacation in Switzerland. I agreed to make arrangements immediately, realizing my thoughtlessness. Time had flown while I enjoyed my home turf for awhile.

* * *

Once more, I said a difficult good-bye to my family. Bobby and I took the train to New York, where I contacted several music agents on behalf of Walter. None offered any encouragement, however, explaining that they acquired their European talent while traveling in Europe, not in the U.S. Walter would have to make it on his own.

We returned to Germany in late January 1936 aboard the Europa, the same ship that had brought us to America, and I retained the same lady to help me care for Bobby.

During the voyage, on a calm, misty sea, we encountered a freighter which at first appeared as if it were a mirage reflected in the clouds high up in the sky. Bobby saw it, too.

Our own ship slowed and then stopped. I wondered why, and soon had an answer. The freighter had signaled, "Very sick sailor on board. Immediate help or die." The Europa signaled in return that it would lower a motorboat with the first officer, to effect the rescue, using its searchlights to illuminate the way.

But the freighter reacted more rapidly. Suddenly, a simple rowboat, with the sick sailor strapped to a stretcher, became visible through the mist close to us. The sailor immediately was taken on board and, while the Europa stood still in the water, the Ship's doctor operated and saved the sailor's life. Bobby will never forget that incident, and neither will I.

The rest of the crossing passed uneventfully, and we arrived in Bremen to find Hans on the dock, waving happily in greeting.

What a wonderful reunion! Hans delighted in hearing his excited little son babbling away in English about his many adventures.

So happy to be together again, we drove straight home to Mannheim and our baby girl, who of course did not immediately remember me. A happy little person, she had grown rapidly during the three months of my absence, and had learned to walk holding onto her crib. Hans and his mother also noticed an interesting change in Bobby. To his friends he spoke only English—but he quickly regained German when they did not understand him.

Not long after I returned, Hitler saw the futility of his death threat against Germans who harbored money out of the country, and rescinded the "death sentence." Immediately, Mother Bohle decided she wanted "her" bonds returned to Germany. For peace of mind and with Hans' consent, I sent George a coded message, and he mailed the bonds to us. Mother Bohle claimed them all, which was unfair to both Hans and Walter, but her sons would not combat her. However, thanks to George's foresight, my trip to America yielded an invaluable benefit. Before returning the bonds, shrewd George clipped and cashed the interest coupons and banked the money. Those dollars eventually paid for our passage home to the U.S.A. after the war.

Within weeks after my return from America, Hitler took a big step on the long road to war. On March 7, 1936, German troops moved into the Rhineland, an area on either side of the Rhine River, which formed the border between France and Germany. The Treaty of Versailles had established the Rhineland as a permanent demilitarized zone.

Hitler claimed his action was necessary to minimize the security risk from a treaty that France and Russia had signed, and he pledged that Germany had no further expansionist aims. For several days we feared that the French would react and thus precipitate a war, but as in previous confrontations with Hitler, they did little other than bluster in indignation. Once again, Hitler had won his bet.

* * *

We moved that spring to the Bentzinger House, a beautiful big stone mansion made over into three apartments. Our landlady, Mrs. Bentzinger, lived alone on the first floor. We occupied the second floor and Karl Elmendorif, maestro of the Mannheim Symphony, took the third floor.

All the rooms were very formal and elegant, with high ceilings. Our entertaining area included a huge parlor with a real American fireplace built especially for a library a balcony and us. A large dining area adjoined the parlor, with two high doors leading to another balcony. The apartment also contained four bedrooms, all with balconies overlooking a small surrounding garden edged with trees, two bathrooms and a grand foyer. Rooms for the maid and the children's nurse were located in the parterre, a sort of half-basement with a garden.

One lovely evening we dined with Mrs. Bentzinger and met Carl and Rita Reuther, neighbors from a few houses away. Beautiful and exotic, Rita's pride and reserve reflected her North German upbringing in Hamburg as an architect's daughter.

More outgoing than his wife, Carl also came from a family with business interests reaching many parts of the world. The Communists had executed Carl's father, and his mother carried on in her husband's place—very unusual for a German woman.

What wonderful friends Rita and Carl became: progressive and engaging. Throughout the war and long thereafter, we remained friends, often defying long distances to see each other once again.

Instead of the ski vacation Hans promised upon my return from America, we decided to attend the 1936 Olympics in Berlin later that summer. We arrived to find all tickets sold. But we stood debating what to do, a woman stepped up and offered to sell us her tickets for the days events, and we accepted happily.

Hitler intended to use the Olympics as a showcase for Aryan supremacy, but the great black American athlete Jesse Owens shattered that plan with his spectacular performances in track and field. Hans and I witnessed his victory in the 100 meter dash.

Hitler and Mussolini, observing stoically from the grandstand nearby, made their disappointment very clear. Hans remained in Berlin on business after the Games, while I took Bobby to a children's spa on the North Sea to seek a cure for the persistent colds that plagued him. I stayed a week, observing Bobby each day without his knowledge, to make sure he was content and well cared for.

Hans and I met again in Berlin to continue on to Mannheim, but on the way we stopped to visit a famous race course called the Nurnberg Ring. A driving enthusiast, Hans decided to fulfill a long-held ambition and drive the track. What a dangerous and exhilarating experience for him—and for me, too, since he insisted I join him. Steeply banked double curves threw the car into greater speed than Hans had anticipated, and it took all of his skill to keep us alive

* * *

Despite the political events swirling all around us, life continued normally most of the time. In the summer of 1937, we took the children to a rustic fisherman's village on the Baltic Sea for a family vacation. We rode the waves in our collapsible boat, ate fish smoked on the beach —even smoked eel, long, fat and delicious— and walked for miles along the seashore. Amazingly, Hans and I also met, in that out-of-the-way spot, a friend and member of the Baptist church in Oak Park, Ill.

The little village may have been tucked away in an isolated area of the Baltic, but the elders knew how to entertain tourists. One of the events we attended was a performance by a group that called themselves "The White Russians." They sang and danced and performed gymnastics wonderfully. After the show, we saw the athletes as they were leaving, admiring the exotic beauty of their ladies.

Hans' career kept him busy. He could spend little time with

the children. But when in town he seldom missed their favorite ritual, coffee and cake at 4 o'clock on Saturday afternoon.

Hans liked lots of fruit in his torte and asked me once to instruct the cook to put more in the next one she prepared. I did, but she forgot. When coffee time arrived on Saturday he took one look and then set down his fork.

"Get your coats, children. We are going out for our treat today just the three of us," he said. He did not need to say to me, "Maybe you will remember next time."

Unsure how to handle the situation, I noticed the children's excitement at the prospect of an outing alone with their father. So I simply smiled and told them to enjoy themselves. That took the "spice" out of Hans' cake for that day, but he got more fruit on his torte the next week.

CHAPTER 9

A Home in Berlin

In his address to the Reichstag on January 30, 1937, Hitler promised that "the time of the so-called surprises has been ended." And indeed, 1937 was a year of calm during which the Nazis strengthened the nation's military might, cemented political ties with Italy and bided their time.

The deceptive quiet ended on March 12, 1938, when German troops invaded Austria, achieving the Anschluss (union) between Germany and his native Austria that Hitler had sought for years. Reports in German newspapers claimed that the Austrian government had asked Hitler to send in troops to help quell rioting and bloodshed in the streets. But thinking Germans saw through the ruse.

And the response of the rest of the world? Once again they sat by and let Hitler win the day, unopposed.

At the same time, a long-brewing situation in Hans' professional life came to a head. The success of his oil company had attracted the attention of a group known as the Kartel, comprised of several large oil companies. Hans had chosen not to join that group, a decision he later regretted. The Kartel resented his independence and achievements. One executive in the syndicate especially wanted to force Hans out. Finally, he found the weapon he needed.

On one trip to Rumania, Hans had bought oil at a very attractive price. It was an unusual buy, lower than they had been able to negotiate. When the traitor leaked word of Hans' purchase to the Kartel, they used their powerful connections in the government to force Hans to sell them half the oil at less than cost. Disgruntled and disheartened, Hans realized that the Kartel would not relent in its campaign against him. Under the prevailing conditions at his firm, he lacked leverage. His family held 49 percent of the assets.

"Perhaps I made a mistake in not staying in America when we first met," he said one night, as we discussed what to do next. "But how could I ignore my father's plans for me here? Perhaps my difficulties with the Kartel are a sign that I should sell out now and move to the United States."

But then came the stunning blow to him, to us. In early 1938, the government denied visas to all German males of conscription age. Another tell-tale evidence of impending war, we realized.

Forced to stay in Germany, Hans gave up the battle against the Kartel. With approval of the Syndicate board, he negotiated the sale of the oil company to another firm—costing the informer his job. As part of the sale agreement, Hans accepted a senior management position with the purchaser, which meant a move for us to Berlin in May, 1938. Already seven months pregnant with our third child, I left for the city to find a place for us to live.

* * *

"I have shown you houses the envy of every German woman," the frustrated real estate salesman said after a morning of inspecting one elegant house after another, none of which met my favor. "What do you want?"

"Something different, unconventional," I tried to explain, not sure myself. "Something refreshingly casual, maybe a countryside cottage. Not a tailored floor plan with a trimmed garden on an immaculate street. Can you show me something in the country?"

At that suggestion, he headed west on the Heerstrasse, Berlin's main east-west axis. I dozed as we drove, then roused when we crossed a wide bridge.

"We are entering a small peninsula, with the Havel River to our left and Lake Pichel to our right," my escort noted. "These two waters meet and form the Wannsee. It is still Berlin, but also country."

We turned onto a narrow street that curved downward past a number of modest, charming country homes set in gardens and surrounded by picket fences. Stopping on the shore of Lake Pichel, we got out.

Wonderful! I loved it! Sassy blue and gray jays flitted from one stand of tall trees to another, and the sun shone on sailboats out on the distant Wannsee. Across Lake Pichel, a mile and a half away, a thin line of tall trees marked the west rim of Berlin. We heard no cars or other noise, just the gentle whir of the breeze and the soft lapping of the waves on the shore, hardly 20 feet away.

Entranced, I listened as the salesman described the area.

"This peninsula has just four streets, three of them leading to the shore: Paddlerweg (Paddler's Street), Schwimmerweg (Swimmer's Street) and this one, Rudererweg (Rower's Street)."

"How appropriate," I murmured, and he continued.

"At the very end of the first dirt road, on the point of the peninsula, stands an abandoned castle, a sort of silent sentinel, marking the division of waters.

"This brown house to our left is the one I wanted you to see," he added. "It's the only brown house in a whole area of white ones, and it also is a bit bigger than the others."

He hardly needed to say more. I loved the whole setting immediately, and the rural atmosphere appealed to me tremendously. He pointed out features such as the balconies with their striped awnings, the large play yard for the children, apple and peach trees laden with fruit and the general good repair of the structure.

A lovely wrought iron gate opened to the garden. Two sets of steps led us to the entrance. Two tiny, mouse-like elderly maiden ladies met us there, leaning against each other and tittering with excitement at the prospect of a sale.

Inside were a few more steps to a hall and stairwell serving all three floors. We passed through a cloakroom into the social rooms, the first of which measured approximately 18 by 24 feet. It had a beautiful parquet floor, corner windows to the right and a glass door that opened onto the large balcony we had observed outside.

The decorating scheme provided a sharp and unpleasant contrast to the architectural details of the room. Stark red paint covered the walls and heavy, cheap, dark green drapes bordered the windows. Sparse furnishings and a small rug completed the decor. One glance, of course, told me all: atrocious!

We walked through a single door to the left into a room the mirror image of the first, even to the decor. I recognized immediately that removing the dividing partition would create an exquisite room with a sweeping, 180-degree vista of the lake.

We continued our tour without comment. Another door on the left opened on a small hall, where a steep staircase led upward and yet another door provided an exit from the house.

"How odd," I said to my agent. "This staircase and door look like an escape hatch. I wonder why?" But no explanation was forthcoming.

We moved on to the dining room, which was spacious but dark since it had but one window. Next came the butler's pantry and subsequently the kitchen, whereupon we found that we had completed a full circle and stood once again in the main hall.

"I'm sorry," the salesman apologized. "The location is superb, but I had no idea of the crazy layout."

My response caught him by surprise. "I'd like to see the rest of it, all of it."

We took the main stairs to the second floor which, we discovered, could be shut off from the rest of the house to form a separate apartment or suite of rooms. Two bedrooms opened to the east, and two to the west, with one bath and a kitchen. The entry was cut short from the south wall by that crazy second stairway we had seen from below.

"The stairway must go, so the floor extends to the south wall with its lovely huge window," I said. "This hallway would then make an excellent playroom for the children. The kitchen could be converted into a master bath."

My agent stared at me, aghast, as he realized that I actually was considering that monstrosity.

We climbed to the third floor, and I saw that it could be made very charming. It had a huge front bedroom overlooking the lake and two smaller ones.

We then descended to the basement, where I found a washroom, a furnace room, a storage room and, of all things, a projection room and viewing room with seating for about 40 people.

I saw great potential in that unusual house, if Hans could buy it cheaply enough to allow for renovation costs. With three floors of living space plus a full basement, it offered ample room for our family, servants and guests. I also loved the location, only a 10-minute walk to a streetcar stop and a country store.

Two days later Hans arrived in Berlin and completed the purchase. We retained a decorator to oversee the renovation.

* * *

My task completed for the moment, I returned to Mannheim to organize the move and await the birth of our third child. The movers took our furniture to Berlin in June. Hans, the children and their nurse went to live in Berlin. I remained with Mother Bohle in Mannheim.

I entered the hospital on July 25, and Hans returned from Berlin for my delivery. When noon came with no sign of the baby, Hans and the doctor left for lunch. They returned an hour later to find our little boy, Dieter, waiting for them.

Five days later I flew directly from the hospital to Berlin with Dieter and a nurse to rejoin Hans and the other children. As I entered the renovated house for the first time, I could not believe the changes. The decorator and Hans had wrought a miracle, a fantastic transformation.

Removing the back staircase and the wall that originally divided the large front room had expanded the dining and living areas. Freshly painted and wallpapered walls, new drapes at the windows and some new furniture transformed the formerly dreary space into gracious, elegant rooms. Even a new sailboat sat in a slip in front of the house. I loved my new home.

What more could a young woman want? A dream home, plenty of good help, fresh air and sunshine, a beautiful lake to watch, a thoughtful husband, a new and healthy baby and two other fine youngsters. We also enjoyed the company and assistance of several of Hans' cousins who occupied the guestrooms on the third floor.

With all my advantages, I still felt misgivings. Was it the added responsibility of managing our new home, anxiety about the prospect of war, post-partum blues, or a combination of them all?

In the evenings, with the children in bed, Hans and I settled in the living room with our houseguests for heated discussions of the political situation. Our new friends and neighbors from across the street, Franz and Wally Grubert, often joined us.

We spent other evenings huddled around the radio, listening to Hitler's venomous speeches. I marveled at his ability to stir the audience to the point of hysteria. "Sieg Heil, Sieg Heil," the crowds shouted, sometimes hardly waiting for the next sentence to begin.

"Those people support him 100 percent," I commented one evening to Hans in exasperation, as we listened alone. "Why do not one of our acquaintance profess such admiration? Our friends all share our skepticism of Hitler and the Nazis.'

"How many people do you think are in that audience?" he asked.

"Oh, thousands. Probably many thousands."

"And what portion of the total population of Germany do they represent?" he countered abruptly, with unaccustomed harshness. "You hear nothing more than induced mass hysteria; Hitler is a master of it."

* * *

By late summer, Hitler's appetite for expansion had put Germany once again on the brink of war. On the heels of his success in Austria, Hitler had begun threatening the Czech government over purported persecution of Germans living in a part of Western Czechoslovakia called the Sudetenland. Although the Czech government made concessions to the Sudeten Germans, Hitler vowed to settle for nothing less than the immediate cession of the Sudetenland to Germany. The Czech leaders stood firm, and with both sides refusing to budge, conflict seemed inevitable.

Mindful of the separation that war might bring, and concerned about the slow recovery of my energy from Dieter's birth, Hans suggested a few days away from home in some quiet spot, to rest in solitude.

And so we departed for the castle across the lake, a lovely, isolated spot. We ate, slept, motored the chain of lakes and walked in the rose gardens and the great untouched spaces surrounding the castle. Eager for solitude, we kept to ourselves—as did the few other guests.

The tranquillity of our surroundings could not, however, keep the ever-worsening political news from filling our minds, and we found no rest. Hitler, on a rampage, obviously intended to press on until he gained his objective—whatever that might be. Would the Allies continue to give him free rein? We speculated on possible consequences—all of them terrible—and imagined many scenarios all-drastic and awful. The quiet of life at the castle only added fuel to our concerns. Each day of uncertainty seemed an eternity and Hans could not reassure me.

In a last-ditch effort to avert war, the leaders of the "Big Four"— England, France, Italy and Germany—agreed to meet in Munich. On September 30, while peace hung in the balance, Hans and I sat silently in the castle dining room at noon, absorbed in our thoughts.

Hearing a commotion, we looked up and saw Mrs. Goebbels, the wife of the Nazi propaganda minister, entering with her entourage, all of them gay and frivolous.

Their spirit and actions were callous, the exact antithesis of the serious happenings of the day. On the decisions of the Big Four representatives rested the fate of all the people, yes, Hans' and mine, too. Their frivolity—was it just outward show? Regardless, it was disgusting, unfeeling and crushing.

"Let's go home," Hans said in disgust. "We need real distraction, not peace and quiet. Tonight, let's go to the acrobat show at the Sportspalast in Berlin."

Only hours after leaving the total quiet of the country, we found ourselves in a noisy arena. The crowd clapped too long and too loud, jumped up and down and moved about constantly in a desperate attempt to blot out reality. One performer was an American girl, tap dancer. I wanted to call out to her, "Go home, young lady, go home while you still can."

The activity on stage and around us held our minds to a degree. We both tried to put down moments of panic and succeeded in short spurts, only to get caught up again in a mad whirl of despair.

When intermission finally arrived, we joined the huge mass of people who scrambled like so many idiots, like a flow of lava, hot and relentless, toward the exits. On the street we heard cries of "Extra, extra, read all about it," so unusual in Germany and reminiscent of my America. Over the heads of the mob, Hans saw the headlines: "The Big Four Have Decided! There Will Be No War."

What pushing and pulling, as the frenzied mob stampeded toward the news vendors! Then, miraculously, the crowd melted away suddenly into the night, all thought of returning for the rest of the entertainment seemingly forgotten. Maybe they had gone to a beer garden to drink down the remnants of fear, to haul together their wits. Hans and I started for home, emotionally and physically drained by the ordeal of the day and thinking only of sleeping and awakening without tension.

Once again Hitler had won without a fight. England and France had agreed to German occupation of the Sudetenland, and had pressured the Czech government into accepting Hitler's terms.

* * *

Despite the agreement reached by the Big Four, the Nazi military build-up continued unabated. Hans and I sought relief with weekend guests and an occasional dinner and show in town after work.

On one such occasion, as I left the streetcar at our agreed-upon meeting spot, I saw shattered shop windows everywhere I looked, with store contents strewn over the pavement. The shop owners stood nearby, sobbing and wringing their hands. Then I spotted Hans, waiting for me near the smoldering ruins of a synagogue

"This is awful," he said in horror. "The vandalism, the smashed shop windows. Look at those mannequins, fabrics, jewels, all sorts of wares scattered in the streets."

We stood caught in horror as we viewed the tremendous damage, knowing instinctively that Hitler's S.A., gone wild and unrestrained, had perpetrated that madness.

Depressed and fearful, we proceeded to the restaurant but ate with little appetite and soon returned home. The next day, the papers attempted to place the blame on bands of Jew-haters seeking retribution for past grievances.

I, too, occasionally erased the nation's problems from my mind, in light of personal security concerns at home. While tending the furnace in the basement one day, I came face to face with a disheveled-looking intruder. Where did he come from, I wondered, and how did he gain entry? I was trapped.

Warily I stared at him, rigid with fear. He, too, stood immobile, seeming as frightened as I was. Then his face turned fire engine red and great beads of sweat dotted his huge head. Without a word or even a sound, he turned and fled through the back basement door.

I bounded upstairs and phoned Hans who immediately ordered new locks on all the doors and contacted a kennel in Mannheim for a police dog.

When we mentioned the incident to our neighbors, we learned that the intruder was the brother of the two elderly women I had met on my first visit to the house. He had spent his time in and out of lunatic asylums, always returning to the house. I was very frightened.

Arno, a huge, powerful pedigreed German shepherd, arrived a few days later. Each evening he began barking between 5 and 6 o'clock, suggesting the presence of a prowler outside. One evening we let Arno out when his barking commenced. The sight of that great animal must have convinced the prowler to give up, because Arno's barking ceased after that night.

CHAPTER 10

A Last Interlude

Christmas soon neared, and with it the end of 1938, a good year for our family. We invited Mother Bohle to join us for the holidays. She arrived, and occupied the guest suite on the third floor. The children, usually bereft of grandparents, were enchanted with her, and, initially, she with them. A beautiful tree, gifts, music, carols and good food lifted our hearts. Snow and ice covered the ground, and heavenly blue skies with sunshine enticed us to sledding and skating on the frozen lake.

Hans and I spared no effort nor expense to make his mother feel wanted and loved. We even purchased three tickets for the Berliner Staatsopera as a special treat. But for all our trying, our guest seemed restless and unhappy.

A few days after Christmas, she informed us of her plans to return to Mannheim for New Year's, where the climate suited her better. "I also hate to leave Otto (her permanent houseguest, the violinist Otto Spamer) alone during the holidays, and he has no one but me. And I also find the holidays difficult since Father died."

Unable to change her mind, we took her to the train station on the fourth day after Christmas. She thanked us with as much warmth as her nature allowed, but her lack of emotional attactment to our family saddened us. On the day of Father Bohle's death, she had exclaimed bitterly, "Nun ist das ganze schoene Leben verbei (now the whole beautiful life is over)." Her life seemed without purpose.

After Mother Bohle's train left, Hans took me home, intending to return to his office. As we opened the front door, however, we received a call from his brother, Walter, whom we had not seen nor heard from in more than a year. I picked up the bedroom extension and listened in.

"Where are you?" Hans asked, excited to hear from his brother again.

"In Berlin, since yesterday."

"Are you staying with friends, or would you like to come and stay with us?"

"I'd love to stay with you, but that's not practical. I'm formulating a program to perform on the Berlin radio station, and I must work in the studio every day. At present, I'm staying at a very good hotel, the Adlon. Do you know it?"

Hans laughed. "Doesn't everybody? It is one of the best. Are you eating alone this evening, and if so, would you like company? Or, when can we see you?"

Walter chuckled in embarrassment. "I need to talk to you about that. I am not exactly alone. Mrs. Rumpel came along. We have theater plans this evening, but are free for tomorrow night."

Huh! I thought to myself that sounded natural. Mrs. Rumpel never let him go anywhere alone, never let him out of her sight. Did he really like that?

"We're busy tomorrow, but why don't you join our party on New Year's Eve?" Hans suggested. "Come early so we can catch up before the other guests arrive."

After conferring with Mrs. Rumpel, Walter accepted enthusiastically, then rang off.

"That was Walter," Hans said, as he was about to leave for the office.

"Yes, I know, I listened upstairs. That young man surely is brainwashed. He really seems to enjoy the company of a woman his mother's age."

"Do you agree with my suggestion that they visit on New Year's Eve and join us for the party?"

"Why not? They can mix with the other guests and we won't have to entertain Mrs. Rumpel the whole evening ourselves. I only hope they don't come too early. My goodness, what if your mother were still here, with the terrific enmity between them? Disastrous!"

"Does Walter ever go anywhere without her? One never gets to talk just with him alone, to know his real feelings," I added.

"Seems not," Hans said. "I keep wondering, as you do, why this much older woman. Why not a lovely young girl of his own age—Mrs. Rumpel's daughter, for instance? And I wonder, too, when he last visited Mother."

Hans left, and I sat musing about Walter and his strange alliance with Mrs. Rumpel. She had first entered the lives of the Bohle family eight years earlier, when she and her husband met Dad and Mother Bohle at a ski resort in Switzerland. The two couples, of the same age, enjoyed a splendid time together in the snow and sun, and everything seemed perfect.

The Bohle's returned full of exuberance about the couple from Leipzig. "We met two lovely people of intelligence, elegance, wealth and position, just the right ones to keep an eye on Walter while he studies piano at the conservatory there," Mother Bohle had said.

Her words proved prophetic. Almost immediately, Mrs. Rumpel began the process of alienating Walter from his "too dominant" (but loving) parents. No doubt she lost her heart to that sensitive, charming and pliable young man and his great art.

And Walter, usually oblivious to all but his beloved music, found her attentions gratifying, not realizing that he had replaced one dominating influence with another even stronger. Mrs. Rumpel's grip never slackened, and Walter eventually became completely alienated from his mother and father.

Despite our feelings toward Mrs. Rumpel, we retained cordial relations with her in an effort to keep open an avenue between Walter and his grieving parents. At least that enabled us to report news of his musical progress to them.

After Father Bohle died, Mother Bohle's separation from Walter became even more painful for her. She had always favored her youngest son, lavishing on him her attention and affection, and his rejection dealt her spirit an irreparable blow. Walter knew that and seemed not to care a whit.

"I am happy. Mrs. Rumpel meets all of my needs and has such a fabulous strength in her way of life," he explained to us once. In his eyes, she could do no wrong.

* * *

On New Year's Eve, Walter and Mrs. Rumpel arrived at 4 p.m., with the rest of our guests due at 7 p.m. Walter walked into the parlor and greeted us with his usual charming, smiling and gentle manner. Then, spying the piano, he sat down and began to play Bach's beautiful "Jesu, Joy of Man's Desiring," that glorious bit of inspired music that could soothe even one's dying hour. I longed to sit and listen, but turned instead to greet Mrs. Rumpel as she came in from the entry, a wisp of frosty air still hovering about her.

Walter stopped in mid-performance and joined us around the coffee table. As we enjoyed hot beverages and a bit of pastry, Hans mentioned Mother Bohle's Christmas visit.

"How long since you have seen her?" Hans asked pointedly. Visibly uncomfortable, Walter squirmed in his seat and sighed before answering.

"It's no use, we cannot see eye to eye on anything. She insists on blaming Mrs. Rumpel for our estrangement, when nothing could be further from the truth. But what's the use of discussing the situation with my mother. She's always right."

Meanwhile, the matronly and very proper Mrs. Rumpel sat listening with an amused half-smile on her lips, attired in her well-tailored, conventional black wool.

"Well, you, too, think you always are right," Hans said, laughing.

"That I am, yes, that I am," Walter said with unabashed egotism reinforced by conviction.

Recalling a story I read as a child, I posed a question.

"Walter, did you ever read of the two mules who met in the middle of a bridge too narrow for them both to pass? It made quite an impression on me and taught me my first lesson in humility. I visualized them fighting to pass, knowing it might cost one or both their lives. Under such circumstances, is backing up not better than going down?"

Walter threw back his head in a paroxysm of mirth, as Mrs. Rumpel laughed softly and discreetly. "I see your point," he said, "but neither Mother nor I ever got as far as the bridge, because it still separates us."

"But if it still stands, is there not at least hope?" I countered.

"It still stands, I suppose," Walter responded, then hesitated before continuing. "However, neither of us seems to know where it is."

Hans suggested that Walter might like a tour of the house, and the two of them left the room, leaving me with Mrs. Rumpel. Suddenly, we heard Arno barking from the cellar, where we kept him when guests arrived due to his unpredictability with strangers. "A police dog!" Mrs. Rumpel said, intrigued. "That I must see. I just love dogs and they like me. Please let him come up."

When Hans and Walter returned, she repeated her wishes insistently. Against his better judgment, Hans brought the dog up on a leash. He first walked Arno over to a clearly-uninterested Walter and then to Mrs. Rumpel, who spoke to him but did not touch him. After noting her scent, Arno proceeded to lie down between her chair and Hans'.

Believing all was well, Hans removed the leash. With one bound, Arno lunged at Mrs. Rumpel and grasped the sleeve of her dress in his teeth, ripping it from the armhole without scratching her skin or tearing the cloth. Hans, on his feet in an instant, took hold of Arno's collar and literally dragged him to the basement.

Strangely enough, Mrs. Rumpel exhibited the least shock and

fright of us all. I admired her composure. I apologized repeatedly, wondering all the while if Arno had sensed our true feelings toward the lady and acted on them. Mrs. Rumpel replied good-naturedly, "I asked for it—you warned me."

Then she and I went upstairs to our bedroom and I sewed the ripped sleeve back into place, leaving no trace of the incident. What a good sport, I thought, hating the subterfuge with which I pretended to like her when my heart blamed her for the separation between Walter and his mother. After all, he was a grown man and bore at least some responsibility for the estrangement. Unfortunately, both his mother and his lady friend insisted on possessing him totally. What did Mrs. Rumpel have in her favor, to keep him so firmly in her grasp? I determined to explore that question.

A casual comment got her started on her favorite subject. "Walter is utterly helpless in everything except his music, and a child about making decisions," she asserted. "He cannot so much as buy himself a sweater, a shirt or any garment."

Her speech grew more animated as she continued. "Walter has a deep psychological need for companionship, and I can devote my time to him. A philosopher as well as a great musician, his mind is so preoccupied by deep wells of thought that he hardly notices events around him. Sometimes I just die watching him cross the street, oblivious to the snarling, swift traffic all about him."

Perhaps so, yet somehow her words failed to reassure me. Clearly, she believed that Walter could not function without her.

Finished with sewing and downstairs again, I continued my probing, but this time in Walter's presence. We learned that he visited the studios alone every day and decided his own programs, and that he drove alone to the conservatory several days a week. He acknowledged that Mrs. Rumpel accompanied him on longer trips to his performances, since she could spare the time and he enjoyed the company.

A bit more grudgingly, he acknowledged that they always vacationed together. Although their travels often took them near

Mother Bohle's residence, they had never stopped. What a sad and unfortunate situation. Our other guests soon arrived. Walter and Mrs. Rumpel entered into the festivities with zest, the incident with Arno seemingly forgotten.

* * *

A few weeks later, Hans and I left for a ski vacation at the Hotel Duchi D'Aosta, one of the famous Tower hotels of Sestriere, Italy.

Prominent people from all over Europe, including many crowned heads, traveled to that remote ski resort. The daily routine for most guests began with breakfast, followed by a trip to the hairdresser for ladies. After a full day on the slopes, it was back to the hotel (and another trip to the hairdresser), a snooze, then up to dress in evening gown and tux for dinner and dancing.

At meals we were surrounded by royalty. Danish princesses occupied the table next to ours, always arriving late. Their breakfast plates held only a single carrot—the secret to their slender figures, perhaps?

Both the Italian crown prince and the grandson of the German Kaiser, accompanied by their respective entourages, were also seated nearby. One evening, emissaries carried notes back and forth between their tables, and we learned later from our waiter that the Italian prince had invited his counterpart to a special party. At first, the German prince had declined, explaining that he had not brought formal attire with him. The Italian prince then had remedied the situation by offering to provide his guest with the needed clothing, and the German had accepted.

Hans spent his days skiing the most difficult runs, while I took lessons on the easier slopes. I delighted to see him enjoy his skiing, but regretted my inability to share the experience more fully. I enjoyed my afternoons at the tea tables, listening to the guests from many lands—some of whom were not very discreet in their discussion of Germany's political situation.

On our way home to Berlin, we stopped in Milano for a day as guests of Hans' school friend, Alberto Keller. We spent the day sight seeing, touring galleries and visiting fine linen shops with Alberto's sister. That evening we enjoyed a superb dinner at the home of Alberto's parents, then adjourned with members of his family to La Scala for a performance of "Aida."

Our late arrival caused no concern, since the audience whispered, rattled papers and paid little attention until the singers approached the high notes. Once the dramatic moment ended, the audience returned to visiting—a new experience for Hans and me but apparently the accepted procedure there. We left the opera before the end to catch the night train for Germany, still in our formal clothes.

Back home again, we returned to the daily routine of work and family. That summer, Dr. Helmut and Lottie Schmitt moved into the house to the left of ours. They, the Gruberts and we became unusually compatible neighbors. Evenings often found us in one or the other parlor, in earnest discussion of the state of political affairs. Although not well enough informed to participate actively, I listened and gleaned much of the history and the general thinking of the German people.

Our neighbors and Hans agreed that the large majority of the labor class in Germany accepted Nazi ideology because Hitler created work for them. Men no longer stood in despair on street corners.

Educated people, the thinkers of the nation, recognized the danger in that dictatorship and saw a likely negative outcome in the event of war. But they felt helpless to prevent what seemed inevitable. Furthermore, the Nazis already had infiltrated every aspect of life in Germany, and stayed constantly alert to real or imagined offenses against the Party. Silence seemed to be the only protection.

By the summer of 1939 speculation of war was everywhere. Hitler had followed up his success in the Sudetenland by seizing control of the rest of Czechoslovakia in March and signing the

'Pact of Steel" with Italy in May. He then turned his attention to Poland, insisting that Danzig and the land along the German-Polish border known as the Polish Corridor be returned to Germany.

On those issues he enjoyed the fervent support of many Germans. No provisions of the Treaty of Versailles were more universally hated throughout Germany than those which created Danzig as a free city and established the Corridor.

Through the summer of 1939, the question of peace or war remained unresolved. Hitler railed against Poland in his speeches and insisted that Germany would regain control of the disputed Territory one way or another. But the Poles stood adamant, and the French and British vowed to support them.

Repeatedly, Hans and our friends debated whether or not Germany should insist on the return of the Corridor. And remembering the American in their midst, they sometimes speculated about the probability of widespread conflict with U.S. involvement. I waved such questions aside, refusing even to consider the prospect.

But I was not without emotion. I felt deep sadness for the many Germans who could find no enthusiasm for that or any war. The only voices raised in support of conflict came from those in the government.

The German people, meanwhile, found themselves forced ever-nearer to a war they hoped to avoid. But if war came, I knew they would fight to defend their country, despite their misgivings. Absolute obedience had been drummed into them for generations and, it seemed to me, they were by nature fatalistic.

I admitted to myself, and to no one else, my wish that Hans and I and our children were back in America. But wishes could not change reality. I had cast my lot with a wonderful man, and I would not leave him. Whatever the future held, we would go through it together.

* * *

With the prospect of war looming ever nearer, Hans and I decided to take a last chance to vacation with our children and our close friends, Carl and Rita Reuther. So we departed by car from our home in Berlin for a three-week vacation on the Isles of Sylt, off the North Sea coast.

Halfway up the coast of Schleswig-Holstein was a rail causeway connecting the island with the mainland. As we boarded the train, Bobby and Irmgard watched carefully to make sure our automobile was loaded onto the same train as us. Once underway, they ran from one side of the coach to the other, nearly hysterical at seeing nothing but water on either side. Our hurried explanations eventually calmed them, as they saw that we also were not afraid.

Emmy, our nursemaid, helped Bobby spot the island first, a fine diversion. The children babbled in excitement, as land loomed larger and larger on the horizon. As soon as we arrived, they jumped down from the train to supervise the unloading of "their" car. How glad we were to have an automobile for even that short two-mile drive. Hans originally had questioned the advisability of taking it. "The constant blowing sand will not be altogether healthy for the engine," he worried, later relenting.

Fifteen minutes brought us to our pension just outside Kampen, about half-way between our arrival point on the channel side and the high cliffs bordering the open sea. The Frieslanders who owned and operated the resort greeted us politely but reservedly. Our drafty rooms contained only the barest essentials of furniture, and a film of sand covered everything.

"I think I want to go right back home," I said.

"The conditions are rather primitive," Hans agreed, laughing. "But even if it falls short of our expectations of comfort, the sun and the sea air will do us all good."

Once more, the subtle suggestion of a last chance, a final respite before the storm, produced a huge lump of fear down my throat.

At lunch, Bobby asked his father why sand covered everything in the room. "Because the windowpanes fit loosely in their frames, and the strong wind blows sand through the cracks," he explained. "If the panes stayed firmly in place, the force of the wind might break them."

"We don't like the rattle." Bobby announced. Hans and I agreed, finding it difficult to tolerate the incessant noise, day and night. More ominous, however, was the roar of fighter planes practicing their maneuvers overhead, from daybreak till nightfall and sometimes later. Not much different than in Berlin!

So why did we stay? In part for the companionship of our friends from Mannheim, the Reuthers, who joined us the next day with their children and nursemaid. Also, we believed another such opportunity might not come along for a long time.

The children loved playing together, under the watchful eye of the nursemaids, which left us parents much free time to enjoy each other's company and make new friends.

At first we shivered in the cold wind, but soon acclimated and enjoyed the briskness. Mornings we devoted to walking the dunes and shopping in the tiny town. Afternoons were spent at the beach on the ocean side of the island, where huge breakers created a deafening roar.

The children played along the water's edge and sometimes ducked under a huge curl, dancing away quickly before the wave broke. Hans swam daily in the heavy surf but I stayed on shore until one day when, goaded by his teasing, I overcame my fears. Without letting him know, I dove into the waves. I quickly regretted my decision as I struggled to fight my way back to shore against the terrible pull of the waves. No one seemed to notice my absence, not even Hans, and I vowed that I would never try that again.

The food was good but very sparse, and left us hungry. Evenings after dinner were endlessly dull. No mental diversion, no news, no radio, no music. Only sand, wind, surf and the planes, with their constant hints of war. To break the monotony, we adults fell into a pattern of walking to a tiny cafe some 20 minutes away for piping hot red wine, but soon that became just another part of the routine.

Boredom never bothered the children, however. They ate and slept well and loved every minute especially when their father made an extra trip to the little town of Westerland for hot plum coffee cake to eat on the beach in the afternoon. The older ones made sand castles, ran the narrow beach with balls and played tag. Watching their eager little faces told me they always would remember that happy time together.

* * *

One evening in the pension parlor, Carl picked up a travel folder advertising daily excursions to the island of Helgoland, a two-hour journey away in the North Sea. Just the excitement we needed, we decided, and two days later we boarded a large ship with 50 other passengers.

On arrival, heavy swells forced us to anchor a safe distance from the island and sailors in small rowboats evidently fathers and sons—ferried us to shore. Vendors with fresh fruit lined the long street to an elevator that took us to the top of the rock. There we stood, buffeted by a fierce wind. Immediately to our right, a high chain link fence guarded the defense mechanism of Germany's mighty rock fortress in the North Sea.

Signs warned all to keep out and threatened violators with arrest. To the left, a narrow street wound around the resort section of the island, past darling little white houses set in adorable miniature gardens. Exotic flowers, plants and birds in cages hung in front of partially curtained windows. Those were the homes of seafarers.

After two hours of sightseeing and a lobster lunch with duty-free French champagne, we returned to the ship for our voyage home. A few days later, enticed by our memories of the interesting sightseeing and the wonderful food, we returned for a second visit. Hans read his daily newspaper on the voyage, searching for information about the current state of affairs.

The ship arrived and Rita and I became separated from Hans and Carl in the crush of departing passengers. I noticed Hans' newspaper lying on a seat, and called out to him, "Honey, do you want me to keep the paper or leave it on board?" Unfortunately, I spoke in English, not German.

Without answering, Hans' eyes caught mine, and I followed his gaze to a sign posted on the wall by the exit that read, "All foreigners forbidden to leave the ship." As I read, I began to realize the gravity of my blunder.

Hans' face lacked all expression, but his eyes locked on me. My heart skipped a beat, or perhaps several. The sign said "forbidden," a very threatening word in Germany.

After one horrible moment of panic, an inspiration came to me. I turned to Rita, laughed, and said in my very best German, "There I go again. Ever since our last trip to the U.S.A., I can't resist practicing my acquired English with Hans."

Rita quickly picked up on my deception, and added, "Das wuerde ich auch tuen (I would do that too)."

A quick glance around me revealed only blank expressions on the faces of our fellow passengers, and my mind flooded with questions.

Who were those people—just tourists or Gestapo? Had they taken my explanation at face value? Would admitting my foreign citizenship lead to questioning by the authorities? Might I and my family as well become suspect? In the event of war, would my nationality single us out as possible traitors, especially if God forbid, America ever became involved?

As the door opened, I decided to leave the ship, despite the risk of detection and detention, and do everything I could to avoid raising further suspicion. Subdued and remorseful that my thoughtless remarks in English might jeopardize Hans and our friends, and mindful of the American passport and identification in my purse, I left the ship and kept my eyes focused on the tourist side of the island, away from the chain link fence.

We saw no one following us as we toured the island and Hans, Rita and Carl acted perfectly normal. I expected recriminations, but heard nary a word. What good friends—I loved them very much. But the hot lobster and French champagne were less enjoyable that time.

As we boarded the ship for the return voyage, and I felt relief beyond measure. But still I wondered, would that end the episode?

That night, back in Sylt with the lights out, I curled up alongside Hans.

"Can we talk about it?" I asked timidly.

"Yes, Cherie, I'm ready," he laughed, using his favorite name for me.

"I'm so sorry, and I hope I haven't hurt anyone."

"You handled it well," he comforted. "Probably nothing will come of it, but something could have."

I reflected through my tears on Hans' patience and understanding with me. He must love me very much, a thought that humbled my spirit. Why did he leave me to decide on board ship, when the decision involved him too? Did he trust my judgment so much? An awesome thought—what if I should make a serious mistake?

Many times in the past I had thought about the chance I had taken in marrying a man from a foreign land. For the first time, I realized that Hans, too, had taken a risk in keeping me in Germany. For his sake and our children's, I knew I must curb my impulsiveness, thinking of their welfare in all my actions. If war came, as seemed inevitable, it would call for much maturity. Dear God, I prayed, stay with me, and give me wisdom and strength.

Hans' words interrupted my reverie. "Did you hear the announcement on board today? That was the ship's last trip. Isn't all that a pretty clear signal of war just around the corner? I think it's time for us to go home."

And so we did, leaving for Berlin the following morning while Rita and Carl returned to Mannheim. Hans and I stayed in Berlin only long enough to settle the children and their nursemaid at home, then departed for a visit with Hans' mother. She was a guest at a spa in South Germany, a long way from Berlin, and it might be a long time before we could see her again.

CHAPTER II

Premonitions of War

Watching Mother Bohle and Hans at dinner that night, I marveled again at how alike—and how different—they were. Even to a casual observer, their outward appearance marked them unmistakably as mother and son. Tall, slender and regal, they presented a picture of elegance and refinement Hans in his finely tailored English-cut suits and Mother Bohle in her carefully chosen Paris fashions.

Both spoke impeccable high German, unflawed by guttural accents; had keen, disciplined minds; shared a love of music and culture; and exuded a gentile aristocracy.

But there the resemblance ended, for in temperament the two occupied opposite poles. Hans was an optimist, with merry blue eyes and a ready smile, full of energy, wit and enthusiasm. Mother Bohle was an introvert, formal and unwilling—or unable to express emotions I suspect she harbored deep inside.

Perhaps those differences helped explain why Mother Bohle always favored her younger son, Walter. Hans lived with the knowledge of her preference for his brother from an early age, never allowing it to alter his devotion to her. And it was Hans she turned to for assistance with practical matters. When a need arose, she never hesitated to request his presence, irrespective of the inconvenience this might cause for him. Hans responded unfailingly to her call, which she took as her due with no expression of gratitude.

During this last week together, however, she had seemed to

feel a stirring of deeper emotion for the son who had come, unsummoned, to offer help to his mother, all alone. We had spent every waking hour with her, keeping vigil by the radio, constantly assessing reports, giving what help and comfort we could. As the time neared for us to return home to our children, she had seemed not only appreciative of our assistance but also sad at the thought of our leaving.

Her emotions were influenced, no doubt, by the ever-worsening prospect of war. Only days earlier Hitler had signed a non-aggression pact with the Soviets. We feared that this development would encourage Hitler to pursue a military solution to the question of Poland, which might bring about war with England and France as well. All of us dreaded the thought of such an outcome.

After dinner on the night before we left, Mother Bohle bade us farewell, declining to see us off the following morning. Her reticence at outward emotional display made her unwilling to risk a tearful farewell in public view. Still, we suspected that beneath her cool exterior she felt pain at the pending separation. True to her nature, however, she chose to suffer inwardly and alone.

Hans and I rose for a 6 a.m. departure. At that early hour, all was repose, the lovely gardens with flowers, the shorn lawns and the many tall pines. It seemed the most peaceful nook on all the earth, tucked away in the southwest corner of Germany. One could easily believe that nothing ever would mar its quiet serenity

For all the spas remoteness, the troubles sweeping across Europe reached even there. Few guests remained, and soon Mother Bohle would leave as well—not for her home in Mannheim, but to visit for a few weeks with a musician friend in Allensbach, a tiny village on Lake Constance.

Then, rather than return to her lonely home in Mannheim, she planned to take rooms in Allensbach and invite her sister Betty to come live with her. That remote location would be safer than Mannheim in the event of all-out war, she insisted firmly. Only time would reveal the wisdom or folly of her choice.

We packed and loaded the car, parked in front of Mother Bohle's windows. Commenting in hushed tones on the beauty of the late summer dawn and the gorgeous gentian blue sky, we inhaled the aroma of the pines. How we wished that Mother Bohle could stay in that beautiful spot.

Ready to go, we both looked up to Mother Bohle's second-story bedroom windows. She never rose that early. Would she just that once make a special effort to awaken, look out and wave her good-bye, not knowing when we might see each other again?

A shadowy figure appeared behind the curtain and we felt certain she stood there watching us, believing herself unseen. We remained a moment, wordlessly looking up at her, then waved with no response. We had to accept it so.

* * *

As we neared a small Esso station, Hans turned off the radio, brought the car to a quick stop at the only pump and jumped out to help himself. An old man emerged from the small shack behind the station.

"Gruess Gott," he said, greeting us with the traditional South German salutation, much like "good day" in English.

Hans responded in kind, adding, "Where is everybody? So far this morning we have not passed a single car."

Before the attendant could respond, Hans became impatient with the meager flow from the pump.

"Is this dribble all the gasoline you have left?"

"You've no doubt tapped the last of it, my man, and now I can put up a sign, 'out of gas,' and go home. There'll be no more delivered for civilian use in a long, long time," he replied. "Aren't you being a bit presumptuous?" Hans asked.

"Might be, but the military has closed the autobahn up ahead to civilian travel. You must take the country roads today."

That explained the lack of traffic—and it also meant a longer and more difficult trip home. More ominously, it seemed another clear sign of impending war.

Hans paid the attendant and walked with him to the little shack for change. They spoke briefly and Hans started back toward the car, then stopped suddenly and retraced his steps. I could not hear their conversation but nodded expectantly when the old man disappeared into the woods behind his shack. He returned a few minutes later carrying a Jerry can, which he quietly placed in Hans' outstretched hand. No doubt the gasoline in the can fetched a pretty price, for Hans was desperate.

As the old man predicted, a barricade halted our travel less than 1,000 meters from the station, forcing us to detour through a forest onto a narrow road that sloped so drastically we rode on a slant. We turned the radio on, the volume low. The reports helped take my mind from the hazardous driving, but brought back with full force the fear that obsessed me.

"Turn it off; I can't bear to hear," I said, then immediately changing my mind. "No, leave it on." Better to know, though the reports offered neither news nor encouragement.

The detour took us through several small villages, as usual all with a church, town hall, restaurants and shops ringing a fountain in the center of town. Villages in different parts of Germany exhibited their own unique character, but almost everywhere the houses fronted directly on the streets, sometimes not even allowing for a narrow sidewalk. Light hues of blue, pink and lavender covered the plastered exteriors of many houses. Others, left white, featured paintings of rural scenes complete with life-size figures. Wrought iron signs hung free from the walls to identify offices, shops and pensions.

Slowing on the cobblestone streets, we wound our way carefully through the crowded villages, past townspeople dressed in colorful peasant costumes. They danced in the streets and squares in Sunday afternoon gaiety. Some of them blocked our way momentarily, just curious or perhaps resentful of our intrusion. Eager to continue, we waved and kept moving.

* * *

By late afternoon we approached the Neckar River near Mannheim.

"Cherie, look. Do you see anything you recognize?"

Almost opposite us, on the other side of the river, sat a hunting lodge where we had spent many happy weekends during our time in Mannheim. The lodge lay amid a small group of two-story houses, home to the forest rangers who guarded the great fir forest and the deer and other wildlife it contained.

On the river's edge stood the house we often used on our weekend visits with friends. The men hunted deer, wild boar and occasionally fox, and roasted the day's kill in an open pit at sundown.

We wives looked for blueberries and wild strawberries with the children. Once we even scared a huge wild pig out of the berry patch. He made an awful racket as he fled, and scared us terribly. We also paddled with the children in a borrowed rowboat. They loved to let their hands dangle in the water and feel the swift current flow through their fingers.

"Can you believe only two years have passed since then?" I asked, as pictures of those peaceful days passed swiftly through my mind. "I wonder who hunts there now?"

Instead of answering, Hans pulled up abruptly in front of a little cafe, jumped quickly from the car and came to open my door.

"Do you remember this place? They always served gooseberry tarts and fantastic coffee here. Maybe they still do. I'm starving, aren't you?" he asked.

Hungry and eager for a rest from the jolting ride on the back roads, we walked through a darkened dining room devoid of guests and onto the balcony where the sun still shone. The balcony extended straight out over the river's edge. We took a table against the wall and looked through the spokes of the wooden banister at the swiftly-flowing current.

The quiet and solitude provided a welcome respite from our

worries and brought out Hans romanticism. Taking my hand in his, he asked, "Whoever would have believed I would marry a brunette, and like it, when in my mind's eye I always pictured a blonde."

And whoever would have expected you to marry an American girl, for love, I thought to myself. German men of Hans' class usually chose a wife for more practical reasons.

"Today, after nine years of marriage, I still would have it no other way—unless you want to become a blonde for my sake?" he teased.

I laughed, but Hans sensed my pensiveness and sought to reassure me.

"Seriously, Cherie, I am so proud of the way you have adapted to life in Germany with its different people and customs and climate. And you have brought to our home the joy of three beautiful children. You must know that I love you as much as ever, and I know I always will," he said. "The future seems ominous, but we will hold together no matter what comes, won't we? For my part I promise, and you do too, don't you?"

Of course I did. Little did we realize, however, how coming events would test our promises to each other.

Our waitress arrived, dressed in a flowered dirndl with a bright red apron and bearing gooseberry tarts, coffee and whipped cream. The tarts tasted superb—as good as we remembered and the coffee was hot and strong. But they failed to distract our minds from our immediate problems for long.

* * *

Most urgently, we needed gasoline to complete our trip to Berlin. We were not even sure we had enough to reach Mannheim but we headed there anyway, hoping to make it to the headquarters of the Syndicate for which Hans once had worked. We did, and there we found fuel. While Hans loaded the Jerry cans inside the trunk, Mr. Schwarz, the company chauffeur, saw us and walked over to talk. He had been the Bohle family driver for many years and had watched Hans and Walter grow into manhood. He also had observed our marriage and had driven us to our honeymoon hotel.

We exchanged greetings and explained the reason for our trip. In response to our inquiry about his family, Mr. Schwarz explained that the Army had called his eldest son into military service, along with most of the youth in the area. "Personally, it does not look as though Germany can keep the peace these days," he said.

His innocent observation led him to look around quietly, wary not of us but of others who might overhear and report his comment. His simple gesture reminded me of the changes that had taken place since Germany had become a police state. Again I felt pangs of fear. Still, I was an American, and believed I could count on my country's protection if necessary.

Taking his leave, Mr. Schwarz bowed and then raised his hand in Nazi salute, for the benefit of anyone watching. He revealed his true feelings, however, by accompanying the Party's exacted gesture not with the standard "Heil Hitler," but with a heartfelt "Auf Wiedersehen und Gute Reise (good-bye and safe journey)."

As we drove away, I said to Hans, "That man is in a state of shock, fearful of what may happen that he cannot control. I wonder how many people . . . oh, I'm a little bit sick myself."

"Me, too," Hans admitted. "I'm afraid we will not have much choice for ourselves from here on in."

Our destination for the evening, the beautiful Mannheimerhof, provided yet another reminder of change. In the past, the hotel always had swarmed with guests and the dining room was never empty. On that visit, however, we took our pick of rooms and found the dining room nearly deserted— despite the elegantly prepared, wonderful food.

After dinner, in our rooms, Hans ordered drinks from room service while I drew a warm bath and enjoyed a pine-oil soak. Next came a whisky soda and, finally, a chapter of a most interesting book about Russia, Das Vergessene Dorf (The Forgotten Village).

Filled with pathos and suffering, courage and heroism, it contained vivid geographical descriptions of Siberia. I became deeply engrossed in the story, oblivious of everything else until I felt Hans' hand on mine.

"Cherie, my dear, why do you cry? Is the book so sad?" he asked. Laughing at myself through the tears, I nodded.

To cheer me up, he suggested we telephone a few friends, but that proved not much fun. Those we reached spoke in hushed and stilted voices, not knowing who else might hear. We quickly exhausted personal topics and, with political talk most certainly not advisable, that left only business to discuss.

So, I listened while Hans talked. Worn down by apprehension and suddenly very tired, I drifted ever-closer toward sleep, barely hearing the click of the telephone receiver as Hans returned it to its cradle.

* * *

The last mist of the night still lingered in the air when we pushed off very early the next morning for the final lap of our trip home. With the gas tank full and the car in good shape, we drove like mad all day. We used the autobahn whenever possible and detoured onto narrow, twisting byways when necessary. We passed only a few gas stations, all of them closed, making us thankful for the fuel we had obtained in Mannheim.

Occasionally we encountered other cars, and narrowly avoided several collisions with drivers who, assuming themselves alone on the road, drove without caution. News on the radio offered nothing new, nothing good. Toward evening the traffic intensified and we returned to the autobahn for the last hour of our journey. Planes zoomed in formation overhead, creating an electric atmosphere that intensified as we neared Berlin.

Finally we turned onto the little narrow rural road that led to our country home. At precisely 6 p.m., Hans pulled to a jerky stop.

"We're home," he said with a happy smile.

The big front door flew open and Irmgard ran laughing down the steps and into her father's arms. Emmy, our young Viennese nursemaid, followed close behind, fairly bubbling with excitement as she took my hands in greeting.

Looking for Bobby, I saw him standing in the doorway, eyeing the scene, a searching half-smile on his face. Hans stretched out his arm to his eldest son, and Bobby walked down to join us.

Together we unloaded the car and headed inside, the children carrying what they could. I noticed Wally Grubert, our neighbor, standing at her garden gate across the street.

"Hello," I called to her. "Were you standing there long? I didn't see you."

"I know you didn't, Ruth, but I saw it all." she laughed. "Are you all right? The children did fine; Emmy is a jewel. Come over for a talk when you're settled."

Nodding, I waved and walked inside. As Bobby and Irmgard danced around in excitement, Emmy disappeared into the kitchen and returned with Dieter, our little one. Sitting on his daddy's lap, he studied Hans' face smiling whenever their eyes met.

Emmy soon announced supper. Suddenly ravenous after eating nothing all day except a few grapes, we headed for the dining room. Hans suddenly stopped and asked, "Where's Arno?"

His question made me realize that in the commotion outside, neither of us had noticed the absence of our big German shepherd. He always bounded to greet us when we returned, jumping up and putting his great paws on our shoulders. But not that time.

Smiles and giggles were suddenly gone, the children looked apprehensive. "Can't we eat first and talk about him later" Emmy asked.

"No, tell me now, Emmy. What's wrong" Hans persisted.

"The kennel master says he jumped into the lake for a swim, caught pneumonia, and died."

Not very likely, Hans and I both thought. Pneumonia at that

time of year, from swimming? With the kennels nowhere near the water? One look at the unhappy faces of our children convinced us to let the matter drop.

"I guess you're right, Emmy," Hans agreed. "We'll talk about it later."

After dinner, with our little brood in bed and order restored, Emmy asked to talk with us. Although she hated to leave the children, she said, with war coming "a girl should join her family." More bad news! The children loved Emmy, and she worked hard, but what could we say? We promised to let her go when we found her replacement.

Worn out from our travels and from the new problems at home, we ascended the stairs for a quick shower and to bed—but not to sleep. I lay awake, mentally drafting an advertisement for a new nursemaid, while Hans mused about Arno's disappearance.

"I don't believe he drowned, " he said eventually. "I think the Army took him. By rights I should pursue the matter with the kennel master, but I'm sure nothing would come of it."

We finally slept, setting aside for a few hours our immediate problems, along with our worries about what the future held in store for us all.

CHAPTER 12

The War Begins

September 1 - 3, 1939

Hans and I rose early the next morning, eager to resume our familiar domestic routine after a month's absence. We dressed, and I headed for the kitchen to help with last-minute breakfast preparations. When all was ready, Emmy carried the steaming casserole of Cream of Wheat, baked with butter and honey, into the dining room. I followed with the coffee.

"Good morning, my little sweethearts," I said to my hungry children, already seated and eager to begin. Jumping up from their chairs, they chimed their greetings, then, according to custom, they stood until we all sat together.

"No paper this morning?" Hans questioned Emmy, as he entered from the living room.

"Not yet, if it isn't here now," she answered. "But we never missed a delivery during your absence."

The gray, cloudy weather lent a gloomy atmosphere to the morning. The children were chattering but the rest of us spoke little as we ate. The silence seemed unnatural, eerie, and then I realized why: we heard no incessant drone of planes overhead in the empty sky.

The doorbell interrupted our reverie. "There's the newsboy now," Hans guessed, as he hurried to the door. But it was our neighbor, Franz Grubert. Hans greeted him warmly. Excusing myself to the children, I joined the two men.

An accountant, very practical and realistic in his thinking, Franisch (as we always called him affectionately) practiced honesty to the point of bluntness. During more than one evening discussion, he had exploded in exasperation that the Nazis could "railroad" Germany into a state of war once again. Worried about his weak heart, and perhaps the consequences of speaking freely, his wife Wally often admonished him to calm down. With a grunt of acquiescence, he would comply.

We loved that devoted couple and could not have hoped for truer, kinder or more considerate friends. From our first meeting, we felt an instantaneous rapport. We accepted one another without reservation, and learned to rely on and cherish each other's confidence.

True Berliners, they could by birthright claim membership in the top echelon of the city's social register. However, they had more or less separated themselves from that group, desiring to free themselves from the bondage of the demanding, often senseless protocol of their status.

One look that morning at our usually jovial friend told me something was amiss. Flushed and fighting to retain his composure, Franisch spoke almost in a bark, as he did whenever he became overwrought. Concerned about his heart condition, we immediately drew him into the parlor and seated him on a sofa.

"Hans thought I was the newsboy, but you'll not get a paper this morning," he said to me. "You won't need to. Turn on your radio."

Hans did. Wally had now joined us quietly, still dressed in hostess gown and curlers. She also seemed alarmed, and took a chair in a corner near the door, motioning me to silence.

Within seconds, the Horst Wessel Song, the approved Nazi rouster, came over the airwaves, followed by Hitler's voice, bringing the long-dreaded news.

"I no longer find any willingness on the part of the Polish

government to conduct serious negotiations with us. I have therefore resolved to speak to Poland in the same language that Poland for months past has used toward us. This night for the first time Polish soldiers fired on us. Since 5:45 a.m. we have been returning the fire and, from now on, bombs will be met with bombs," he announced.

Franisch and Hans stared silently into each other's eyes, and tears coursed down Wally's face. I sat in stunned silence, until Emmy's voice penetrated my daze.

"Frau Bohle, gnaedige Frau, ist kaffe gefaelling (Mrs. Bohle, would you like coffee)?" she asked.

"Yes, yes, just the thing," I responded automatically to her suggestion.

I took the tray she carried and asked her to send the children upstairs to their playroom. No school for Bobby that day!

Filling the cups and passing the hot beverage gave me something to do, and for the moment I found myself master of the situation. But a sickening despair quickly took hold of me, as it had in proceeding months with the advent of each new crisis. I just could not bear the thought of living through a war.

While I replenished Hans' cup, he lifted my hand to his lips. His caress reminded me that times were no easier for him than for me. I shuddered, horrified at the thought of what might possibly stand before us.

"What shall we do, what can we do?" Franisch asked, breaking the silence. "Does anybody know? After months of talking about what to do if this day ever came, I still don't know, do you? My mind is full of fear, and by God, I am not a 'fearing' man."

But none of us offered an answer to his question, as we lapsed into a long silence, each busy with private thoughts.

I was new to the whole experience of war, but the others remembered all too vividly the last global conflict, and realized that their country had not fully recovered from that great bloodshed. Franisch and Wally had hoped fervently to spare their daughter

Renata, their only child, the hardship of war. But that hope was gone.

For a moment we remained quiet; then Franisch rose, with a huge sigh, to leave for work. But Hans suggested an alternative plan. "I'd better show my face at the office today, too. I wonder if we can get through?"

Nodding his good-bye, Franisch left with Wally. Hans made the trip into Berlin without incident, finding the center city quiet, nothing much stirring. He later told me he found the few people on the streets subdued, sad and totally lacking the "righteous indignation" so pompously proclaimed by the radio announcer.

* * *

After Hans left, I sought the balcony with its view over the lake. Sad and reflective, I noticed once again the absence of fighter planes in the air. For months we had endured their presence as they practiced their loops and vaulted about in simulated war. The ceaseless drone of their engines had jogged our equanimity and provided an ever-present reminder of the precariousness of our peace. With the start of the war, of course, they all had flown east, to join the fighting.

Germany no longer could count on a bloodless victory—if a victory at all, I thought. All of our hopes for a peaceful settlement of the issues of Czechoslovakia and the Polish Corridor were dead.

I reflected on the aggressiveness of that so-called "common man," Adolph Hitler, whose rise to power had begun at about the time when Hans and I were married. No one had anticipated how rapidly he would complete that climb, or that he would accumulate the strength to proclaim himself president of the Reich.

Years of consternation had followed, but also moments of joy and exaltation. If Germany finally was emerging from the economic havoc caused by the Treaty of Versailles, she was, on the other hand, falling into the clamps of a deadly situation.

But many of Hans' countrymen found it hard to discern the

danger, since the issue had two sides. Hitler had brought success and rehabilitation and a newly-acquired self respect and worldwide status for Germany. The thinking people of the country, however, realized the peril of being under the influence and the power of an unscrupulous tyrant surrounded by criminals.

What would the coming war mean for our family, I wondered. Irmgard and I held American citizenship, but Bobby's birth had preceded the change in U.S. law that allowed U.S. citizenship for foreign-born children of an American parent. And what of little Dieter? Before leaving for our vacation on the North Sea, I had sent a request to the U.S. State Department asking American citizenship for him, also.

Remembering a pile of unopened mail on a tray in the parlor, I hurried downstairs, sorted through the letters and, sure enough, found the reply. In fear of a possible refusal, I hesitated momentarily, then tore open the envelope, unable to bear the suspense.

"I take great pleasure . . ." the letter began. Blinded by tears, I walked the floor, clutching the treasured confirmation. Then, regaining my composure, I finished reading the document that gave our baby the coveted status of U.S. citizenship. What it might mean I did not fully know, but the news gave me the hope I needed, and instilled me with courage and strength.

Perhaps naively, I believed with all my heart that with the support of my own country, no evil would befall me or my family. That conviction girded me like a suit of armor.

It had been Hans' wish as well as mine that the children receive U.S. citizenship. But the American law of 1934 did not include our son Bobby. Nor had a special trip with him to the U.S.A. in 1935 given us any hope for a change in his status. Bobby and his father were Germans; the rest of us Americans. How might that complicate our lives?

At repeated intervals during the day, the radio broadcast instructions ordering a complete blackout at nightfall. We felt certain that our wooden window blinds, which we rolled down every night war or no war, and our heavy drapes would suffice. To erase any doubt, we joined our neighbors, the Gruberts and the Schmitts, in an after-dark inspection tour. Our houses all faced westward and bordered the lake, and even the tiniest miscreant beam of light could prove disastrous for the whole area if things really got bad. Improbable, perhaps, but we took no chances.

* * *

We awoke the next morning to a beautiful, golden Saturday, the lake reflecting the azure blue sky and the fluffy white clouds.

At breakfast, Hans said the wind and waves seemed perfect for sailing. Some time on the water might help us forget, at least momentarily, our worries about what lay ahead, he suggested.

But it was not to be. As Hans started up the stairs to get into his sailing togs, the doorbell rang. Answering, he found a woman who introduced herself as a representative of the distribution center for food and clothing rationing.

We invited her into the house, where with brisk efficiency she sorted out ration coupons for each family member, seeming to know all our names. Finished, she gave Hans an infectious smile and added the inevitable "Heil Hitler" as she turned for the door.

Hans saw her out, then returned to me in the dining room. Pausing from inspecting the coupons, I asked, "Where did she get such accurate data on the family? She didn't even consult a list, at least not in here."

"From the police department," he said. "She probably studied a list before she came in the gate. It's rather sobering to realize how well that department knows each family. And it leaves no doubt that Hitler anticipated war a long time ago."

Looking through the ration coupons, my heart sank as I realized that, overnight, the old days of buying unlimited supplies of foodstuffs had disappeared.

"Butter supply down to 70 grams per person per week, for spread and for cooking. Bread, milk and meat? We'll be a little hungry until we get used to those amounts," I said, thinking aloud.

Fresh fruits and vegetables were not an issue, since except for cabbage, onions and potatoes we could buy them only in season anyway. Potatoes, a German staple like wheat in America, were not rationed, but I found no supplementary sugar or salt allotments for preserving foods.

"The apples and peaches from our trees will last us until spring," I continued. "Maybe you still can get a few sacks of potatoes and a barrel of sauerkraut somewhere. And if you find some eggs, I'll put them up in 'water-glass' in my big crock in the basement."

"That's a good idea," he answered. "And I see here that we can obtain eggs and cheese occasionally. We'll have to watch the newspaper for the announcement. That's why the numbered blank coupons, isn't it."

"What about poultry and fish? I don't see anything here for them," I said, looking questioningly at Hans.

"I'm sure they count that in with the meat supply."

"Yes, it seems so. I just hoped I had overlooked something," I sighed.

Keeping three growing children happy and healthy on our meager food allocation would take careful planning. But the real shock came with the clothing cards. Each of us received a different allocation, depending on our age and sex. As an adult male, Hans received an allotment of 150 points for the year. An overcoat required 75 points of that total, and a suit 120. Shirts and underwear required no points, but shoes took 15 and socks eight. To make shoes last, they could be resoled twice a year. Sheets, pillow cases, bedding and other household necessities could be obtained only as replacements, and claims would be checked for authenticity.

I found the idea preposterous. "Do you mean they will really walk into this house to see whether we need what we ask for?"

"Yes, I think they will," Hans said. "Remember, in Germany a bride's dowry includes enough of those items to last a lifetime. So a request for more might seem suspicious."

"As for clothes and shoes, we are not badly supplied, and maybe the war will not last so long. England and France may not carry out their threat, and this whole conflict might soon end."

Rising, Hans added, "We still should have quite an assortment of canned foods in the storage room in the basement. I have not been down to look for a long time. Let's go and inspect."

We did, and found a large supply of gourmet foods, which we kept on hand because we lived so far from food markets. Hans often brought business friends home for dinner on short notice, leaving little time for shopping and preparation. With little, if any, impromptu entertaining in the offing, those supplies might help extend our rationed foods for a year or more.

* * *

Back upstairs, both Hans and I felt the general let-down that comes with fear. Rationing came as no real surprise, but the government's speed and efficiency in implementing their program amazed us.

Overcome for the moment by resignation and acceptance, we played with the children instead of facing the difficult task of putting our heads together and planning ahead. But that provided only a temporary respite from questions for which we had no answers. Had we been too optimistic, wooing ourselves into thinking war would not occur? Should we have stockpiled food and clothing? Should we have risked the death penalty and left money out of the country?

And with rationing in place, should we turn to the black market? My instinct said no. Better to endure some hardships than risk serious trouble with the German authorities. They could never discover that Irmgard, Dieter and I were American citizens.

As Hans and I became increasingly wrapped up in our thoughts, Emmy sensed our perplexity and stepped in to lighten the mood.

"Bobby, Irmgard, come, let's go into the kitchen. I have an idea," she said.

The children ran joyously with her, and we heard them laughing and exclaiming. Hans paced the floor, then stood at the balcony door, looking out over the lake.

Turning to me at last he said, "I wonder what that idea was. I think I'll go in and see." I resisted the desire to go too, but stayed, preferring to play with Dieter, who was quietly enjoying his toys at my feet.

In time, delicious aromas wafted my way, and soon they all reappeared, shouting "surprise." Hans carried a tray laden with dishes, silver, coffee and cocoa, and Emmy held a plate of hot luscious Vienna apple strudel. Bobby and Irmgard, their eyes big and bright, trailed behind, fairly dancing on their toes with anticipation. And baby Dieter sat smiling in delight, eager to play a part in it all.

How wonderful to see our children so light-hearted, gay and mischievous, free from the tensions of the time. We soaked up the love and happiness they so freely gave—while keeping our ears tuned for any unusual announcement on the radio.

Finishing his treat, Bobby turned to his father. "Dad, may we go for a ride in the big car?" he asked hesitantly. Irmgard added a plaintive "Please?" and Emmy, as if on cue, said, "Let's take Dieter, too." But their carefully orchestrated scheme met with failure, despite Han's reluctance to disappoint them.

"Not today," he explained. "I don't have the necessary permit, and gasoline is scarce."

The children didn't really understand, but settled for a compromise—taking turns with Hans at the wheel of our car in the garage and calling out imaginary stops as they used their imagination to turn disappointment into joy.

Han's emotions were not so malleable. Restless after the stressful driving and terrific pace of the previous several days, he found it difficult to unwind. As night approached, he suggested the two of us take a streetcar into Berlin for a show.

"Why not?" I agreed. "It might be quite an adventure. I can't remember when you and I last rode a street car."

As we left the house, total darkness enveloped us and I could see nothing. Reassuring me that my eyes soon would grow accustomed to the dark, Hans took my arm and we set off for the nearby streetcar stop.

After a short wait in the chill September evening, we saw the faint blue searchlight of the approaching streetcar and a tiny light glowing inside. We boarded and sat snuggled close together for warmth in the unheated car. I recalled our last such ride long before, during our engagement in America, and whispered to Hans, "Just think, it's been 10 years since we did this."

In Berlin, we found that the blackout made it difficult to get our bearings. People brushed against each other passing in the pitch dark, laughing and embarrassed. "Oh, verzeihung (beg pardon)," one heard constantly. The few cars on the streets moved slowly, their headlights covered with heavy black paper slit in the center to let through a minimum of light.

We continued on, Hans grasping me tightly by the arm. I laughingly let him continue to guide me, enjoying the novelty of the moment. Still, I was glad when the show ended and we sat in the streetcar again, homeward bound.

At our stop, Hans and I stepped down from the streetcar onto a cement island in the middle of the Heerstrasse. Before us in the black night a seemingly endless column of foot soldiers marched past.

We saw nothing and heard only the shuffle of their feet and the swish of their arms as they passed. I closed my eyes, since I could not see, and listened as the sound of their measured tread punctuated the stillness. How many of them will return?

At last the moving formation ended. We were free to leave, but remained rooted to the spot, listening to the sound of the last boot gradually fade away. Then we stumbled down the curb, crossed the thoroughfare and, groping our way through the darkness, finally found the little road that led us home.

* * *

After a fitful night's sleep, I woke Sunday morning to the sound of blaring news. "It's not a nightmare; we really are at war," I thought, wincing at the realization.

How I wished I could stay in bed, avoiding the problems of the day. Hans was already awake, intent on the radio news reports, so I propped my pillows up next to his and we listened together." No announcement of any kind from England or France, Cherie," he informed me. "Let's listen for a few minutes more and then get up and go sailing." Pointing out the window, he added, "Look at the boats. It's a glorious day." Ten minutes later, Hans headed for the shower. 'How about taking the children with us today?" he suggested, then added after a pause, "And let's ask the Schmitts, too. I'd feel safer in the boat."

We both laughed at his last remark, as he continued with a grin. "I know, I am still too clumsy with the sails. That's where the Schmitts come in. We can learn from their expertise."

Following a leisurely breakfast with Hans on the balcony overlooking the lake, I rose to go next door.

"Auf wiedersehen, darling, bis nachher (good bye, darling, see you later)!" I said.

He looked up from his newspaper and the amused glint in his eye made me laugh. I was teasing him a bit, for I knew he refused to speak German with me. "My English is much better than your German, so we will communicate with each other in English," he had declared long before.

When I arrived at the Schmitt house, Lottie greeted me warmly and inquired about our trip. The conversation soon turned to news of the war.

"No special bulletin from England or France yet, as you probably know," she said, rising to lower the volume of her radio.

"Yes, and I keep hoping it might stay that way. Once Poland falls, maybe that will be the end," I responded.

"You really are an optimist," she said, but I could see that she hoped for the same result.

I asked Lottie and Helmut to sail with us. She laughed, knowing of our misadventures on the water. "Helmut is due back shortly from a house call; I'm sure he would like to go sailing."

The radio interrupted our planning with an announcement that the Fuehrer was about to speak. We stood together, tense, as Hitler began with his usual salutation, "Volksgenossen und Genossenin," which loosely translated as "Men and women of the Party." Then he came right to the point, conveying the dreaded news in a low, guttural, rough and very angry voice: England had declared war on Germany.

The news, although expected, made Lottie's eyes swelled with tears. "There goes my wishful thinking," she burst out. "This time it did not work. With nothing but verbal opposition until now, Hitler believed he could retrieve all of our lands without war. Did you notice how angry his voice was?"

Lottie's agitation demonstrated how strongly she must have hoped for a different outcome. Like many of her countrymen, she believed the disputed lands should be returned to Germany—but not at the cost of war.

Rising, she walked to the window, then turned to face me again. "How can Germany face three opponents on two fronts—all at once? You can never know how it felt to be vanquished in the last conflict. You cannot know what it means, this loss of our precious youth. And all of this so soon again. God help us now! And God help you, too, my dear American friend."

Such comments were uncharacteristic for Lottie. In our group discussions, She seldom spoke her mind, more apt to listen attentively and sympathetically. Yet this time her overflowing heart precluded silence.

She spoke openly about her feelings, secure in her trust of me. Bach of us—the Schmitts, the Gruberts and Hans and I—had said much in recent months that we could have been used against each other. But none of us would betray the others.

Later, to take advantage of the beautiful day and because we all needed diversion, we sailed. The weather soon reflected our spirits, however, as the wind rose and the water became rough.

We returned home in time to hear Hitler announce that France had joined the hostilities against Germany. His statement was again concise and to the point, his voice subdued and echoing bitter disappointment but this time, devoid of any rancor. He hadn't believed it would happen.

CHAPTER 13

The "Blitzkrieg" Becomes the "Sitzkrieg"

September - November 1939

The days following the declarations of war by England and France passed with an illusion of normalcy. Hans continued to be permitted to use his car for business, and Bobby returned to school. Still, reality intruded at each meal, as we adjusted to food rationing. And each night as we lowered our wooden roll-blinds, we wondered how soon air raids would begin.

The radio brought news of quick and startling victories in Poland and the prospect of a rapid conclusion to the war there. In the stores and on the streets, people began to express guarded hopes that England and France might not act once Poland was conquered.

"Wishful thinking again, isn't it, Hans?" I asked, hoping for a possible refusal.

"Maybe so, but hope never hurts," he replied.

He shared my uncertainty, although he kept his doubts to himself. Whenever he felt unobserved, he disappeared into the garage. Locking himself in to ensure no interruptions or detection, he searched for foreign broadcasts on the car radio, an act still punishable by death. He took the risk—even knowing that he could do little for the moment with any knowledge thus gained—in hopes it might prove useful later on.

Despite Germany's initial success in Poland, the government began to prepare for a lengthy war. Welfare authorities registered empty rooms as possible housing for refugees. A few young fathers on our street wore uniforms. One of the wives, left alone with two little girls, stopped me as I returned home one day from marketing.

"All the young men around here are soldiers except your husband," she said, eyes flashing bitterly. "He still drives around in civilian clothes as though he had no part in the war at all."

Although stunned by her anger, I understood her. "Please, do not judge by what you see," I implored. "My husband is doing his part even though as yet he wears no uniform."

Hans' company dealt in oil, a commodity needed for war, and he spent his days helping facilitate the transfer of operations from civilian to government control. When the conversion was completed, only about 15 percent of the former civilian staff would remain, he predicted.

"It is like sawing off a tree limb while sitting on it," he told me one evening. "Will I land on my feet, as one of the 15 percent? I don't know, but I doubt it. The authorities probably will choose those above conscription age.

"At 33, even with a family of three children, I still have military status, and we must face that fact."

How easy to say, "We must face it." During the day I fared better than at night. In the quiet of the dark, I had nothing to interrupt my thoughts. Was Hans worried? He was so disciplined he did not discuss it.

In a matter of days, success of the "counteroffensive" against Poland had been assured in a German "Blitzkrieg (lightning war)." The Luftwaffe destroyed Poland's Air Force and pounded strategic targets with bombs. Meanwhile the Army, led by Panzer (tank) divisions, swept into Poland from three directions and annihilated their defenses. In less than a month, resistance all but ceased.

Once German victory was assured, Russia invaded Poland from the east. Warsaw finally fell on Sept.27, 1939 and Hitler and Stalin divided Poland according to the plan they agreed upon earlier. The battle had been fought with only token involvement from either England or France.

Hitler's radio addresses to the nation praised the military for the great victory they had won for the Fatherland. He also proposed peace, which England and France rejected quickly. Yet they did nothing in retaliation, and the end of the Blitzkrieg in Poland ushered in a time of calm that lasted for six months and became known in Germany as the "Sitzkrieg (sitting war)."

* * *

While Hitler and the Nazis celebrated their success in Poland, a more immediate concern for our household was the need for a new nursemaid to replace our much cherished Emmy, who had returned to her home.

Hans traveled on business much of the time, and I struggled to take care of the house and children alone. With the huge acceleration in my household chores, the days just flitted by with little time for musing.

With Hans away, the black nights seemed interminable. At least we were spared air raids—for the time being. Hans phoned me whenever possible and Franisch and Wally stopped by every evening. Helmut Schmitt also checked often to make sure everyone was all right. The children loved their "Onkel Doktor" and clamored around him during his visits. Sometimes Lottie came with him, and they stayed to chat.

A few days after I advertised for a nursemaid, the postman brought a reply from a young woman named Klaerle Feiss, who lived in the Black Forest. She enclosed a three-year reference from a family in England, which described her as conscientious, honest and deeply loyal. The photo she sent showed a plain young woman about 22 years old, with an expression that suggested a gentle and warm nature.

The prospect of a new nursemaid left me with mixed feelings. I had begun to enjoy caring for the children myself, and they enjoyed my company, but the care of all three children plus the house overwhelmed me. I sent a railroad ticket to Fraulein Feiss, in hopes she would come and we would like each other.

With no further notice, Klaerle stood at my front door one morning, bare-headed and clad in a neat, becoming suit, with a light suitcase in her hand.

"Gruess Gott! Frau Bohle?" she asked shyly and a bit breathlessly.

I knew her at once from her photo. "Fraulein Klaerle? Please come in."

She came hesitantly, a bit frightened by the strange house so far out in the country.

We moved to the parlor and I offered refreshments, which she accepted gratefully, obviously tired from her travels. As we talked, she revived, asking questions and offering information about herself. I decided that my assessment of her photo was correct, and that the plain, quiet girl sitting at my window matched the person described in the references from England.

Too often in the past I had tried to make friends of servants, rather than remaining the mistress of the house. Some had misunderstood and taken advantage of my friendliness. But I felt instinctively that with that young woman I could be myself, with no loss of face for anyone. I wanted her to stay, but knew the final decision was hers.

At my call, Bobby and Irmgard came for introductions. Both greeted her politely, although Bobby's curiosity showed clearly while Irmgard was shy. I invited her to see the rest of the house, including her room, and meet baby Dieter. Her first glimpse of the sleeping child sealed the bargain. Catching her breath, she gasped, "Oh, my, how sweet," fairly itching to get him in her arms. "I'll stay."

Hans returned for the weekend and liked Klaerle immediately. We asked about her stay in England, which evidently she had enjoyed very much.

"My English mistress was truly a lady, very kind and very fair, more generous in her thoughts and judgments than anyone I have ever known. I answered your wife's advertisement in hopes that working for an American might bring a similar experience," she explained.

Klaerle evidently found what she sought in our home, and accepted willingly her role as the only helper in the house. Her quiet serenity and her efforts to correlate German thought with a wider world view elevated her above a typical servant, and she soon became as much friend as employee.

* * *

With household assistance assured and with Hans home more often, we resumed a more active social life. Willy Faessler, whom we had met originally in Mannheim as newlyweds, became a frequent visitor to our home. An engineer, Willy had recently supervised construction of an important scientific facility in China before returning to Germany for reassignment. Since he expected only a brief stay, he had left his American wife in China, but delays in obtaining permission to travel outside the country, with war imminent, had kept him in Berlin.

Handsome and with the dark skin and hair typical of Germans from the Southern provinces, Willy became a favorite with our children. Every weekend they asked, "Will Uncle Willy come to see us today?" When we answered yes, they watched for him and ran to meet him when they saw him walking down our street. He spoiled them with ice cream. Where did he get it? His black eyes flashed with pleasure when he saw them, and his natural charm lit up the house whenever he walked in.

Beneath the smiles, however, we sensed his troubled spirit. Already a victim of one war—he had never filly recovered his health after serving in World War I—he faced the prospect of victimization a second time, albeit in a different manner.

Hans listened sympathetically as Willy described his struggles with the Nazi bureaucracy. 'One office will not grant me a new visa because of the war. Another office, in the same building as the first, refuses me coupons for winter clothing because I might leave any day—even though I have only summer clothes with me. Why can't they get together? Even with my firm's assistance I cannot untangle the red tape.

"When I get back to China, I will send Dana back to the U.S.A.," he continued. "And Hans, I advise you to do the same for Ruth. Who knows how all of this will turn out?"

Before Hans could respond, I answered. "I know of no way for me to go. How could I leave Hans and Bobby alone?" "And the other children?" Willy asked, suddenly intrigued.

I had said more than I ever intended, so I evaded his question. But the subject left me heavy-hearted.

Both Hans and I feared that Willy's disgust with the "wooden officials at the helm," his anguish over his unfinished work and his concern for his wife might undermine his already-shaky health. But we could do little for our friend other than provide moral support, encouragement and occasional distraction from his worries.

* * *

Winter arrived by mid-November, with gray, icy days and high, choppy waves on the lake. Still, thankfully, the "Sitzkrieg" continued, letting life go on in a semblance of normalcy.

Willy helped us bring our sailboat into dry dock and clean and store the sails. Wally Grubert pruned her prized roses and Lottie Schmitt finished her preserves. We picked the last fruit of the season from our trees in the back yard and stored enough of our apples and peaches to last us until spring. But what then?

Miraculously, Hans came home one day with 10 pounds of

honey, a huge amount in that time of rationing. Our temporary good fortune stirred a sense of urgency to somehow find our own solution to the food shortage problem. But how? With our small yard and in that northern clime, could we grow enough of anything for a full winter's supply? And if we raised chickens or rabbits, what would we feed them?

As we pondered the possibilities, Klaerle's face glowed with excitement. "Why not let me take the children to my home village in the Black Forest for a few weeks, to assure them ample food and let them escape the tensions of the city, so close to war?

"We could stay at an excellent pension in town, and you could visit. With no housework, I could easily care for the children, no problem at all. You know I love them dearly, and would take good care of them."

Torn apart at the thought of separation from our children, I objected. "Dieter is only 18 months old. How can I let him go?"

I saw from Han's eyes that he shared my doubts, but he also understood the difficulty of our circumstances. "We could try this arrangement for a few weeks, and continue only if it proves advantageous for the children," he said. "And you could visit often to make sure all is well."

After further discussion, we allowed Klaerle to contact her relatives and Frau Hock, the owner of the pension in Schonach, Klaerle's home village. Soon a message arrived for Klaerle from Frau Hock, quoting a rate so low that I questioned the quality of the food and accommodations. But Klaerle offered reassurances.

"The bedrooms are not heated, but the dining room is," she explained. "Except during their short busy season, they have long stretches with no guests, so the children and I would have the run of the social rooms.

Frau Hock's niece, a fine person who apprenticed in the best Danish hotels, does the cooking." Frau Hock wrote us, too, a letter filled with amusing dialect and misspellings, and I loved her sincerity.

"Klaerle tells us the children are well-mannered, and for that reason I will accept them without their parents, and will help Klaerle as much as I can," she said. "We are enclosing the huge verandah with glass, to enlarge the dining area, and expect to finish by the first of the year. You may plan accordingly."

Somewhat reassured but still reluctant to send our beloved children away, Hans and I chose to defer a final decision until after the holidays.

CHAPTER 14

Terror from Above

November, 1939

Air raid! The words still leave me numb as I recall the terror we felt on the night when invading English bombers made their first appearance over Berlin. Hans was traveling on business. Alone, Klaerle and I did our best to protect the children and calm their fears.

We hurried downstairs at the first sound of the warning siren. Our well-equipped basement bomb shelter contained cots and blankets, running water, food, medicine and, gratefully, a toilet facility. Suitcases packed with extra clothing, valuable papers, dry food, medicine and money stood ready if we had to leave. Three separate exits provided vital avenues of escape unless the whole house toppled.

Unfortunately, we could not block out the noise when the anti-aircraft guns from across the lake responded with earth-shaking booms. Seeing the terror in my children's eyes, I searched frantically for an activity to occupy their minds.

"Let's play ball," I suggested in desperation.

"Yes, please, Mother," they responded immediately, near tears.

A frantic search failed to turn up a ball, but a pile of coal briquettes offered a possible substitute. Picking one up, I looked at the children, who shrieked with near-hysterical excitement as they grabbed at the black stuff for a crazy game in their small basement confinement.

Such giggles, laughter and hearty anticipation. The children delighted in an activity so ridiculous—and under ordinary circumstances utterly prohibited! Only Dieter could not play, so he sat nearby, wide-eyed and wistful, holding his breath with each toss.

With every miss, the briketts chipped or broke into pieces, and soon coal dust covered us all. The crazy intensity with which we played left the children no time to think. Even so, their moods wavered constantly between laughter and tears. Maybe that is why they begged, "Please, Mother. Let's do it again and again, and every time, shall we?"

The all-clear signal finally sounded, and we trudged upstairs. My poor, brave little children fell into bed, exhausted.

* * *

As the air raids continued, other parts of Berlin suffered heavy damage. On the west rim of the city, we were more fortunate. We also learned that the bombers seldom flew on moonlight nights, because of the increased danger of detection. Thus, on one especially beautiful and bright evening, we anticipated a respite from the relentless British attacks. But the raiders surprised us, flying despite the clear weather. The warning siren sounded as usual at 8 p.m., telling us that in 12 minutes the planes would arrive.

"This time, let's stay up here on the first floor, turn off the lights and raise one of the wooden blinds just one-half inch," I said to the children and Klaerle. "We all can stand here and peer through. The moon is so bright we may see something. If need be, we'll quickly lower the blind and go downstairs."

The children loved huddling together to look through the tiny aperture. The moon provided fantastic for visibility, and the air was still and breathlessly quiet. The usual 12 minutes passed with no sign of planes, as we waited in the dark.

Suddenly the crack of anti-aircraft guns across the lake shattered the silence, and a powerful shock wave nearly knocked us on our fannies. We heard a terrific crash not 100 yards away. Looking toward the sound, we saw red-hot flames shoot up high into the sky, and we watched in silence, fascinated.

"Klaerle, you and the children hurry downstairs, more planes may be on the way," I ordered. "I'll come down presently."

But I stayed to watch instead. Would air currents over the lake blow burning embers onto our house? Would the great fire attract more planes, that time with bombs, perhaps incendiary ones? The phone rang. "Are you okay?" Franisch asked urgently as I picked up the receiver. "Look out the window on the lake side. A downed plane is burning on this side of the Heerstrasse right near us."

"My God, my God, that was close! Better watch for sparks, though. As soon as the 'all clear' sounds, we'll check thoroughly with you outside. For the moment you seem to be all right."

"Thank you, Franisch," I said. "I will join you later. You also seem to be all right, but I'll keep an eye on your house. I have a full view of the flames now. It's all terribly spectacular, but I ache for the pilot who died in those flames."

CHAPTER 15

The Struggle to Stay Warm

December, 1939 - January, 1940

Playing ball with the briketts during our nightly visits to the cellar soon alerted me that our coal allotment for the year fell far short of our needs. The abominably cold weather and wind off the lake made matters worse. To conserve heat, we closed the vents to the bedrooms, lowered the temperature in the rest of the house and left the wooden blinds down day and night on the lake side of the house. But even those measures seemed to make little difference. Our coal supply dwindled rapidly.

The lake already was frozen over, unheard of so early in the winter, but the thought of good skating and ice sledding helped compensate somewhat for the discomfort. Also, our ration of fats was increased slightly, an encouraging sign. And England's delay in waging all-out war fueled speculation that they intended only a token response, and we would have peace and normal life again soon.

Still "sitting on the limb that he is sawing off" at work, Hans relied on his innate discipline to restrain his impatience. Meanwhile, I took a mandatory course in Red Cross first aid. Even though I realized the value of the knowledge, I lacked enthusiasm and hated every minute.

"How about shooting? I love it, Hans. I am a natural, but I

did not need to come to Germany to learn to use a gun," I exclaimed, drawing a laugh from him. "I will never use one except in defense of my family or myself."

One day while Hans was away I received a visit from two Nazi Party officials. They came to invite Hans to join the Fuehrer's National Socialist German Workers Party, they stated proudly, as though they were crowning him with the greatest of glories.

Knowing Hans' sentiments and anxious to discourage a return visit, I explained that he traveled on business almost constantly, and I could not predict when they might find him at home. Apparently, they assumed he was on some secret war mission, because they left respectfully and never returned.

Each day the fuel situation became more critical for us and for all civilians. Even the schools closed. Bobby returned home one morning and reported that the teachers gave them lessons for a week. "We're supposed to do them at home, where it's warm," he said laughing, appreciating the irony.

With no classes for Bobby to attend, the children spent their days skating (under Klaerle's supervision) on the lake, coming into the house only for food and occasional warming. Wally Grubert and I joined them now and then, also on skates, or for sledding on the ice—great fun, so fast and exciting. Each day the sun dazzled in a sky more azure blue than I had seen anywhere except in the heights of the Swiss Alps. The trees looked like crystal, each tiny twig covered with ice.

Our supply of coal had dwindled so badly that we doubted it would last through the Christmas and New Year holidays. What would we do then? Coax? Cajole? As the holidays approached, I knew we would need the Christmas spirit in our hearts more than ever. With no buying power, how would we obtain gifts for the children? Would we have a Christmas tree? Would our Christmas be interrupted by an air raid?

Yet despite our many problems, we still had Hans with us, and for that I was exceedingly grateful.

The holidays soon arrived and turned out better than expected.

Hans managed to secure a small tree, and the children trimmed it themselves with colored paper ornaments. We sang our favorite songs, played games together and even enjoyed a few improvised gifts. Our neighbors, the Gruberts and the Schmitts, joined us for an hour to be with the children.

After Christmas, a large distribution of fish became available, allowing us to buy an unlimited amount of carp. Thus, we carried on the Bohle tradition of a New Year's party, begun so many years earlier. The invitations went out a bit belatedly, but we were pleased to bring a bit of joy to our friends in that uncertain existence.

* * *

As 1940 began we faced, as anticipated, an acute coal shortage. Hans' several visits to the Spandau Fuel Distribution Center finally netted us 10 zentner (1,000 lbs.), enough only for 10 days without even more severe conservation measures, which we implemented immediately.

When the coal arrived, the deliveryman dumped our long-awaited coal at the entrance to our street, at least 1,000 yards from our house. I begged him to reconsider, fearing that others desperate for fuel would steal it. But he ignored my entreaties, explaining that his three-wheeler could not plow through the deep snow.

A small sled could. Running back to the house, I instructed Bobby to put on heavy wraps and go guard the pile of briketts, then sent Klaerle and Irmgard to the basement to fetch the sled and a bushel basket. Always anxious to help, Irmgard turned the task into a game. "We can build a house with the briketts on the sled, then we can play ball with them again in the basement tonight if there is an alarm," I overheard her say excitedly to Klaerle.

Luckily the baby slept soundly and for the moment did not need us. Dashing to the basement, I found a ladder and some tools, and with difficulty pried open the small window above the black, soot-covered coal bin. I had to climb into the dirty bin to accomplish the job. By the time I finished, the children returned with the first load, and together we dumped our precious cargo into the window opening.

Caught up in the fun side of the situation, we became rather noisy, even boisterous. Wally Grubert heard us and came to investigate.

"I've got an idea," she said suddenly, turning for home. I stood watching her walk away, puzzled, but Irmgard interrupted my speculations.

"Mother, Bobby won't help us load the coal. He says he must stand guard against all those people who might steal it. He walks around, shoving folks away who are not even there. That's not fair."

Amused, I turned to Klaerle. "Can you handle that?"

"Oh, he'll be all right, I'm sure. I suggested that once he frightened away all those imaginary thieves, he would get awfully cold doing nothing, and it might warm him to help us."

We spent the better part of the day bringing in the coal, with no further sign of Wally. That night, however, Hans returned home from the office just in time to see Wally and Franisch trying to hoist a small coal stove onto a sled in their lighted garage, and ran over to help.

"It's for you, Hans," Franisch explained. "How long do you think 1,000 pounds of coal will last in a furnace? If you put this little gem up in the children's playroom and connect it to the main chimney flue, you will have at least one warm room. "As for sleeping, I guess we all must learn to sleep cold again, like our forefathers did. By the way, we got one for ourselves, too," he added.

Enthusiastically, the men hauled the little iron stove up to the children's room. With a pickax they chopped a hole in the main flue to the chimney, while our red-cheeked children stood by excitedly, so proud of their participation in the project.

"Heating just this one room will keep you warm and stretch your coal supply for at least two months, maybe longer," Wally said with a satisfied smile. "And you may keep the stove as long as necessary."

Practical Wally always knew the best way out of any dilemma, I thought gratefully. When finally the room began to warm, Hans fetched a bottle of French cognac for a toast to the thoughtfulness and generosity of our dear neighbors. Later, warmed and happy, Franisch and Wally decided to go home in anticipation of a possible air raid.

"Take enough warm clothing to the basement tonight, "Franisch reminded as they left. "It will be mighty cold."

*   *   *

For the next seven years, we fought an incessant battle to keep warm in winter. That night, however, the little coal stove afforded us at least a partial victory, if only in one room.

At dinnertime, Hans went down to the kitchen, where Klaerle had been preparing dinner for the last hour, and helped her bring the food upstairs. I noticed her shivering as she laid out dinner on the children's play table.

"Klaerle, you look frozen," I said. "Doesn't the electric range heat the kitchen just a little bit?"

"Not much, she laughed. "I spilled a few drops of water on the floor and they froze on contact, so I guess you know how cold it really is. Next time, I'll put on my ski togs," she added with another laugh.

"Not a bad idea, and gloves, too," I agreed.

After a quiet evening spent reading and listening to the radio—no air raid that night—Hans and I sat quietly discussing what our days would be like from then on.

"Living in one room is no catastrophe," he said. "I worry about the number of hours you and Klaerle will have to spend away from warmth while you wash clothes, carry coal, cook, stand in line to shop and take the children to play outside. And you won't ever return to a really warm room."

"But spring will soon arrive to relieve the strain. Just a few more months. Long months, I know," he smiled. But he was troubled that the schools were closed, making parents responsible for their children's education.

* * *

At the end of January, a letter arrived offering an unexpected diversion from our dull routine and the gray, cold weather. Rosmarie Lawrenz, our dear friend who cared for baby Dieter during the first weeks of his life, was getting married in Mannheim, the invitation said.

We wanted very much to attend Rosmarie's wedding, but hesitated to undertake a long journey in an unheated train in the middle of an acutely miserable winter. Then a letter from Hans' mother, addressed to him personally, decided the issue. She planned to attend the wedding, and wanted both Hans and Walter to come as well. "Do not disappoint me," she wrote.

"I feel I must comply," Hans said. "The times demand we seize each opportunity to be with one another. Please, Cherie, go with me."

Rosmarie's glittering military wedding was beautiful and romantic, and we found ourselves genuinely moved at seeing so many old friends once again. Underneath the forced gaiety of the event, however, ran a strong current of foreboding. One saw it on every face. Enjoy, cherish the moment while you may, their expressions said.

During the reception, Hans and I congratulated Rosmarie's parents—"Tante Lise and Onkle Petz" to us. Their joy on that important day was heightened by the presence of their son Hans Joerg, an Army officer on special leave. Yet their constant babbling revealed their struggle to overcome hidden emotions.

We joined in the levity as best we could, despite the premonitions of doom. Many of the male guests wore military uniforms and we knew that they, too, fought to cover the fears they felt.

Our worries proved well founded. Years later, we learned that Rosmarie's gifted, handsome brother had fallen during the Baffle of Stalingrad. Her husband was taken prisoner and later murdered in Czechoslovakia, and Rosmarie, with her two year old son in hand, had been sent to but escaped a Czech concentration camp. Exhausted, sick and heartbroken, she walked with her little boy most of the way back to her parents' home in Germany. Along the way, she had suffered a miscarriage on some lonely byway, alone and uncared for.

We had little time to visit with Hans's mother and Walter during the reception, so when the party ended we invited them to join us in our hotel rooms.

When all were assembled, Mother Bohle made it clear that she had summoned her sons to make an announcement.

She began, "I have no intention of honoring your deceased father's appointment of Hans as executor of his estate, nor of the division of his estate into three equal parts (as suggested in his will). If you challenge my decision legally, I will disown you as my sons forever.

"I want all of the capital in your father's estate to use as I please. If you do not fight me, you can share the remainder after my death."

Continuing, she provided a clue for her absolute defiance of her husband's wishes.

"Walter is no longer my son. His loyalties and allegiance belong solely to another family, a situation I cannot and never will accept. I would rise up in my grave if ever a penny of mine or your father's fell into their hands.

"As for Hans, he always has been a dutiful son, but that is no more than what I have a right to expect. While Father was alive, I always needed to ask for money. This I will no longer endure, nor do I wish to look to either of you for permission to use my own initiative. I can take care of myself."

Bitterly, she declared her love for her family "gone." She felt alone, betrayed and bitter, for which we could thank Walter and his close affiliates, she added. Once more family Rumpel had touched our lives tragically. Her tirade finished, she departed with a cold "auf wiedersehen (good-bye)," leaving Walter with us to decide what to do.

All too aware that his actions had triggered his mother's hostility, Walter soon left as well, giving Hans permission to handle the situation as he saw fit.

Hans and I sat down to a conference of our own, which began with a long, thought-filled silence.

"I understand your mother's hostility, but not her unfairness toward you," I finally ventured. "Does all this hurt you terribly?"

"Maybe just a little, but her actions and words were meant to prevent me from administering Father's will, not as a personal attack," he said. "I will not fight her. She can have the estate, but I wonder how long she will stay solvent if she handles it herself. Father always said that money slipped through her fingers like water."

Trying to cheer him a little, I suggested, "Perhaps given the chance, she may show more business sense than we imagine." But neither of us believed it.

During the long journey home in the slow, unheated train, I thought about how quickly a beautiful home can dissolve. It will not happen to us, I vowed.

CHAPTER 16

Assignment: Poland

February, 1940

Home again. After less than 48 hours away, we unlocked our front door and, hearing, the children came running. "Mommy, Daddy," they cried happily, their little arms holding us tightly.

Klaerle reassured me that everyone was fine; no air raids had occurred in our absence. Then, while I answered the children's breathless questions about Rosmarie's wedding, Hans looked through the accumulated mail without even removing his wraps. One particular envelope he opened in great haste.

"Monday . . ." he murmured, still reading.

"Monday what, Hans?" I asked.

"Oh, I must leave on Monday for . . .

"The Army?" I interrupted, instantly near panic.

"No, no, darling," he assured me, encircling me in his arm. "Allay your fears, Cherie. It's a civilian job, not the Army, at least not yet. Isn't that something to be grateful for?"

"But where, and why. . . ?" I stammered, still stunned by that sudden development.

"I must go to Posen, in Poland, the part that is now German and called 'the Warthegau.' I must report to a government agency called the Treuhandstelle, established by the German government to dispose of confiscated Polish property. Here, see for yourself," he said, handing me the letter.

"And when that is done, what then?" I asked.

"Who knows, but that may take a long time. So much can change quickly. Why worry needlessly?"

Of course he was right, but the idea of "taking it as it comes" always put a lump in my chest. I preferred to anticipate possible problems and prepare for them. Perhaps we both were wrong, or both right? Maybe, too, Hans thought ahead more than I knew, and could relax while doing so. After voicing my opinion, I left the decision to him and went along with whatever happened.

Another letter, from the German Welfare Agency, brought up a subject on which we agreed totally. The agency planned to send a group of children—ours included—to a camp in Czechoslovakia to spare them "the fright of bombing and the loss of sleep." As we both read, we knew we could delay no longer.

"Cherie, we must send the children with Klaerle to the Black Forest immediately," Hans assertively. "Under no circumstances can we allow them beyond our own jurisdiction. The idea of sending them into occupied hostile territory is preposterous!"

"What if they became sick," I questioned. "Could we go to them in Czechoslovakia?"

"No, of course not," Hans said emphatically. "And separation from everyone they know would frighten them much more than the bombing they have had to endure right here.

"We must keep them where we can see and be with them at will. No, no. Most definitely no! He raged." "We will send the children out of reach before the officials can come for them."

At supper we showed Klaerle the letter. "I can prepare to leave with the children as soon as we get confirmation from Frau Hock," she said.

Then we told the children, who seemed to understand the importance of the trip. They loved Klaerle and felt no alarm, but still dreaded the separation from us. They also knew their daddy would leave within days for a lengthy stay in Posen, and we all rejoiced that a civilian job, and not the Army, would take him there.

"Will you come and visit us often, even stay weeks and weeks and weeks?" Bobby asked. We promised.

Again that night we sat freezing in the unheated basement during air raids that lasted several hours, wrapped in blankets and trying to sleep on deck chairs placed close together for warmth. No games that time—too few briketts—but Hans' presence calmed the children. Finally, the all clear sounded again, marking the end of a strenuous day. We all went upstairs cold, but it hardly mattered. At least until the weekend we were all together.

* * *

A week later, I sat alone in our cold, empty house. Hans departed first, with all of us taking him to the streetcar to say goodbye. Bobby and Irmgard fussed over the right to carry his suitcase and finally agreed to pull it on the back of Dieter's sled. After kissing them each good-bye, Hans slipped aboard the streetcar.

The children smiled and waved, in good spirits. Fortunately, they did not realize the seriousness of events around them. They responded well to common logic and seemed to understand our deep concern for them. Our slightest show of affection brought out bursts of love.

The following day, Klaerle and the children left for the Black Forest. Bobby and Irmgard looked forward to their "adventure" with excitement, but Klaerle read the doubts I could not help showing. "You need not worry, Frau Bohle, I will take good care of them. You can have faith in me," she said.

Klaerle had come to us only a few months earlier, and I believed providence had directed her to us. A product of a simple country upbringing, unspoiled and with sound principles, her plain appearance belied her beauty of character. In times of stress she maintained calm and clear thinking, conveyed love and understanding and put the interests of the family ahead of her own. To me she was a jewel of great price, and I believed she would lay down her life, if need be, for our children.

True to her promise, she sent me a telegram the day after they left. "Arrived Triberg 18 o'clock. Three-mile trip to Schonach in car of friend. Much snow. Well and happy; visit us soon."

I spent my lonely days preparing to close the house completely and my nights thinking about my husband and children. While the war continued, I would divide my time between Hans in Poland and the children in the Black Forest. The little coal that remained would help me when I stopped at the house en route from one destination to the other, a round trip of several thousand miles.

Shortly before leaving to join Hans, I received a phone call from a hospital in Berlin. Willy Faessler was scheduled for surgery that morning, a nurse informed me.

At the hospital, a nurse met me in the whitewashed, sterile, unfriendly waiting room. In response to my questions, she said that Willy's condition was serious, and that following surgery he could not have visitors.

"He just asked us to keep you informed," she explained. "He also insisted that we not inform his wife, fearing she would attempt the hazardous journey from China. The mere thought of that terrifies him," the nurse added.

How awful to leave him alone to deal with his problem! I explained to the nurse that Hans already had left Berlin and I soon would follow, and gave her our address in Posen. She promised to update us on Willy's condition.

We did indeed keep in touch and several weeks later when Hans and I returned briefly to Berlin, we visited Willy in his apartment. Delighted to see us, he explained that he had given up hope of seeing his wife again until after the war. Neither of them could obtain a visa to get in or out of Germany.

Willy blamed his illness on a Chinese amoeba, which caused an intestinal tumor and obstruction. He seemed cheerful and on the way to a good recovery. Later in the year, however, we received bad news. No longer able to care for himself, he had left Berlin for the home of his parents in a little village deep in the heart of the hills and forests of South Germany. There his life finally came to an end. Our friend, and our children's beloved "Onkle Willy," lies buried in the little churchyard of the village of his birth.

* * *

Several days after Hans arrived in Posen, I received his first message. Settling into a cozy chair in our living room, near a window facing the lake I eagerly opened the envelope and began reading.

"My own darling, it is now a full eight hours since I left you and the children at the streetcar corner. I ate earlier, and now am sitting in a cold single room in the only, and certainly far from posh, hotel in Posen. But I cannot sleep. So much is going through my mind. "It has been years since I had the opportunity or the desire for so much reflection. Much of it, I'm sure you can guess, concerns my business future. I have some visions but can form no real conclusions until this conflict ends.

"However, things will right themselves. For the present, I must stay here and learn as much from the experience as I can. Have you heard from the children? I hope you will close our home soon. Let me know the time of your arrival. You must do that, since I need to meet you at the station.

This is no place for a woman alone. The trip was interesting. I arrived just before the train departed, as I prefer, and found a seat in a compartment with two fine military men, one of them a doctor. Tell you all about it and you will meet them soon. Wire me at the Treuhandstelle, Posen, Warthegau, date and time. Hurry!

Love, Hans."

"One more night in Berlin," I said aloud to myself, finishing the letter. "Tomorrow night I will be with Hans."

My last day at home sped by, shortened by a pleasant visit from Wally, who saw the smoke from our coal stove and needed the warmth. "Come over tonight if we have an air raid," she said as she left hours later.

A bit of warmed-up soup was enough supper that evening. I hurriedly fixed the fire for the night and retrieved a down comforter and pillow from my bedroom, expecting to curl up and sleep on the living room couch, where I felt less alone. The telephone sat on the floor beside me for company.

But just as I slipped under the warm comforter, eager to reread Hans' letter to ease my apprehensions about an air raid, the telephone rang, startling me. Almost simultaneously, sirens signaled advancing bombers. I snatched up the phone, and Franisch said, "Come quickly, this one is for us." He always seemed to know, and was never wrong. How could he be so sure, I wondered.

No time to hesitate! Quickly I slipped into my robe, fur coat, shoes and overshoes. With my comforter, pillow and suitcase full of valuables, I ran through the thick snow to my neighbors. Their basement was no warmer or safer than mine, but at least we would be together. Maybe we would be spared and once more could say triumphantly, "We are still alive."

It was a bad night. The anti-aircraft guns across the lake sounded louder than ever and, if not for the wooden shutters covering the windows, the panes would have burst into thousands of splinters. More than one fragment of shrapnel, sharp as a knife, penetrated the shutters and scorched the wood.

The bombers seemed to target the military installations in Spandau, a few miles north of us. Still, the house shook and trembled so violently that we ducked our heads, expecting it to collapse and crumble. We held our ears, closed our eyes and prayed. Finally, we heard the awesome sounds move further and further away—perhaps toward the center of Berlin. Surely we would soon hear the all-clear signal, we thought, and for a moment we relaxed.

Franisch asked if Hans' letter mentioned anything definite concerning his assignment. "No, he only said that the trip to Posen was interesting and asked me to come soon. I only know his job involves resettling German refugees from the Baltic States."

Wally suggested that a history book in their library upstairs might provide additional information about the Baltan refugees, but no one wished to leave the basement. An outgoing plane still could drop one lone, unejected bomb on our heads.

"Anyway, we don't need a book," Franisch remarked. "I am familiar with the situation, although I do not understand the reasons for it. It seems Germany and Russia have divided Estonia, Lithuania and Latvia in half longitudinally, with Russia controlling the Eastern halves and Germany the Western halves.

"If one can believe the reports," he continued, "the Russians have committed terrible atrocities against all Germans living in the Russian sectors, forcing them to flee for their lives. Germany has set up the Treuhandstelle to provide homes and jobs in Poland for these German refugees—homes left vacant by the Poles who fled to England and France."

Intrigued by that insight into Hans new responsibilities, I asked, "Do the Baltan Germans bear any resemblance to the Volksdeutsche (border Germans)?"

"No," Franisch responded. "Germans who live close to the border of another country take on some, but only some, of the traits of their neighbors. The Baltans, however, invaded Estonia, Lithuania and Latvia many generations ago and became fully assimilated. Many of the German Baltans descended from families of nobility, and amassed great wealth. They lived in luxury and taught their young to do likewise.

"Thus, the Baltan Germans in Posen today bear little resemblance to the hard-working people of the Third Reich. They are used to leisure, largess and servitude from all sides. The meager resources of the Poles can in no way compensate for the immensity of their loss, and one cannot help but wonder how they will adjust. Hans certainly will have his hands full trying to satisfy that group," Franisch concluded, shaking his head skeptically.

CHAPTER 17

Together in Enemy Territory

February, 1940

At 5 o'clock the next evening I finally boarded a train for Posen. The dim light on the platform illuminated little more than the outline of the people with whom I mingled.

Inside the coach, passengers stacked their luggage on the rack overhead. Some kind soul, without waiting to ask permission, grabbed mine and hoisted it too, and I took the empty seat below. Looking around, I saw no other women in a crowd of silent men. Some wore uniforms, others dressed as civilians— like my husband, I thought.

My seat companion showed no interest in conversation and all around me the other passengers slept. So, wrapping my arms around my big purse, I closed my eyes but, wound up and apprehensive, sleep eluded me.

We headed east, out of Berlin. No air raids impeded our progress, although we would not have halted anyway.

After an hour, we made an unannounced stop. I looked out the window for a sign indicating our location, but saw nothing in the poor lighting on the platform. What if the conductor announced none of the stops? How would I know when we reached Posen? My timetable said the trip took four hours, so I decided to get off at the first stop after we had traveled that long. But what if the train arrived early, or late, and I got off at the wrong place? How would Hans ever find me?

At the appointed time, I rose from my seat and barely grabbed my suitcase before the crowd of departing passengers swept me toward the exit. I became part of a vast melee headed down a long, long ramp. The light was better there than in Berlin, however, and then I saw a happy face and an arm waving above the crowd as Hans fought his way slowly against the mainstream toward me.

"Cherie," he said, joyfully grabbing my arm and the suitcase at once, "It is so nice to have you with me again. I do so miss you and the children."

"I know, and we miss you too," I answered, looking up into that shining countenance.

Hans guided me through the station to a waiting droschke, a rickety two-wheeled shay with a ragged top and side flaps to keep out the wind. The driver, wrapped in a cape of tattered sheepskins and with a sheepskin cap practically covering his face, stood hopping from one foot to the other and flinging his arms around to keep warm.

"It's this or an hour's walk through the abominable cold and snow to my apartment," Hans explained. We climbed in, and the driver mounted the seat above us.

"Here, wrap this awful blanket around you," Hans said, helping to tuck me in. "It's probably full of fleas, but you'll need it before we get home."

"How long will it be?" I asked, shivering despite Hans' warming arms around me.

"Not too long," came his disconcertingly unspecified answer. "It depends on the decrepit old horse. He can't keep his head up any more, he's so starved. He'll stumble all the way on these icy streets. This buggy with three people in it is too much for him. But for us, it's the only way. You didn't want to walk for an hour, did you?" he teased, knowing my aversion to cold temperatures.

We sat in silence, listening to the echoing, irregular hoofbeats of the emaciated beast and the driver's occasional encouragement.

Suddenly, a man's voice, singing loudly, ripped the still darkness. We stiffened and peered around the flaps as the voice came nearer. Without warning, a young man jumped up on the small step on my side of the buggy, hanging on with one foot and one arm for the ride. Obviously intoxicated, he peeked around the flaps and, seeing us inside, used his free hand to doff his cap with exaggerated grandeur, as he mumbled unintelligibly.

Hans just pressed my hand to reassure me and, like the driver, silently allowed our "hanger-on" to ride along. After a few blocks, tired of his adventure or perhaps numb from the cold, he jumped off again.

"I'm surely glad that ended without an unpleasant incident," Hans commented. "Life here is unruly and unpredictable.

After another quarter hour of slow travel, we reached our destination, a two-story house on the far west side of town. A jarring sound of a big key in the lock announced the entrance to it. We entered a cold, dreary hall, and again came the sound of a key in a lock. That time we walked into the long hall of Hans' apartment.

"The door to the left is ours," Hans said, as I preceded him. Opening the unlocked door, I felt along the wall for a light switch and, finding it, turned it on and looked around the room.

One glance took in two large rooms, a wide archway separating them. A meager light bulb hanging from the middle of the ceiling of the first room revealed walls bare of any decoration, uncovered floors, two chairs, a table, a bed and a nightstand supporting a small lamp. A small stove occupied one corner in the front room, but I saw no evidence of a fire to warm the miserably cold apartment!

Noticing my surprised reaction, Hans said, "Not much to look at, I know. I don't need much, since I spend little time here other than to sleep and eat breakfast. But now that you are here, I will have a few briketts put in the stove each morning to try to take the chill off the air."

Hans said the apartment belonged to a Polish couple with a 16-year-old daughter. "Any Polish family with intact walls must take in members of the occupying forces," he explained. "In most cases, this leaves little living space for the owners. This family of three occupies a 12-foot-square kitchen where they eat, sleep and live. One bath serves both them and us."

Expressing my shock, I said, "What a deplorable lack of privacy for them, Hans, especially their daughter. We need no more than one room.

Hans responded with a curt, "I did not make the arrangements, and I find it wiser not to question them or make changes."

At breakfast the following morning, I met Mr. and Mrs. Druczinski and their daughter. After Hans left, they invited me to see their domain, which consisted of a coal-burning cook stove, one single bed, a kitchen table and three straight-backed chairs. They kept the room shiny and clean, and took turns sleeping on the floor.

The Polish woman was very sweet but sad. The husband was polite but his eyes glared with suppressed hatred.

* * *

During the next month, my days fell into a familiar pattern: breakfast with Hans, a second snooze, puttering in our two slightly-warmed rooms, then dressing to take a street car downtown and meet Hans for lunch. Often I got off before my destination and walked the drab dull streets.

Although Posen had suffered very little physical damage during the war, the city exuded an atmosphere of gloom and despair. No greenery brightened the streets, and the shop windows held little but dust and dead flies. Advertisements painted on the sides of buildings showed ancient fashions. The predominant colors were gray, beige and black. Even the beautiful blue sky hid behind the bleak winter clouds.

Mealtimes provided a much-anticipated respite. The restaurants showed the same lack of color and imagination found in the shops. But the crowds of noisy, exciting people who filled them were another matter.

During my first week in Posen I met many of Hans' friends and acquaintances. We seldom ate alone, and I enjoyed the stimulating conversation, although for the most part I listened. Hans, too, often restrained from voicing an opinion.

Much of our time we spent with a group of four interesting and very different men, each from a different province of Germany: Hugo Frohne, the cool, quiet but pleasantly observant banker from Hamburg; Waldemar Steinecker, the black-eyed, temperamental and handsome architect from Berlin; Captain Hermaun Brandt of the Posener Barracks, a gentle and sensitive man with top connections to Persil, a famous German soap company; and the very puzzling Hans von Papen, who represented International Harvester's Eastern European division under another name.

Hans had met them at luncheon on his first day in Posen, when they invited him to their table to take the only available place in the crowded restaurant. He quickly fit into the group, and when I arrived they accepted me also. We often dined with them and others. After our evening meal, we always lingered, over wine and talk, to enjoy the warmth of the dining room.

I enjoyed hearing them describe the male world of business, with its brutal, calculating and manipulative competition. As I listened, I marveled at their shrewdness, their insight, resilience to intrigue, retaliation, their jubilation at each success, even their ever-differing views.

They spoke freely in my presence, which surprised me since German women seldom participated in their husbands' professional lives. In turn, my interest in their conversation astonished them.

* * *

Our clique also included Oberleutnant (first lieutenant) Horst von Valtier, whom Hans had met on his train ride to Posen. Evidently they had enjoyed a pleasant and interesting trip together. Hans and Horst had become fast friends.

Of all the personalities I met in that cold, drab colorless city, Horst fascinated me the most. Vibrant, warm and kindly, in every way he exuded class and fine family breeding. In conversation he was quick-witted and charming, although he sometimes exhibited a bit of arrogance that seemed to fit his regal manner. Slender as a ramrod, his movements graceful, he presented a handsome figure in his uniform. I never saw him in civilian clothes.

Yet he also was something of an enigma. Although an officer in the German Army, Horst's name suggested French ancestry, not German. His long, lean and angular face had a slender nose and an almost effeminately well-formed mouth that narrowed to a thin line. His rabbit-shaped jaw contrasted sharply with the wide curve almost all Germans possess. He wore his thin, carefully trimmed medium-brown hair flattened and combed away from his face.

During group discussions, Horst listened without disclosing his own conclusions or convictions. What did that mean? Was he, as he appeared, a dedicated German officer? Or was that only a pose? Did his true sympathies lie elsewhere?

One night when Hans and I sat alone, I reminded him of his promise to tell me more about the train ride to Posen.

"There's really not much to tell," he said. "You already know how entertaining Horst can be, so you can imagine that the trip was not dull. He's really quite a person, but I can't help but wonder about one thing."

Hans' words brought a twinkle to my eye.

"He looks more French than German, and his name sounds French, too. On the train, he said he was born, raised and educated in Koenigsberg, East Prussia, and I thought the location strange for a French family. I have speculated that perhaps his ancestors were Huguenots who fled to Germany from France to escape religious persecution or to avoid conscription into the Foreign Legion. That's only conjecture, of course, but still possible and intriguing.

"Horst and the doctor and I exchanged family pictures during the trip," Hans continued. "He seems to be quite a devoted family man, with a very beautiful wife and four sons."

"Then why a military career?" I asked.

"I presume his family never gave him any other option."

"And so, with no choice, whether he likes it or is inherently suited, he must wear a uniform for the rest of his life," I said, sympathy for Horst's fate welling inside.

Hans smiled at my observations, seeming to share them.

"Regardless, I truly like him, and you do too, Cherie. So let us enjoy him, with a bit of caution, and we will learn."

"And what of Dr. Kleeberg?" I asked.

"I've heard nothing more from him, although I think Horst has. We will surely meet the doctor again, and I know you will like him. He is totally different from Horst, but so are the people I deal with each day."

My curiosity aroused, I pressed Hans to explain, hoping to learn more about his work and the people he assisted.

"You know, Cherie, much as I regret having to leave Berlin and my business there, this whole milieu with its 'swarm' of Baltan German people and their diverse personalities, is a rare experience. They are no longer like us of the Reich.

"You already have met one of them—Baron von Taube," Hans continued. "He was the first of the resettlement group to visit me, and came to my office on my first day of work. He said he was from Estonia, and of course I knew why he was there.

"He led our conversation in German that had taken on the vernacular of the country that had nurtured him and his forefathers for centuries.

"He was pleasantly relaxed, and gave no sign of being downed by the stroke of tragedy so recent in his life. In fact, he acted quite pretentious. I wondered, was he that good a loser, or was he possibly thinking of the 'pieces of eight' he had pirated across the border, with maybe another heaping supply still tucked away in some private cave? He was a new kind of experience for me. I wonder if he typifies all Germans who live close to the northwestern border of Russia.

"The difference between him and the German of the Reich extends beyond the personal, the exterior man, right into his business methods, which are very subtle. On that first day, his main motive was to make a good impression on me, his benefactor. With his personality he was trying to imbue me with a strong desire to give him favors. He was careful, since his objectives were high.

"We talked easily together, he and I, mostly about his past, his way of life, his interests. And then, having become acquainted with me, and I with him, he decided he had accomplished enough for the day and rose to leave."

I found Hans' description fascinating and told him so.

"But that is not all," he said. "As the baron was about to grasp the knob of the door to let himself out, the door flew open and our racy friend Horst marched in, still in uniform.

"So this is where you are,' he said to me. 'I've been looking for you.' Then, turning to my visitor, he said, 'Guten tag, Herr Baron. How are you today, my good man?' Seeing my surprise, he explained, 'Yes, yes, the baron and I have met."

Hans paused and chuckled, seeing my eagerness for him to continue. "Before I could stop him, Horst then introduced me to the man with him, Waldemar Steinecker—whom, of course, I already knew—and invited me to join them for dinner.

"I accepted, glad not to be alone. The baron, poor man, was caught in the interplay and coolly and quietly took his departure. He had not been invited. It really was quite funny." Hans chuckled again, and so did I.

"Before leaving the office for dinner, I walked down the hall to Horst's office and found him gone already. But I made a new and interesting observation: the gold letters on his door identify him as the appointed liaison officer between the Treuhandstelle and the Chancellery in Berlin. Now, Cherie, what do you think of that?"

"I don't know what to think," I admitted. "It's just another mystery about Horst to puzzle over."

* * *

Hans spoke again about the baron one evening while we sat waiting for our regular dinner companions.

"These newcomers are hardly modest in their expectations, and insist on the equivalent of what they left behind," he explained. "Of course, we cannot meet their demands, even though we do our best. The baron and some of his fellow refugees from Estonia now occupy furnished dwellings vacated by wealthy Poles who disappeared into Western countries just prior to the German onslaught, but still they are not satisfied.

"A few days ago, hoping to reassure Baron von Taube that I appreciated his loss and our comparatively inadequate compensation, I suggested he and his family join us for a weekend of sailing the lakes at home in Berlin. And what do you suppose the baron said?" Hans asked.

Before I could answer, Horst interrupted as he slid into the seat next to Hans.

"I'll bet I know the answer," he said, his confidence undiminished by not knowing the substance of the question.

"You do?" Hans queried with a grin, not at all surprised by Horst's impetuousness. "Yes, I can imagine his reply to any question. What did you ask him?"

"To sail the lakes near Berlin with us for a weekend." "That's it? Well, then, this was his reply. 'For a weekend? My dear Mr. Bohle, that could hardly interest us. We Baltans are used to pleasure sailing on the Baltic for a week or more at a stretch. No! Thank you, but that would not interest any of us.' . . . correct?"

"Exactly," Hans laughed, listening as Horst continued.

"These people still have not pulled in their belts, and seem incapable of accepting a lower standard of living," he said with a hint of disdain. "They eat the finest, and believe me, I know. They keep servants and entertain lavishly and apparently have abundant resources cached somewhere. Unafraid and confident, they expect much from us."

Both Hans and I wondered how Horst knew so much about the Baltan Germans, but we hesitated to ask.

"Horst, your comments suggest you may have attended some of the baron's social functions. We have received an invitation for two evenings from now," Hans said, as I looked up in surprise at the news. "Tell us what to expect."

"Go, by all means. The invitation is a compliment. You can expect a very formal evening, and as for the rest, find out yourselves." Despite our entreaties, he refused to elaborate.

Thus, on the appointed evening, Hans and I entered the banquet room of the Posener Hof. There we found a group of about 15 couples, all dressed beautifully in formal evening attire. Baron von Taube, our host for the evening, awaited us. With great ceremony, he placed in our hands a tall thin glass of vodka like the one he held—a sign of things to come—then introduced us to his other guests.

That dinner party remains vivid in my memory because we could not compete with the drinking. Those notably handsome, intelligent, refined and beautifully dressed people began their evening with a six-ounce glass of straight vodka, followed by a second and then third glass before any food was served! Yet it might have been water they drank, for all its effect on them.

Then came another shock—hors d'oeuvres—followed by fish and fowl, each with the appropriate wine. Small portions, admittedly, but how did they obtain such delicacies in that time of rationing?

Despite the generosity of our host and the pleasant company of our dinner companions, Hans and I felt increasingly uneasy at the ostentatious display. What if a spy observed us and reported our presence to authorities? We left early, allegedly to catch a streetcar but really for our own peace of mind.

* * *

As time progressed, more and more new faces—secretaries, wives, sweethearts, other men showed up in the restaurants at noon and in the evening, and their conversation made for good listening.

Sitting with three male companions in our" restaurant one noon, I noted their discussion with great interest.

"There's Novatzski sitting at a table over there in the corner, with his back to us," Horst said. "I would greet him, but I think he wants privacy."

Following his gaze, I saw a nondescript man sitting with his face to the wall, his broad shoulders bent forward over his food and his feet curled around the legs of his chair. He wore a frayed jacket the same color as his unkempt, sandy hair, and heavy coarse tan brogues.

"I wonder what he is doing in Posen today?" I heard one of my companion's say. "Business with the Treuhandstelle, I suppose. He developed a process for dehydrating fruit and vegetables, and produces these foods under contract for the German Army at a factory off in the plains somewhere. No personal food problems for him. Lord, how I envy that."

Horst added, "Some believe his ancestors all were German, although others say he may be half-Polish. Regardless, he serves the Nazi regime loyally. But he doesn't talk—or maybe won't, I don't know which. He just listens, and when you finish talking he says good-bye with his eyes."

The drab loner they discussed soon rose to leave. There was a glimmer of recognition in his eyes as he walked out past our table, but he said nothing.

To myself, I speculated about his possible feelings at being forced to employ his invention to benefit Poland's conquerors. Although he served his masters well, who could say about his true loyalties? Always under suspicion, he could not afford to be drawn into the web of intrigues in Posen. In his place I would muzzle myself too, I concluded.

Each day in Posen an unhappy transition gained momentum. The original department managers of the Treuhandstelle were a refined, intelligent and knowledgeable group, with clear and meaningful directives. Gradually, however, Nazi fanatics began worming their way into positions of power. Their agenda soon became clear: there was meant to be no justice for either the Poles or the Baltan Germans—or even central Germans like Hans who were assigned to duties there.

The original department managers soon found themselves unable to enforce their decisions without risking reprisals, endangering not only their own lives but those of their families as well. Hans decided to simply "ride out" his assignment, avoiding confrontations with "the new bosses."

"How do you keep so cheerful?" I asked, worried.

"I have you, don't I, and the children? Things will work out somehow. Just believe that," he answered, with characteristic optimism.

"Is that fatalism or faith?" I asked, but he smiled his most charming and disarming smile and stifled my question with a hug.

But he wasn't happy. The others, too, whom we had come to know so well, all adopted the same attitude of fatalistic complacency and waiting.

For us in Posen, the war seemed far away. Our concerns focused on a more immediate danger, rumors of uprisings by Polish survivors against Germans. News reports described killings, beatings and a general lawlessness undeterred by threats of punishment, banishment and even death. A death struggle seemed to exist, not only German against Pole but also Volksdeutsehe (border Germans) against Pole and even Volksdeutsche against Volksdeutsche, sometimes pitting brother against brother in a battle of guns and wits.

Comfort and security no longer meant anything, and everyone seemed to live by the motto, "Don't cross your neighbor, he might shoot." Were we afraid? Yes, all of us, and not most of the time but all of the time. We lived in fear, but lived on.

The nights were worst, with their unlighted streets and blacked-out windows. Tram service ended at 9 p.m., when one either walked or rode a lousy droschke—if available. For the Poles, 9 o'clock also brought the nightly curfew, after which they needed identification and a permit.

* * *

Despite our fears, Hans and I joined those out after 10 p.m. each night. We took the risk to sit after dinner in the restaurant and chat with friends and maybe enjoy a glass of wine—and for the need of warmth.

One night as we returned to our rooms, we heard crying and found Mr. Druczinsi waiting for us in the hall. Sobbing, he rushed to us and dropped to his knees.

"You must help us, you must help us," he cried, over and over, grabbing my hands and covering them with kisses and tears. Pushing past him into the kitchen, Hans found the women huddled together; they, too, sank to their knees and implored.

"Please, please don't let them deport and separate us. All our neighbors are gone, with only an hour or two notice. Tomorrow the S.S. men will come for us. Please, please do something," they wept, beyond consolation and lost in grief.

"No one knows where they go—they take a few clothes, a blanket, no food, some sick, some old," Mr. Druczinski sobbed into his hands. Then, as a new realization crossed his mind, he looked up in terror. "My lovely daughter, wat dey do wif her?"

We finally calmed them, saying they should not borrow trouble until it came, but of course that only amounted to pouring oil on troubled waters. We knew Hans could do nothing for them, and we dared not let them know that we feared for ourselves as well.

Each day thereafter we returned to the house expecting to find them gone, but they remained. They marveled at the miracle and may have connected their good fortune with us, but spoke no more about it.

The wife and daughter remained sweet and demure toward

us, but Mr. Druczinski now became more bold in expressing his hatred. Until then he had kept his place, and we had exchanged little more than an occasional greeting. But one morning while using the bathroom, I heard shuffling footsteps in the hall. Looking over my shoulder I saw his leering eyes pressed hard against the milk glass of the door, watching me. I screamed, and he left.

"I thought we might eventually have problems with him," Hans said when I told him of the incident. "One word about this to the proper person would send him on his way, and he knows it. But I cannot cause more hurt in their lives. I do not fear him myself, but I am afraid for you, Cherie.

"Maybe this is the right time for you to visit the children and confirm Klaerle's good reports. What do you say?" Of course I saw the sense in that, and Hans offered to arrange a vacation in June and join us.

That evening we attended a dinner party hosted by Dr. Walter Kleeberg, Hans' traveling companion from Berlin to Posen. It was their first meeting since, and the very first for the doctor and me.

The genial, tall, sandy-haired physician greeted us at his door, then introduced us to his young, lovely—and very pregnant wife. "Charlotte soon will present me with a daughter," he said happily.

"Horst will join us shortly, along with his wife, Eva, who is visiting him," our host explained. "Because we are so many, the food will be sparse, but good," he said jovially, his face lighted by the famous grin that Hans had described to me often.

We recognized and appreciated the irony of his last comment. Was it not already remarkable that they would share or had the doctor, with his winning ways, coaxed some extra by a bit of black marketing? No matter! We loved him, and his wife, too.

Our rapport was instantaneous with those very fine young people, and with Horst and Eva as well. The atmosphere that evening proved jolly and relaxing. A great and important friendship began for all of us that night which we kept faithfully, despite the greatest odds, throughout the war years

CHAPTER 18

A Refuge in the Black Forest

March -May, 1940

They came down to meet my train at Triberg on a toboggan sled. Their cheeks were ruddy and burning little children stretched out their arms in greeting. Klaerle stood off to one side, enjoying the scene, then approached and offered her hand.

"Gruess Gott, Frau Bohle. Welcome to the Black Forest."

I returned her greeting. "A village friend will drive us up to Schonach and we can pull our sled behind. I had a hard time convincing him to help me, because these people are so very shy and stubborn, too. There he is, over there waiting in the car."

Together we crossed the street and met her driver, who acknowledged the introduction with a touch of his cap, too shy to leave his seat or speak. His old black car was of unrecognizable make, a composite of several years and models, probably assembled by the driver himself. Any apprehension I may have had about its safety was dispelled, however, by Klaerle's confidence in it and my rush of exultation at seeing our "bunch" again.

"The children are fine," Klaerle reassured me in her quiet, modest manner as the motor started and we drove away. The steady hum of the engine reassured me that the car was safe, and I turned to listen to Bobby.

"Klaerle takes us for long walks through the forest. Yesterday we walked 12 kilometers and weren't even tired," he boasted.

The others nodded in agreement. "Yes, that's right, and we love it," Irmgard added. Chubby little Dieter just listened attentively.

"Twelve kilometers?" I questioned, looking skeptically at Klaerle.

"That is no particular feat at this altitude, as you will see," she answered.

I admired the scenery as we moved along. The tall hills were covered almost continuously with white, glistening trees that came right to the edge of the narrow, curving road. The scenic picture blotted out for awhile the memory of war and the intrigues in Posen. I decided, then and there, to give my heart and mind over to enjoying the purity of that glorious, quiet white world and the love of our children as long as I could.

With an effort I turned my attention away from the beauty around me.

"However did you four manage to maneuver that small sled on these sharp mountain curves?" I asked.

"Oh, that's easy," Bobby volunteered. "Three of us have ski boots on, and we sit tight up against each other with our legs outstretched and use our heels for brakes. It's simply heavenly when we go fast," he added.

"And, may I ask, how do the heels of your ski boots look?" Sheepishly, they glanced down at their boots while I, too, examined them.

"How many trips before they need new heels?" I asked Klaerle. "Can you get them at all?"

They huddled and snickered self-consciously, expecting a reprimand. But I fooled them. "May I go with you the next time?"

Surprised and overjoyed by my comment, they hardly could contain their excitement and enthusiasm as immediately they began making plans for the following day. "We'll use two sleds, because with Mother along we'll need that many," Bobby insisted.

"And we'll stop," I suggested, "for a nice hot chocolate somewhere before the long haul back up?"

Klaerle warned me with a glance. "Hot chocolate? Is there still such a thing? We never even thought of that. But why not try? Yes, and I think I know just the place," she added with a decisive nod of her head.

"But we better make that ride soon, because we are due for the big thaw. Some night real soon a foehn wind will blow in over the Alps from Italy and in the morning the snow will be gone and spring will be only a few weeks away."

After a 30 minute drive we reached a wide open plateau surrounded by hills and the car drew up in front of the Pension Sonnenbichl.

"Das is unser haus (That is our house)," Dieter said, speaking for the first time since my arrival. He looked at me quietly, studying me with his innocent, big blue eyes.

Four of us climbed from the car, then Klaerle lifted Dieter out and unhurriedly led him by the hand across the street. Plainly, she took good care of the children and treated them kindly, and they loved her.

The driver left without waiting for payment, while Frau Hock, the proprietress, came forward to welcome me. Klaerle introduced us and we shook hands.

"Sie is unsere mutti (She is our mother)," chimed in Dieter, looking up at Frau Hock with the same quiet, sober face he had given me.

"I know, dear heart, I know," she answered. Then, turning back to us, she abruptly instructed Klaerle to show me to my room. I followed her up a flight of narrow stairs in the direction that Bobby and Irmgard had taken earlier, dragging my suitcase between them. They were still up there, giggling.

Thinking I might be embarrassed by Frau Hock's abrupt manner, Klaerle explained that our hostess sometimes seemed a bit crude, in keeping with her big strong physique, but that her intentions were good. I assured her that I understood.

She then briefed me on the routine at Pension Sonnenbichl, where we were the only guests during their between- seasons period. Klaerle explained that Frau Hock heated the glassed-in verandah much of the day and evening, and it served as the only warm place in the house.

Hot baths were a once-a-week luxury, Klaerle said, because of a shortage of wood for the stove that heated the water and turned the bathroom blessedly warm. The rest of the time, everyone got by with ice cold tap water.

The children did not seem to mind the cold, unheated rooms. "We take our books down to supper," Irmgard explained. "Will you read to us tonight before we go to bed, as Klaerle usually does?"

Although the conditions fell far short of the comforts of our home in Berlin, I endured them gladly because in Schonach the children escaped the horror of war. Sons sent off to fight—and perhaps die—for the Reich, provided the only reminder in that remote little village of the conflict that waged across Europe.

In the year and one-half that our children stayed at Pension Sonnenbichl, only one air raid occurred. It happened during my first stay there, as Allied bombers passed overhead on their way to Munich. The alarm ended almost as soon as it began but it caused almost unbelievable fright. Frau Hock, who often boasted loudly that no war ever could affect her, became livid with fear and trembled for hours afterward.

* * *

On my first evening in lovely Schonach, I enjoyed the wholesome, home-cooked food prepared for us and savored the peace and quiet, grateful that we could make that arrangement for our children. What did it matter if they lacked many "essentials" from our former life? That place offered peace of mind, quiet, plain but adequate nourishment, clean beds, beautiful forests, skiing, sledding and even schooling after a fashion.

That night, as I struggled to get warm alone in my bed, I thought of many families separated under circumstances far worse than ours. Although grateful for our good fortune, I could not help but wonder how long before. . . ? I dared not think about how things yet might turn out for us. Better to look forward, as did the children, to Hans arrival for a vacation in June.

From the next morning on, I lived in ski clothes, just like Klaerle and the children. We continued to follow the established routine. Bobby left for school at eight and Irmgard and Dieter performed their little chores in their room while Klaerle did the washing as necessary.

The rest of each day passed more quickly than I would have thought possible, with a good walk in the forest before noon, a nap for the children after lunch and homework for Bobby after school. We also enjoyed visits to various points of interest in the neighborhood, including the cuckoo clock factories and the woodcutters and carvers. We took a toboggan ride to Triberg for the promised cup of cocoa and made the long, hard walk up the hill again. At factories in Triberg we watched craftsmen make gorgeous, perpetual-motion mantle clocks encased in glass and saw a frozen waterfall nearby.

On one special outing—that time without Dieter—we made a four-and-one-half-hour climb on skis up the terrifically steep slope of one of the highest summits in the Black Forest. There we found a lovely, typical mountain chalet.

"I'm hungry," Bobby complained upon our arrival, and we all concurred quickly. We adjourned to an intimate little dining area which contained few other guests, where we satisfied our hearty appetites with thick slices of hot corned beef on huge, home-made buns. Hot broth and hot milk supplemented the delectable food.

Then, we settled back to rest in the warm room and enjoy the unforgettable view. From our vantagepoint on the mountain peak, dense forestland spread below us in every direction as far as the eye could see.

"I'm tired," Bobby soon sighed.

"Me, too," Irmgard added, and truthfully I also felt extremely fatigued.

"That was my longest and most arduous climb ever. Aren't you tired, too, Klaerle?" I asked.

My comment and question spurred her to action. Jumping up hastily from her chair, she told Bobby and Irmgard to put on their wraps.

"I'm afraid you're feeling the effects of the good and ample food and the warmth of this pleasant room," she warned. "Come quickly, let's go. The way home is long and strenuous and we cannot allow anyone giving in to fatigue."

She was right. We left immediately with a burst of speed on the downward slopes. But before long each stroke of our skis and sticks became a terrible effort. We constantly called for a rest, but Klaerle would not allow it. She explained that a rest could lead to sleep and we could freeze to death, and so pushed us forward relentlessly.

The way seemed endless. Four exhausted people slid into the pension at dusk, none too soon before dark, almost too tired to eat our evening meal. We all went to bed early that night.

Most days we planned no specific program. Often we enlisted a villager as a ski teacher and practiced our technique on the Winterberg, the very tall but gently sloping hill close behind the pension. Then one night true to Klaerle's prediction, a warm wind blew in from the south. It sighed and whined miserably throughout the night, bringing a feeling of mystery so disconcerting that I could not sleep. In the morning, the snow was gone and the ground shone black and brown and bare. Tiny rivulets ran everywhere, merging together into miniature streams.

The following days were mostly overcast, which affected our moods. But after about 10 days, warm sunshine came again and brought a new miracle. From its base to its peak, Winterberg, so wonderful for skiing in the wintertime, began showing tints of green. Before long a solid sea of emerald pasture grass, interspersed with wild flowers, waved in the strong, sharp breeze.

The improved weather and the beauty of spring proved harbingers of even better news, as a letter arrived from Hans confirming his vacation plans beginning in the middle of June.

"Frau Hock, will you please accommodate my husband for a two week visit about the 15th of June?" I asked at the supper table that night. 'He wants to rest and see his children."

"Of course," she answered, her reply nearly drowned out by the cries of joy from Bobby and Irmgard. Even little Dieter, usually a silent but most attentive part of their world, chimed in. His joy at the news seemed almost overpowering. With a gleam in his eye and a smile on his lips, he caught his breath and held it again and again—he was so happy.

As I watched, I thought that maybe he found the separation of family hardest to bear. It brought tears to my eyes and an ache to my heart and I, too, could hardly wait for Hans' arrival.

CHAPTER 19

A Brief Family Reunion

June - July, 1940

June 15 finally arrived. At 5 p.m. the children stood waiting at a bus stop near the pension for the bus that before long would bring Hans up from the railroad station in Triberg. The bus finally pulled up to the stop, the doors opened and shoppers and workers from Triberg poured out.

Then came Hans with his luggage and a happy smile. As always, the children welcomed him wildly and ecstatically, and with no end. Irmgard climbed up on him and Dieter reached up with his little arms. Bobby held back a bit, then extended his hand, but Hans swept him up in a bear hug. Klaerle and I waited at the pension entrance, leaving the reunion stage to the children and their father.

"Come now," Hans said at last. "Let's go over to Mother, shall we? I also must say hello to Klaerle, and then you can show me to my room."

With Dieter in one arm, he picked up his luggage and crossed the street, then dropped his bags again where I stood. After putting Dieter down, he greeted me with a kiss.

"Cherie, my dear, you look fine and the children, too." Turning to Klaerle, he shook her hand with a smile and a remark of approval. Then into the house we went, up the stairs to "Mother's room," where two beds stood, one "just for Daddy."

As we got ready for the evening meal, Hans shuddered—more for me than for himself at the cold, damp chill.

"Does this room ever get really comfortable?" he asked. I didn't tell him that it was much warmer than during the wintry days of March. "But then you probably don't need to spend much time here, do you, darling?

"I keep hoping that before long we can return to Berlin, but doubts assail me," he continued, encircling me in his arms. "I cannot project, even though in my position I should have some idea."

Then I told him, 'That's what bothers me here, Hans. We cannot keep up with events on the outside. The only radio in this house produces just a jumble of noises. It's exasperating because well—time just stops here."

Laughing, my husband remarked, "There's a saying that even in our small land, some areas—like this one, like Tegernesse, like the mountains of Bavaria—are so remote that people do not even know that the last war ended."

Then, after some reflection, Hans' mood turned sentimental. Taking my hands in his he said, "But we know it, don't we, dear. In that little interval between wars I found you, and together we have established our own little empire that we are trying so hard to keep intact, even as we miss each other."

His words implied an unspoken appeal for continued patience, despite the ordeal of our separation, and a request for pampered me to dig in and call up my own hidden strengths. Moreover, for once he had exposed his own need for reassurance, for a boost to his spirits that were serene only on the surface. I sensed a mood of foreboding and pessimism so unlike him.

Yet how could I evaluate the depth of his present problems, which stemmed from a political antagonism which he dared not show? Hans always had shielded me from the unpleasant, but to whom could he turn other than me for relief from his own emotional tensions? And how could we overcome the long stretches of absence from each other, for the children's sake, with no change in sight? We could not cut short or end an ever-widening war.

My heart reached out to him. His lot was harder than mine. Time for an about-face, I told myself. My turn to help him, if I could, if I could. So, I tried to reassure him with my love and confidence. I told him that he was my life, that my thoughts and spirit stayed with him every minute of my waking hours, and promised him patience and the will and strength to hold together. I could give nothing more, and I hoped it would comfort him enough.

* * *

At the supper table that evening, Frau Hock came to greet Hans and brought her niece, a lovely young woman who did the cooking. Frau Hock seemed much impressed by Hans, since she reiterated repeatedly that anything she could do for his family she most surely would, he had but to indicate.

With the children finally in bed, Klaerle and Frau Hock and her niece joined us at the warm stove to ask for news of the various fronts.

Frau Hock knew little of the world beyond her own tall hills. Her niece, however, who like Klaerle had worked "outside," understood and liked people of other countries, too. Just the same, Hans gave a straight account of the news and left the opinion-forming to them. While waiting for him to begin, I thought how incredible that communities still existed in our modern world that depended entirely on news from the Town Crier.

"Herr Bohle, tell us about the struggle in the East," Klaerle began.

"Struggle?" Frau Hock interrupted. "We're done with the Poles. We've taken our Corridor back again—and about time. If they thought...." She stopped as her niece reached over and laid her hand on her aunt's arm.

"Auntie, dear, let Mr. Bohle tell it —now you listen."

Hans laughed and said, "We did win back our Corridor, but

the Poles are not yet totally pacified. Insurgents continue to create trouble, although the Army manages to control them for the most part. However, the West, not the East, is the focal point of interest."

He explained that after Germany's conquest of Poland, Russia had invaded Finland. Hitler then had used that as a pretext to enter Denmark and Norway on April 9, 1940, ending the six-month-long "Sitzkrieg."

Hitler claimed he had acted to protect those countries from possible Russian onslaught, a pretense to save face for Germany, Hans said. In reality, Hitler had wanted to gain access to Norway's iron supplies and her ports, airports and roads.

Denmark had capitulated in a single day, and success had come quickly in Norway as well, Hans said. In the opening 24 hours of battle, coordinated attacks by land, sea and air had enabled German forces to take and hold all the principal Norwegian coastal cities from Skaggerak north.

By early May, Allied forces had been forced out of central Norway, and the Norwegian king and his government had fled into exile in England.

"All this already is old news, every speck of it reported in some newspaper," Hans said, surprised at our lack of awareness. "Do you really lack access to this information? What about your radio?"

"Wir hawe keine Zeit zum lese," Frau Hock said, to which her niece countered quickly, "Yes, we do—I do. I have time to read, but the radio could bring us more if our reception weren't so jumbled. It's no use to listen, although we keep trying—it's frustrating."

"That's true," I substantiated. "Reception is so poor I've given up trying."

"Sage Sie weiter (Tell us more), Herr Bohle," Frau Hock interjected, adding, "Hauptsache wir gewinne (Main thing is, we win)."

To that we all laughed, because of her delightfully comical dialect, or because her unswerving confidence left no room for doubt in her mind about the eventual outcome of the war. Hans just could not believe we all were so unaware, and I saw a gleam of mischief in his eyes as he continued.

"You know that with considerable daring, and an overpowering air attack, Germany struck Holland?" Frau Hock nodded, either acknowledging the news or agreeing she had known.

". . . and then Belgium." Again she affirmed with a nod of her head.

". . . then Luxembourg, and that it all ended. . . ." he waited, and Frau Hock took over.

". . . bis ende Mai, gel (By the end of May, right)?"

"So you do know," Hans laughed, but Frau Hock, her niece and Klaerle, too, interrupted each other with "Ja, das wisse wir, aber wie es halt zuging, das wisse wir nit (Yes, but not how it happened)."

"Well, that I do not know either, but someday historians will tell us, if we live that long. But by now you know that Germany trapped the French and Belgian armies, and the British at Dunkirk also, making their only hope evacuation.

"The British accomplished this by using all sorts of sea transports for four days and succeeded largely due to a sudden and unexplained halt in the advance of the German Army. However, Dunkirk fell, the Germans caught the French in a military tidal wave, and General von Kuechler's 18th Army occupied Paris."

"Un' was macht der dumme Mussolini? Den brauche wir nit," said Frau Hock in sudden heat. "Wir hawe schon den Franzosen fertig, die Anere sin' erledigt, un' den Englaender hawe wir nach Hause geschupst. Da is der Kneg wohl alle, gel?"

"I agree, we don't need Mussolini," Hans said. "But I am afraid that just because the French, Dutch, Danes and Belgians are what you call 'finished' is no reason to believe that England won't fight back. Nor do we know what Hitler has in mind.

"No, I'm afraid I cannot agree with you that now the war is over. But for the next two weeks I'd like to forget it a little bit and enjoy my family and your lovely countryside."

Hans made that comment in his usual charming manner, but we all gladly ended conversation about war when Frau Hock's niece brought a tray with glasses of hot red wine "to put us in the right mood for a good night's rest."

* * *

During the next two weeks, the sun shone a little brighter, the air seemed balmier and gentler, the trees in the forest a little greener; in fact, all of nature surrounding us gave assent to our happy togetherness. We roamed the hills day in and day out. On longer trips we left Dieter at home with Klaerle, but Bobby and Irmgard never found the way too long, too far or too difficult.

Both children responded to every change of scenery: the clouds and shadows, the lovely tall pines, the bugs, the birds, the toadstools and mushrooms under the beds of pine needles, the rivulets and little sparkling pools, logs, tadpoles, the lizards, the deer, the foxholes and the badger lairs, the delicate flowers, fallen pine cones, the rock scale and every mood that makes the Black Forest such perfect Hansel and Gretel country.

Hans separated himself from his burdens in Posen, renewing himself in the fresh clean atmosphere. He hated to miss a single day with the children, but he felt compelled to visit his mother before returning to his duties. She was still staying as a guest at the spa in Glotterbad, which had remained open against all expectations.

Hans called his mother to propose a day-long visit, and she asked me to come along and bring Bobby and Irmgard as well. So, as Hans' two-week vacation neared an end, he reluctantly bade little Dieter and Klaerle farewell and the four of us set out for Glotterbad.

Lacking a car, we were forced us to rely on local buses. Although they operated with scheduled routes and departure times, the buses stopped wherever and whenever a passenger requested or someone stood waiting by the roadside. Most of the passengers were local residents, and often their relatives came down out of the remotest folds of the tall, tall hills to meet them. The people of those mountains dressed in costumes indigenous to the particular area in which they lived. They seemed quiet, undemonstrative, retiring and actually very shy, and reminded me of a remark Hans once had made about remoteness being "less the distance away than the lack of physical contact with humanity."

The mountain people only came out of seclusion when the rural bus arrived, to exchange messages quietly with the driver or greet a visitor. And in their entire lifetime, some of them never left their tiny obscure area at all.

We changed buses after an hour or so and then boarded a third bus after another long ride. Finally at one stop, a middle-aged stranger poked his head in the door and quietly asked the driver if he had passengers with our name.

On hearing that, Hans walked forward, talked to the man, and then beckoned us to leave. The stranger led us to a waiting private car, and we climbed in. Not long afterward, the car pulled up in front of the spa where Mother Bohle stood waiting expectantly.

"Na, da seid Ihr (Well, there you are)," she said, using the phrase with which she always greeted us. She laughed her child-like little chuckle that always seemed so incongruous coming from a woman of such tall, regal bearing. We thanked her for providing the ride to the spa.

"Yes, that was clever of me, and you may pat me on the back for inveigling someone into using a private car and gasoline for something other than a military purpose. But I expected to find you in military uniform, Hans."

The children immediately began to tell their grandmother all the events of their lives since they last had seen her more than a year earlier. Finally, Mother Bohle said, "I can see that you, Bobby, and Irmgard are very hungry. You will not have long to wait." It amused her—and concerned her as well—when Irmgard put her hands to her stomach and rolled her eyes to the ceiling. Bobby chimed in, 'Me too!"

During the evening, mother and son discussed family affairs, mostly matters of finance that concerned her most, relieving her of the burden of making lone decisions. We had seldom seen or heard from each other since the disastrous meeting with her and Walter after Rosmarie Lawrenz' wedding in Mannheim. For some reason, maybe the war or perhaps reconsideration of her own drastic moves, her attitude toward us seemed mellowed. But she made no mention of Walter, and neither did we!

This time, instead of accepting Hans' help as a form of duty, she expressed genuine gratitude for the several hours he spent with her. We belonged together, she and we, I thought. But the spa was no place for children, and she considered the Black Forest region where we were staying too "primitive." Thus, we left her alone once again when we departed the next day. Hans headed for the East and the children and I somehow found our way back to Schonach.

In our absence, Dieter had become ill and Klaerle scarcely had left his side. We also had missed a visit by Carl Reuther, our dear friend from Mannheim, who with his wife had joined us on the trips to Helgoland, just prior to the beginning of the war with Poland.

Disappointed at not finding us at home, he had left a warm and substantial greeting in the form of a beautiful cake. A cake! We couldn't recall when we last had seen one, nor could we imagine where he had found it. The father of four, Carl knew how we would welcome such a gift and how endearing it would make him. His special friendship was most precious in times like these and especially touching as we returned to our lonesome, bland routine.

We spent our days missing Hans and waiting eagerly for his letters, which brought a happy glow and joy to our lives. Along with irregular reports from the fronts, they provided the only news that reached our sleepy little town until August when the summer guests arrived from Alsace-Lorraine, across the Rhine.

After spending several months with the children, I needed to inspect our house in Berlin, and from there, go again to Posen. So, I gave up my room and took the train northward from Triberg to Offenburg, where I changed for an express to Berlin

CHAPTER 20

Posen Again

August 1940

As I walked from the streetcar stop up the road to our house, I reveled in the beauty of our country setting. Wally and Franisch Grubert, our beloved neighbors, spotted me and came to greet me, linking their arms through mine, as they had many times before, in a gesture of joy and welcome.

"Are you coming back?" they wanted to know.

"Just checking on our property," I said, and they left me alone to inspect the quiet house. I moved from floor to floor and found nothing amiss—no broken pipes, nothing taken from the storerooms. All was so still, so undisturbed.

I opened the windows and doors to the balcony to let in the sparkling sunshine and the breeze from the lake. The sounds of waves lapping gently at the shore and mourning doves cooing in the nearby timber of the marshlands reached my ears. Blue and gray jays chased each other in the tall trees nearby, raucous and fresh as ever. So far, the houses out there on the western rim of the city seemed intact and undamaged by air raids.

Restless and suddenly horribly alone, I impulsively closed the house again. Still packed, I simply picked up my luggage and made tracks across the street to my dear neighbors, the Gruberts, joining them for afternoon coffee and improvised Streusel Kuchen.

"How is living now?" I asked. "This delusionary quiet, how

deceiving? Any children remaining in the area? How often do the raids come, and how long do they last? What do you think of the German situation now?'

Franisch's views remained unchanged. A good German who loved his country but not the regime, he said life was tolerable, so far. He also claimed he could follow the route of the raids. When the 12-minute warning sounded on our little peninsula, he could determine immediately whether the planes would remain at a distance or continue on toward Berlin.

At first, he would not say how he knew, but after awhile he dropped his guard and led me into a separate room. There, on a table about six feet square, sat a strange-looking device.

"It's called radar," he explained. "Only a few people have it, Ruth, and I wouldn't trust many to know that I do."

"But Franisch, where did you get it?" I asked.

And so for the first time I learned of his brother in the high command of the Luftwaffe, who gave the radar set to Franisch. "Of course, you must swear to secrecy,' he said. "Now you know that my military and political assessments reflect some of my brother's deductions, as well.

"He says that for awhile, Germany enjoyed a strong position against the Allies. But then an unaccountable delaying tactic ruined the final possible victory. At the very least, he says, it afforded a turning point in favor of the Allies," Franisch added.

"Strange, Hans told Frau Hock and the others in the Black Forest the same thing, but he didn't know what the 'unaccountable reason was," I answered.

"My brother's idea, and maybe mine, too, is that Hitler hoped England would accept the subtle peace offer he made in his last speech," Franisch said. "He gave England time to accept—too much time, a very grave mistake "

Much influenced by that point of view, I found Franisch—and his unknown brother shrewd and fair. The end of the war, years later, proved their fantastic insight into the outcome.

As our conversation continued, I shared confidences with them about what I saw and felt in the East and some of Hans' interpretations. They shook their heads in disbelief, and Franisch said, "We are doomed. How can it be otherwise?"

"I have heard that many times," I countered. "I also hear 'right or wrong, my country,' or 'what is right and what is wrong?' and 'why must we take on the whole world?'"

Wally and Franisch wanted me to stay. But with my mission in Berlin accomplished, and eager to see Hans again, I left for Posen to surprise him by arriving a day early. However, my unexpected appearance made Hans furious, not happy—as angry as I had ever seen him.

"Have you lost all sense of danger?" he raged. "You know Posen is unsafe—I've told you repeatedly. Where would I have looked for you if you hadn't shown up? What would have become of you if you had fallen into the wrong hands? If you could not remember that I love and need you, at least you might have thought of our children."

Crushed, entirely subdued and filled with remorse, I accepted his criticism and promised never, never to do that again. He forgave me, and I fell into his comforting arms that night, ready to resume the Posener routine.

* * *

I awoke the next morning determined to master my fear of staying alone in our rooms with the Druczinskis and eager to see old friends and meet new additions to the Treuhandstelle forces. At noon I joined Hans for lunch at "our" restaurant. I spotted Horst and moved up behind him, unseen. "'Tag, Horst," I greeted him.

Recognizing my voice, and knowing I was not due until the next day, he wheeled around on one heel, took a long look at me and then glanced at Hans.

"Did you know about this?" he asked.

"No, a big surprise!"

"Gruess Dich Gott, Gnaedige Frau," Horst greeted me. He suddenly clicked his heels, took my hand and with his usual German military gallantry, bent over and kissed it. "Come, we must celebrate!"

And so, with my arm drawn through his and Hans bringing up the rear, he led me toward the back and through a door to a small private dining room. A big round table stood in the center, where two gentlemen sat in deep discussion. Hearing us enter, they stopped suddenly, looked up and then stood at attention.

"May I introduce, Frau Bohle, Herr Guenther Brink and Herr Baron von Gagman." Of the two new young faces, I judged the baron as the older.

"High time you returned," Horst began, turning his attention to me once more. 'Hans is lonesome without you, and that is not good around here."

"That does not make having to leave again any lighter," I rejoined.

"Must you? He asked, looking questioningly at Hans who, in his quiet way, answered, "The children."

"Yes, I guess you cannot help it. It's a great existence, isn't it?" Horst said, his touch of irony failing to disguise his disgust. He motioned us to a seat.

I took one opposite the two newcomers and, leaving the ordering to the men observed. The usual questions intrigued me. Who were they, and why were they there? The baron, I thought, plainly seemed stuffy, conceited and sure of himself. Medium in build, with a hard oval face, he wore his colorless hair cropped closely and peered out through thick glasses.

His companion was tall and broad, with soft dark eyes and thick, wavy blond hair, on the unruly side. Despite his suave manner, he slouched in his chair as though he found it difficult to sit erect.

Seated again, they resumed their conversation in muffled tones, with the baron doing most of the talking. His clipped, military way of speaking amused me and I wondered what bill of goods he sought to sell. I thoroughly I disliked him immediately.

I turned my attention back to Horst. "Tell me about Eva and the children, and about the new people we passed on our way down through the restaurant," I asked.

"The children remain in Berlin," he said. "Eva leaves them with her mother every now and then and comes to visit me, just like you do Hans. Regarding newcomers, perhaps you observed the beautiful auburn-haired wife of your architect friend, Waldemar Steineeker. They found rooms on the outskirts of town near Hans'. Otherwise, no new developments, only worse and disturbing ones.

"Don't quote me on that," he added, "nor this. We just mark time, watching progress in the West as closely as possible and wondering what will become of us, all of us."

So then I knew! They trusted few and kept their counsel. And more and more I believed that Horst lacked the conviction of a dedicated Nazi.

As usual, we found the food lacking in quality and quantity, but as we all put it diplomatically, "It was lunch." Only occasionally could we enjoy a special treat, Baltic Sea eel with dill sauce, that the men and I liked so much.

With lunch finished, the men returned to work while I again spent the afternoon hours visiting various shops whose proprietors I knew, to ask about their new merchandise and to while away the time until night. Oh yes, there was the battered- down cathedral to visit and other bits of historic monuments. Also, for awhile I took an occasional afternoon tea with Frau Baronin von Traube, but those times became less frequent, as Hans grew increasingly opposed to my social fraternizing. He became very choosy, no doubt with good reason.

I tolerated all the "do nothing" in good weather, but became miserable when the weather turned bad. And so no one blamed me much when, during the last week in August, I pulled out for Berlin and subsequently the Black Forest, where my room was available again with the end of the summer season.

While in Fosen I had longed for the children, and once back with them I longed for Hans. Why buck it! I could do nothing. But oh, how to choke down the exasperating frustration that engulfed me. Although I promised Hans patience, I lacked that inherent German virtue—and their sense of fatalism as well. Like a typical American, I wanted to get out of the jam I found myself in—not someday, but immediately! Yes, but how? No way! This time the "thing" was too big for me

CHAPTER 21

A Respite from War Worries

September - December, 1940

On my return to Schonach, I found the children and Klaerle healthy and happy. Bobby had started back to school and I began private French lessons.

I took stock of the children's clothing. The point system allowed little possibility for new clothes. Instead, everyone remodeled old garments and handed them down to younger children. But Klaerle and I hit upon an ingenious idea. We would buy as much cotton yarn—trachten wolle, the locals called it—as we could find. The thick string had always been used to knit the sweaters, vests and socks of the native dirndl costumes. We could knit garments for the children, and when they outgrew them we could unravel and re-knit.

As we knit, I learned the many stitches peculiar to the Black Forest. That new interest helped pass the time. But before long our days once again became a tiresome sameness, especially since we lacked the diversion of reading material or news. One evening, while we all ate supper, the special ring of the long-distance operator interrupted our routine. Frau Hock, our landlord, answered, then called to me; "Mr. Bohle is calling."

"Are you all right?" he asked over the wire. "I hardly can hear you How good to hear his voice again, I thought, but I wondered also if he would be delivering any bad news.

"Yes, dear," I finally got it out. "I'm fine."

Then he told me the reason for his call. "Cousin Lisel has invited us to her wedding in Trier on October 26. Can you meet me there? I can arrange a few days extra over that weekend."

"Yes, Hans of course I can make it," I said. "It will give me something to look forward to."

I waited breathlessly. Did he not want to tell me anything more? I lived in constant fear of what might happen to Hans in Posen. Underhanded intrigues, especially against anyone suspected of lacking devotion to the Nazi cause, occurred constantly; the reason always personal gain and self-preservation.

"How are you and the children?" he asked, bringing me back from my momentary contemplation.

"All fine. The weather is cool, rainy and changeable; we need heat soon." What nonsense we talked just to hear each other's voices.

"Posen, too." he answered. "Miss me?"

"Intolerably."

We said good-bye and hung up. I breathed a huge sigh of relief—a reaction that reminded me once again of the burden of apprehension under which I lived.

Then I thought of the village telephone operator. She had listened in on Hans' previous call and heard us talking English. Immediately, she had informed Frau Hock that she harbored a spy in her house. If the operator had listened that time—as she no doubt had—she had heard the kisses Hans had sent over the wires to me and the children. To alleviate her fears, we had spoken only German, which made our conversation so unsatisfactory, so stilted.

"Was that Daddy?" Dieter wanted to know. "Is he coming again?"

"Not for awhile," I answered. Then I told them about Cousin Lisel, whom Bobby and Irmgard remembered from a visit in Berlin. They listened keenly when I told them about her upcoming wedding. I explained that I would go, but that I would come right back.

Extremely contented with Klaerle in the hills, the children did not ask to go along. Nor could I take them due to the risk, already great for Hans and me. Trier lay on the far western border of Germany and faced, I assumed constant alarm. I really did not want to go, but Hans did. And after all, had not the war already forced me to join the ranks of fatalists? We would hope for the best, I thought as I sat through a meal of hot browned-butter homemade noodles, with steaming hot applesauce—good, but far from enough.

So Klaerle and I continued with our knitting, walking, eating, sleeping, studying and getting what little war information we could. Of the latter, we knew that the two remaining Western adversaries, Germany and Britain still faced each other in direct confrontation. Hitler's speech in the Reichstag on July 19 had seemed a masterpiece of appeal for peace, directed to the common folk of both countries. But he also had said that if Britain refused his terms, they would bear the responsibility for continued war an implication that had angered England's leaders, Churchill in particular.

For awhile, everyone had hoped for an immediate peace. But as the wait for England's answer lengthened, it had become plain we hoped in vain. Once again the combatants were at each other's throats—not on land but in the air and on the seas. British bombers flew raid after raid, bringing hellish reprisals to our big cities, and destruction widened from military objectives to personal property.

I understood fully, therefore, the unpleasantness I might encounter when I left the children and Klaerle for Lisel's wedding. But still I went, entrusted with a million kisses for Daddy from his affectionate puppets and a great bear hug for Lisel. Promising to return immediately after the wedding, I urged them to order snow during my absence.

"Then we'll start skiing and practice real hard. We'll show Daddy, when he comes at Christmas time, that we can keep up with him on ski trips, long and short, won't we?" Oh, yes, they liked that!

* * *

To manage the trip would be an accomplishment under any circumstances, but particularly so during war: bus to Triberg, mountain rail to Offenburg, day coach to Koblenz on the Rhine and another inland, west to Trier. That little town on the Mosel River marked the gateway of the old Roman Road. A huge, centuries-old stone gateway marked the entrance to the city.

The journey lasted 12 hours, but I arrived in time for a short visit before bedtime with Lisel's parents, Hans' Aunt Emma and Uncle Karl. Several years had passed since my last visit and I enjoyed seeing them again.

All keyed up, Lisel eagerly showed me her new home, created by remodeling the family residence to add a separate entrance and staircase to the third floor. The renovated rooms had wonderful lighting and a view, and the furniture overflowed with gifts. Lisel acknowledged that some were not new, but came from friends' own possessions—a necessity during war rationing. The linens, silver and dishes were from her parents, saved for that purpose for years. "Thank God, our home still exists, as yet spared the destruction of bombs and fire," the happy bride said.

I delighted in her happiness and good fortune, since for so long Lisel's parents had contested the marriage of their daughter into the Catholic faith. But the young couple's love had prevailed and finally they stood on the eve of their wedding.

Leaving her in her own new rooms, I descended to find Lisel's brother, Hans, ready to take me to my hotel. The family hoped I would not mind sharing my room with Cousin Ursula (Uschi), arrived from Essen. We had never met, but with hotel reservations difficult to obtain I did not mind—although I wondered privately where Hans would rest when he arrived at 5 o'clock the next morning.

A key in our door awakened us out of a sound sleep. The door opened and Hans stepped inside with a happy grin on his face, while we sat up groggily in our beds and rubbed our eyes.

"Sorry, my dears," he said. "The hotel has no other room for me, so I thought of a solution—'The Besuchritze.' How about it? I traveled all night and stood all the way."

I laughed out loud. Of course, I knew of the standing German joke calling for three to occupy two single beds, pushed tightly together with the guest occupying the center over the uncomfortable wooden rims. I volunteered to give my tired Hans the better part of the bed and cuddled up happily. Only a few hours remained before dawn.

As required by a unique Old Trierer tradition, horse-drawn glass carriages called for all the guests at noon and carted us over the cobblestone streets to the chapel. All Trier knew from the noise of those wood-rimmed wheels and the clip-clop of the horses' hooves that a wedding party passed outside. In house after house, doors flew open and men, women and children in every conceivable get-up hurried out to wave and share in our happiness.

Of course we waved back, Hans in his midnight-blue tails and tall hat with gloves and I in my apricot slipper-satin with furs. For just a little while, we found ourselves transformed into a Cinderella wonderland, and it felt so good!

The carriages finally deposited their occupants in front of a quaint chapel. It sat within the confines of an ancient monastery guarded by two rings of walls, with lovely grounds in between. The chapel was small, intimate and exquisitely fashioned, with stained glass windows of amber, red and blue. We loved it the minute we entered.

As members of the wedding party, Hans and I accompanied the bride and groom to the altar for a lengthy and dignified ritual. Not once during the ceremony, nor during the beautiful dinner that followed at the home of Uncle Karl, were we disturbed by flyers. Toward evening an alarm sounded, but it ended quickly, either false or unimportant.

We took a few hours that evening for a fine family chat. Then, with a kiss for the bride and a handclasp for the groom, and our heartfelt thanks for including us in their beautiful celebration, Hans and I left for Cologne. We longed for a quiet weekend of our own before separating once more until Christmas.

Monday morning came all too quickly, and I retraced the arduous journey to Schonach. Stepping from the bus into the beginning of a whopping snowstorm, I unexpectedly found the children waiting for me, happy with expectation. Irmgard and Dieter stood huddled together, ducking their heads and hunching their shoulders against the wind, laughing as the big flakes plastered their eyes, noses and mouths shut. Bobby stood aside, hands in pockets, with a cap of snow covering his thick, curly blond hair.

Seeing me they called greetings and crowded around, grabbing my hands, my arms and my luggage. Together we ran across the street and down to the pension. Indoors, they shook off the snow and peeled out of their woolen outer garments, then began bombarding me with questions.

"How was it? How did Aunt Lisel look? What did you do at the wedding? Would Aunt Lisel and her new husband come to visit, if we wrote them that Schonach has snow?"

"Yes, they plan to do just that, and real soon," I said.

"And did you have alarm?" That last question came from Frau Hock who, on seeing my negative head shake, added, "Well, you just had luck"

*　*　*

During the night the wind abated, yet at dawn the snow still fell. In my icebox-like room, my breath steamed in the air but I stayed toasty warm under my thick down comforter. Oh, how I hated to climb out of the feathers—a daily battle. Knowing I would have to face the cold eventually, and that the verandah already would be warm, I rose to dress fast, fast, fast in my ski togs and get on with the day.

But I still blew and stamped and fussed over the icy water and the tooth-brushing ritual. That miserable, horrible old war—if one could only turn it off, or give the terrible battle back to Hitler and his henchmen to fight themselves.

Those conceited fools, I thought, what did they expect to gain? We, the people, wanted to go home to a normal living routine. We wanted our husbands, our children and a chance for a future. Aloud I said, "Ah, yes, I know, I am being unreasonable." But it felt great, and gave me a bit of release.

The storm lasted three days and three nights. Bobby went to school the first day, then no more until the roads were cleared. We quickly ran out of games and stories and grew tired of dominoes and checkers. With our ideas for fun depleted, it became difficult not to lose our sense of humor.

Then on the fourth morning, we at last arose to see bright sunshine in a sky of most exquisite blue. The entire world below was covered with mounds of glistening, untrammeled, pristine white snow. Can anything compare with the pure, clean, quiet air following a snowstorm? Even the gentle wind carried its own sound, as if voices from the astral planets surrounded us, filling the ears of those who would listen with the mystery of another world. I felt my spirits lifting and resolved to remain patient.

We hurried through our morning chores, then strapped on our skis and quietly took the road in single file. Before long we struck off into the nearby thinned-out pine forest, breaking trail in the deep powdered snow and winding slowly in and out among the trees until we thought by the sun that it might be noon.

Day after day we followed that pattern, and it took many such outings before the magic wore off. Then once more we hired a villager to instruct us in skiing. He taught us to mount the tall Winterberg without sticks and slalom down through gates formed by our ski sticks. In that way November quietly and quickly slipped into December and, before we knew it, thoughts of Christmas and the arrival of Daddy filled our minds.

For the second time in our lives, we enjoyed the privilege of picking our own Christmas tree out of the forest stand, cutting it down and dragging it home. Frau Hock provided tinsel and lights, and even she roused more abundant enthusiasm in herself from the spontaneous good cheer of the children.

Little Dieter soon knew the words to the carols and learned a few poems from the indomitable Irmgard. He enjoyed that, and wholeheartedly took part in all the preparations. And, of course, time flew faster as the days became shorter, the mornings later and the nights so early.

On the day before our Yuletide celebration, Hans arrived. Like every coming and going the children turned it into an event. They clung to him and no one dared mention the New Year's Day that would send him off again.

Nothing too special happened in those next 10 days. We enjoyed good weather and made lovely skiing trips in the snow. The wonderful togetherness was a joy heightened no doubt by the hurt of parting so soon again to come.

And it did come, as it had to. The day dawned unusually warm, dull and gray, seemingly on the verge of a January thaw. Once more the bus door closed and the moving vehicle took away the light of our lives. It left all of us with heavy hearts, wondering about the New Year, already several hours launched.

CHAPTER 22

Shuttling Between Posen and the Black Forest

January - April, 1941

After seeing Hans off, I returned to the pension and huddled near the just-warming stove on the verandah, waiting for Klaerle and the children to come downstairs.

"Mr. Bohle enjoyed a much-needed stay here, didn't he?" asked Frau Hock's niece, as she set the table. A discerning person, that niece. For the next few minutes we reviewed the activities of the prior 10 days, including a visit to one of the village wood carvers who had mechanized his Christmas story figures on a room-sized platform.

We talked also about the new ski jump, and the wonderful performance of the villagers. I recalled the fun of tobogganing to Triberg on a small sled with Hans and Dieter, and how our speed had robbed Dieter of his breath, scaring us.

Suddenly realizing that we had spoken only of my activities and interests, I asked, "And what about you, my dear? Aren't you ever tired of staying here and doing the same things, day in and day out?"

"Yes," she agreed. "I get weary of it all, but as long as my soldier husband does not come home, I appreciate staying busy.

"I wonder if I shall ever see him again? Ja, Ja," she sighed, hurrying away to warm the milk and the coffee as she heard the children scurrying down the stairs.

Unlike the previous year, when everything in the Black Forest was new to us and every incident an experience, time hung long and heavy. We felt glad when the magic foehn winds melted all the snow in early March, bringing an early spring.

The children seemed happy enough, but I felt restless, knowing I should check again on the house in Berlin. I did not much relish the idea, recalling the cast-off feeling from my last visit and realizing that the weather still would be unfriendly so much further north. But it needed doing, so I went.

Each trip had become additionally complicated, and I no longer saw any novelty in traveling under very trying conditions—no seat, no heat, long hours and distances. Not the least of the hardships was the ever more plausible prospect of finding oneself in the midst of an air raid.

As always when I returned to Berlin, I first greeted the Gruberts, then went over to inspect the house. This time as I entered, the icy still air held a morbid feel, like entering a morgue. '

Phew, this is not much fun," I said to myself as I dropped my luggage in the hall at the entrance door. How should I proceed. basement first?

All seemed in the best of order. The pipes contained no water so they could not freeze—but neither could we heat them. Everything looked fine in the storeroom, and I noted a layer of ice three inches thick covering the "water-glass-mixture" in the huge ceramic egg crock. Three hundred eggs lay stored below the surface of that ice—maybe also frozen—but still good and a treasure.

Upstairs? All seemed well. I dragged out a down comforter and pillow and decided to sleep, as usual, on a couch in the unheated parlor. Frightened but determined to conquer my fear, I cooked a simple meal in the icy kitchen. Then as I prepared to crawl under the covers, the sirens sounded. Two minutes later Franisch phoned.

"Get your pillow and your comforter and come quickly," he said. "This one is for us."

Franisch and Wally met me at the door, and a few minutes later we huddled together in their cellar, where we stayed the whole night through. We held our breaths each time as the house trembled, shuddered and swayed, and we expected that in another second it would collapse totally. Again, hot splinters flew in all directions, hitting the house mainly on the west side. Repeatedly, Franisch disappeared to check the roofs for flames. Not until after 4 a.m. did we hear the first signal, the usual 10-minute forerunner of the "all clear." Eight long hours of that horror—a prayer with every breath.

"Well, we weathered another one," we agreed, the fear still in our uncertain voices. We're still alive, or almost."

What irony—our victory. How many more would it take? Would it get worse? We hardly dared hope—only wondered about the eventual end.

Fully exhausted, we all slept. I dropped, wrapped up in my down comforter, onto a couch in the Gruberts' spare bedroom. No one stirred until late that morning and then, sleepy-eyed and bedraggled, we gathered in the kitchen for a cup of hot ersatz coffee containing the grounds of a few real coffee beans. Franisch laughed as he said, "We seem to come by some extras now and then, lucky for us."

"Well, you are angels to share it," I said.

* * *

I took the late afternoon train for Posen. Having learned my lesson earlier, I had notified Hans of my arrival and he was waiting at the station for me. He had spent a worry-filled night, fearing I had again been in an air raid in Berlin. Even his correct supposition that I would take refuge with the Gruberts had given him little comfort, since that afforded scant protection.

During that visit I again met Guenther Brink. He enjoyed

rapport with his Treuhandstelle co-workers, who included him in many social gatherings despite the SS uniform he wore. "You have risen in rank, I see, Herr Sturmfuehrer (Mr. SS officer)," I addressed him quietly. He laughed.

"Think nothing of it, madam, just let us say they forced it upon me."

I found his modesty charming and assumed that, as most young Germans would, he no doubt felt honored by his selection as one of Hitler's elite guard. Yet his laugh and the expression of his eyes seemed almost mocking, not wild or free but choked back with an intake of breath that brought second thoughts.

When I mentioned that to Hans, he said, "Guenther tells everyone that, and no one believes him. Maybe that explains his incautious remark. It took me three months to wheedle out of him the story of his promotion to rank and, believe me, it's quite a tale. I'll tell it to you some day, Cherie."

But Guenther told us himself one night, in the back room of our regular eating place where I had met him originally. After our evening meal, Hans and I lingered with friends until they left. We then decided on one more hot toddy before the long, cold walk back to our icy sleeping quarters. Moving to the back room, where we expected to find some other friends, we saw Guenther sitting alone.

Usually he was accompanied by a very devoted young woman whose quiet attentions he accepted a bit tritely, I thought. He was a tall, very attractive, well-built German, close to his thirties, beautifully mannered, a bit lackadaisical, who could without seeming effort spread his charm impressively.

That night, however, he sat by himself. He had also drunk too much, abandoning himself out of loneliness to a state of despair he normally kept under strict control.

As we entered, he rose uncertainly from his chair in greeting and acknowledged us courteously. Taking a seat next to mine, he crossed his arms upon the table, both to support himself and to more easily peer directly into my face. A few strands of his thick, wavy blond hair hung down over his furrowed forehead and he looked a bit bedraggled.

"Hans, I like what you have here," he said. "Where'd you get her? The lady is no German. Sure she's your wife? American! Ha!" he laughed. "Sure enough, it's written all over her! Well, you've got nothing on me."

Slouching back in his chair, he continued. "I'm sort of a foreigner too. I am a 'Volksdeutsche,' a 'border German.' You, my dear lady, don't know what that means, so I will tell you and then you can tell me about yourself and how you happened into this beautiful land, into this 'bee-u-ti-ful' war."

In his somewhat inebriated state, Guenther insisted on telling me all about what that meant, all about himself.

"You know," he said, "my life has been going through my mind all evening. Want to hear? Maybe then, just maybe then I can stop thinking."

Since neither Hans nor I objected, he began.

"I came from quite a spread in Poland, something to take pride in, just this side of the German border. My parents were German, my father a rancher and a good one. My eldest brother took over when he came of age, and luckily he too excelled at it. So the estate was, until now, in the best of shape.

"Hans, you know how it works over here the eldest son always inherits the land. I accepted that because I wasn't the type for it anyhow. My father saw that and steered me through the university and law school. Just the thing! Did you know that I earned a law degree, and can practice in Germany? So ask me—will you—what am I doing here?"

We sat in uncomfortable, straight backed chairs with wooden arms. Guenther kept slouching, then straightening, sliding his left hand up and down the smooth arm surface while he talked. The long fingers of his right hand wrapped around an empty glass in a vise-like grip.

"Guenther," Hans interjected, "Do you really want to talk? I don't think you feel well. Want us to take you home?"

"No!" Bracing himself and facing me, with his soft easy smile, he said, "I want this lady to know about us Volksdeutsche, and what great and steadfast people we really are. You think only Reichdeutsche are strong and stable, don't you? Well, you have nothing on us. I can tell you a great story. Want to hear?" he asked again.

Without waiting for an answer, he launched into a tale, broken by many sighs and pauses.

"Well, the Germans in our little town formed a club, just at the edge of our ranch, purely a social club with few members. We Germans there were not too numerous, but we held together. For years the Poles accepted our club unconditionally for what it was, just fun and games.

"But as the war with Germany grew nearer, it became another matter. The Poles became suspicious—and why shouldn't they? Thought we'd become a nest of spies. We should have closed that building and quit the club, but it seemed more incriminating to do that, so we let it alone.

"I was the club president when the war finally broke loose—the devil's own luck for me. What made it worse, I crossed the border into Germany daily to get to work. So the Polish town officials pegged me as an informer. And I was—not because I wanted to, but because the German authorities pressured me.

"'Guenther, my boy,' they'd say to me, 'what's going on in Poland these days?'

"I said as little as I could, since I did not want them to use me. I had no quarrel with the Poles, neither with the Germans for that matter. I just wanted to be left alone, but no one understands neutrality these days. Back at the ranch in the evening, the Poles would come and they'd ask, 'Guenther, my boy, what's doing in Germany these days?'

"Can't you just hear them? They'd threaten me if I did not tell. Trying to evade them just brought out their ire and they began to hate me and bide their time. I knew that, and I know now what I should have done. Too late!"

He paused to consider, then continued. "Finally, the German offensive started. With that, the Poles ceased all discretion. They swiftly interned me as a spy, and 'stacked' me away in a dark, dank old prison. Du lieber Gott, what a hole—cold, sunless, no cot, no chair, cement floor, a slop pail and a tin cup for water. In Poland, one never drinks unboiled water. Remember that, young lady, remember that. It's full of bugs that crawl in your liver." He gesticulated, making the news very graphic.

"Food? Not fit for swine! They knew I couldn't eat that vermin-filled weak old cabbage soup. They counted on it. They expected me to wilt and die. But you see me, don't you? Did I die? No! But I did wilt—a little.

"Still, I got out of there. I got out!" His derisive tone held rancor and more than a touch of arrogance. His laugh was not pleasant. "How do you like it so far?" He addressed the question most directly to me, bitter and pungent.

"Guenther," I urged, "You need not relive this for our sakes, unless it helps you to get rid of it."

"Rid of it? Do you think I shall ever rid myself of it? Want to know how I got out of there? I'll show you!"

Guenther pushed his chair away from the table, drew up his right trouser leg and pulled down his sock.

"See where they fastened the chains?" he asked. "Yes, ball and chain—my right leg chained to the left leg of an old decrepit man. That's because the jailers got scared of the German air onslaught. They thought the German Army would soon liberate us and they wanted to keep us prisoners.

"So one dark night they brought us into a very large room and chained us, always two together. Then they started us, with armed guards, on a three-day-and-night trek from our prison to another in Lublin. That's on the Russian border, you know. A cute trick, wouldn't you say, nailing me to a feeble old man?

"Up and down those guards marched, looking for the laggers as we stumbled along. I did my best to prop up the old man and keep him moving. Whenever the guards got close I muttered a warning, let go of him and kept my eyes averted. Any sign of dragging on that long walk and to the rear of the column you went. Then two shots and you knew that two of you were out—finished—kaput."

With a cynical laugh, Guenther continued. "Not me! Dear God, not me—they weren't going to get me. But can't you visualize us on the march? Outside feet forward, inside feet dragged up with ball and chain, over and over, limping along mile after mile, hour after hour—inside, outside, inside, outside, a murmur with every breath to keep the old man coordinated, to keep him from a fatal tumble, to keep the guards from seeing and, my God yes, to keep us both alive.

"Lord, what pangs of hunger and thirst we endured on those hot, treeless plains during the day. And, all sweated through, how we shivered during the cold September nights. The ankle chains rubbed through the skin and we began to bleed. My old man often seemed near collapse.

"Du lieber Gott, that would have ended me, too, but every time the guard walked by I got the old fellow ready and the rest of the time I fairly carried him. Ja wohl! I did just that!"

Guenther's thoughts focused somewhere in the past, as his face suddenly lighted up with his next question.

"Hans, have you ever seen Stukas at work? They flew over often, every day, all around us—fantastic, awesome, absolutely unbelievably grandiose. What courage sat in those pilot seats! How could they stand that terrific dive-pull and remain conscious enough to make the uptake at the right moment?

"They surely lived through one kind of hell, and just watching them face that dangerous mission with daring defiance brought me a new courage to grapple with my own dilemma.

"How I wished I could signal those pilots in some way, but whenever they got too close, the guards forced us to lie down quickly in the dirt alongside the road. How frustrating—instead of waving to the pilots, we hid from them."

He paused, and I ventured, "Did you get any food or water, Guenther?"

Scoffing, he replied, "Prisoners, no! Guards, yes! They ate in full view of us, relishing every moment of torment it caused us. They'd reach out a crust to us, their own mouths full and smiling as they munched, then draw away quickly with a 'ha, ha.'

"But why grab for it, with our swollen gums and tongues? Yet a bit of water, just a swallow, if no more—how we needed that. Once when we passed a pond, they stopped us and allowed us to fill our cups and then quickly knocked the cups from our hands, spilling the water. Those sadists! Mein Gott, mein Gott, how I despised them."

Guenther became very agitated. "How I hated them. More than ever I vowed I would survive this. I would, I would, I must. I crushed every creeping bit of doubt from my mind."

He paused, and then with plenty of venom in more quietly spoken words, he began again. "Some day, I said to myself, some day, you heartless monsters, I'll come back and I'll finish you off."

Guenther straightened up, but his face did not lose the brooding expression of terrible memories.

"Three days and three nights like this. It seemed an eternity. Well, we made it, the old man and I, alive, moving like automatons, outer feet forward, two middle ones dragged up, step by step, only slower and slower.

"They put each one of us who entered that prison into a cage by himself. We received water and a handful of dried beans—hard, uncooked beans, day after day. I sucked on them the whole day through—the best I could do."

As I sat there, barely breathing because of the horror I felt, I found it hard to imagine men with swollen gums and tongues trying to chew hard, dry beans. It seemed that would only encourage an accumulation of stomach juices and added hunger. During a pause in Guenther1s narrative, I suggested that, and his eyes widened in a gleaming acknowledgment of just that fact.

"More torture, my dear lady," he said, peering into my face and slowly punctuating each word, "Just a little more torture.

On what Guenther figured as the 11th day after their arrival, an attachment of the German Army entered the prison, announced the capture of Lublin and set them free. The prisoners boundless joy lasted only moments, however, as the Poles re-took the prison when the German soldiers left and re-incarcerated the prisoners. Guenther hardly could endure the heartbreak. Two more days passed before German officers came again, that time in total victory.

"Du Teufel," exclaimed our friend, "Can't you just see us, each prisoner looking out of a cage down three or four stories into the well of the covered prison court, seeing one of our own officers and hearing the news? Now we could believe it.

"Then, just as if someone had triggered it, simultaneously a shout of the old German national anthem, 'Deutschland, Deutschland, Uber Alles,' spilled into a scream of ecstasy from every throat. You just cannot imagine! 'My God, my God,' I cried aloud in thanks. You have not forsaken us."

Rising to a shaky stand and with his empty wine glass still clasped tightly in his right hand, Guenther raised it in salute. Simulating that memorable day, he began shouting out in song the old German national anthem, right where he stood. That brought a number of people rushing from the front of the restaurant to our door, the proprietor among them.

But Hans jumped up and pushed them away gently. Then, stepping out and closing the door behind him, he asked the proprietor for a pot of coffee with some real coffee beans, not only ersatz. "Please, the SS man is very sick, and needs help," Hans explained.

I sat alone with Guenther as he slumped back into his hard wooden chair, his face feverish and extremely drawn.

"That's a beautiful song, Guenther," I said.

"Beautiful, really beautiful," he reiterated, shaking his head thoughtfully in consent.

"But tell me, Guenther, why the German national anthem? Why not the Nazi Horst Wessel song, the Party rouster?"

"I don't know, I don't know," he said in wonderment, sitting up suddenly. "I never thought about that. All of us must have reverted involuntarily to the elementary, the comforting and meaningful, in our hearts." And while he wondered about my unexpected question, I pondered over the emotional conflict that had dwelled in the bosoms of those stalwart men. Were they really Nazis, or just German?

"But, Gnaedige Frau," he turned to me and asked, oh so gently "was I not as brave as any American?"

"Yes, Guenther, and you saved the old man."

"That I did, that I did, but I wonder what became of him."

"What happened to you?" I countered.

At that moment the door opened to our little room and Hans reentered, bringing a pot of coffee and three cups, enough for all of us, thanks to the magnanimous proprietor. Although not pure coffee, it contained a few real beans and gave both warmth and healing. For the first time that evening, Guenther relinquished the empty wine glass in favor of a cup of steaming brew, and momentarily took on new vigor as he more calmly continued his tale.

"I don't know about the others, but a group of German officers interrogated me. That done, they asked me what I wanted most right then. I said something good to eat and drink.

Du grosser Gott, you should have seen me! In prison fatigues with shorn head, my face no doubt as gray as my garb, I could barely walk. They supported me to a restaurant and gave me exactly what I asked for—boiled lobster and champagne. To my amazement, it was available and they let me have it."

He lifted his head and shook it in utter exasperation. "Those thoughtless simpletons actually gave lobster and champagne to a man with a stomach suffering from scurvy! That pretty nearly finished me for good.

"Weeks later, I awoke and thought myself in heaven. Everything was white, and everyone wore white. I lay on something soft, warm and white, surrounded by a golden glow of sunlight. Where else could that be, after this miserable earth, but heaven? How I wish it had been," he wailed. "But my life was not meant to end quite that simply. The bugle call had not yet sounded for me.

"And so I must stay on this damned earth yet awhile. I can no longer fight in combat; my health is 'futsch,' ruined. I'm not worth anything to myself or anyone else—my lungs are gone, my ankle still hurts and I belong in a sanatorium. The Reich would pay my keep there, but that's so boring.

"For some reason the Nazis feel I deserve compensation for my suffering. Since I refused the sanatorium they decided to 'honor' me with this SS uniform, which I do not want. I simply do not want it. Don't get me wrong, I am a good German, but not a. . . ."

Hans hushed him and he finished his sentence quietly with, "I do not deserve honoring, and I just do not want this uniform! Maybe," he mused, "I should go to a sanatorium anyhow, then I would not need it or could even get rid of it. Otherwise, tell me, how can I refuse it?" he asked with a hopeless gesture.

He got up and straightened, saying, "I've got to go—I've got to leave. I need sleep; I've got to sleep."

Hans and I saw him home that night, and our relationship continued in an impersonal way. We saw him occasionally and he always seemed friendly. But he never made mention of the night we sat together over his story. As if it never happened.

The authorities eventually gave Guenther an office and evidently found his services with legal problems satisfactory. But he found no cure for the sickness in his soul. Realizing the divided loyalties of the Volksdeutsche, we understood his resentment of the SS uniform. However, we hoped he would not proclaim his antipathy so loudly or he would find himself in a Nazi prison and that time for good.

* * *

Hans and I still roomed at our original lodging in the home of Mr. and Mrs. Druczinski and their daughter, but we hardly ever saw them. Each time I returned to Posen, it seemed as though I had never left: we found breakfast waiting as soon as we arose and returned at night to a cleared and cleaned room.

Day in and day out, the routine held a stultifying essential sameness. Even the ever-dull weather seemed unchanging, and the endlessly flat and uninteresting landscape offered little variation. And yet, I felt a sphere of contradiction that strangely fascinated me, a lure to which I responded instinctively—not only in the land, but also in the Polish people. Their Slavic souls seemed capable of the highest peaks and lowest depths, but more often they dwelt on the tragic rather than the sublime.

I looked constantly for a sign of softness or vulnerability in their character, and often found it, but tempered by a flinty hardness and surprising resilience. That I found remarkable considering the injustices and brutalities they suffered in their never-ending fight for life, against both Russia and Germany, again and again.

My growing fondness for that land made me less and less anxious to leave again. But the incidents of each day seemed to point out what we would eventually have to do.

"Chere, I cannot find one of my ID. cards," Hans said one noon. "It must be in my gray suit. I changed this morning, do you remember? Right after lunch, please go home and get it for me, won't you? I need it."

How many hours since I had left our rooms that morning four? In that short time, they had been stripped and now echoed with emptiness. Only one old, dilapidated, single iron bed remained, its springs and mattress held up by a board braced from the floor.

A few light blankets lay rumpled on top of the bed. Off to one side, on the floor, sat our travel cases open and piled high with our clothes in jumbled disorder. And crawling over the floors of the entire apartment I saw countless cockroaches.

At last the deportation that Mr. and Mrs. Druczinski and their daughter had dreaded so greatly must have caught up with them. They were gone—where or why we could only guess.

Apprehensively, I rummaged through Hans' tumbled suits and found the I.D. card. If I hurried, I could catch the streetcar returning to town. Clearly, Hans and I immediately would need a new sleeping place and we would need to return before long for our possessions.

That event resulted in my return to the Black Forest, but with a new idea in mind. Hans took single lodgings closer to work. Both of us dreaded the long separation; and the war, instead of ending, was taking on new dimensions in the Balkans. Perhaps our hearts ruled our minds, but we left each other with the idea of reopening our Berlin home immediately, so I would be closer, regardless of the risk, if we could gain any assurance of enough fuel to keep warm the ensuing winter

CHAPTER 23

An Aborted Return to Berlin

May-June, 1941

Klaerle could not suppress a grin when I asked if she would like to return to Berlin. "It would be great," she answered, "a relief from mental stagnation. Being so isolated has begun to annoy me. At times I've thought I'd just burst."

Then, pausing, she added, "But what is best for the children?"

I understood her concerns and shared them. With spring already here, at least we wouldn't need to worry about heat for several months. But safety from the air raids? Another question.

"Perhaps we will not always think so well of our decision," I acknowledged, "but I believe we are brave enough to stand whatever comes. And the outskirts of Berlin lack strategic interest for the bombers compared to other sections of the city.

"Also, other factors speak for our return, and I believe the welfare office will leave us alone. They have changed their minds about many things. Shall we try it? I will precede you and phone you when the house is ready, and you can make arrangements as you see fit for comfort and safety."

We said no more about it, either to the children or to Frau Hock, and before long I headed homeward. My heart fairly sang with joy as I marched down the little street of our beloved peninsula. Wally Grubert, clipping roses, heard our gate open and bobbed up from behind her fence, gloves on and pruning shears in her hand, to see who it was.

"Was du sagst? (Now what do you say?)" Her surprised expression broadened into a wide smile when she saw my happy face.

"You look positively bubbly. What happened? Did you win in a game of lottery?" she asked.

"I won in a game of consent! We are coming home."

"The children too?"

"The children too!"

"When did the war end?" she said with gentle sarcasm. "You mean that little old war?"

"You win," she laughed. "Tell me all about it."

I did, and added that I had come to get the house ready. She objected strenuously. "Please don't clean it alone; let me call Mrs. Meyer in Spandau. She needs work."

This time the silence in the house did not frighten me. I banged the door noisily, dropped my bags on the reception hall floor, drew up the blinds, opened wide the doors to the balcony and sniffed the good air. Then I heard a ring—the telephone? Who would know of my return before I hardly knew myself?

"Hello," I said, then heard Klaerle's voice on the other end of the line.

"Where are you, in Schonach?"

"No, in Villingen! Please, Frau Bohle, don't be frightened, but Bobby suffered a little accident. For safety's sake, I brought him here to see the doctor.

"The doctor," she continued, without giving me a chance to interrupt, "is sitting right next to me and wants to talk to you. Then you can talk to Bobby so you'll know he's all right."

The doctor came on the line and introduced himself, and at my urging to leave nothing out, proceeded to tell me that Bobby had been hit by a car. His injuries included four broken ribs, two banged-in front teeth, a concussion and shock.

"He needs lots of rest," the doctor added. "He really should stay flat on his back for a month before we move him from the hospital."

Anticipating my next questions, he continued. "You need not come now; he's in no danger. The hospital is a good one. The X-rays I took show no other discernible injuries."

Despite his reassuring words, I decided to return immediately, and informed the doctor of my plans. Then I asked him to put Bobby on the line.

"Hello, Mother," Bobby piped in. "It's really wonderful here."

We spoke briefly, and hung up. "Well, that changes things!" I said aloud to myself as I put the receiver back in its cradle. I was proud of myself for maintaining control of my emotions while we spoke, but oh, how my heart pounded.

Then I thought of Hans. Could I reach him before I had to leave? If not, I would ask Wally to try. He would surely telephone me that night. What would he think if he couldn't reach me?

About nine that evening, I boarded a southbound train, on my way to Bobby. As we sped through a blackout, shades covered the windows and the only illumination inside came from dim blue lights. Passengers crowded all the compartments, and those of us without seats occupied all the floor space in the cars. After several hours some seated passengers offered their seats to those who stood, hoping to get them back eventually. Others slept where they stood.

Eventually I tired and sat down on my suitcase, which sagged and so did I. On my right, a sailor dozed, sitting on his pack, and eventually his head fell against my shoulder. To my left a soldier sat with his head in his arms, trying to rest. After such a night, I breathed a sign of relief just to see the dawn break slowly on the horizon.

In Offenburg, I changed to the mountain rail that took me past Triberg and Furtwangen and far up into the deep heart of the Black Forest. But the scenery held little fascination for me that morning. Hungry and very tired, I focused my thoughts on my mission.

* * *

At 8 a.m. I left the train and began the long walk to the hospital. I would see my boy first, food would come later. Food? Still an optimist. Once more I dragged my heavy suitcase, with no conveyance of any sort to help—it was wearing me out.

The small hospital seemed neat, clean, quiet and efficient. I found Dr. Duschl already in his office, and a sign on his door said he functioned as administrator as well as head physician and surgeon.

"Frau Bohle, you got here very quickly," he greeted me pleasantly. "I assure you, your son is getting along fine. If you will precede me, I will come to you soon." He rang for a nurse to show me the way, but I preferred to go alone.

"Mother, Mother," screeched a young voice in a room a few doors down. "I knew it was you, I just knew it, I could tell by your walk. Mother, Mother!" he exclaimed repeatedly, beside himself with joy.

His idea of lying flat on his back meant we were in for a difficult month. I gently pushed him back on the pillow, but immediately his head bobbed back up, supported by his elbow.

"Please, Mother, get me a game or a puzzle; I have nothing to do here," he begged.

"Bang, bang, bang!" he pretended to shoot a nun passing his door, and she stopped and came in.

"He's shot everyone within earshot ever since he arrived," she laughed, adding that evidently a game of war had led to his accident.

I turned to Bobby.

"That's right. At the top of the hill, the boys suddenly tried to lasso me. So I ran down toward the pension and jumped from the slope past the high bushes into the street. But I landed on the hood of an automobile instead of in the street. I didn't see it, but they tell me that's what happened, and I don't know anything more."

The sister nodded to me. "Well, don't worry. In a few days he will calm down, and we will watch him."

The doctor came soon after, and assured me that Bobby would recover. His broken ribs and concussion would heal with bed rest, perhaps in a month. With their nursing staff exceedingly thin, the doctor offered to put a couch in Bobby's room for me if I would nurse him myself and I agreed.

That evening Hans called, much concerned. Despite my reassurances, he insisted on joining me. "I shall arrive by Saturday night, so that we can make our decisions together, okay?"

Hans arrived and met Dr. Duschl, and the two men liked each other immediately; nevertheless Hans worried about Bobby's excitability, and wondered that the doctor did not seem to find it strange.

The next day, Hans telephoned his mother—only a few miles away but a full day's journey without the use of a car. She suggested summoning a specialist from Freiburg for consultation, but Dr. Duschl said it only would waste the specialist's time and our money. So we abandoned the idea for the moment.

Not long after Hans left us, Bobby suffered a severe stomach upset. I blamed the hospital food, limited in quality and amount but the only kind available. The good doctor, however, feared appendicitis and wanted to operate immediately. "It's minor surgery, and then you know for sure," he said.

"Let's try baby foods for a day and if that does not help, I'll give you my consent," I countered, unconvinced.

"If it is not too late," he patiently retorted. No doubt he hated the responsibility, but he consented to try a different diet, at least for one day.

My meals were also a difficulty. The hospital's food supply could not accommodate guests, and I learned quickly that if I fed Bobby at his scheduled hour, and then walked the 20 minutes to town, the restaurants had no food left. No matter how many coupons I offered, they turned me away flatly.

As a result, I found myself one mid-morning in town, sitting on a curb, fighting a fainting spell. Spotting an inn just across the street, I rose, made my way wearily inside and collapsed into a chair, hoping maybe someone would give me something to drink and a roll. Butter? It did not even occur to me.

"Bitte, broetchen, tee, and quickly please," I said to the astonished waitress setting the tables well in advance of lunch. She walked away, then returned. "Marken," she said, holding out her hand.

Oh, yes, without coupons, nothing available, I thought, handing them to her.

Finally the giddy feeling began to leave me, and before long the waitress returned with a roll and some sort of herb tea—the real thing was not available. But it tasted hot and good, and I was able to make it back to the hospital.

*   *   *

As Bobby healed, he became more and more difficult to manage. His treatment required him to rest quietly, lying down—a difficult task with few distractions to occupy his mind. The little town was deplete of games, crayons, paper and pencil, even scissors for cutting figures. We had to devise entertainment out of our own minds and imagination, and we soon ran out.

He completely ignored my admonitions to be quiet, and since his condition did not allow for corporal punishment—which he really needed—I was at wit's end. I worried that my image as a good mother and disciplinarian suffered in the eyes of those around me, but the understanding doctor gave no sign.

One afternoon Dr. Duschl came to check on Bobby and genially spent more than an hour with us a welcome change in my daily routine, someone adult to talk to. Instinctively I liked and trusted that good man, that graying doctor, with his easy grace and outgoing, comforting and cheering manner. Bobby liked him too, and so we welcomed the doctor eagerly that day.

After settling himself on the couch, he announced he wanted to talk. Bobby lay back on his pillow, quietly expectant, and I found a restful spot at the foot of his bed. I wondered if the talk would focus on Bobby, but it did not start out that way. The doctor said it was his first breathing spell since my arrival and he wanted to get better acquainted.

"Your nursemaid acted very promptly and very wisely with Bobby. You must excuse me if I probed a bit into the family background and why she was here alone with the children. Our lives today are a little bit sad with homes disrupted and families separated.

"Fraulein Klaerle told me you are an American. Not many American girls marry our men and stay in Germany. You must miss your homeland very much and sometimes feel most apprehensive about the future, with this war still widening."

He did not know it, but even a suggestion that I might not like some aspect of life in Germany made me wary. I wanted to trust the doctor's motives, but I could not risk being thought of as against the Reich. Nobody could know that, for my own sake and my family's safety. And so I answered vaguely.

Then gently he tried to appease his curiosity. "Had you ever visited Europe before, or did you meet Mr. Bohle in America?"

Just maybe I dealt not with curiosity alone, but with a romanticist? The heart of every fine German man seemed to feel a stir of romance toward a girl who would leave "the land of opportunity, the land of milk and honey" for a German and love to live in his country. That part of his question I did not mind answering.

"Hans and I met in the United States, in fact in my own home," I said.

"His father and mine shared a business acquaintance. They both worked in the coal business, which Hans planned to enter. Hans and I felt ourselves drawn to each other instantly, especially through our love of music.

"In many ways he is inherently an artist in that field and an enthusiast. My first judgment of him was surprise that anyone with such beautiful hands would go into business."

I paused in my tale and glanced up at the doctor. "Funny, isn't it, that his hands were the first thing I noticed about him?"

The doctor rose from his seat and walked slowly over to the window, where he stood and peered out. Did my remark cause him to thrust his hands into the pockets of his surgeon's coat?

"I find nothing strange about first judgments of people," he said, still looking outside. "Sometimes they miss the mark, but I believe that for the most part they are right."

Turning to me, he continued. "Your husband pursued a business career because it was offered him and he proved good at it, but that does not negate the artist that you found in him. And this so-called chance acquaintance with the man in whom you saw the artist—did that not unfold compatibility's that could lead one to believe in predestination?

"Does it not seem logical, then, that you should continue your lives together in Europe?" he asked. "If you want to look at the philosophical approach to marriage, my dear doctor, yes—an arrangement, so to speak, which must embody certain advantages. For me that was secondary," I responded.

"Then you considered emotions first, and the language presented no barrier. But where then did you finally develop such excellent German?"

Perhaps the story of how I learned good German would amuse that . . . that romanticist, I had concluded. Actually, I thought, he would love my tale. And so I told him how during the first year of our marriage, reading provided our primary enjoyment—along with skiing. I said that Hans had insisted I learn good high German and had read to me each evening so my ear would absorb the sounds.

"Excellent," breathed the doctor. "I too know a bit of English and a little about your country. I spent one year, 1938, as guest physician in one of your famous American research centers, the Mayo Clinic. I knew just enough English to get by, and I profited much from the experience. I brought back to this hospital many of your better innovations, one of which is the recovery room."

To my look of astonishment, he added, "Oh, yes. I can read your thoughts. Many people wonder why I 'bury' myself in a little town in the Black Forest. I do not discriminate. The high and the low, they all need help. I wish to devote my life to medicine and that is the only way to do it.

"This is a fine hospital, accredited in every way and revered by all surrounding specialists who assist whenever needed. In no way do I feel 'buried.' But I wonder how soon the Army will snatch me away from here and send me to the front."

"Did you see this morning's paper? The Luftwaffe has destroyed thousands of Russian planes in a hangar or some storage place. Old planes and new ones. So easy—doesn't it make you wonder? Were those real planes, or decoys?"

I told the doctor that during our telephone conversation the night before, Hans had mentioned that one endless string of heavy duty Army trucks, equipment and soldiers filled the main roads through Poland, on their way to the newly-opened Russian front. Hitler had invaded Russia only days earlier, and newspaper reports indicated that German forces were progressing eastward rapidly.

The doctor and I talked some more about the Warthegau, Germany and German history—what we should have learned from it, about Russian winters and what the armies faced.

Then he said, "But now, I am not worried about the war, nor about Bobby, but about you. Tell me, when did you last enjoy a real warm meal?" I gave him an idea of the situation.

"Just as I thought," said the perceptive physician. "Tonight you shall dine in town with my wife and me, as our guest. We will come for you shortly before 7:30."

Thus began an all-too-short friendship, the many thoughtful attentions of Dr. and Mrs. Duschl bringing relief to the monotony of the long days at Bobby's bedside. Finally the doctor pronounced the words we had waited to hear. Bobby could make the trip to our home in Berlin, provided we got to Offenburg without using the very shaky mountain rail.

To comply with the proviso, I needed official sanction for transport by car. Even with the doctor's specific order, it took several visits to small town dignitaries and long and powerful persuasion. Everyone feared reprisals, punishment for overstepped boundaries—no one trusted anyone.

But finally I won. We drove to Offenburg, where we met Klaerle, Irmgard and Dieter and secured a sleeper berth on the train to Berlin. But it was not an easy trip, and required a sleeping potient to subdue our overly excitable Bobby for the whole, long journey

CHAPTER 24

Together Again in Berlin

July - December, 1941

Our joy at returning home again was tempered by the need to find the right method for reestablishing discipline for our son, Bobby. We always had tolerated his tendency be like a loner and, at times, act like a rebel, but after four weeks without any rules, he had become impossible to live with.

Hans agreed with me that a doctor should examine Bobby again to make sure his long trip had yielded no ill effects. After that, strict demands for obedience!

That proved none too easy, as Bobby devised new and original pranks. When his Latin tutor bored him, he set fire to the teacher's chair. When his father, on a Sunday morning, swam across the lake in rough weather, Bobby secretly followed. Forbidden to use the short cut through the marshland in front of our neighbor's home, he made it his favored route to school or to visit friends.

Bobby never complained against rules and regulations, he just quietly and slickly ignored them. His teachers in school found him exceptional, but willfully uncooperative.

But Klaerle understood. "He is forcefully shoving aside every obstacle to the freedom he enjoyed so much while roaming the hills of the Black Forest," she said. "Remain patient and do not worry. I think I can help him find the way back."

On the positive side, our return to Berlin meant that Hans joined us at least one day and one night a week. Each weekend he made the long train trip from Posen, his journey more strenuous because he lugged a terribly heavy suitcase always packed tight with meat and sausage instead of clothes.

In addition to the physical labor, he bore the worry of discovery with his load of contraband. How grateful we felt, for we could not conceive making it through each following week without the wonderful extras he brought.

No doubt nervous tension wore away any fat our bodies might have stored, almost as much as the lack of nourishment. We probably could have survived without a bit of black marketing, but barely. Most people found a way to supplement the food cards. However, one dared not get caught.

Occasionally, we received visits from friends who knew of our return. The Krumeichs, whom we had met during our last family vacation on the Isle of Sylt, journeyed from Potsdam. From Posen came the von Valtiers, Hans von Papen, and our architect friend Waldemar Steinecker and his wife. The group also included a number of Hans's close associates from his former oil company—in fact, whoever did not mind the long trail to our house by streetcar.

Of course, our good friends and neighbors, the Gruberts, still lived next door. Dr. Helmut Schmitt, however, had become a soldier, and his lovely wife Lottie had returned home to stay with her parents.

The government confiscated our sailboat, our car with all extra tires and our skis and equipment. But they left us our flatboat (collapsible boat), and it provided freedom on the lake. At times the children and Klaerle paddled out not too far from home, or I paddled alone diagonally across to visit acquaintances.

Once, returning from such a visit, I lay down in the boat and let it drift while I watched the clouds. My wandering mind came back when I heard the dip of oars nearby and arose to view a shore delegation come to investigate the unpropelled, unpiloted boat.

"Thank God, lady, you scared us," they said. "We thought we'd discovered a drowning."

We expected air raid sirens at all times, but the children stayed calmer, more stoic than previously. We finished the rounds of measles, chicken pox and whooping cough before Christmas. When cold weather came, we dealt with the heating problem by filling the pipes with hot water no higher than the first floor and sleeping cold upstairs. Not too bad, at least after Pension Sonnenbichl in the Black Forest. My electric oven still worked, but only after I agitated extensively with the Spandau electrical department to repair a snapped wire.

"Electric appliances, who uses them?" they scolded. "Crazy idea—verruecktes Frauenzimmer (crazy female)!" Although nervous and impolite, they did repair it.

* * *

The addition of the Russian front led Hans and most of his colleagues to anticipate serving in Posen for at least another year or even two. Having seen the sabotage by the Poles and the guerrilla warfare on the Russian-Polish border, they knew the problems that German soldiers and civilians would face in Poland, the supply storage center for the German forces in Russia.

One weekend Hans came home with the news that, despite the risks, Horst planned to take his family to Posen. Hans suggested we consider doing the same.

"We could rent out the house furnished and still take enough with us to keep house well," he said. Perhaps right then I should have resisted, but I did not and he continued.

"For one thing, and this is well worth considering, food and clothing are much more plentiful in the East, and surveillance and rationing much more lenient. For example, one can buy or resole children's shoes there. In Berlin, it's strictly twice a year for resoling. And new ones? You cannot get them even with coupons. Think it over, Cherie."

He sat quietly in thought, but roused when I asked, "Hans,

don't you have a more pertinent reason for wanting us to make the move?"

His glance toward me shone with appreciation, for he guessed my thoughts just as I read his. "Yes, my dear, I am sick of missing you and the children. Posen won't be our peninsula, but we'd be together again, and I think you need me, too."

Indeed I did, more than ever. Just days earlier, on December 7, 1941, my worst fears had been realized. Japan's attack on Pearl Harbor had brought my homeland, the U.S.A., into the conflict against Germany, my adopted land, and I found myself in enemy territory. I could stand war with all else, but with America too? That hit much too close.

Hans returned to Posen again, and I walked around the house in a daze, wanting to talk to no one. How complicated things had become. I felt trapped, and strained against that feeling. In my heart I knew that with the United States. as its opponent, Germany could not win and that more death and destruction lay in our paths before the war could end.

No doubt many circumstances would arise requiring keen judgment on my part. How frightening! I vowed to try to remain in the background, make no move to call attention to myself—the safest way. Somehow, some way, if God stayed with us and guided us, we eventually would fulfill our dream of returning to America.

I drew comfort from my perpetual belief in my own survival and that of our children. But what of Hans? What did the future hold for him? The thought of him being drafted and of losing him brought tears, as too easily I conjured scenes that we had managed to brush aside for the last several years.

I thought of my parents and especially of one of my brothers, an officer in the U.S. Army Reserve and already probably part of the great conflict. He, too, loved his wife and children. It crossed my mind that, although unlikely, he and Hans might someday face each other on the battlefield. I forced myself to erase the thought from my mind.

How must my parents feel, I wondered, with two children in

a terrific life struggle? They could only wonder, hope and pray. Still worse, from now on they could receive no message from me, since contact with them would bring censorship and attention to me, to us.

So I hardened my heart against writing to those dear ones so far away. I knew they would worry and maybe someday assume us dead, and mourn. That hardship we both would have to endure, perhaps for a long time. I resolved to remain strong, and ever hold before me the thought, "Americans possess courage, else how should they have discovered their own great country. They do not die without a struggle, and I am one of them.

* * *

As if on command, my first test materialized one that in the end stiffened my purpose and belief in myself. A call from the Spandauer police demanded my presence, naming the date, place and time and leaving me no choice.

Upon my arrival, they offered me a chair and with no preliminaries began interrogating me about my American citizenship.

"I was born in America and I married a German. According to your law, do you not consider me German?" I answered.

Maybe they anticipated my response. The two men looked at each other with gleams in their eyes and a half smile. One of them let off a "Ja, Ja," in full accordance with my statement.

"She is right," said the other, a deep throated, burly man. "Congratulations, gnaedige Frau, and see that you keep it that way." Therewith they dismissed me.

I did not like it, and called it luck. Those two men, naive or maybe just good-natured, seemingly knew nothing of American law, which required that I not express or show allegiance to any other country. I would live in accordance with American laws, I decided, and also never lift my arm in Nazi salute, the exacted gesture of the Nazi Party. Never!

The children seemed to note my distress, and stayed quiet

and good. Most evenings, Klaerle and I read quietly, but one night my dear little nursemaid ventured to comfort me.

"I always have been glad for those three years in England, which taught me to know and understand people other than my own," she said. "That is why I feel I understand you now. In these days, the tragic fate of a nation becomes the fate of a wife from another land.

"Last night, for a long while, I could not sleep. I thought about you and Mr. Bohle, how two people of two entirely different lands can create a marriage of such wonderful harmony. If only countries could do the same. Of one thing I am certain, if I could find someone whose love I could return, I too could sacrifice...."

I could not refrain from interrupting. "Thank you, dear, dear Klaerle. I sincerely hope you some day find that love. But when you do, you will realize that nothing is a 'sacrifice,' not even leaving your country. In fact, you will not take into account what a war or anything else would do to you. You will think only about that love and the gain of being together.

"And how could I expect anything but happiness from a people who produced a person with the qualities for which I love my husband?" I added.

Suddenly wound up, I continued. "The majority of the German people possess good and wonderful qualities, and do not share the views of those in authority. But they are too fatalistic and submit too passively to the ways of men in high places, even evil ones. The original aims of the Nazis were not totally wrong. But power turned the once harmless cubs into vicious lions.

"I get pretty mixed up at times. I never dreamed as a young girl, sitting through my history classes, that my interests would someday widen forcibly to include world political events and that I would be caught up in such a whirlpool of mixed emotions. There are so many good people among the bad."

It amazed me that so many of our friends and acquaintances, even people we hardly knew, found the courage and the means to express to me their sorrow that our two countries faced each other in mortal combat. Not a living soul among them uttered an unkind or disparaging word. Everyone felt sad and depressed at the new burden. Russia, the United States, England, France, nearly the entire world, aligned against their little land? Impossible, they said.

It came to me, as I pondered that awesome truth that Hitler, too, must be thoroughly frightened at Germany's new situation and be filled with deepest, darkest regrets.

CHAPTER 25

The Family Moves to Posen

January – April, 1942

The Christmas days we made as happy as we could for the children's sake. We had finally decided to rent out our home and take rooms in Posen, and we did not know when we would enjoy another holiday together in our beautiful house on the lakeshore.

Right after the New Year, in response to an ad, a caller visited and fell in love with the house and its rural setting. He worked for Organization Toct, a group set up to build all kinds of military installations. Money seemed no object; he loved the house and its lovely furnishings. A lease guaranteed us the best of care for the property and inventory—and the use of the third floor in the event we should ever need it.

Hans then looked for and found an apartment in Posen, one right in town and near his work. Toward the end of January, therefore, a van pulled up to the door of our home and took away those pieces of furniture we needed in Posen. In the meantime, Hans bought a small, inexpensive dining room set and some children's bedroom furniture—still possible only in the East.

The children, Klaerle and I remained in Berlin until word came that our belongings had arrived. Then we took the train for the Warthegau. We reached Posen at night and Hans and Horst von Valtier met us at the station. Horst stood holding two dozen long-stemmed red roses, his welcome to Posen.

"Where in the world did you find roses at all, let alone at this time of year?" I asked.

Horst put his finger to his lips and looked around him. Whispering, he said, "Any and everything is available if you want it badly enough."

As always, Horst greeted me with military gallantry. Then, turning to the children, he leaned toward them, shook hands with each one separately, calling them by name. It was an enchanting scene.

But what a drab old apartment house we walked into. The front door opened onto a dull, bare foyer, and I noted the cheap, thinly painted wood. A spiral stair led up the whole four flights, and a dome of glass covered the large stairwell. Due to the blackout, we used flashlights for the climb to our floor, the third, where a double glass door opened to the entrance hall of a 12-room apartment.

The huge rooms lay all in a row to the outside of the building and pivoted around the corner. An inside running corridor served all the rooms, with two kitchens, side by side, at one end and two baths, also adjacent, at the other. The one entrance, exactly in the middle and at the point of the pivot, served the whole.

"We share this apartment with Baron von Gagern and his family," Hans explained as we entered. "Each family has its own six rooms. Come see our large parlor." I heard the pleasure in his voice.

Indeed enormous, with three large French doors leading to small balconies, it contained both living and dining areas and easily accommodated our concert-size grand piano. Our rolled-up oriental rugs, pictures, furniture, glassware and china all sat dumped in the center of the room. The beds were set up and waiting in the respective bedrooms.

Continuing my inspection, I saw in one corner a huge hole gaping in the wall, showing the plaster over laths and stuffing of coarse straw. Cheap ornate frescoes decorated the room snug up against the high ceiling, and the walls badly needed paint.

The parlor also contained the only heating facility in the apartment, a large delft hearth, called a "kachel-ofen." We would again sleep cold, but when I saw Hans's joy at having his family again, even that made no difference. Our kitchen was nothing I would care to work in, but Horst assured me help was no problem.

However, we faced a problem of another kind, as one look at the children told us. They sat on the piled-up rugs, looking at each other glumly.

"Well, you young folks, what's the matter?" I asked.

Bobby finally volunteered, "There's no lake, no forest and only big buildings. Oh, Mother, this is awful."

They were right, and with a pang of regret I realized that we had not even thought how they might feel about the move.

"Let's all just eat and go to sleep, and tomorrow we'll begin looking around for other ways to have fun, shall we?" I really meant that! We always had found a way to make life a joy before, and we would again.

* * *

On the morrow, quite early, the doorbell rang and an emaciated little old Polish woman presented herself. Horst meant what he said and had found me a maid.

"This little woman looks like she is ready to fall apart," I said to Hans. "How can I possibly ask her to work?"

"Probably hungry," he answered.

"Ask her in!"

"What is your name?"

"Michaline Kubiak," she replied.

"How old are you?" I continued.

"Sixty-nine, but strong—work all my life," she answered in broken German.

Her little round face featured high cheekbones and tiny deep-set eyes and she wore her colorless, stringy, thin hair pulled back neatly to a tiny knot on the crown of her head. Her shoulders rounded as if burdened.

"Please, gnaedige frau, please try," she said. "I show."

"Go ahead, try her," Hans suggested. "With a bit of food in her, she will no doubt work out okay."

"Yes, I will try you, and pay better when I see what you can do," I said. "If you wish to start now, please go and get your things and put them in your room."

"Danke," she said. Then, like a peasant used to old fashioned servitude, she grabbed my hand and kissed it as she fell on one knee. Rising, she slunk into the kitchen.

Later in the day two men came to us and moved the carpets and furniture into position. A painter also appeared to patch the hole in the wall and give two rooms color—unheard-of privileges since the war had begun. In the East, some wheels truly still went 'round.

Michaline shopped for food on our cards and I did the cooking with no comment from her. In 10 days' time, my new maid began to fill out and, for her years, exhibited an astounding toughness. In spite of her diminutive size, she was far stronger than I. Little by little, she became less distant, even friendly, and one day offered to do the cooking.

"Can you cook, Michaline?" I queried.

"Yes, I once cook for very noble family," she answered.

Could she cook? We had found a gold mine! She was an expert in the kitchen and served at table equally well. Moreover, she made the fire each morning, cleaned and, in fact, stayed busy and happy the live-long day. And her face literally shone at the sight of food.

But then the time came when her own need for nourishment grew less urgent. As her heart responded to her less fortunate countrymen, she began surreptitious "hand-outs" at the door. Although I knew I never would be able to completely control her generous impulses, I made a visible effort so that she would realize I knew of her actions. Only in that way could I hope to keep at least a check on the outflow.

I really liked Michaline, and I felt she liked me too. A shrewd little old woman, she quickly figured out my American heritage. She behaved a bit bolder with me than with Hans, whom she saw as "the master."

At no time did she show any protest over requests, only willing compliance, even with Klaerle, whom she served with the children in the manner of a household accustomed to a nursemaid or governess.

With my household well organized and the children in school, I found myself with much free time. So once again, after several years, I took up my music. In Munich at the beginning of our married life I had studied the German Lieder with one of the leading sopranos of the Munich Opera. Later, in Mannheim, I had continued under the tutelage of the conductor of that city's excellent orchestra.

In Posen I began on my own, trying at first to bring volume and evenness back into my register. The vocal cords needed careful rebuilding and I made splendid progress. Before long I would need an accompanist willing to do repetitious work until I gained the feel of accompaniments often far different than the solo parts.

On occasion, music from the apartment above us intruded rudely upon my practice. Since the interruptions happened at various times of the day, I interpreted them as an intentional poke at my musical efforts, a ploy to discourage them completely. I found the inference unfriendly, aggravating, actually hostile. Who lived up there? We never saw anyone from the fourth floor except an occasional man who, with his brief case, slithered hurriedly up that extra flight of stairs.

Thereafter, we heard routine vocal exercises and songs sung by a male voice already cultivated, not at all in need of instruction. We became almost certain that something subversive occurred upstairs, covered by recordings. I dropped my own ambition to sing again, thinking it wiser to remain anonymous than provoke a fermentation of hatred. Hans and I later concluded that the fourth story of our building housed the center of the Polish underground.

*   *   *

Life seemed smooth enough until one day when Hans returned from work in the middle of the morning "to pack and be off." He avoided my question about his destination and just said not to worry, he would be back. I guessed that regardless of the importance of his "mission," in times of war it was best not to probe too deeply, and so I asked no more. Had he not promised to return?

However, a few days after Hans left us, a very strange encounter interrupted my so-called "smooth existence." One morning, too early for our usual guests, the doorbell rang—a bit too stridently. I stood stock still in the middle of the living room and glanced at my watch. Eleven o'clock—the hour for a formal call, according to German custom. Who could it be? Formality was no longer popular in those difficult war times, in the middle of an icy cold winter.

Michaline gave me little time to reflect, however, as she admitted a stocky middle-aged couple without announcing them first, only murmuring "If you please, madam" as they entered.

The striking elegance of those two strangers— black attire, furs, silk scarves and spats for his shoes—seemed incompatible with the privation of our times, and a sudden feeling of revulsion welled up within me. Yet I admitted to myself that they looked beautiful and exhibited impeccable manners. The gentleman gave Michaline his fedora, cane and gloves, while the lady hurried to me in a most ingratiating manner to offer her hand.

"I am Frau Rottman, Frau Bohle," she said. Then, stepping aside and nodding to the man behind her, she added, "This is my husband."

"Guten tag, Frau Rottman," I said wonderingly, motioning them simultaneously to seats together on the sofa near the warm hearth.

Mrs. Rottman quickly opened the conversation. Her voice came breathy, her round, pink-cheeked face upturned with a frank clear smile. She looked rather appealing under a gorgeous fur turban.

"What a pleasure to meet you," she said, "and bring to you warmest greetings from Frau Professor Rumpel in Leipzig."

"Yes, yes, and from her husband, Herr professor himself, ja wohl," put in her husband importantly, trying to impress me with the prestige of that association, his monocle eye watching my reaction. I fully knew of Professor Rumpel's prominence and considerable influence in the scientific world, and I quickly smiled my appreciation.

But the name "Rumpel" struck cold to my heart with the explosive force of a bomb. I knew the professor only slightly. But his wife? Oh, yes, indeed, I knew her, and mistrust and fear accompanied my dislike. Perhaps that gave me an advantage for the moment. At least it prejudiced my feelings toward my guests enough to make me wary. Knowing her also made me wonder as to what kind of people the Rottmans might be. If their friendship with Mrs. Rumpel really was on the level, it meant "caution double caution."

"How kind of Professor and Mrs. Rumpel to think of us, and good of you to stop by," I said. Then, begging their indulgence for just a moment, I left them to finish something in the kitchen that could not wait. "It will take but a minute," I promised.

I employed that ruse to gain time. I needed to think and steady my nerves and impulses—rude of me, perhaps. But they conceded to my momentary absence graciously. I repaired to the kitchen and requested that Michaline not leave the apartment before our guests departed. Then, I remained in the kitchen for a few minutes, leaning against the door, deep in thought.

As I quickly reviewed our whole previous association with family Rumpel, I recalled the occasion of our first New Year's Eve party in Berlin. Mrs. Rumpel had come with Hans' brother, Walter, and insisted on seeing our police dog, Arno. A disaster! The dog had sensed our mutual dislike and jumped on her, ripping the sleeve out of her dress. Had the memory of that incident left her with an undercurrent of desire for retaliation of some sort? At the time it had not seemed so.

For two years or more, no communication had passed between us and Walter or the Rumpels. How then could they know of our move from our home in Berlin to Posen? No one knew except one of our Berlin neighbors not even the renters who leased our house in our absence. Had these people checked our address in Berlin? What had brought them to Posen? People did not travel in such class those days without an objective. My doubts really put me on the defensive—something definitely seemed unsavory.

More than a year before the war began, fear had become a reality that I lived with subconsciously every day. Occasionally, an event—such as the unexpected and unwelcome visit from the two strangers in my parlor—caused my fear to erupt.

But had I ever really met fear, stark naked and head on? Perhaps not, because my feelings seemed mixed with anger maybe the American in me was coming to the surface. My pioneering grandfather and his wife had set an example of courage, and I resolved to follow their example. Thus, I returned to my guests with no conscious awareness of my fear.

"So now I am entirely at your disposal," I said as I reentered the living room and seated myself across from my guests.

"Schoen, schoen," they answered politely, their eyes still lustily observing points of beauty in my parlor—the delfi hearth, the overlapping oriental rugs on the floor, the various sofas, my beloved Lady Chippendale desk. Aloud, they commented on the enormous height of the three large windows that really were doors, asking if they led to a balcony.

"Yes, they do, and in the summertime we open them and let a full shaft of sunshine in."

"Do you still practice your music?" ventured Mrs. Rottman, nodding at my black concert grand standing off in one corner.

"Rarely, but we do not lack for music. A vocal instructor— a lady—lives above us and gives lessons. Of course, we listen and it does get monotonous at times. But the children like to sing and I play for them. So the piano is a great asset, and since the large room can accommodate it plus our dinette set; we practically live here.

"Then, too, you no doubt noticed that the room is none too warm. With only a few briketts for heat each day, we need all of them right here, except for those we use in cooking."

Mr. Rottman suddenly shoved himself forward on the seat of the sofa and commented, "We all must contend with such conditions now, but warm or not, it is a lovely room and we are not. . . ."

". . . We are glad we followed Mrs. Rumpel's suggestion and came to see you. She made us promise, you know," interjected his wife, her rude interruption causing her husband's face to flush an angry red. Had she kept him from saying something he should not?

"Did Mrs. Rumpel give you any particular message?" I asked, hoping they might mention Walter. "It's wonderful to hear the latest, you know."

For a moment the conversation stopped, as my question seemed to catch them off guard. Mr. Rottman sat silently, as he caught his monocle in his left hand and flicked away a tiny speck from his fine, gray spats with his right. His composure restored, he looked up at me, smiling.

But his appearance contrasted sharply with that of his bright-eyed "wife." His bold eyes, wide-gapped teeth, straight, glossy black hair that he wore brushed flat, and his too-thick brows and lips seemed suggestive and not quite so harmless looking. I doubted they really were personal friends of the Rumpels. But an iota of uncertainty remained . . . the setup seemed so perfect, even to the hint of a Saxon accent.

"Particular message?" Mrs. Rottman reiterated, catching up. "Nothing except to tell you that they are all well and concerned about you, so far from your native land, so alone among the hostile Poles. When we return shortly, they will want to know all about you. Tell me, my dear, do you hear from your parents in the U.S.A.?" the fair lady inquired.

With that question, the trend of the conversation became dangerous. I did not like the inference about America and knew I had to give them the impression that, having cast my lot as the wife of a German, communications with my family in the United States seemed less important. They must not know (but maybe they did anyhow) whether or not I heard from my parents. After all, with the U.S.A. on the "other side," I was in enemy territory. So I dared let no anti-Nazi suggestion appear in my answer.

Searching for the right words, I hesitated, wishing I could avoid responding. And I succeeded, as my prolonged silence took away some of her composure. Instead of quietly awaiting my reply, she continued.

"And this privation, lack of fuel, food and unsettled political situation—does it ever worry you about what will become of us? Of course our Army has performed magnificently and the decisions from high places have been incredibly correct. It just proves, does it not, that we are the 'master race' and when this conflict is over—oh, but what do you think about this subject? Can you bear the events of the interim, you and your children with your husband away in the service of his country? Do you hear from him?"

How did they know Hans was away? Furious, I thought to myself what slithery horrid people!

Amazed, I just could not believe they failed to realize the clarity with which they had revealed their actual mission. The situation had nothing to do with the Rumpels, I realized suddenly. I felt sure they knew only of a supposed friendly relationship between us and that family. How fortunate that my initial caution and my thorough dislike of Mrs. Rumpel—of which my two visitors obviously lacked any knowledge—had prevented me from letting down my guard. And how fortunate that their formality hindered them from beginning their visit with the usual greeting of "Heil Hitler," since my refusal to respond in kind would have marked me.

What a deadly game we played! Sadistically humorous! I wanted to laugh, and then I wanted to cry. Such an evil strategy, I thought to myself. They used the name "Rumpel" to soften my defenses, and the smiling smug beauty across from me sought to seduce me into an indiscretion so her dark, sinister companion could carry me off. Concentration camp for the little American, another possible enemy out of the way, and a pat on the back for them—good work!

Then another possibility entered my mind. Could they be priming me for an assignment in a spy ring?

My heart pounded like a trip-hammer in my chest. Through my anger and fear, I saw that I could not let the encounter continue. I could not allow them to inveigle me into an inadvertent wrong word, expression or gesture. Under no circumstances could my guests suspect that I had read their real intentions, that in their clumsiness they had fumbled their mission.

As if inspired, my words just tumbled out. "So many questions! You have given me much food for thought. I accept day-to-day events, as do my friends, in the belief that in time all will clarify itself. As for your visit, I must say, it was unselfish of you to give me your time, especially since you plan only a brief stay in Posen."

I could no longer contain myself without motion. Rising from my seat, I slowly wandered over to the piano, then turned to face the pair who looked up at me expectantly.

"At this time of day, we all no doubt would welcome an aperitif, which I would gladly offer you were not my supplies long since depleted. I know you understand the difficulty of replacing such luxuries today."

"Oh, how well we know and how hard to get used to when one has lived the good life. But that time will come again, you must believe it!"

"I do believe it," I replied, a safe answer since I did not say where the good life would begin again, or when! They took the hint and rose to leave, but first interjected a final word.

"Are you sure we can be of no service to you in any way may we contact your parents for you?" They cleverly showed no sign of disappointment when I responded that I would wait with that for awhile.

"And what shall we tell the professor and his wife?" they asked.

"Tell them how I appreciate their concern. You see that I live as well as anyone, maybe better than some and surely better than the soldier in the field. Tell them also that I pray for their safekeeping." The latter remark just in case their story contained any truth and Walter should sometime hear.

The Rottmans feigned a cheerful mood as they moved toward the parlor door. Why did they not seem disappointed or show chagrin? Part of the pretense! Michaline, hearing our approaching voices, appeared with the gentleman's fedora, cane and gloves, but I personally escorted them to the entrance to make sure they left my apartment.

"Auf wiedersehen und alles gute," they said, to which I smilingly nodded. Again, why did they not say "Heil Hitler?"

Once the door closed upon them, I leaned heavily against it, trying to still the pounding of my heart. Their visit marked my third confrontation with the Gestapo. The first had come through a summons from the Spandauer police. Then, shortly after we moved to Posen, another summons had arrived, that time from the Berlin police, no doubt a more sophisticated group. It had been sent to our Berlin address and forwarded to Posen. Frightened, I had asked Hans what to do.

"If you go to answer the summons, I go with you. But why don't you write them a letter stating that you now live in Posen, the Warthegau, and will come to Berlin if requested. They may turn the matter over to the officials here, or they may even drop it completely."

I had followed Hans' advice and had heard nothing more until the visit from the Rottmans. I told them nothing, and my anger conquered my fear. My U.S. citizenship, which sometimes seemed a hazard, still provided my armor of protection because I believed in it so strongly. But what of the future? It seemed there was no future, only the past and the present.

While spending those few minutes at the door, strumming up my courage, music from upstairs suddenly startled me. Involuntarily I jerked to attention and looked upward, my exasperation spilling and in a choking voice I rasped out. "Up there are your villains, the people you seek. The men who slink quickly and silently up those stairs with a briefcase full of what?"

But hush. Michaline would think I had lost my mind, venting my feelings in English which she could not understand. A Pole, she sensed my innermost feelings and convictions. She knew without my saying that I longed for America. She dared to face me with it occasionally.

"Madam will go back to America when this war ends, I know, I know," nodding her head and smiling in self-assertion, as she shuffled about in her "carpet-cloth" slippers, doing her work.

With the "guests" gone, the children came running, needing the warm room. I preceded them and Klaerle back into the parlor.

"Do-me-so-do-sol-me-do," Bobby quietly mimicked the arpeggio we heard from upstairs, as we walked. Then he ogled Irmgard, and they laughed. I tried to laugh with them, they were so funny.

But with the door once more shut and the children at play, my thoughts continued to whirl as I reflected on that last experience. The same man's voice sang the same vocal exercises and the same songs day after day. Some sort of intrigue continued upstairs—the Polish underground. Hah! We lived right in the middle of things: the Gestapo at our door, the Polish underground one floor above us. There the Rottmans could have cornered their quarry.

But why no sound from upstairs while the Rottmans visited? Did Michaline warn them? Was she in league with a spy ring? I assumed so, but the puzzlement would remain every time I thought upon that encounter.

Oh, how I wished Hans would come home. I needed him to comfort me because I felt more endangered than ever. Posen always had been a hotbed of intrigue. But now this? Should I tell Horst in the meantime? Maybe not. Silence and waiting in such times seemed best. But where was Hans, and when would he return?

CHAPTER 26

An Interlude in the Country

April - December, 1942

When Hans finally returned home to us, we learned that his "mission" involved a temporary assignment as manager of a winery, with supplementary fruit and vegetable plantations, located in the middle of the Polish plains.

"On my trip I made an initial inspection and must return in a few days," he explained. "The good news is that you all will join me there for the summer."

Glad at the prospect of escaping Posen for awhile, we listened eagerly as Hans described what we would find in Kruschevitz.

"The little town boasts only two industries, the winery and two sugar refineries, offering employment to men who, with their families, may number about 1,000 Polish souls. Along with these are hardly 200 Germans.

"Kruschevitz lies at the end of a lake stretching about 60 kilometers south in a band at least one and one-half kilometers wide. The land on either side lies flat with hardly a rise, and grasses and wild flowers cover the nearly-treeless terrain. Tall rushes edge both shores of the lake.

"Except for a plantation some 12 miles away, the surrounding countryside is uninhabited other than by sunshine, as lovely and serene a landscape as the heart could wish.

"The winery buildings sit in a semicircle, facing the lake, and in this way form a wall that separates the enclosure from the rest of the town. A huge gate, locked at night, gives access to delivery trucks by day," he continued.

"We will occupy one of the houses in the semicircle, with room enough for us all, including Klaerle and Michaline. The dwelling is most primitive and scarce furnishings—only a table, chair and bed for each, but I surmise you all will spend your time out of doors for the most part and will not care.

"The surroundings offer good swimming and paddle- boating for the children and for us adults, good fishing, hunting, sailing and the use of a beautiful glass carriage with two separate span of splendid horses, plus groom and coachman.

"Given a truly friendly relationship between the Germans and the Poles, a permanent setup such as this could be fantastic. Three plantations furnish every kind of fruit and vegetable imaginable for the winery, its manager and the maintenance people living within its confines. Surprisingly, this comparatively small complex comprises a town complete in itself. Every sort of labor exists there to take care of any conceivable need or emergency."

To my feeling of apprehension at being so isolated in enemy territory, Hans commented, "You need not fear the Poles, for they will do you no harm. Their number includes some really splendid people. If we keep to ourselves, and they see that I am fair and understanding in my management, all will go well."

Time proved Hans' philosophy correct. He gained the respect and cooperation of the workers, and they paid Hans the highest compliment they could extend to any German—who, no matter how good or fair, still was an enemy.

"Mr. Boss," one eventually said, "We like you very much. Of course, once the Germans lose this war, as you must, we will find it necessary to annihilate you. But of one thing you can rest assured. Because you have been fair and kind, we will not torture you first." Cold solace, that!

The summer proved delightful. We gave up our milk and butter coupons and received in their stead a cow. We made our own butter and drank quarts of buttermilk and good rich cream, but could save none without refrigeration. Each day the gardener came to the house to ask Michaline her choice of fruits and vegetables then picked and delivered them. Workers also hauled and delivered wood for firing in the cook stove. Michaline cooked!

The little old peasant woman really was almost gay. "I stay here now—no go back to Posen," she proclaimed. Then immediately she changed her mind and shook her head, and one-suspected tears in her flushed face. "No, no—I go back to Posen someday, with you."

Never before in all of the 69 years of her life had she left Posen, or even crossed the Warthe River. Upon our departure, as the train moved onto the bridge above the water, she had become nearly hysterical with fright. In Kruschevitz, however, she allowed herself to be coerced into sitting in a rowboat. Her little face beamed with delight, even if she still felt somewhat afraid.

The plantations provided an abundance of fruits, berries and other delectables: gooseberries, currants (red, white and black), cherries, raspberries, strawberries, blueberries, pears, peaches and apples. All of them yielded juice and wine. Also, more than 200 bee hives provided hundreds of pounds of honey, used to create a rare wine called met (mead). Experimental gardens boasted every conceivable type of melon, winter-hardy Canadian apples, every kind of vegetable and herb, and fields of poppies for poppy seeds. Cows and bulls roamed the pastures.

Every other day a barge drawn by motorboat left for the berry plantation, some seven miles away, and brought back barrels full of choice fruit and honey. Sometimes Klaerle, the children and I made the journey too. While men loaded the fruit on board, we enjoyed a dish of huge, juicy, freshly-picked red cherries with fresh honey in the natural comb.

On other days we took the overland route to another plantation to watch the workers harvest apples, peaches, pears and melons, which they brought back to the winery by means of horse and wagon. Sometimes they allowed me to take the reins on the homeward trip.

Other than to make the trips to the various plantations, the children and Klaerle and I did not mingle with the Polish employees of the winery. The bargemen for the lake trip and the driver of the wagon remained distant and made no attempt at conversation. Nevertheless, they remained alert, attuned to our wishes and very considerate.

The Polish workers in the little town vied in a strange manner for prestige with those employed at the two nearby sugar refineries. Hans told me that it was extremely necessary for us to visit back and forth with the managers and owners of the two factories, to exhibit friendly rapport between us. The importance the workers felt in themselves depended on the social prestige of their employers.

Consequently, when visiting, we all took pains to dress only in our finest. Coachmen in livery drove our beautiful carriages, pulled by a fancily-accoutered double span of horses, even for the minimal distances between our establishments.

Occasionally we let the word spread that "the bosses and their wives" would sail on the following Sunday, or that we planned cross-country sportive span driving for a holiday. They liked that, those peasants, who did not covet the extravagances for themselves but found exhilaration in the knowledge that they worked for "men in high places."

How did Hans feel about all of that? He said, "It is just part of a protective shell, easily broken with one false move, but an integral part in the handling of the personalities and management of my job."

As for me, I noted without much concern that Hans still kept a loaded Belgian Browning revolver on his night table. I doubted it would provide much actual help. But our friend Wily Faessler had told us that in China, the knowledge that the "whip" lay right at hand kept mutiny in check. Perhaps the same applied in Poland? I hoped so.

Still, I did not realize the depth of Hans' feeling of insecurity until an incident occurred one day in the middle of our stay. The wife of one of the sugar refinery managers fell ill and needed a companion for the 30-mile trip to the railway station. I volunteered. We used our carriage and horses, and on the return trip I was alone with the driver. When dark arrived, long past the time Hans expected me back, he became terribly overwrought. He blamed himself for anything that might have happened to me, for allowing me to travel alone and unprotected at the mercy of a coachman he hardly knew. On the other hand, I had loved the whole idea of my adventure.

* * *

Along about that time, the winery fell short of cherries. Hans decided to tour the surrounding countryside in search of more to buy, and asked me to accompany him. Of course such a trip held hazards, as did letting our children stay behind with just a German maid. But was it not already risky being there at all?

Occasionally a coolness surfaced between a former Polish manager of the winery and Hans, but Hans seemed to know how to handle the situation. As for me, I consulted with Klaerle and then took Michaline into my confidence with an appeal.

"Michaline," I said, "Mr. Bohle and I want to leave you and Klaerle here alone with the children for a few days. Do you know of any reason why we should not?"

Klaerle and I both watched her face. She fraternized with a few of the Poles within the winery grounds in her spare time and, naturally, sympathized with their cause. Yet I believed she loved our children sincerely and surely would voice any doubts she might feel. Instead, she said, "Klaerle watch children. I cook and keep house. We take good care."

To Klaerle we explained that the "sugar people" knew of our intended trip, and that two shots fired into the air would bring help at any time.

But Klaerle said, "I am not afraid. The workers like the children and somehow know their names. They look at Dieter in particular when we walk through the grounds to go swimming or paddling, and they smile and say with affection, '"klein Dieter."'

Michaline had told her why the workers loved our little boy, and Klaerle paused for a moment in thought before explaining to me. "Frau Bohle, I believe you witnessed the incident. You remember that a group of men came with a two- wheel cart to get blocks of potato sugar out of storage in the basement beneath our house? You saw Dieter climb up into the driver's seat and take the horse whip, wave it in the air and shout, 'Giddyap' to the men pulling the cart—playing 'horse' with them?"

"Why yes, Klaerle, I remember that the men laughed and played along with him, and afterward Dieter climbed down off his perch with all the dignity and air of a master, and they just loved it."

* * *

One beautiful summer day Hans and I set out for a ride. We headed north and east, and for many miles enjoyed open country—flat, flat, flat! All alone on the road, we passed little villages with cobblestone streets. Mud huts (some with unrepaired holes) and primitive frame houses bordered the cobblestones.

Everywhere we saw scrawny geese and children in rags. Black-clad women walked the streets with shawls wrapped around their heads in a manner to accommodate carrying a baby on one arm, leaving free the other for carting food, wash or kindling wood. Always the same picture, until one place it was different.

"Hans, what in the world is that structure, way back in the field, surrounded by high barbed wire?" We both examined the large four-story building as we drew closer. We saw many door and window openings with apparently no doors or windowpanes to fill the frames.

"Probably a bombed-out building," I thought out loud. "See anyone?"

"Not yet. But it would not surprise me if people once lived there. I suspect it was a camp for prisoners."

"But a building in such condition affords no protection, no sanitation, probably no water. How could people possibly be so confined? And in winter. . . ?" I said, really concerned.

"Yes, I know," Hans agreed. "But so far I see no sign of life. I guess it's empty."

We rode on in silence, each with our own thoughts—in reality pretty much alike. Had people really been confined there, and if so, where had they gone? A grim picture formed in my mind, and my speculation was as good as confirmed before the day ended.

Near noon, we approached a fruit orchard. The cherry trees were loaded with fruit, but Hans decided, "No use to buy these— too poor in quality to process. Let's just keep going until we find better ones."

The afternoon passed uneventfully. We had seen no other car on the road. As evening neared, we found ourselves on what appeared to be the entry to the main street of the city of Lodz. Our progress slowed to a snail's pace due to a sudden rash of oxcarts, dog carts, bikes, wheelbarrows and pedestrians. We saw not a single car other than our own.

As we continued, two great enclosures, completely fenced in high barbed wire, bordered the rather narrow street on both sides. A steel bridge over the street connected them. We decided they also were prison yards. Immediately behind the fence and running parallel with the street sat small one-story cement houses, seemingly shops. Far to the rear stood huge houses with apertures for doors and windows, but again, with no glass or wood in them, not even in the framework. They resembled the huge structure we had seen that morning.

But in those two large treeless spaces, hundreds of drab, unkempt humans milled about. Some of the men bartered excitedly over some commodity in front of the shops. They squatted or sat on the grassless ground, no chairs or tables in sight. The women stood or walked about in dark, drab long clothes, mostly black, their heads covered with shawls. Little children sat leaning quietly against the wire fences, peering out with their big, sad, soulful eyes.

The realization descended upon me, lightning quick, that I was gazing down from the untold luxury of an automobile—even an extremely poor one—on the unmitigated misery of a ghetto or concentration camp. A million thoughts seemed to converge in a terrible feeling of guilt, an awful, deep, personal guilt, so that I choked and turned away.

I could not meet the eyes of the people inside. How could I possibly view their misery without an agonizing cry of sorrow and a strong arm to help? And I could do nothing. Brought up to believe in one's own immunity and protection within the law, it pained me to confront the realization that not everyone enjoyed the priceless gift of freedom.

Those little children, innocent victims of a burning hatred. The Germans hated the Jews, the Poles hated the Germans, and so on and on.

I thought of our own children, who knew nothing of the reasons for the war, knew nothing of the animosities of one nation for another, or even one man for another. They were alone in enemy land. Would their naivete' and their inherent kindness, their natural consideration and respect for those around them, protect them from harm? I wanted, all of a sudden, to go home, and yet I did not want Hans to see the depth of my fear.

"What are our chances of getting cherries tomorrow south of here?" I asked with all the calmness I could muster.

"Equal, if not better than today's. And, too, I feel I should see Novatski's dehydrating plant as a possible innovation for use some day. It is a coming process, and good to know about."

Not one word did he mention about the scene just passed. I knew it hurt him terribly, and he could not speak of it. Hans often had said, "The day of reckoning will come." But for the moment, we complied with orders and weighed each of our own acts in the light of personal survival.

Hans decided we should carry on instead of going home to the winery. So we stopped for the night at a dreary little hotel on the south end of Lodz and stilled what hunger we could with very simple food. We then walked to a miserable, long, narrow concrete structure called a movie house and sat way up in back on concrete steps to watch a picture of no significance whatsoever, in a vain attempt to keep from thinking. Everywhere the Poles quickly and surely classified us as Germans. They treated us with tolerance and kept their distance. No one offered a welcome. I felt hated.

The hours from midnight until dawn passed in one long misery. We tossed and turned, awake and apprehensive. After what we had seen, the town seemed ugly and dangerous, and we waited only until the first light of dawn to depart.

* * *

The weather continued beautiful and we found cherries which were ripe and sweet.

Hans bought them on the trees, delivery time estimated. With mission fulfilled, thank God, we could go home. But instead, Hans directed our car toward Novatski's factory. "Hans, do I know this Novatski? The name sounds familiar, but why?"

"Perhaps because you heard me talking with Horst and Hans von Papen about him the last time Novatski came to Posen. Do you remember we talked at lunch about his process for dehydrating food for the Army?"

In a flash I saw once again the drab figure, slouching in frayed coarse clothing, alone at a table in our favorite restaurant with his face to the wall, shunning all association, and recalled the comments about him:

> " . . . He wants to be alone.. .he never talks, just listens and then says good-bye with his eyes.. .They say he is a Pole, or partly so.. He serves the Nazi regime loyally and well.. wise to be a loner, out of reach for intrigue. . . ."

At a crossroads, we found the Novatski factory. Along with his residence next door and a few workmen's houses nearby, it formed a complex alone in the center of great, flat, empty plains. Mr. and Mrs. Novatski had just finished afternoon coffee in the garden and sat lazily soaking up the rare, hazy sunshine when we arrived.

That day I found no slouch, but a well-dressed man of quiet dignity, with a touching gentleness as he introduced us to his slender, dark-eyed wife. Leaving me with her for the afternoon, he invited Hans to tour his factory, then insisted quietly that we remain for supper and for the night.

After the evening meal we retired to the arbor of the rose garden, and the man shed his acquired drabness under a glow of romanticism. With almost a feminine delicacy, he insisted on personally serving us a rare treat of fresh raspberries, grown on the land adjacent, with cream and demitasse. As he did so, he fascinated us with tales of his early childhood.

"My father," he said, smiling inwardly at his recollections, "soon learned the uselessness of keeping me in school. I refused to conform, to sit quietly. I longed for the open air, and freedom. But he wanted me educated, and, therefore, finally assigned me to the care of a tutor. Together the tutor and I occupied an apartment in my parents' home.

"The gentleman in question was a great person, intelligent and shrewd, not at all dismayed at the task of teaching a rebel. We became fast friends, and as somewhat of a rebel himself, he soon understood my problem."

"Sounds just like Bob, our oldest son,"

I said, laughing. "I see you understand," answered Mr. Novatski. "And so the solution in my case may interest you."

"That it will," Hans commented.

"A quiet talk with my father brought the promise of an exchange of the four walls of the classroom for the great vault of the heavens. From then on, and for many years, all learning took place by word of mouth, on treks across the plains, through marshlands, the forests, or on the rivers. Hunting, fishing, swimming, out in the open air in every kind of weather.

"Free! How I loved it, love it now. Would you believe that in due time this course prepared me for an honorary college degree?" To our words of astonishment, he smiled and continued. "Then I met my wife." He glanced lovingly at the delicate woman at his side and explained that altogether they had brought five children into the world, only to lose four of them at birth and the fifth after six months. Those tragedies saddened them and left them again without a family, especially deplorable because his wife so desperately wanted children.

To my blurted words of sympathy I added, "And talking with Mrs. Novatski this afternoon, I am ashamed to admit I spoke of missing and worrying about our three youngsters, who all are healthy and well."

"How could you know?" Mr. Novatski sighed. "I have my own philosophy. The times are hard on children, and parents bear an extremely heavy responsibility. Who knows? Maybe we are better off. At least that is what we must believe."

The next morning at leave-taking, they showered us with gifts to thank us for our visit, quite a switch from the accepted form of hospitality and so very heartwarming.

"Welcome anytime," they said with their voices, their hands and their eyes. How many people knew the polished gentleman who could pose as such a slouch? Charming and affable, in perfect German, with not the slightest trace of a Polish accent, he had kept the conversation the previous night strictly on a personal basis. We still did not know whether he was Polish, German or of mixed blood? But for us it mattered not. Nor was it Hans's mission to get him to reveal such obscurities.

More than two years later, as all Germans in Poland fled back into Germany before the pressing onslaught of Russian tanks, Horst von Valtier burst into our apartment with the latest rumors concerning Novatski: "According to a most reliable source, he was trapped contributing to the intrigues of the Polish underground.

Supposedly, he used his wife's post as a radio announcer for a cover. They are jailed in separate cells, and Mrs. Novatski reportedly is dying of tuberculosis."

Those few of us who knew the Novatskis speculated that the Nazi authorities would forget about them in their frantic, almost ludicrous scramble to save their own skins. Maybe then their Polish compatriots or even the oncoming Russian soldiers would release our friends. We had decided that Novatski was indeed Polish. But what about his loyalties to the German cause? Maybe he carried mixed blood. What disloyalty had he really committed? Maybe none at all, since all too often in the East some Nazi fanatic picked an apt victim to denounce in the hope of strengthening his own stand in the Party.

We needed to leave Poland, and quickly. I never learned what became of Novatski and his beautiful wife.

* * *

My worries about the children proved unfounded. On our return, we found all serene and good. They had continued boating and swimming in our absence, loved every second, and looked rather wistfully at one another when Hans and I began talking about our return to Posen. Even Michaline shyly showed regret, wishing the summer would never end.

Hans stayed on at the winery and once I had reestablished our little family in Posen, I returned to be with him for a few days at a time.

As autumn arrived, the beautiful, colorful countryside enticed me to long, lonesome walks, shuffling through the fallen leaves. During my visits with Hans, I fell into the habit of an afternoon stroll alone—without Hans' knowledge—onto the small wooded peninsula, about an hour's walk from the winery complex.

One day, as I neared the point of the projection, a shot sounded behind me. I stopped short, and strong air pressure next to my left ear told me that a bullet had just passed near my head.

"Phew! That was close," I said aloud, and pivoted around. "Some lunatic with a gun," I continued with emphasis, angry but seeing no one. My shuffling feet, turning up the thick bed of fallen leaves, should have warned the hunter of my presence, I thought.

I looked around, expecting to see a dead bird very near my feet, or a bevy of birds maybe ducks, fluttering into the air in frightened disarray. Quickly I faced the lake again to see. No! No birds, no dead ducks, no sound, not even a deer crashing through the underbrush.

The obvious conclusion came to me with the speed of the gunshot. I, and not some animal, was the intended target. The shooter was no dilettante with a gun, but a marksman with a deliberate threat, a warning for me to quit my walks.

Was it one person's idea or an act on behalf of all the Poles in the small settlement? And why? Had I unknowingly trespassed on a hunting reserve, or was it just another sign of the boiling hate all Poles felt for the German intruders in their land?

I grasped the meaning of the incident and began my retreat, returning the way I had come. I realized that I might come face-to-face with the gunman. Nervoulsy I searched for any movement ahead of me.

But it seemed that my "hunter" had taken cover. Aware that he might be watching my every move, I forced myself to continue my retreat at an unhurried pace trying thereby to persuade him that I lacked fear. What other choice did I have? But the vulnerability and aloneness I felt were totally contrary to the solitude I originally had sought there.

My contemplation widened as I marched along, still very much aware of my surroundings. One thought consoled me: he did not mean to kill me! The German Treuhandstelle would take terrible revenge for any violence perpetrated against its employees. The hunter, no doubt a Pole, surely considered that. Of course, the government's revenge would not have done Hans or me any good!

I regretted that we Germans and the Poles could not become friends. Neither Hans nor I bore any animosities toward those people. Could we convince them of that? No, they might believe us, but still we were Germans, their enemies. They were the defeated, the vanquished, the dispossessed, and they suffered agonies.

I finally reached the complex without seeing anyone, and thus could accuse no one. I decided not to tell Hans of my experience. Maybe some day I would tell him where I had gone and what had happened, but for then he needed no more worries.

So, no more lovely, carefree tramps for me through the trees and the autumn colors. Nowhere before had I encountered such a lovely place to walk, to enjoy solitude, to kick through the thick bed of leaves, and to lift my arms to the wind as it brushed my face, swept through my hair and cleared my mind.

Despite all fears and hostilities, I had learned to love that countryside and its charms, and enjoyed living there. Could Hans secure a permanent position as manager? No, the government held that post as a reward for a veteran SS man. Hans could not aspire to the job even if he wanted it.

Consequently, not long before Christmas, Hans' term of duty at the winery ended. He and I returned to Posen with an unknown future facing us, since the Treuhandstelle could offer him no new assignment.

I wondered if a certain government official had influenced the "no more assignments" decision. The prior summer, he had visited us at the winery and Hans had guided him around the factory. Then, while Hans tended to urgent matters, the children and I had endeavored to entertain him.

I suggested a boat ride to the peninsula, so we could climb the tower there, which afforded a gorgeous view. He agreed enthusiastically, and stepped gingerly into the rowboat. The children offered to row, and since they were careful and experienced, I did not object.

Our guest enjoyed the splendid view from the tower, and the children pointed out many points of interest to him through a telescope. Then very suddenly, black thunderclouds appeared on the horizon, traveling in our direction at enormous speed. In great haste, we climbed down the spiral steps and back into the boat for the five-minute crossing. With Bobby and me at the oars, we arrived easily and safely, and the children and I even enjoyed the pelting rain.

But not our guest. Bitterly angry, he contended that we risked his life. "I cannot swim," he announced belatedly. He left us standing there in utter consternation. There had been absolutely no danger.

Did that incident create a raging antagonism in him against Hans? Or perhaps he had sought a weapon to use against my husband, and found one? Anything seemed possible. Maybe he resented what he called my American accent or background. Was that the Gestapo's way of getting at me through Hans? A horrible thought.

In any event, with "no new assignment," only one thing could happen to Hans. The Army would get him, and that it did.

CHAPTER 27

Hans Becomes a Soldier

February - August, 1943

One Sunday morning in early February, as Hans and I lay dozing, the doorbell rang at exactly 9 o'clock. At the sound of the bell we both sat bolt upright in bed, in fullest realization of the only thing it could mean. A few seconds later, Klaerle knocked at our bedroom door.

"A registered letter for Mr. Bohle," she said.

Hans asked her to bring it in. She knew what it contained, and as she handed him the slip for signature said, "I'm so sorry, Herr Bohle."

"The usual cordial invitation to join the Army," said Hans, as he read the missive. "They give me a week to get ready. And so this is it at last." Oh, misery, how sick we both felt inside.

The news soon spread and brought friends for visits during the next days. For those closest to us, I held a dinner party the night before Hans' departure. We allowed the children to join us for a few extra evening hours. Dressed up in their Sunday best, they looked wonderful. They also practiced their very best behavior and made their presence a joy for everyone.

We kept the conversation light, deliberately trying to make the occasion happy, and avoided the reason for the gathering. Our guests stayed until the wee hours of the morning. Then Hans and I crept under the covers for a few last hours of rest together. I gladly would have crawled inside him, to keep him with us, especially since I was three months pregnant with our fourth child.

But once again nature balanced everything. Just when I was filled with grief at our parting, and Hans was beside himself, feeling he was leaving me unprotected from the hazards of our time and place, an unexpected kindness came from an unexpected source. On the morning that Hans took his leave, Waldemar Steinecker, with whom Hans had worked at the Treuhandstelle, "popped in" to wish Hans "Godspeed" and to make him a special offer.

"If bombing ever threatens Posen, your entire family can join Barbara and me at our home. You can rely on that."

That tiny settlement, two hours by rail from Posen, offered relative safety from bombing and a refuge out in the vast Polish plain. The Treuhandstelle had assigned Waldemar, an architect and interior decorator from Berlin, to manage a lumber mill and furniture factory there.

Very sophisticated, clever and ingenious people, Waldemar and Barbara often came up with rather rakish ideas, as they had in securing living quarters in Hazelthal. Rather than occupy the mill manager's villa, which sat some distance away, they had bought an abandoned old railroad coach and set it down near the mill.

While leaving its outside appearance untouched, they had refurbished the interior and sectioned it off into a rather luxuriously-appointed and very livable dwelling. The manager's villa remained unoccupied, and it was that space Waldemar proposed to offer the children and me.

We appreciated Waldemar's generous offer, but it could not, no, nothing could relieve my pain at the parting. My hopes for bidding my husband farewell like a brave wife washed away, as tears not only stood in my eyes, they poured down my face. We were both in agony.

The children did better and Bob a brave 12-year-old now, taking his father to the streetcar, found the right words for the occasion.

"Dad," he said, "Don't worry, you'll return. I know it just as well as I know I would." Quite a philosophy for so young a lad.

* * *

Somehow my whole life needed readjustment. After living mostly for Hans, I threw myself into the task of rearranging my way of life to spend more time with the children.

I also gave them new privileges, such as eating supper with Klaerle and me and an hour of togetherness before their bedtime. I found those times greatly rewarding, as the children conjured up programs to present during that special hour. Irmgard, who was studying ballet at the Royal Ballet School, made use of what she saw and heard and came home with good ideas. She drew her two brothers and little Baroness von Gagern, who lived in the rooms adjoining ours, into the play. They all enjoyed themselves and helped me forget for a time the sharp pang of longing in my heart.

Eventually mail began to arrive from my soldier. He wrote his messages in English, and they arrived uncensored, filled with love and hope. No longer a "foot soldier," he was being trained for wireless communication in an open tank. He added that, with the intent of misleading the enemy, the Army moved erratically and thus they might not reach their destination for quite awhile. He could not provide an address where I could write him; I must have patience, he said.

A full two months passed before I received an address that would bring mail to him. Then came a note telling of a short furlough. He would come by way of East Prussia, a long trip, and stay barely 24 hours.

Filled with anticipation, we could hardly wait. The children dreamed up new programs and danced about the house eager-eyed and hopeful. But on the appointed day, our brave Hans arrived dead tired, wanting only rest and quiet. Many all-night marches had supplemented the full day's training.

His exhaustion was mental as well as physical, stemming from the constant humiliation involved in the training program.

"I am the father of three—soon four—children, and have stood in life for years as a leader, employing hundreds, getting along well with them. But these young 19 and 20-year-old sergeants, these whippersnappers, take a special delight in breaking our pride. Finding imaginary specks of dust on our gloves brings a penalty for which we must crawl in the mud. Then, they detain us from furlough to clean our dirty uniforms. They take pieces of equipment and throw them away in the fields and tell us to go find them, which sometimes takes hours. And so it goes on and on. I sometimes wonder whom I hate more, them or our so-called enemy."

It must be awful, I thought to myself as I listened, because it was so unlike him to complain.

"Hans, my dear," and to my next words he smiled assent, "This time will pass, and it is still better than being at the front."

* * *

A few of Hans's special friends heard about his return and came to visit. Delighted, he welcomed them and offered champagne. We still kept a supply of that, and Michaline surprised us with a flat of Hans's very special Plum Kuchen. The children joined us for that special treat and then, as the conversation veered to the political, they scampered off to their playroom.

Hans, apparently not bound by secrecy constraints, mentioned he was no longer stationed in East Prussia. Captain Brandt was still stationed at the barracks in Posen, but wondered for how long. As for Hans von Papen, his return from a business trip in Eastern Poland had left him with much to tell.

I listened while the three men huddled together and talked, ever mindful of the possibility that our apartment might be bugged. They shook their heads over the fiasco at Stalingrad, where after long and bitter fighting the Russians had forced the German Sixth Army to surrender. It was just the most recent in a long string of setbacks on the eastern front, where the war was going badly for Germany, the men said.

They also talked of the North Africa campaign, and let their sympathies run rampant for Rommel, the idol of every German.

After taking command of the nearly-defeated Afrika Corps, he had won one dramatic victory after another and nearly had pushed the British off the continent. The Allies had rallied, however, and Rommel was struggling to hold on in North Africa, one of the men explained.

But violent disgust shook us all, and a terrible fear tore at our very souls, when Hans von Papen told us he had witnessed personally the massacre of Jews in the Bast.

"If anyone had seen me stumbling onto the horrible scene," he said, "I would not be here to tell it. All I can suppose is that the perpetrators, engrossed in their frenzy of power and hate - and, I hope, guilt—lost awareness of anyone other than themselves and the thing at hand.

"Oh, yes, I saw it all and heard the cries and whimperings of those herded into the waiting freight cars as those huge doors closed upon them. The scene will haunt me to the end of my life."

"Hans," I asked, "Could that have been a concentration camp that we stumbled upon?" He heard, but ignored my question. It all seemed too terrible to comprehend.

Finally they leaned back again, quietly absorbed, and as the day drew to a close, I invited our guests to join us for a modest supper. Hans concurred heartily, and so they stayed.

* * *

In the morning Hans left us again. From then on Captain Brandt came to visit often from his barracks a few blocks away. Sometimes he brought a comrade, sometimes he came alone. At times he stayed to dinner and helped Klaerle and me put the children to bed. He even offered to sit with them, when I enjoyed the theater or a movie with friends. He said he needed the atmosphere of a home, the one he missed so much, his wife and his own two little daughters.

One late afternoon he surprised me by arriving in civilian clothes, which of course violated all regulations.

"I obtained tickets to a play," he said. "Want to go?"

"If you don't mind my appearance," I countered, referring to my quite apparent maternal state. But it did not deter him, indeed made him more reverent, gentle and kind. Then one night, as I accompanied my tall fine friend to the door after an evening together, he paused.

"Frau Bohle, tomorrow my stay in Posen ends. We go to the western front, and I already know that I shall not survive. I thank you for the kindness you showed a lonely man. God be with you, your Hans and the children."

I stood transfixed, choking out an emotion-laden "God be with you too, my friend." How then did one bid good-bye to a soldier so sure of his impending death, who despaired for the safety of his wife and daughters?

A few weeks later he fell during heavy fighting in the West. I grieved for him and his family, and for all the others who somehow knew they would not survive. Death had become such a personal thing. My own Hans—how would he fare?

New visitors appeared in our home. Mr. Ohly, a business associate of Horst von Valtier's through his Treuhandstelle liaison, came from Western Germany with his wife, Lilo, and their two children. Kind, good people, they helped me much in every way. Other new friends included Mrs. Bode, a young widow with one daughter, and many others we came to know through Hans' Treuhandstelle associations. Horst's family also had moved to Posen.

Changes also occurred in my own apartment. The Army called Baron von Gagern, the nobleman who with his family had shared our apartment, into the service shortly after Hans' induction and he died in action almost immediately. His wife returned to live with her mother, the Countess von Essern, at her estate on an island in the Baltic Sea. Their furnished rooms stood empty until Hans' cousin, also named Hans, took over several of them. His young wife expected their first child, and they came reluctantly, for reasons of expediency.

* * *

The months passed, and the middle of July arrived with Hans still in East Prussia, nearly finished with his training. As my delivery time neared, I felt very low, mentally and physically exhausted, which frightened me. I kept to my bed a good deal of the time out of sheer necessity.

On the morning of July 24th, I roused from a light sleep at 3 a.m., and by 5 a.m. I knew I had to go to the hospital. Rising, I summoned Klaerle.

"Please phone for an ambulance," I asked, and she did, since no streetcar, taxi or other conveyance was available. By 6 o'clock we arrived at the admittance room. Since the ambulance driver refused to take Klaerle back to the children, she left to begin the long, long walk home.

"Personalien aufschreiben (Here are forms to fill out)," said the clerk, shoving a form and pen my way. That finished, a nurse took me to my room and left me to fend for myself. I waited, and the pain became intense and urgent. My ring for a nurse brought no quick response, but eventually she came. For the next hours in the delivery room, I screamed at the top of my lungs. With no rest, no ebb and flow of the pain, I despaired of ever delivering myself of my burden. The nurse coldly bade me save my energy, and I begged, begged, begged her to call the doctor.

But my reluctant little Hans Bernhard finally arrived, long and thin and weighing seven and one-half pounds. Immediately I was returned to my room for a short rest period—very short, it turned out. No interlude of recovery and quiet for me. With the nursing staff "too slim to care for mothers," they got us up to care for ourselves.

Oh, how I longed for Hans. The Ohlys came by and promised to get word to him, which I hoped would gain him a furlough. But Hans neither came nor sent word. He seemed gone, lost, and I felt sure he had not received our message. All week I waited.

The baby did poorly because he could not retain food. I nursed him inadequately and the nurses evidently supplied no supplement. His weight decreased constantly and his little face and body became covered with an unsightly rash. The children came to call but, denied admittance, stood outside my window. They alternately threw kisses and, teasing, pretended to weep unshed tears, to convey their sadness that the promised little sister was a brother.

"Doctor," I said one day as he came to visit, "May I please go home?"

"When do you wish to leave?" he queried.

"As soon as friends can come get me." He nodded in agreement, and with miraculous speed I found myself sitting with Mr. Ohly, waiting to leave. The pediatrician brought me the baby and examined him, then pronounced him healthy and well. At that, Mr. Ohly shook his head.

"How scandalous," he ventured. "It takes no medical experience at all to see that the baby is far from well."

The two men faced each other, eye to eye, hard and flinty. Wordlessly, the doctor shoved a form into my hands to sign, releasing the hospital from all obligations.

"Don't sign it," said Mr. Ohly. "Don't you sign that."

But against his protests I did sign, and after the doctor left, I explained. "Don't you see? It's the only way to save the baby. I must get him out of here."

"Looking at it from that point of view, I agree," he said. And so we picked up baby and luggage and drove home in a borrowed car.

Still no word from Hans—no fault of his, I knew, but it made me miserable. Dr. Kleeberg's wife, Charlotte, who was studying medicine during her husband's absence at the front, came to visit. She looked at the ailing child and said, "Poor little worm, if only I knew how to help."

I fed my little fellow thin formula, or sometimes thick, it made no difference. A few minutes after he swallowed, up it came like a gusher and he cried with hunger. After three weeks, he weighed 300 grams less than his birth weight. What should I do?

Quite by accident a few days later, I learned of a small but excellent children's hospital right in Posen, with a brilliant young doctor heading its staff. Why had I not known that before? I packed up my child and went unannounced to see him. He listened and then growled at me.

"That child needs mother's milk. Why don't you do something about it?"

The young doctor treated me gruffly. In his opinion, I was neglecting my child. But I could not nurse. Fatigue showed in every line of the doctor's face and in his bearing. He cradled the baby in his arms, looked down at him for a long, long time, then called a nurse.

"Take this one up to Division 7, and feed him 30 grams every two hours, day and night. I will send up a half pint of his mother's blood. He must receive it intravenously."

I looked up anxiously as he prepared to draw blood from my arm with a syringe.

"Don't worry," he consoled at last. "Your blood type and his are still compatible and will mix. Now go home, and tomorrow bring me 300 grams of mother's milk. You want to save the baby?"

Scared and worried, I wandered out of the hospital and walked toward town. A hand on my shoulder —I wheeled around on one heel to face a nurse from the maternity hospital.

"You look unhappy, maybe just tired?" she asked. "How is the baby?"

"He will die unless he gets mother's milk, and I can give him none. I am desperate."

"Not any longer," she soothed. "I can help! A mother at the clinic produces enough to feed her child and another. Come in the morning, and I will give you some."

Very early the next day and for the next month, I took the long walk to the maternity hospital for a quart of mother's milk, trudged back to town center, continuing on to the far opposite side of the city to the children's hospital. Most of each day passed that way. But each day I saw through the window that, little by little, my baby filled out and his skin cleared.

CHAPTER 28

Destination: The Russian Front

September - December, 1943

At last, at last, one day Hans stood in the doorway.
"Hans, Hans, where have you been?"
I fairly threw myself into his arms, and a weight of responsibility seemed to slide off my back like a garment. In spite of my effort at self-control, the tears poured down my face as we stood, holding each other tight, for a long, long time.

Quietly he said, "I knew your time had come and gone, and you must know how terrible I felt not to be with you, not to help you in any way, not even let you know my whereabouts."

Hearing his voice, the children came running.

"Daddy, Daddy," they called as they hugged and kissed him. He took them, all three, into his arms, as always with no letting up of the show of affection. Finally, he said, "Now take me to see the new baby."

"Did you get the message of his birth?" "Yes," Hans said. "Not right away, but no matter. I was on a mission and could neither come nor write, and endured in agony the knowledge you needed me. Now, where is our baby, and what have you named him?"

Out came the sad story of our little one. On that same day Hans and I visited the hospital to see our son—but through a windowpane, held up by a nurse. Still, better than nothing.

He looked handsome, that husband of mine, in his black Panzer (tank) uniform with cocky black cap. So tall and slender, browned by the sun and with such an easy grace, he looked happy to be home with us.

"What a beautiful uniform, Daddy," Irmgard remarked when she saw him. "Can you keep it, and stay with us now?" I noticed other admiring glances, too, as we proceeded home from the hospital by way of the Treuhandstelle and the bank, where he greeted old friends.

But time was all too short, and after a few days with us he had to leave again, for France. How did I feel about that? Anywhere but Russia, I thought, hoping all the while for something unforeseen to put and end to the war before total disaster occured.

With Hans at home, we discussed a problem concerning Bob. Our eldest neared his thirteenth birthday, at which time the Hitler Youth would claim him automatically. Neither Hans nor I wanted the boy indoctrinated, but how could we prevent it? Hans saw only one way: try to find an opening in one of a few German Home Schools in the country.

Surprisingly, those schools avoided any Party affiliation. Hans left it to me to locate such an opening by writing to the headmasters of their various locations regarding possible admission. Then we would make our decision in that urgent matter!

I took Klaerle into my confidence one evening after the children retired.

"I bear no love for Nazism, as you know," she said. "I understand that the Party uses the Hitler Youth for many corrupt activities, and I hear reports of terrible things. You are wise to try to get him into a boarding school outside Posen."

Then the conversation turned in an unexpected direction.

"This brings up a difficult subject," Klaerle said. "I have gone out evenings quite often of late, with your permission, of course, in the company of a young man who interests me and who seems to like me too.

"His occupation, police work with juveniles, also interests me. The department has accepted my application to train as a policewoman, provided you release me." Rushing ahead, she added, "Before you say 'no', let me emphasize that the youth of this town need me in a way that your children, with their good home, do not. I can help you more on the outside than in."

"Oh, Klaerle," I lamented, "How can I give you up?"

To say the least, that removed another support from my world. Where would I ever again find a girl like Klaerle? I knew that in the end I would have to let her fulfill her greatest service, and so finally promised to find a solution.

A few days passed. I made inquiries about admission for Bob to a school not too far distant from Breslau. All "German Home Schools" were accredited and had non-political orientation. The expense was not prohibitive, but I wondered how well the young folks there ate. Mrs. Ecker, a Posener acquaintance whose son attended that same school, said she sent extra food once a month to him. Since she owned a food shop, she offered to include some for Bob.

When we eventually enrolled Bob there, we gave as a reason to the school authorities in Posen that he had learning disabilities and needed very special attention (at least I left them with that impression). Luckily, they accepted that excuse, which let us sidestep his absolutely mandatory admission to the Hitler Youth. Parents who objected to membership often were jailed and the child was forcibly removed from the family to Nazi care. Why the authorities allowed a private school to remain "non-political" puzzled me, but we took advantage of the situation.

Klaerle's problem also came to a head. A policewoman appeared at my door one morning and asked me to release Klaerle from service. I consented, provided they would help me find someone to take her place, and they agreed to try.

The following day a telephone call came from the employment center telling me that I could interview a possible replacement for my present nursemaid that same afternoon at 2 p.m. I agreed to that arrangement and at the given time met Maria, a Polish girl of 27, refined and neat. In fact, I found no reason for not wanting her, except that I preferred a German girl. Since I realized that was practically impossible, I consented to try Maria, if her credentials seemed in order.

"Maria has no credentials," they told me. "We hoped to avoid this request. You see, Maria is a nun, from a nunnery dissolved by the government. She always has worked with children and is extremely capable."

Capable, but probably bitter, I thought. But if so, she concealed it beautifully. Anyone that clever would bear watching, I thought. Yet why worry —I still headed my household. I could try her, and if my doubts proved unfounded, so much the better. I asked Maria to join Michaline, Klaerle, the policewoman and me in conference, and then I made my decision.

* * *

The next month saw two arrivals and two departures in our household. Bob left for school and Klaerle began her training—although she returned often to visit. Meanwhile, Maria joined us as Klaerle's replacement, and little Hans Bernhard came home from the hospital.

"You must keep your son in a room by himself," the doctor warned. "No one shall visit him but you. Furthermore," he admonished, "do not talk to him until he shows that he accepts you, his mother, in this new environment. Feed him every four hours from morning until evening very slowly and above all quietly."

We followed the doctor's orders strictly, and before long our baby responded to my quiet love with a gentle smile and soft cooing, his voice growing stronger as he gained confidence. After a few weeks, I allowed Irmgard and Dieter to visit him and, at her request, let Irmgard give the little one his morning bath.

Reports from Bob indicated he was homesick and sad, and even "a little hungry." But with Christmas not too far off we decided to wait until then to determine whether or not the school provided the proper place for him.

I had gone for a long time with no message from my parents or two brothers in the U.S.A. Undoubtedly, they thought us still in Berlin, but we received no mail forwarded from there due to censorship, no doubt. In light of that probability, I decided for safety's sake not to send any letters home, not even through the Red Cross, at least for awhile. Our silence would worry my family, I knew, but I felt I must coldly ignore that fact.

Food became our biggest problem, and we thought constantly about how to get more without detection. Several acquaintances in Posen owned food shops, and sometimes helped augment our larders without coupons. When the inspectors were not around, we lurked near the back doors of the shops, hoping for extras such as ox-blood and barley sausage, marrow bones for soup, tiny cutaway scraps of meat for stew, dried fruit or sometimes very dry cottage cheese made of skim milk. Unpalatable, perhaps, but nourishing and likewise filling.

Like most Poles, Michaline excelled at utilizing every speck of food value economically while contriving ingeniously to make each little bit delectable. Her creations included goose-blood soup with sago, with small bits of fruit floating on the surface; soup made from dried crushed rose petals, also thickened with sago; poppy seeds, crushed and combined with sugar and hot skim milk and poured over bread; borscht; crab soup made from crayfish we collected from the banks of the Warthe River; soup of marrow bones with cream of wheat dumplings; and many other dishes satisfactorily prepared and nourishing. Unfortunately, the portions were diminutive.

Maria seemed happy and at ease and fulfilled my expectations. The children liked her, and I watched my faithful little ones warily. I still cared for baby Hans Bernhard exclusively, and on good clear days I wheeled him out along the streets in the sunshine.

On one such day in late October, the top Nazi figure Himmler came to town to give a speech and preside over a huge military parade in his honor. Forgetting about the parade, I took the baby for a walk as usual and became caught up in the crowd. Five deep, they lined the main street with arms outstretched in Nazi salute, occasionally bursting into shouts of "Heil, Sieg Heil."

Curious, I wanted to observe the events. But since I refused to raise my voice or arm in Nazi salute, and dared not call attention to my rebellion, I remained very much in the background and busied myself with baby. Focused on fixing his blanket, I almost jumped out of my skin when someone tapped me on the shoulder.

Barbara Steinecker begged my pardon for the unintended fright. She too stood to the side, watching, as the parade finished and the crowd dispersed. Barbara introduced me to her daughter and her mother, Mrs. Armsberger, who stood there crying. Barbara explained that she and her family had been forced to change their place of residence. After a difficult search, they finally had found new quarters for themselves and their daughter, she said, but with no sleeping accommodations for Mrs. Armsberger.

"I'll take her," I said. "Apparently the von Gagerns left without informing the housing authorities. Of course I hold no right to dispose of their rooms, but one has furniture stored in it. Come over and see if it will do."

"Not necessary. We'll take your word that it will work out. Thank you so much." Barbara gave me a hug.

The sweet elderly lady dried her tears and smiled, relieved.

"My mother can stay with us during the day, and then Waldemar can bring her to your room for sleeping," Barbara thought aloud.

"Do whatever you find convenient," I returned. "But please, let her stay for breakfast with me, won't you?" The company of such a lovely refined person would do me more good than she knew. Her presence would make an added reason for wanting to arise in the morning. Does that show my mental state, my diminishing zest for living? If so, I recognized it too, and made every effort to overcome it.

* * *

To that point, Posen had suffered no air raids, and we slept undisturbed. But about three weeks before Christmas, I received an alarm of my own, in quite a different way. Maria routinely left the locked apartment at six each morning to attend early mass, using the key I laid out for her nightly on the dining room table. On that morning, however, long before her time to leave, someone knocked at my bedroom door. I roused and thought I had dreamed, but a second rap came loud and clear.

"Who is it?" I called, but received no answer. Nor did I find anyone standing outside my door when I looked. At first I suspected Maria, searching for the key. But it lay undisturbed, on the table.

I moved from room to room, switching on the lights, but saw not a solitary soul. So I returned to my bed, leaving all the doors ajar and all the rooms fully lit. To say the least, I slept no more that night, and after breakfast the following morning I confronted my maids in the kitchen.

"Which of you knocked at my door last night?"

They appeared astounded. "It must have been the spirit of some departed soul," they both speculated. "You will soon have a message," said Michaline.

"That spirit was flesh and blood," I countered, but they insisted, all sympathy with 'my situation.'

"I left them without further comment. But that night I not only closed my door, I locked it, leaving the key in the lock. At the same hour as the night before, I experienced a repetition of the foregoing night's event, except that the intruder violently poked at the key, which fell out of the lock on the inside and skipped across to the floor to the foot of the bed. Although terribly frightened, I jumped up in a flash, lighting my way. But my investigation revealed no sound, no sight. The front door still was locked from the inside and the back door likewise.

The next day, I phoned Klaerle. She came and consulted with

me, but warned against calling in the police. "Do not focus attention upon yourself, if you can help it. We must find some other way." Then I phoned Horst von Valtier, who also came and loudly spoke of his method for keeping spirits from wandering too far afield at night. But quietly he said, "We'll work it out over a glass of champagne this evening, shall we?"

What finally worked the wonder I never will know, as the spirits quieted for the most part at night. But they accomplished their aim, and left me in a terribly nervous and apprehensive state that grew harder to control each day. How long could I manage a cool outward surface? How I longed for Hans with me, for him to come home.

And then one day he stood there in the doorway, his happy smile a blaze of light. He dropped his gear and flew me around in circles, his strong arms wonderful to feel. With his kiss and his hug, my troubles suddenly evaporated—as always!

"Great," he said, putting me down. "I can stay for 10 whole days. The rest get just a week before they leave."

"How did you manage?" I asked, leading him into the parlor, where we let ourselves down onto the inviting sofa.

"Extra guard duty," he explained. "Now that I'm here with special time, it all seems worth it. Lots of the men hate night guard duty, but I don't mind. You know that I need little sleep, and I see very well in the dark, so I helped out quite a bit.

"One day the lieutenant said to me, 'Say, Bohle, what's the angle—all the extra night duty?' I told him I hoped for some extra time with my family at Christmas. You see, I knew we'd be heading this way anyhow, and I just couldn't bear passing by and not seeing you."

"Passing by? You mean through Posen? Going where?" I sat up stiff and wide-eyed, with apprehension.

"To Russia, darling. My division heads east real soon. After Christmas, my travel orders will come, enabling me to catch up. I know this is not happy news, but for my sake as well as yours, let's not think about it for a few days, shall we? Please? Where are the children?"

Hans' words filled my heart with dread. The few reports of battle that reached us described fierce and bloody fighting, with heavy German losses. And the Russians were known for their savagery and brutality—intensified, no doubt, as they defended their homeland. German forces achieved occasional victories, but the overall direction of the conflict seemed to favor the Russians. And Hans was being thrown into the midst of what might already be a losing battle. I was sick with fear.

"Hans, before we start 'forgetting' for a few days, tell me something," I said. "When you set out to find your division, do you go alone?"

"Yes, alone! But I'll travel with many other 'aloners' most of the time. Don't you worry about that. When does Bob come for the holidays, and where are the young folks?"

"The two elder children went for a walk, and baby Hans sleeps in his crib. Go look."

I watched Hans bend over his sleeping child. It seemed like something final . . . a last chance . . . No! I had to put that out of my mind, blot out the realization of his new destination, at least until the time I could no longer avoid it, which would come quickly enough. But could I? I knew what to expect—a growing panic, strengthening as the time for parting drew closer day by day.

Back once more in the parlor, out came the story of my nightly visits from roving spirits. Hans grew very angry.

"We'll put a stop to this nonsense before I leave. Beginning this very night, we'll sleep on these two sofas in the parlor, instead of in our beds, and I'll keep a loaded revolver on the table."

But, of course, our omniscient ghosts immediately sensed the end of their game. No more doors opened and closed "operation thin air." Nor did we hear any more unaccountable noises down the long corridor or see erratic light flashes from indiscernible sources.

Hans and I concluded that our "spirit" was none other than

Maria. In retrospect, my first instinct against hiring her seemed on target. Uprooted from her true vocation as a nun for political reasons, no doubt she felt compelled to avenge herself in some way. Before Hans left us again, he made sure the employment service knew of the happenings in our home, and they agreed that Maria should leave us. That really did put a stop to spiritual escapades for all time.

* * *

Bob joined us for the holidays. Quiet and uncomfortable, he hated the idea of going to school away from home. But Hans thought his dislike stemmed more from unloved discipline than his absence from us, and insisted that he finish out the school year there. Besides, what alternative could we pursue if we wished to keep him free from Nazi indoctrination?

Music provided our greatest pleasure during those days before Christmas. Our collection included many records, but we longed to hear new ones. Yet where would we get them with none on the market, not even for money?

"Just for fun, let us try for a trade," Hans suggested. "Let's advertise our smoke-eater it in the daily paper as a trade for records and see what happens." Although it was a lovely piece of Chinese porcelain and a gift from Mother Bohle, the smoke-eater failed to capture our fancies and we never used it.

We placed an ad, with incredibly fast results. Before long a lady stood at our door, smiling and holding out a pack of records, and we reached for our smoke-eater. In two seconds, with no asking or quibbling, we made the exchange, the lady left, our door closed and in our hands we held 15 records—good ones, mostly classical. From then on, new music filled the hours, one after another, and how fast those hours sped by, how unceasingly they passed on to posterity, until the time came for us to face reality.

Hans left to pick up his orders one morning, but came home

without them. "They must first locate my division," he explained. "That gives you and me another day."

That good fortune came to us three days in a row. But on New Year's Eve, Hans received orders to proceed to Warsaw for further instructions regarding the next lap of his journey. The children did not fully understand the seriousness of his leave-taking, so they remained in high spirits. But for me, that New Year's Eve brought no festivity, only a lonely vigil at home, trying to keep warm hugged next to the dying heat from the kachelofen.

Hans spent the holiday eve waiting in the drafty, unheated railroad station at Warsaw, from where he phoned me once more to say, "So long my love. Keep a prayer in your heart." What a contrast between the cold, darkened, empty room of that night and the parties of previous years. Only longing and fear filled my soul. Was it Schumann who set to the loveliest melody the words, "None but the longing heart can know its pain"?

A few days later, time came for Bob's return to his studies. His train left at six in the morning, and he and I walked through the blacked-out streets of Posen to the railroad station. After he boarded, I saw him seated, sad and withdrawn, a lone figure in an almost-empty coach. He hardly acknowledged me when the train pulled out. I walked home in the growing light and buried my feeling of unease until 10 p.m., when I phoned his school and learned that he arrived safely. I hoped some day he would understand.

CHAPTER 29

My Wounded Soldier Fights for Life

January - March, 1944

Finally my soldier husband was in Russia, from which nine out of every 10 German soldiers never returned. Other friends and acquaintances also served there, among them two doctors our good friends Dr. Krumeich from Potsdam and Dr. Kleeberg, our neighbor in Berlin.

For myself I thanked God for our children and for the company of Barbara Steineckers mother, Mrs. Armsberger, who still joined me for breakfast every day. During that early morning hour, we read accounts in the news about the various fronts, true human interest stories: geographical descriptions of the areas of fighting; the winter fogs that helped as much as they hindered the discovery of opposing forces; and the sights and sounds at night, such as the distant campfires of the Russian armies and the singing of their troops. We shared experiences, hopes, fears! Each day I hated more to see her leave.

I appreciated, too, the many other ways in which I received mental and emotional diversion through friendships and thoughtful invitations to the theater, shows and teas. These treats helped turn off my mind. Yet I felt no relief from the horrible foreboding, the terrible desolation, and so I succumbed to fits of despair and weeping, chiding myself for my weakness.

One cold, gray, forbidding Saturday near the end of January, I just could not contain my grief and became hysterical, my tears flowing without stopping. Hans cousin and his wife finally forced me to join them on a long, long walk. Afterward, I crept into bed and fell into a deep, deep sleep.

The next day passed in a daze and by Monday morning the sun shone clear again and I felt better—even a bit foolish about my lack of control on Saturday. Yet I wondered! I had never experienced such uncompromising mental agony before. Was something wrong with Hans or Bob? Did I believe in strong spiritual connections, a transmitting of mind to mind through vast spaces, recognizing no barrier? My mother once had told me that she knew of an accident to me when it happened, long before I told her. Could I receive such spiritual messages?

As I sat with Mrs. Armsberger, Michaline brought in the mail. "How wonderful—three letters from Hans and one from Bob. Let us see what our son says," I said, opening his badly scribbled note and reading aloud hurriedly.

> "Dear Mother, I am here in a hospital. I broke my arm and they have no one to set it, so I must wait. Besides, I can help the nurses with my good arm. Mostly old people and children are in my ward. They all need help. Your loving son, Bob."

I must go to the boy," I said. "Imagine no one to set his arm! I will bring him to the hospital here where he can receive good care. Now let's see what Hans writes."

> My own darling, I am on my way back into Germany, headed to the hospital in Neumarkt, Lower Silesia. You must

> not worry about me, for I will be all right soon. Your one-legged warrior, Hans."

I felt myself flush hot and cold, and looked up from my reading to meet the inquiring glance of Mrs. Armsberger. Unable to talk, I gave her the letter to read. He is alive and coming home, I thought, and will not need to go again. Dear God, how wonderful. But at what price! My poor, poor Hans.

Quickly I realized what matter one leg or two? We needed his spirit, and he was alive, alive! He would return to us again.

Why read the other letters, what could they say that mattered? And still I opened the envelopes. One contained a letter from the doctor who had amputated Hans' leg, with a brief preamble from Hans:

> "The soldiers arrive here thick and fast; the doctors work day and night, yet this one finds time to console the wife of a lowly soldier who has confided in him his fears of how his wife will take the blow."

Then I read the doctor's letter.

> "My dear Mrs. Bohle: A shell splinter lodged in the vein beneath your husband's right knee, and remained undiscovered at the sanitation tent at the front. The three-day trip to this hospital took too long, and his right foot and ankle already were black when he arrived. To be surer of saving his life, I felt compelled to remove the leg far above the knee. I must warn you that all amputees experience moments of great discouragement and inadequacy. May I hope that you, his wife, will bring understanding and love to a solder as fine as yours."

I gave Mrs. Armsberger the other letters to read, and sat there waiting wordlessly, with tears brimming over—not altogether unhappy ones.

After reading the letters, Mrs. Armsberger spoke. "According to these dates, your husband already is in Neumarkt. You must go to him and to Bob. I wonder how he found the strength to write you after such a surgery, and that they risked transporting him back so soon thereafter. Can you leave the children alone here?"

"No, I hardly think so, but let me telephone some friends and see what I can do."

Mrs. Armsberger left me, promising to send her daughter, Barbara, and I sat down to make a few telephone calls. First I phoned Horst von Valtier, who after a few of my agitated words, cut me short with, "I'll be right over." As I hung up, Michaline scuffled over to me, having heard. She sank to her knees and, broken up, wept as she took my hands and kissed them.

"Unser Herr," she repeated over and over. "He is such a good man, that something so terrible should happen. Gnaedige Frau," she cried, "what can I do?" She scrambled to her feet and, bent, broken and sobbing, returned to the kitchen where she mourned aloud. Her show of emotion surprised me.

Summoning Irmgard and Dieter, I had begun to tell them of their brave daddy when Horst and Mrs. Bode arrived, interrupting me. Mrs. Bode cried openly and Horst appeared mightily shaken. They both brought flowers and fresh fruit—gifts for Hans, they said, with their best wishes for a speedy recovery.

Mrs. Bode volunteered to take Irmgard and Dieter, and hoped I could leave the baby with Michaline. Horst offered an escort for me to the railroad station at 4 a.m. the following day to catch the train for Breslau, where I would connect with another that would take me into the interior of Lower Silesia by mid-morning.

After making arrangements hurriedly and bidding my children and friends good-bye, I walked with Horst through the pitch dark, quiet streets to the train station. There we waited in the wee hours of the next morning for the train from Warsaw to pull into

Posen. In addition to my suitcase, I carried the gifts for Hans. These boxes loaded me down far beyond my strength.

What a queer sensation, to "rub elbows" with people I could feel but not see. When the train finally stopped, the milling crowd pushed and shoved unmercifully, sweeping me toward the unseen steps and door to the coach. Stumbling forward, I entered an already-crowded gangway and quickly realized the futility of trying to penetrate further into the interior of the coach. So I stopped where I was, lucky to be inside but dreading the next hours.

The train moved forward and time took on the aspect of eternity, even though my mind mulled over a multitude of thoughts. My cramped quarters and the lack of any view made the trip doubly fatiguing. In Breslau, after an hour's wait, I boarded a tiny, primitive "Toonerville Trolley" for the remaining two-hour ride. It surprised me, on arriving at the station in Neumarkt, to find myself still out in the open country.

Apprehensively, I followed the many whom exited there, and with them clumsily boarded an already overloaded waiting omnibus bearing the sign "To Neumarkt." Unsure of my decision, I addressed the lady standing next to me.

"I did not realize the town was so far from the station." "Yes, several kilometers . . . four, I believe," she said, smiling. "You have someone in Neumarkt?"

"Yes, my husband. This is my first visit here."

"It's my third, and I should mention right now certain things you must do when we reach there."

She told me that five military hospitals were located in Neumarkt, and the little town was hard-pressed to accommodate the resulting stream of visitors. Thus, following her advice, I made the housing office my first stop on arrival. There an official assigned me to a room in a nearby inn, and told me I could stay only three nights.

After stumbling around in the business section of town for awhile, I finally found the right "Stube." The innkeeper took my assignment slip and gave me the key to room #6, across the court.

The room had neither warm water nor heat, he explained, but I could sit in the warm cafe during the day when not at the hospital. The cafe served warm broth continuously, and I could buy as much as I wanted, without coupons.

I thanked him and walked to my room. After a sleepless night on the train I longed for rest, even in my ice-cold room. Instead, however, I deposited my luggage and headed immediately for the hospital.

When I arrived, I found not a soul in the hospital lobby, and a big sign that said, "Visitors from three to five p.m. only—no exceptions." So, slowly and reluctantly, I retraced my steps to room #6 at the inn. I tried to rest lying on the bed fully dressed—coat with hood, mitts, black suede boots and all. But the cold and damp, and my own overwrought emotions, kept me from sleeping or even resting quietly. When I began shivering violently, I decided to get up and return to the warmth of the cafe.

Lunchtime neared, so I took a little table off in one corner that looked just right for me, where I could sit alone and unobserved. Just one room, the little cafe seemed friendly even if quite dark and poorly furnished. Other women sat about, no doubt on the same mission as mine, with a few male guests interspersed—probably the town's merchants in for lunch.

Through the partially stained glass window in front, I saw ox-drawn carts arrive periodically. The carts—really just great flat boards on skis—were covered with hay a foot thick. The drivers sat squatted in one corner, engulfed in full-length, dirty sheepskin robes.

The drivers unhitched their beasts and led them to hay, then entered the cafe, peeling off their tattered, flea-infested furs and hanging them on a nail behind the entrance door. Then they gravitated to the first unoccupied table, too shy to look about despite their big, burly physiques. Eventually I learned that their shopping trips to town provided the sole means of transportation to the inland hamlets of Lower and some of Upper Silesia. The innkeeper always struck the bargain between them and prospective passengers.

I ordered some broth—which arrived good and hot so I asked for more. The luncheon menu, typed up neatly in an effort to lend it importance, offered no choices. I simply said "Me too" and accepted the skimpy plate of food as it came.

After lunch I sat and watched the people for awhile and then took a walk to kill time and subdue my agitation. The town offered no diversion, nothing new or unique to see. The only virtue of that poor, backward settlement lay in its isolation, an advantage for its five military hospitals.

* * *

Promptly at 3 p.m., I climbed the steps of the entrance to Hans' hospital, so excited by the prospect of seeing him that I could not still the pounding of my heart. Entering, I asked directions to Hans' room. "Second floor—end of the hall to the right —#10," the receptionist said.

Instead of the quiet of a typical hospital, I found bedlam, a madhouse. Recuperating amputees and others played ball with their crutches in the halls, as nurses' aides laughed and scrambled with them. All the doors along the corridors stood ajar, and several loudspeakers blasted schmaltzy songs—a different tune on every floor.

Nearing #10, I encountered a group of soldiers smoking and playing some sort of a dice game, occupying the hall floor. They arose to let me pass at my request, never once looking up from their play, and I stood in the doorway of my husband's room.

He lay on a cot in the right back comer—one of four wounded soldiers in the room. When he saw me, he tried to lift himself to a sitting position but could not maintain it. I rushed to him with words of cheer and comfort, but after I kissed him he suddenly burst into tears and turned from me to the wall, ashamed. Nor was he interested in the gifts I had brought from Posen he did not want the flowers and could not eat the fruit.

Hans now explained the reasons for his misery. His medicine gave him dysentery, and no one bothered to clean him. Nor could he eat the hospital food. He had gone from one hospital to another for 10 days, too keyed up to sleep day or night. The bandages on his open wounds had dried on, and at the prior hospital, the interns had torn them off without benefit of anesthesia or painkiller. To top it all off, the cacophony from the screeching loudspeakers—one of which hung just outside his open door—threatened to drive him crazy.

"If only something would put me to sleep," he moaned. "I just have to sleep or I'll lose my mind."

"I'll talk to the nurse," I said. "What nurse?" Hans replied, his laugh a mockery. "There's only one, and she comes only with the doctor when he makes his morning call. And the nurses' aides spend all their time playing with the fellows who can be up, or going to the movies with them in the afternoon."

Hans introduced me to his three sick comrades. The one next to him wore a brace that held his arm as high as his shoulder. Able to lie down only with great difficulty, he sat on the side of his bed, obviously in a great deal of pain. The other two lay facing the wall, quiet. The room offered space only for a cot and a chair apiece. Hans' chair contained the soiled dishes of a late dinner, so I sat on the foot end of his cot.

"Tell me, Hans, what did they serve you for dinner?"

"Bean soup, but I could not get it down, so the fellows finally ate it."

"Do your nurses' aides know that you cannot eat?"

"No, they just tell me I'm spoiled and take it away. This way the boys get a little extra to eat, and God knows there's not too much anyway."

"What do you eat?" I asked, really concerned.

"Nothing to speak of" volunteered the neighbor boy, rocking

in pain. "There's no choice. Either you eat their God-damn soup, or it serves you right if you starve."

"Do you ever get tea or coffee?"

All four laughed, a sour sound.

"Remember that bottle of champagne Hitler promised every hospitalized soldier, as his personal gift?" continued the little rocking soldier. "Those God-damn interns intercept them and revel every night. We've never tasted a drop." Groaning, he tried to lie down but could not stand the pain and sat again, unable to find a comfortable position.

At 4:30 p.m., a big, bustling nurses' aide came in and shoved a thermometer in each mouth, then left. She reappeared in 10 minutes and took Hans' chart from its hook on the wall.

"Huh, fever again. What are you doing to yourself? Nothing pleases you. Such a spoiled one," she nodded to me.

Turning to the rocking soldier, she said, "Why don't you lie down? Here, take this," she added, offering a painkiller. But he refused, saying the medicine nauseated him. "All right, have your old pain; see if I care," she snapped. The poor soldier, busily wiping the perspiration from his brow with his one useful hand, hardly took notice of her.

Supper arrived shortly before time for me to leave, causing the noise in the halls to subside; the loudspeakers fell silent. The evening meal consisted of a bowl of watery soup, placed on each chair, the ways and means of eating it left to each individual soldier.

I left the hospital after darkness fell and made my way back to the cafe—empty except for a few customers, those making hospital visits. We ate in silence, downcast and sad. Like me, some tried to be brave and constantly choked back the tears. So much to think about! We felt sympathy, one for the other, without caring to talk or introduce ourselves. At 9 p.m., I returned to my frigid room and crawled, fully dressed except for my boots, under the single thin blanket and tried to sleep.

Cramped from huddling my knees trying to get warm, I tossed and turned all night. My black broadcloth, seal-lined coat looked anything but chic the next morning, so I turned it inside out while I washed with icy tap water and combed my hair. Teeth chattering, and grateful for the one warm room I could go to, I headed for the cafe and a breakfast of a roll and ersatz coffee.

Afterward, I walked to the shopping area looking for some kind of stationery. Then I returned to an obscure corner of the cafe and wrote Mother Bohle a letter. So far she did not even know that Hans had served in Russia, since she could do nothing for him and we never worried her needlessly. But I felt she should know things as they were, and I thought we needed her prayers.

The time until 3 p.m. dragged on interminably, with nothing to do but wait. But at last I sat beside Hans again. This time he asked about the children, and I told him I planned to pick up Bob on my way back to Posen, and why.

"Cherie, would you please get a pan of water and wash me a bit?" he asked later. "I haven't been washed since leaving the Russian front, and it might help me sleep. Besides, I feel filthy."

So I did, careful not to get near the bandage on his sawed-off leg. Afterward, he seemed more composed and content just to have me near.

But the next day brought a reversal. Terribly restless, he hardly could keep his body quiet. His head and hands moved constantly, and he sighed and fussed. Finally, he burst out, nearly incoherent in his distress.

"Please go home, go home, go home," he begged. "I must have an outlet for this pain. I need to cry, but I cannot in front of you."

Alarmed, I resisted leaving him in that condition but finally acquiesced to his wishes. As I rose to leave, I bent forward to kiss him farewell. But he stretched out his arms, holding me away, and closed his eyes as big tears welled over the rims. The agony I felt at leaving him then defies description. Unable to hide my own tears, I tramped the halls in an effort to regain my composure. He saw my torment, and yet insisted I go.

Back in my dark, cold room #6, I knelt by my bed and sent up prayer after prayer, plea after plea, for help and hope. Even more,

I asked for the belief that I so sadly needed, the belief that it was not meant for Hans to die. That night I received no answer to my supplications, my constant entreaty, my cry for help. All night long, in my little cold bed, I stifled my choked-up sobs with one more plea. How could I leave Hans? What could I do for him? Until I knew, I would go to Bob.

* * *

I returned to Breslau the next morning in a mental fog, hardly knowing what I did. Somehow I boarded another "Toonerville Trolley" leading off into Lower Silesia at a different angle. I eventually arrived at Bob's school after a long walk from the train station in that little town, and explained my plan to the headmaster.

Another long walk brought me to the hospital, where I found my son up and in a ward that accommodated all ages and both sexes. Apparently enjoying himself he gave no clear indication that my arrival mattered much to him. I obtained his release, and the nurse said they would miss him, since he had made himself useful.

Together we carried more heavy luggage to the station and took the train to Breslau, Bob helping with his "good arm." His broken arm was held to his chest with a sling. We spent the rest of the day and evening sitting, walking and waiting outside the station for the train from Vienna to Warsaw. Hoping not to be hounded by air raids and wishing for something to eat, we wondered if the train, when it finally arrived, could accommodate the huge crowd already assembled on the platform. Why were all those civilians going east?

As it grew dark, blue lights shone along the tracks, offering some visibility. The fates answered our hope no alarm. But food? None! Not even for coupons. We would have to wait until midnight in Posen.

Two weary, hungry people arose to meet the train when it finally hove into sight. As we approached the entry to a coach, a mighty, frenzied crowd caught us in its tide, so strong we were powerless against its direction. It forced us so close to the edge of the platform that I feared we would fall down upon the tracks beneath the coach. In my terrible fright I cried out loudly, my voice rising clear and strong above the sound of shuffling feet.

"Stand back! Have you all gone mad? You are throwing my child down onto the tracks, and he has a broken arm."

My words spurred an instantaneous reaction. Quite as quickly as the rush for the doors had begun, it stopped. As those around us made way for our safe entry into the car, I regretted the anger induced by my anxiety. A crowd could exhibit kindness as well as thoughtlessness, given the right guiding power. It was something to ponder over as once again we sat on our luggage in the cold gangway, next to the frosted window, while the train moved ahead.

X-rays at the hospital in Posen the following day revealed a clean break in Bob's arm, not too much displaced and already somewhat knit. The doctor asked for a day in which to consider the advisability of a new break, and I left Bob in his competent hands.

At home a telegram from Hans awaited me. "Your signature necessary on several business matters," it said cryptically. That very queer wording made me realize that something was desperately wrong.

I phoned Horst and then Mrs. Bode, who said all was well with Irmgard and Dieter. Baby Hans Bernhard seemed fine as well and Michaline shone with joy at being allowed to care for him.

So, after telephoning an agreement with the doctor concerning Bob, I once more rushed off into the eerie darkness of the blacked-out streets of Posen at 4 a.m., that time without escort.

After arriving in Silesia, I barely contained myself until 3 p.m., when I could see Hans. The housing office had assigned me to a room I shared with seven other women, all of us sleeping on a bed of straw on the floor, each with one blanket. A washstand and a pitcher of cold water, that was it! But it made no difference to me, I hardly noticed. I left the room to walk the streets in my agitation, wishing the time would pass.

Fifteen minutes prior to visiting time, I turned my steps in the direction of the hospital. Suddenly, I heard the rumble of a heavy truck and the scream of brakes and tires hard-pressed. I turned and saw a tiny child in the street, in the pathway of a huge supply vehicle, the youngster's terribly frightened mother already "flying" to the rescue. But the seconds passed too quickly. Knowing herself trapped, the mother scooped up the child and threw it to the nearest bystander on the curb as the wheels of the truck caught and crushed her.

Her long, drawn-out wail trailed off to silence, as she lay dead in the street. The dull-witted bystander had failed to catch the child, its head had struck the curb, and it too lay dead. The truck came to a full stop in seconds, but too late. The driver, jumping down from the cabin and seeing the tragedy he could not avoid, leaned against the radiator, head in arms, and wept. So did the crowd that gathered, and so did I.

Oh, dear God, I prayed, is there nothing but death and destruction everywhere? How, or where, would I get the composure I so badly needed to comfort Hans, to give him the isle of security he did not feel? Did just a wisp of happiness and sunshine exist somewhere? Must it get darker yet to bring on the dawn? I waited and walked a long time before I ventured to Hans—until I felt sufficiently in control to meet him calmly.

Of course I arrived late, and Hans no longer expected me - which perhaps made him more grateful when I appeared. He did not ask why I came late, and I volunteered no explanation nor gave any hint of what I had witnessed. Engrossed in his own urgency, Hans hardly noticed the state of my emotions.

Papers to sign? The wording of his telegram had served only as a necessary ruse to make the hospital send for me. He barely got out a greeting before he began a desperate plea.

"You've got to do something, get me out of here. I'm sure I have blood poisoning, and I can tell by my failing strength that I have just three days to live. And oh, how badly I want to live.

"Look at this latest contraption," he said, referring to a device attached to his severed leg. "I just can't stand it, it's driving me mad, out of my mind. I've got to sleep; somehow I've just got to get some sleep—I cannot stand this much longer. No one around here seems to know what to do for me, to help me, so I must get it from somewhere else. Please, Cherie, do something. Call Horst, call somebody, before it's too late."

His fever rose, and his agitation with it, primarily due to the doctor's latest treatment idea. In an effort to keep the flesh of Hans' severed leg from receding from the bone-end, the physician had glued a stocking onto the sore flesh around the stump, then attached a weight to the stocking with a string.

No doubt the doctor knew what he wanted to accomplish, but the method seemed crude. Worse still, Hans said, a ring of inflammation four inches wide had formed around the stump. In one place it had drawn up into a long, thin line of red. Immediately I knew that Hans was suffering from a clear case of sepsis, and when the red line completed the circle, my man would be dead.

Each night Hans' temperature soared, he said, returning to normal by morning. Just like that his father had died, I thought, beside myself as I recalled that experience of a few short years earlier. What could a lone wife do against a German military machine? How could I get him out of there? A stupendous task. With no idea what to do, I decided to find the doctor.

That proved daunting. No one seemed able to provide definite word of his whereabouts, which suggested to me that he, with one colleague, headed all five military hospitals in the area. So I spent hours walking from one to the next, hoping that someone could and would tell me how to find the doctor.

When night fell, I finally resolved to go to his home. Although I felt reluctant to disturb his privacy after a full day's work, the urgency of Hans' situation allowed no delay. Fortunately, I found the doctor at home, and he received me.

After I stated my mission, he scrutinized me carefully, then said, "You are an American."

I neither confirmed nor refuted his statement, nor did I need to. After a pause, he added that his mother, too, came from the United States. Then he suggested that I return to the hospital immediately, promising to join me once he had made a number of important phone calls. I left and walked back to the hospital alone.

A half hour later, in Hans' room, the doctor unbandaged the stump and showed it to me. Pus dripped down on the dressing, and the red stripe had moved up near Hans' groin. The doctor said he could do nothing but rebandage, but he decided to leave the weight disconnected for the night to ease the pain.

"It is true that he is a very sick man, Frau Bohle," he agreed. "For that reason, you shall have morning visiting hours as well as those in the afternoon."

"Is that all that can be done?"

He looked at me, but gave no answer, and his manner said clearly, "The man will die." From that doctor I knew I could expect no more help.

* * *

Back in my new quarters, I begged the innkeeper to let me put through a "blitzgespraech" ("lightning" special telephone call) to Posen. Although it would cost 10 times the normal rate, it afforded the only way for a civilian to make a long-distance call during those times. And, thank God, I had the money. I put up as collateral a 20-mark piece, and the innkeeper promised an "okay" to the operator for the use of his phone.

Luckily, my call to Horst found him at home. I sobbed out the story of Hans' condition, and begged Horst to send a doctor who would know what to do.

"My dear Ruth," he replied, "I cannot get a doctor for my own baby right here in town, let alone send one to you so far away. Then too, only a physician with proper military rank would dare enter your hospital."

We both wasted precious minutes in silence, wondering what

to do. Finally, Horst said he'd give the matter his deepest consideration, and I had to settle for that.

Imagine my surprise, therefore, when at nine the next morning Horst and Dr. Walter Kleeberg, both Hans' special friends, approached my breakfast table in the cafe. The two tall, handsome officers sat down beside me to tell me of their plan. Amazed and unable to find words, I just sat agape, and a great hope welled up within me. There sat a doctor and a friend, each with a military rank.

"What rank does the doctor hold?" Horst asked me.

"Lieutenant colonel."

Horst looked from my downcast face to Walter. "That's one higher rank than yours, isn't it, my friend?"

"No matter," Walter replied confidently. "We'll find a way."

Turning to me, he continued. "Listen well, dear Ruth. Last night I returned from Russia to take a cure for a case of sciatica that I acquired in the last months on the front. I phoned Horst, heard about Hans, and asked immediately for permission to postpone my cure and come here to see if we cannot save Hans' life.

"Now this is our plan. As you may know, Horst's mission as liaison with the Treuhandstelle gives him a little influence that he will use if necessary. But first, he will try to bluff his way in. If he succeeds, I will take over.

"I understand they post no sentries at the hospital, so we can enter Hans' room quickly. If I get in, and you want to come along, you are welcome, right?"

Together we left the inn, walked to the hospital and entered the large tomb-like lobby. Walter and I seated ourselves on the lone stone bench that stood in the middle of the floor, while Horst ascended the eight broad steps leading to the main corridor. But immediately as he turned the corner, a door opened and then banged shut and a loud, gruff voice yelled, "Who are you and what are you doing here?" I recognized the voice as that of the doctor in charge of the hospital.

Horst's heels clicked in salute. "Zu befehl, Major von Valtier, sent her from the Chancellery in Berlin to ascertain the condition of Bohle, room #10."

My heart pounded with fear. Sent from the Chancellery in Berlin? What bravura! I never expected such courage from Horst on what authority did he make such a statement? In a flash, I recalled their plan to bluff their way in. But what if the doctor asked for Horst's orders? Then we would be finished, or.. would we? I glanced at Walter, who sat motionless, keenly alert, showing not even the tiniest sign of fear.

The doctor reacted to Horst's explanation with friendliness and acceptance, and made no request to examine Horst's credentials. He told Horst to proceed, and said he would come up to Hans' room after rounds.

That outcome, far better than I anticipated, left me wondering. Perhaps it simply confirmed my initial suspicions about the doctor's competence and demonstrated that he ran the hospital badly. Or maybe, recognizing the poor quality of care given to Hans and the other patients, his conscience smote him. Or, was Horst's assertion so preposterous that the doctor could not believe it anything but true? No matter, it had worked. We heard a door close, and Horst returned for us.

With quiet, rapid strides we walked to Hans' room, entered and closed the door. The doctor's rounds took longer than we expected, and by the time we heard his approach down the hall, Walter knew all he needed to about Hans' condition. Call it more luck, if you will, but the doctor did not enter. Instead, he knocked and called from the hall, "Major von Valtier, please come out."

No doubt Horst felt none too comfortable, but he pulled off the bravado elegantly. He was a very elegant man anyhow, with enormous presence in his uniform and fur-lined overcoat. He joined the doctor in the corridor, and we overheard their incredible conversation.

"Your name is that of a nobleman; it sounds familiar."

"Possibly," Horst replied. "Baronial estate East Prussia." That identification labeled him lavishly, I knew.

"Yes, yes," continued the doctor, "I have one here in Lower Silesia, where I spend my weekends. You'd probably appreciate its beauty immensely. I suggest you visit me sometime and go hunting."

"Delighted, sir," Horst replied in a manner that suggested an end to the conversation.

The doctor paused, then continued. "And as for Bohle, had we known he was related to the Gauleiter, we would have treated him with a little more favor. I already have ordered a boiled egg and some applesauce for him."

Inside the room we just gasped. Clearly, the doctor believed that Horst's visit was prompted by a familial connection between Hans and a top Nazi official also named Bohle. What must those three other poor fellows, Hans' sick roommates, feel to hear a remark like that?

Horst took advantage of the doctor's erroneous assumption to press our case.

"I've brought a physician with me, Dr. Kleeberg, to take over the care of the patient," he stated in a tone that brooked no disagreement.

"Fine; I shall send in the nurse for instructions."

Horst clicked his heels again in salute, thanked the doctor and re-entered the room. Almost immediately the nurse joined us. She remarked to Walter that from the very beginning she had thought Hans suffered from Erysipelas (blood poisoning) and had reported that to the doctor, but he had seemed unable to make up his mind.

Without committing himself further, Walter gained her support. She promised to put Hans in a room away from the loudspeakers, to administer as Walter instructed, and to tell me each evening what I should relay to Walter via long-distance telephone. Together, she and Walter then proceeded to the hospital laboratory. There he found a shocking minimum of primitive, rusted equipment, insufficient to run even the simplest of tests, give a transfusion or take a cardiogram. More unbelievable and beyond comprehension to Walter, however, was the doctor's willing acquiescence.

At noon, Walter, Horst and I left the hospital and walked back to the inn. We sat in somber conference in a side room, over a miserly bite to eat. Horst decided to leave: having paved the way for Walter, he thought his job complete. Walter agreed, and to our pleading faces he voiced the opinion that a "horse cure" of sulfa, a new and sometimes-effective drug that he had brought with him and given to Hans, represented Hans' only chance. Hans might live if his heart could stand the drug, Walter noted grimly, but he could offer no promises. And it remained imperative to remove Hans from the hospital to one where he could get adequate care.

As Walter finished, we suddenly became conscious that a distinguished, white-haired gentleman stood at our table. We had not noticed his presence earlier.

"Excuse me, please, I just wanted to say, I could not help listening as I sat across the room. I can see and hear that the lady is in great trouble. May God be with you." He bowed and backed away respectfully, and we thanked him, so very touched by a stranger's sympathy.

Horst rose and departed to return to Posen. Walter and I went back to the hospital, saw Hans put into another room and sat with him the rest of the afternoon.

At dinner that evening, the innkeeper came to Walter.

"You are a doctor?" Walter nodded in affirmation, and the innkeeper continued. "My wife is very ill, and I can get no help anywhere. If you will see her and tell us what to do, I will repay you in any way possible."

Walter immediately followed him and examined the woman. Fortunately, he understood her trouble and could help. Afterward he returned to the table, and both the innkeeper and I knew that day how lucky we were.

Only one more train left Neumarkt that evening. Walter wanted to take it, but the station lay four miles away through open country and he needed a conveyance of some sort to get there in time. With no bus or car available, he asked for a bicycle.

"My son made one himself," the innkeeper offered. "It is small for such a big man as you, and tends to ride a bit to the left, but it has a light. If you can use it, take it and leave it at the station. We will pick it up tomorrow.

Walter instructed me to phone each and every night to report and receive further briefing, then set out for the station. He made quite an image—a very tall man, riding a much-too-small bike with his long legs akimbo and the ends of his fur-lined military coat trailing in the wind. The dim light barely penetrated the pitch black night, and the frail little bike did, indeed, steer left. But no matter; he made his train on time.

* * *

The next day I returned to the hospital and observed that the nurse followed Walter's instructions carefully. Hans received a cup of real tea, and some oatmeal. At last, food he could eat! I reported that to Walter that night when we spoke by phone.

During visiting hours the following day, Hans met my greeting with a querulous look in his eyes.

"However did you manage?" he whispered, explaining that he had just received word of his proposed transfer to Posen, scheduled for the next day. I hardly could believe it—a real miracle.

That night, during our "blitzgespraech," Walter said he knew of Hans' impending transfer and advised me not to question, but accept the turn of events. Suddenly, however, a great wave of responsibility descended upon me. I feared that Hans would not live through such a trip, and felt I would bear responsibility for his death if I made the wrong decision.

I shall therefore be forever grateful for the advice of the innkeeper. Seeing my distressed face at the supper table, he came to talk to me. I told him my fears, and he replied, "Dear lady, why not leave it to your husband to decide. He knows what he can stand, and it is his life."

Early the next morning, I acted upon that sensible suggestion and received a convincing answer from my husband. "I will die if I remain here," he said simply, and that ended my doubts.

The orderlies came in soon thereafter to prepare for Hans leave taking, and we both begged them to allow me to accompany the transport. At first they said no, but then changed their minds.

We left by lorry to catch the early train at Neumarkt for Breslau. At the station, the orderlies carried Hans stretcher on board and laid it in the aisle on the floor. We arrived in Breslau 45 minutes late, but the express train from Vienna bound for Warsaw still stood waiting. It waited some more while two volunteers transported Hans stretcher from one platform to another and hoisted it through the window of a private compartment.

In Posen, a Red Cross ambulance stood at attention on our platform, ready to finish the journey to the Posener Military Hospital. I knew that facility was marvelous, and the ensuing days proved it so again.

In a time of war, with one life meaning so little, the whole procedure seemed incredible, a real miracle, and I had no choice but to view those events as an answer to our prayers and supplications. It was a time for belief, not reasoning.

How did it all come to pass? By coincidence? For me, it was divine intervention. Horst had sat next to a man of influence on his return trip from Neumarkt to Posen. As we all did in those days, and especially with his heart so full of concern, Horst had burst out vehemently against the conditions in the hospital and told the stranger about Hans. His outrage was not lost upon the fellow traveler, who then told Horst that he was the doctor in charge of all medical installations within a 100 kilometer radius of Breslau—including Neumarkt. He made no comment that exposed his true feelings about conditions there, but promised Horst he would transfer Hans to Posen immediately.

Things improved immediately and dramatically for Hans at

the hospital in Posen. Soon after our arrival, the head doctor put him in a nice warm bath. Then he sat by Hans' bed and for the next hour reviewed his case history—perhaps wondering also what had made his unprecedented transport possible. That finished, he ordered the nurse to give to Hans anything he might request to eat or drink, no matter how ridiculous the request or inopportune the time. Then he placed Hans in a large room with two other very sick men and gave him many transfusions. Hans' room, and in fact the entire hospital, seemed so quiet that my tiptoed footsteps echoed off the walls.

Day after day our Posen friends came and sat outside Hans' room with me, often bringing whatever bit of extra food they could get that might tempt his appetite. Dr. Kleeberg came to Posen too and conferred with the resident physician, and together they agreed on the method of treatment.

About a week after his arrival, Hans greeted me tremulously, all excited and happy.

"I actually slept for one whole hour," he reported, his eyes gleaming once again. Then his countenance clouded, and he continued. "But what if it doesn't happen again? I'm afraid to hope or expect too much."

Such concerns failed to dampen his spirits for long, however, as the sleep had brightened his entire outlook. For the first time, he asked for the children. But he could not yet see them, since even the strain of quiet conversation with me left him drained. He spent most of his time lying quietly, taking note with his eyes of events around him. His face was losing its deathlike pallor, but even so he remained so gaunt and wasted that he hardly bore a resemblance to the robust soldier I had sent off to war.

Hans' progress pleased the doctor, however. One day he finally allowed Hans his children for a brief five minutes, then 10, then more, and then other guests as well. But he admonished us to patience, "much patience for the long hard pull."

Ten weeks after Hans had fallen in battle, he still could not sit up in bed. My world in those dark days centered almost solely on my husband. I knew little of current political or military developments, focusing all my energies and attentions on helping Hans get well. He continued to improve, as did the weather as Easter neared. The hard, bitter cold gave way to sharp, cutting spring winds that whipped across the Polish plains from Russia. When the sun came out from behind big, fleecy white cumulus clouds, it offered warmth—and a hope for better days.

CHAPTER 30

Allied Bombs Blast Posen

Easter 1944

Easter soon came—our second in a row with Daddy not at home. But at least we could visit him, and for the whole afternoon—all except baby Hans Bernhard. Our little one was doing quite well in Michaline's care overall, but was suffering from a slight cold.

To my delight, Easter Sunday dawned warm, windless and beautiful—perfect. I placed our small one in his buggy and wheeled him out onto the balcony to enjoy the sun. How we lapped up every ounce of precious, rare solar rays.

I was beginning to feel secure for the first time in many months, so I hardly could believe my ears when the air raid sirens sounded a 12-minute warning. Searching the blue azure of the heavens, I saw nothing alarming. Surely on such a clear day, one could easily spot enemy planes as tiny silver flecks in the sun. But I saw nothing. Probably the enemy was once again dropping ammunition for their forces to cache in the nearby woods. Everyone knew that between us and the first line of German defenses in Russia, large-scale guerrilla warfare progressed.

I sent Michaline and the children to the basement for their safety and promised to come, too, if it proved necessary. They left immediately, carrying knapsacks and sheets. Once in the basement, they filled a laundry tub with water so they all could immerse the sheets and quickly cover themselves with the dripping cloth, in case they became trapped in a flaming basement and had to walk through the fire to gain an exit.

A few scant minutes after they left for the cellar, a bomb whistled past and hit directly behind the house, jolting me out of my composure. Stifled with fright, I grabbed my sleeping child out of his buggy and ran for the spiral rear steps. As I descended, more bombs struck farther away. The earth rose and fell like a wave and the huge four-story structure in which we lived shuddered as if ready to crumble. The shock threw me down perilously close to the metal hand-railing that provided no guard at all against the open stairwell three stories down.

In fact, as I slid down the steps, out of control. My body lay sideways and my feet came ever closer to the edge. With baby in one arm, and with all the effort I could muster, I rolled over onto my face toward the wall, trying desperately to guide us away from the stairwell. Using the tips of my toes, I tried to slow my swift downward slide on the curving steps. Baby remained silent, too frightened to cry.

"Someone please help me," I sobbed, but no one heard or saw. An eternity passed while I slid down to the door and the wall of the second floor landing, which finally halted my fall. For a moment, all remained quiet.

I shoved back into the corner on the floor, catching my breath and cuddling little Hans Bernhard, who wanted to cry and searched my face for reassurance. My fears reached the heights of panic, but somehow I managed to summon a smile—albeit a rather screwed-up one—that told my little one all was well. I realized I must reach the basement very quickly—more bombs might fall any second. But I trembled so terribly that I could hardly come to my feet.

Poor little Irmgard and Dieter. They too felt frightened, but they were safe. We all were, and no more bombs fell. The all-clear soon sounded and we returned upstairs. Investigating, I saw that the first bomb luckily was a dud. But another, an incendiary bomb, had exploded in flames over the city and I saw a great column of smoke rising in the direction of the military hospital.

That beautiful Easter Sunday brought Posen its first bombing, and once again we felt anxious about Hans. Irmgard and Dieter knew no rest until we started on our way to him. What a terrible revelation for them to climb pile after pile of rubble, walk around tall buildings aflame, and see crowds of people crying and wringing their hands. Only after we had passed the thickest destruction could we see that the hospital lay beyond and their daddy was safe.

We hurried on, hoping to see him, but no Hospital personnel bustled about, returning the sick and wounded to their rooms from the basement air-raid shelter. No time for visitors.

The events of that day changed much for us. With the threat of more bombing, the hospital authorities decided to vacate the building in Posen and move all patients to an established hospital in the tiny village of Pudewitz, two hours east by train toward the interior of Poland. I wondered about the advisability of moving so much closer to the Russian front. But the authorities considered air raids the greater risk and thought Pudewitz a far less likely target than Posen.

Waldemar and Barbara Steinecker visited the following day and, true to their earlier promise to Hans, offered us their extra house in Hazelthal. Waldemar owned and managed a lumber mill and furniture factory there that provided employment for all the residents of that little Polish settlement.

I hesitated to accept their generous offer, realizing how often I would have to leave the children to visit Hans. However, I felt Hans would want me to accept.

* * *

For the next six months, therefore, the children and I lived in Hazelthal, occupying an improvised second floor apartment in an empty villa that Waldemar owned. At first, we drew our meals from the mill kitchen. When the mill whistle blew, we stood in line with all the town's people, food pails in hand. Eventually, the German authorities refused to allow us to continue that procedure because we lacked a connection with the mill.

Since I could purchase only a few staples in Hazelthal, I found it necessary to travel to Posen each week and bring back food supplies. The local residents relied on the mill kitchen or food grown in somebody's back yard during their short summer.

Traveling to and from Posen by train with my burden of food posed difficulties even on those infrequent trips when I could find a seat. An equally nagging annoyance was the constant military control of civilians as well as men in uniform: "Your travel permit, please! Your identification, please. Anyone carrying black market products? What's in that suitcase?"

I encountered the same aggravation at every major stop. Nor did it cease once the train got underway oh, no! They stalked through the coaches with surprising alacrity, looking for irregularities —spies, maybe. And the further eastward one went, the stricter the search.

Once, however, a rather coarse but jolly peasant woman relieved the grimness of the ritual with her daring. She wore a scarf, a tight, short wool jacket and at least six very long woolen skirts. When she sat, her abundant skirts gave her the appearance of a person with very heavy thighs.

The inspector eventually made his way to her side, and apparently suspected she hid something beneath her skirts. "And you, on what are you sitting?"

"Two hams," she replied, and then she giggled.

"For shame," said the blushing inspector, as he strode onward. Those of us seated in the same compartment laughed along with her, since she indeed sat on two big, beautiful smoked hams. We enjoyed her welcome show of courage in a very hostile land, so near the front.

Days drifted into weeks in Hazelthal, where we spent our time safe and happy. But it grew monotonous with nothing much to do, and we all just tried to live through the experience. In the end, either we would survive the devastating war or we would perish. But I believed firmly we would survive. Pondering that great question never proved fruitful—ideas and thoughts for our survival came from somewhere beyond ourselves every time we reached a low point. We followed something bigger than ourselves —I called it faith without understanding.

The children missed their father, whom they could no longer visit. To compensate for his absence, they dictated short messages which I took along on my trips to see him. At least once a week I joined my husband and delighted at his progress.

Hans shared a room with four young soldiers, all in about the same stage of convalescence as he. They really liked each other and constantly laughed and flung remarks and jokes back and forth. Sometimes, however, their taunts grew aggravating, a result of their pent-up frustrations and their emerging need for a more active life. Occasionally they even became explosive, and pillows, food and everything flew across the room.

"It is wise to knock and wait, even to open their door only a slit at first to announce oneself," the doctor told me smilingly one day as we happened to meet outside the closed ward, both wanting to go in and visit.

On my first visit to Hans after our move to Hazelthal, he asked for all the news. How were the children? Who was staying with them while I was with him? What was Hazelthal like—the food, the rooms?

"Hazelthal is two dozen simple, unadorned houses, a mill, one small store and a railroad station, all set down in the middle of a great prairie," I told him." The town boasts just one long street that turns to mud six inches deep in rainy weather and dries into stiff deep ruts when the rain stops. There's no paving anywhere, not even a sidewalk.

"The small populace has a limited supply of electricity and must boil and cool the water for use of any kind. What's more, I'd wager that no one in the village—except the Steineckers, of course—

ever heard of a bathtub," I said, laughing lightly. "Luckily, we have toilet facilities inside the house, although we must climb the narrow, very steep stairs to reach them."

As I spoke, Hans took my hand and intertwined his long fingers with mine, toying with my wedding ring and my diamond engagement ring, which both hung loose on my fingers. Then his face became troubled.

"What a way to spend your time, to pass your best years," he said. "No music, no literature, no singing for the children or you, no dancing for Irmgard, no piano or records. Still, we must be grateful we are alive." He sighed, and seemed withdrawn.

"And since we cannot furnish the music ourselves, we have it provided," I told him. "Listen to this, my dear, and tell me if it is not made to order. A Russian prisoner camp sits directly behind our house, on the edge of the settlement. Every evening at sundown or thereabouts, the prisoners sing.

"And how they sing.. sometimes sad, sometimes wild. The final song is always the same, full of longing for their freedom, their homeland, their loved ones. Their beautiful voices, so high in the tenor and so deep in the bass, are wondrous to hear, and we never miss it. Each night we wait for our serenade, and then we go to bed. Some day they will gain their freedom again, and so will we. All we can do is wait."

Hans liked my story, but suddenly became apprehensive.

"What if they escape and take refuge in your rooms? What you do? Oh, you really need me, and here I lie so unable to would help."

But I calmed him down and told him we were unafraid. "If the men did escape, they would immediately head for the Warthe River, visible on the horizon. They surely would not stay near enough to be caught again."

And then without waiting for his reaction, I gave him, as I usually did before leaving, the little notes from his children. If they filled him with nostalgia, he covered it well. He only smiled once more, squeezed my hand and said, "Our sweet bunch."

Yet I felt I detected a mute look of longing in his eyes. He felt thwarted, I knew, since he still had to lie and could not help.

On my next visit, I found Hans sitting on the edge of his cot, getting used to a vertical position.

"This is not the first time, and each day I can take it a little longer," he said. We could look forward to the beginning of crutches, he hoped.

As my visit ended, I promised to bring a surprise for Hans and his roommates on my next visit. They needed something new to think about, to anticipate, no matter how trivial. Then, when I stood to leave, Hans pressed into my hands an envelope, thick and sealed, and asked me to read it on the train going home. I agreed, and hurried off to catch that train.

Seated and settled an hour later, I opened Hans' letter and read. It contained all his pent-up longings, the more poignant because he had chosen his own native language to write in what he could not say. His beautiful command struck a chord deep in my being.

"Meine liebe, liebe frau (My dear, dear wife)," it began, "How shall I ever thank you enough for my life, for your love and for our children?"

Three full pages of devotion, so tender, so total, so simple and so fraught with meaning, followed by a terrible urge to be up and well again, to resume his role once more as the head of his home, the protector and provider.

How deeply he showed the almost unbearable frustration of the long, long convalescence—with nothing to do, nothing to see, nothing to hear or read, from morning till night only thinking, thinking, thinking. It was maddening, he said, especially in the light of increasingly menacing war developments. Would he get well fast enough to help us avoid being overrun by the Russian hordes—which, in his secret heart, he felt we would face eventually?

Hans' last paragraph contained a promise. He would make every effort to hurry his recovery. Given time and the chance, he would get well and strong and totally ignore his handicap. Just one more thing, however, I had to know: he faced another surgery as soon as his physical condition allowed.

I thought Hans would forgive me if my reflections upon finishing his letter extended beyond him and our children to include other family and friends: my parents and loved ones at home; the many in Germany and Poland who had become dear to me; and even the Russian prisoners, who sang away their woes each night before they fell asleep. With the world so terribly enmeshed, how would it ever untangle itself?

CHAPTER 31

A Slow But Steady Recovery

April - October, 1944

Each time I made the long trek to visit Hans in Pudewitz, I questioned the need to relocate his hospital so near the Russian front, with its dangers, discomforts and inconveniences. But my doubts came to an abrupt end on Pentecost Sunday, seven weeks after the first Allied bombing of Posen.

I began that day at our apartment in Posen. I had arrived a day earlier to find the town serene and quiet and the apartment clean and inviting, as always. My good cook Michaline was busy in the kitchen baking tiny cakes, using a windfall of shortening and flour and a few extra eggs. I planned to serve the delicacies to Hans and his roommates, along with real tea, as my promised surprise. And to make the treat extra-special, I decided to carry with me my best china tea set, a bit of refinement to contrast with the habitual hospital crockery.

At noon I started for the Posen railroad station, laden with my goodies. Just as I reached the entrance, the air raid alarm sounded. Only a few people stood nearby, and those with tickets ran for the trains. Those without hurried to the two ball-shaped air raid shelters bordering the wide ramp just outside the station entrance.

A quick decision sent me running to the ticket office. All trains would leave, regardless of schedules, to clear the station before the 12-minute warning ended. If I could yet reach my train...

Quick as lightning I bought the ticket and flew to my train's designated ramp. I arrived, scared and winded, just in time to see the doors close and the train move out, without me.

"Oh, no!" I cried aloud. "Couldn't you wait that one more second?" I called after that horrid train! My only remaining alternative was one of the just-passed shelters—quickly!

The first tiny concrete shelter was filled to capacity and locked; the second nearly so and desperately I squeezed inside the crowded shelter. No one made even the slightest suggestion of refusing me as someone barred the thick door.

In the quiet we waited fearfully. The children seemed especially terrified, packed so hard up against the standing grownups. Fortunately, light came through two tiny longitudinal slits high up in the concrete, not more than six by 18 inches, designed to give air as well as light.

"Here comes the first one," said a soldier standing in front of me. "An incendiary bomb—hear it?"

It struck nearby and the earth heaved, bouncing the shelter like the ball it was. A few people whimpered and cried softly, while others tried to comfort the terrified children, but no one screamed. Voluntary body functions became involuntary in those tense moments when more and more bombs fell and the slits in the room let in smoke instead of air. The stench with the smoke became intolerable. We coughed, sputtered, sneezed and gasped for breath, each long draw only increasing our agony. In short, it seemed no oxygen remained. We all swayed together, woozy, leaning against each other for support.

"That's all for now, open the door!" the soldier commanded. Someone questioned weakly, "The all-clear has not yet sounded."

"Open the door," he repeated, more forcefully. "We can close it again if they return this way."

Someone obeyed. Thank God! Air! Draft! Even if smoky!

"Close the door now," commanded the soldier once more. With

his good ears and well-trained hearing, he had detected our tormentors coming back. The tense moments and the fear returned, so terrifying I did not see how I could stand it. That time the bombs fell further away, and then—silence. A waiting and an anxious silence!

Finally, the "all clear" sounded. Spared once more, alive but numb, I realized that I still held my awkward package in my cramped hands, and all for nothing. No trip to Hans that day! Drained, I decided to go home and sleep.

The shelter cleared promptly, but I left less hastily. Vaguely I noticed air-raid wardens, dressed in special uniforms for protection, walking about in search of unexploded bombs. I had forgotten that possibility, and realized I should watch alertly for such a find as I dragged along.

Michaline overflowed with compassion when she saw me. "I hoped you had made it," she said. "'Der Herr' will know about the raid and worry if you do not appear at visiting hours. Can you not get word to him?"

I appreciated her genuine concern and explained that I knew of no way to contact Hans. He would have to trust for my safety and wait until the following day. Then, instead of sleeping, I phoned Horst and Eva, who likewise phoned others. Their spirits seemed as low as mine, and we all decided to meet and see a show or play, or anything. But even for that we could muster no enthusiasm. We felt washed out and on the verge of something dreadful. If Ivan ever got close enough, God help us. All of us knew it.

The next day I managed to make my way to Hans. Although he had worried a little, he had filled the time of my absence constructively.

"What do you suppose he did yesterday?" asked one of his buddies.

Georg Donner, the sunniest of them all, piped up with, "I died a thousand deaths just watching him, and today he wants us to go through the torture again he wants to demonstrate to you. I shall lie down and face the wall. I just cannot see him break his neck."

And then I saw the crutches leaning between the wall and the bed, and Hans gave me a mischievous smile.

"Want to see? I'll show you," he said, making an impulsive grab for the crutches.

"Not alone, for God's sake!" shrieked the boys. "Good God, ring for an intern."

The intern came and took the situation in stride—not a first, I gathered. He gave Hans the support he needed, but only that much. Although weak and horribly wobbly, Hans refused to give up.

"Open the door, I want to try the corridor," he insisted.

"My God, screamed Georg, "Don't let him take the stairs. He's likely to want to try them too."

A double amputee, Georg saw his own coming trials in his pal, for whom he had developed esteem and affection. I sat in the room waiting, and they confided to me that the doctor had promised Hans a vacation from the hospital, for a full week in late June, provided he developed enough dexterity with his crutches and his health continued to improve.

"Hans does not mean to tell you this," one of them said. "He wants to make sure first and then surprise you. He thinks you might worry, because afterward he must undergo another surgery. But you can take it, can't you?"

"Thanks, dear fellows, you bet I can take it. If the operation is inevitable, the sooner the better. I'll respect your confidence. He won't know that I know until he elects to tell me himself, okay?"

That time I felt relieved to leave Hans. Watching his "tottering progress", as his buddies put it, had unnerved me. With his rehabilitation begun, I knew he would plod on until he succeeded.

My description of Hans on crutches brought peals of laughter from the children when I rejoined them, and the tale provided a fine antidote for the sadness they had experienced during my absence.

Then their turn came to tell me the story of how some of our Russian prisoners had managed an escape. One of them indeed had taken refuge on our property, two had cut across the plains to the North on foot, and two had tried to swim the Warthe River and drowned in the whirlpools. Prison guards had caught the surviving escapees, returned them to the camp and whipped them thoroughly.

"Oh, Mother," our little Irmgard and Dieter cried simultaneously, as they alternated in describing the subsequent events. "They get whipped now at 'sing' time every night, and they cry. Wait, Mother, you'll hear. Such nice men. You know how they used to smile at us each morning as they marched by on their exercise. They have not marched since. Why do the guards punish them when they only want to go home?"

Poor little children! They sobbed, heart-broken over the fates of their "friends," while I wondered if I had left them at home unprotected and in danger? Barbara and Waldemar, whom we saw every few days, did not think so. They passed over the incident lightly, and since they too had a lovely daughter whom they cherished, I relied upon their judgment.

The reports I brought back of Hans pleased the Steineckers, and they thought it wonderful that before long he would leave the hospital on a visit.

"The steps of your apartment are too steep for Hans; he will not yet possess sufficient skills with his crutches," Waldemar commented. "I will arrange for a room in the mill for him and you during that week. Just let me know in time when he will arrive and we also will provide transportation from the railroad station."

Barbara, like myself, needed a bit more excitement in her life, so she looked forward to a few games of chess with Hans and a few evenings with "supper at our place."

* * *

Hans' anticipated vacation became a sort of open secret, and great fun. On each of my visits, Hans showed miraculous progress, yet he mentioned nothing. The boys, his roommates, watched with intense interest the little drama between us.

The day finally arrived. All excited, they shouted after him, "auf wiedersehen" as we entered the shay that took us to the train for Posen, where we would spend the night before proceeding to Hazelthal.

The two-hour train ride, the fuss and bother of shays before and after, and the steps to the third floor apartment in Posen left Hans extremely exhausted. But my soldier did not complain! Michaline welcomed Hans at the door by dropping to her knees and taking his hand in both of hers. Again and again she kissed it, as tears rolled down her cheeks. "For a German, he is such a good master," my little Polish cook later confided to me apologetically.

That day, no wish of his was too much. Michaline scuffled through the room, read his wants from his face, often before he asked, beaming with happiness. Hans wanted music, music, and more music—Brahms, Beethoven, Schumann, Chopin, Bruckner, Reger, symphony after symphony all afternoon.

Dinner was as tastily prepared as obtainable food allowed, and we indulged in our plentiful stock of champagne, letting it trickle down our throats in pure joy at our reunion. After dinner Horst phoned, and I answered.

"Thought I'd take a chance on finding you in Posen. Are you lonesome, need a champagne friend?" he asked.

"A delightful companion is here with me, Horst. Why don't you drop in and get acquainted?"

"Hmm," Horst said, speculating on my caller's identity. "I'll wager you'll not regret the effort. Come and see. Auf wiedersehen," I sang into the phone, hanging up without giving him time for a comeback.

If I knew Horst rightly, he'd die of curiosity and arrive quickly, and so he did. Michaline answered the ring, and barely managed to keep her balance as Horst swept her aside impulsively, literally tearing down the hall to the parlor door. We heard him hesitate. He knocked, then slowly opened the door, poking his nose around the corner. The two men faced each other grinning, Hans from his seat on one of the sofas. Without a word, Horst entered the room very dramatically and walked toward Hans, his eyes fastened on him, his hands behind his back.

"So that you know my joy to see you alive and well again, please accept my gift of a bottle of red champagne." He drew it forth and handed it to Hans, then could not restrain himself any longer. Putting both arms around Hans, he hugged.

"Nein, ist das schoen," he murmured. He turned sharply to me. "I said it was wonderful," he barked in mock anger, staring at me then hugging me tightly too, remarking how nearly it had all turned out otherwise.

With immense feeling, Hans told his friend that he knew of Horst's contribution to his survival. But Horst just stood looking intently at Hans.

"May I use the phone?" he asked.

"Gladly, yes."

And so it came about that more guests spent that evening with us for a sip and a chat. It seemed like old times, if you took it at face value and forgot for awhile about the war.

The next day we reached Hazelthal, where we spent a happy week even though it rained every day. The dust ruts in the street gave way to deep, slimy mud that caked our overshoes. Our clothes stayed damp and the rooms seemed cold; even the food was thin. But we were together!

Hans devoted himself to the children, who climbed up and about him, loving him, begging for games and stories. Before Hans' return, I had prepared the children for a daddy with one leg and on crutches. They took it just as I had described it—all except Bob. Older, more understanding and extremely sympathetic, he seemed a bit shy around his father.

"Dad," he finally asked one day, "What happened to your leg?"

Hans told him that a shard of shrapnel had hit his leg and made it real sick. "And anyhow, that leg always seemed to get in my way, so I told the doctor to snip it off." He laughed, but Bob did not, and I could not read his quiet inward reaction.

"And what did he do with it then? Throw it away?"

"Threw it away—in a trash can, or so I guess."

The children looked at each other and laughed, and Hans did too. I stood there devastated by his casual manner. Maybe having spoken with his fellow soldiers for so many months, perhaps such a flip conversation seemed commonplace, maybe even a consolation. But not for me.

However, the children dropped it just like that, and occasionally I saw them go to him and touch his trousered stump, then look up into his face tenderly.

As for me, I could only remember hearing Hans tell me that in East Prussia, where his sick leg was removed, the wounded soldiers had arrived by the hundreds, and the doctors had mended, sewed and amputated night and day unceasingly. Could I help visualizing all the arms, legs and whatnots assembled and sticking out of trash cans behind some hospital, so that the dream harassed me day and night? Until then I had never even considered that.

The stay in Hazelthal benefited Hans. True, his strength was sometimes taxed to the limit, but his resilience improved and he quickly "measured up" again. When the vacation finally ended, he refused my help for the return trip.

"I am a soldier, not a baby, remember? I don't need you! Maybe in a week, after the second surgery. With the nasty business over, I will look forward to seeing you, at least I expect so."

Those terse words did not sound like my Hans. At first I felt hurt, but should I? Was that not the philosophy of a strong man, with his confidence and equanimity recovered? It seemed so. To make sure, apparently he planned to use the trip back to the hospital as another test, a difficult one, of managing on his own.

If he mastered that, and he would, the new surgery and its aftermath could no longer frighten him, I thought to myself. It seemed he finally had realized how much courage it would take to get well, and he was gathering it.

When next I sat at Hans' hospital bedside, I saw no evidence that he had just undergone another operation. I did not need to ask of his health, since he obviously felt fine and in good spirits.

Waldemar Steinecker drove me for that visit. With his family away for the weekend, he felt lonely. Also, he wondered about Hans' welfare. Bob came with us, and although happy to see his father, he begged off from a sick visit to search for a water hole somewhere where he might get a swim.

The men quietly talked about the war. Earlier that summer the Allies had crossed the English Channel and invaded France, and were making steady progress against the German forces. News was equally grim on other fronts. The Allies had driven Germany out of Greece and were advancing steadily up the Italian peninsula, despite fierce resistance from German troops. And in the East, Russia was advancing steadily toward Poland.

Waldemar then made a disturbing announcement. Government officials had forcibly converted his mill into a glider factory, he explained. Whether he wanted it or not, that made him an integral part of the war effort.

In light of what both men believed lay ahead, Waldemar feared that a conqueror might some day hold him accountable. Most surely, he would eventually lose the property, with no possibility of reparation.

Devastated and feeling helpless, Waldemar had needed to talk with someone and thought of Hans. That, and not just loneliness, had motivated our trip to the hospital. But no matter. Waldemar was a pleasant companion and the ride equally as nice, requiring less expenditure of my own energy and giving me more time to visit with my husband.

As visiting hours came to an end, my escort rose to leave. Going from bed to bed, he shook each soldier's hand, sincerity emanating from him as he wished them well. They returned his good wishes warmly, and one especially spirited young soldier smiled up into his face.

"I don't see how Hans can stand to see his wife leave and go home with you." They all shouted with gaiety and Hans let off a roar.

"Don't worry, he'll take good care of her."

"That's just what I thought," answered my champion," and what chance do you have, Johnny boy, flat on your back?"

Waldemar laughed in appreciation. "Can't you see we have Bob for a chaperone?"

A few days later, I traveled to Posen for replenishment of food supplies. When I arrived at the apartment, Michaline said a gentleman had called twice, asking for me without leaving his name. The call came again.

"Here Carl Reuther," said the voice. "Is that you, Ruth?"

"Yes. Whatever are you doing in Posen, Carl?"

"Had a little time and thought I'd come and see you and the family. I am staying at the Posener Hof."

"And are you comfortable there?" I asked.

"Quite so."

"Well, then, please do join me for supper. But why wait until then? Can't you come now for a chat and a cocktail before dinner?"

He arrived wearing a uniform. Although not a combat officer, his duties kept him away from home. Rita and the children remained in their mountain villa in Bavaria, where they escaped the ravages of war but not the shortages of food and clothing nor the pain of separation. Somehow Carl managed every few months to pick up something extra for their hungry mouths, a situation not unlike ours when Hans had been in Posen and our family in Berlin.

Carl and I sat and chatted, enjoying a fine liqueur. As evening approached, we listened to records or just sat quietly, and I felt him soak up the home atmosphere. Later, Michaline served us a good supper. She served well, but somehow managed to convey her lack of sympathy for a male guest sitting in "her master's place."

Determined to enjoy his few remaining vacation days, Carl offered two interesting suggestions.

"Let's go visit Hans tomorrow; I'd really like to see how he's doing. And then in the evening, why don't you invite a group of your friends to join us, as my guests, for dinner at my hotel? We'll celebrate my birthday."

Noting my hesitation, he continued. "Nothing fancy, just a dinner consistent with wartime tradition. But we must celebrate, even if modestly, so long as we can. You said so yourself didn't you?" So I made the necessary invitations by phone, and Carl returned to his hotel.

As planned, we left the next morning for the hospital to visit Hans. I shall never forget the look of surprise and joy on Hans's face when Carl walked into the room. The reunion stirred the emotions of both men, those two good friends of many years. Cautiously, Carl drew Hans out in conversation, and as always, the topics veered toward business and politics. Then the doctor put in his appearance, and the subject turned to medicine. The doctor, whom I liked more each time we met, expressed much optimism about Hans and foresaw total recovery. Still, he doubted that he could dismiss Hans from care until November. Even then, he said, Hans might need to report to the hospital once a week for observation.

Our evening at the Posener Hof? Great! Our party of eight occupied a room to ourselves. As always, Horst and Eva arrived late, and the others seemed a bit formal with Carl, whom they had never met before. Carl told them of our visit with Hans that afternoon and the doctor's pronouncement.

When the missing guests arrived, the tension eased. Always a merrymaker, Horst kept any party he attended from falling flat. Of course, he also allowed himself "poetic license," which he expected his wit to excuse or cover, and for the most part it did. True to himself that night, and in excellent form, he bubbled with mirth.

When he angled his tall, slight figure into contortions demonstrating the humor, the laughter found no end.

With the dinner finally over and much wine imbibed, Horst stood with a full glass of champagne in his hand.

"Will you all join me," he began, "in a toast to our host Carl Reuther and his hotel."

"Happy birthday, Carl, and thanks for the food and drink," we all said with Horst, but then I added, "This is not Carl's hotel, he just stays here."

"Just so he stays here and not with you."

Did I not say that sometimes Horst could be a rascal? But then, sensing he may have overstepped the boundaries of propriety, he mumbled, "Don't see why he should have it any better than I do."

That lovable, presumptuous rogue, I thought, but Carl just laughed. Changing the subject, Carl announced, "I hold in my pocket a few real coffee beans."

Horst, maybe a bit grateful for the gentlemanly rejoinder, quickly and with mock-surreptitiousness pulled a small, flat bottle of brandy from his side pocket. "Let's go to Ruth's house and have Michaline cook coffee and spike it with brandy," he suggested.

A day later, Carl returned to Berlin for new duties, never telling me their nature. Again, I did not ask, sure of the futility of doing so. I only knew that they disallowed the time for a visit with his family in South Germany. Thus, Rita traveled to see him, a visit with hazards. Berlin was experiencing the most horrible of air raids.

Rita came to see me on her way to Berlin and stayed in our Posener home as my guest. She remained for several days, quietly, serenely, going to the hospital with me to see Hans. She then persuaded me to travel to Berlin with her for a day, despite my terrible fear of the alarms.

On the day of our leaving, we sat and chatted, fully dressed and ready to go, resting on the sofas in the living room until 3 a.m. Then we walked the long way through the dark, dark streets of Posen to the railroad station—another trip for me at that ungodly hour.

Carl still sat at breakfast when we reached his private quarters in Berlin, but before long he left for his duties. Rita and I slipped into his unmade bed for an hour of rest, but we could not sleep. The remainder of the day we spent wandering through the nearby ruins. Our luck held, and all day long no alarm sounded—not during supper, nor even before both Carl and Rita put me aboard the train for Posen at 9 p.m. that night. Hungry and very tired, I felt a huge relief when my train moved out and away from that big, vulnerable city.

*   *   *

Midnight in Posen. How I dreaded that half hour walk alone through the stark darkness from the train station to our apartment. My alert ears caught no sounds other than the echo of my own shoes as I hurried down the middle of the deserted streets. I would not relax, I knew, until I entered my own apartment. Even the spiral steps leading to it lay shrouded in pitch blackness. I could have passed anyone and never known.

A small light burned in my parlor, and a note lay on the table! "Come at once, baby very ill. Grandmother Armsberger with maid and children.

"Oh, no," I said aloud, letting myself down into a chair beside the table. Dog tired, I wanted nothing more than to fall into bed and sleep, but no use to contemplate that. A sick feeling of fear arose once more in my throat. What was wrong with our baby? Did the Steineckers call a doctor? Did Hazelthal even have one, I wondered, realizing I never had questioned that before. How quickly could I get there, and what could I do once I arrived? Whatever, I had to return to the train station at once.

I wrote a note to Michaline and rose wearily to gather a few belongings. Then, leaving the light burning, I closed the door behind me and retraced my steps in the dark. After two days and nights without sleep, I was far too tired, and too worried about baby Hans Bernhard, to feel afraid.

A dim blue light provided the only illumination in the empty station, forcing me to stand only inches from the slate schedule board to read the chalked-in listing of expected arrivals and departures. Leaving for Hazelthal at 2 p.m., it said —12 hours later. That would never do, I thought, looking around.

At the one ticket window still open, a tired, elderly man leaned against a post half reclining on a stool. I walked over to him.

"Excuse me, sir. I have a problem. I must get to Hazelthal fast."

Without answering, he pointed to the blackboard.

"My dear sir, can you help me figure out a quicker way? It's an emergency."

"Emergency, emergency," he muttered. "Always an emergency. Well, let me see."

He leaned over and brought up from under his counter a little blue book, and began leafing through the pages. "Hazelthal, Hazelthal," he repeated, licking his thumb with its claw-like nail, trying to loosen the thin sheets, one from the other.

"Well, now," he said at last. "A train leaves here at 4 a.m. going to Warsaw. Take it as far as Wreschen and change to a train going back on an angle south-southwest to Hazelthal. You should arrive at 10 o'clock yet this morning. That's the best I can do."

"Thanks; that sounds fine. I'll take a ticket."

Sleeping soldiers filled the train I boarded that morning, floor and all. A seat? I didn't even get that far. The aisle near the door would do. I sat on my suitcase, knowing it would bulge and might even break under my weight, but I did not care.

As it grew light, the soldiers roused and stretched. Those nearest me seemed surprised to find me in their midst. They said little, but smiled a sort of "good morning."

One by one they hauled rations out of their knapsacks and munched their breakfast. Next to me an observant young man noted that I did not do the same, so he drew his knife and sliced a nice fat piece of bread for me from a long loaf. A slice of sausage came the same way. It would have been unkind to refuse, although I hesitated to take food from a soldier who might need it so much more than I.

To the question in his eyes, I answered I was on an emergency call to my sick baby and dreadfully worried.

"I know how you must feel," he said quietly. "I have two of my own. My wife is with them." A prayer filled both our hearts, how appropriate at this moment were the words of the lovely Negro spiritual "Let us break bread together upon our knees."

When my station came, my new friend bade me a quiet "Auf wiedersehen and alles gute," which I returned.

* * *

On arriving, I found Grandmother Armsberger with the children. Hans Bernhard had suffered convulsions but was better, they said. He recognized me and smiled sweetly as I greeted him, but he looked sleepy and weak, and the eyes that gazed back at me from his puffy face lacked alertness.

No physician was available at the moment in Hazelthal, and Grandmother Armsberger agreed with me that the baby needed one. I knew I had to get him to Posen, but taking him on the train presented a frightful risk. The noise and confusion might bring on another attack, and then?

I determined to beg Waldemar to take us in his car, recently converted to a wood burner due to the lack of gasoline. All that wood smoke and soot swirling in the air around us would make for a messy drive, and the journey would require frequent stops to stoke the boiler. But it offered my only hope.

On a workday, I knew I would find Waldemar in his mill. However, since he manufactured a war commodity, I also knew that a Nazi liaison probably watched him carefully. How could he possibly take time, I wondered, to do something for me, requiring use of his car, even though it involved no gasoline?

When I finally gathered the courage to make my request, Waldemar's ready assent surprised me. I admitted my misgivings, and he quickly reassured me.

"Such an act falls under the category of assisting the family of a severely wounded soldier," he asserted bravely. "Gladly do I assume any resulting risk."

We drove to Posen and met with a medic, a friend of Dr. Walter Kleeberg, who had promised to assist us during Walter's absence on the Russian front. He examined Hans Bernhard and told me what I must do for my little one. For the next week, Michaline and I watched him constantly, and no more attacks occurred. The baby's illness prevented me from visiting Hans for awhile, but he received my letters giving account of our progress.

We returned to Hazelthal once more after the baby recovered, but not for long. Doubts about the feasibility of a further stay, in light of the baby's illness, constantly gnawed at me. Then, a sudden assault of illness suffered by Irmgard confirmed my decision to return to Posen. High fever and nausea hit her without warning, and her abdominal pains became so severe that she cried and pleaded with us for help.

That time we found a doctor in Hazelthal and he responded to our summons. A very little man, he settled himself on a straight-backed chair, his short legs dangling, but refused to either diagnose or prescribe. As a Pole, he would not lay himself open to criticism, fearing I might have him shot if his handling proved incorrect. I insisted that such a course had never entered my thinking. But he remained unswayed, and only suggested we take her to Posen or Wreschen—even though he knew no trains ran at night. Angrily, I dismissed him.

What should I do? Might her illness be appendicitis or perhaps an amoeba? Did high fever such as hers accompany appendicitis? I thought not, and so assumed she probably had contracted an amoeba.

I sat with her through the night, knowing nothing else to do and not wanting to try the wrong thing. Toward morning her fever fell a bit and continued to recede throughout that day and the next. Her pain also left—but why? Was that dangerous? I did not know.

Irmgard continued to brighten and on the fourth day asked to get up. On the fifth, we left for Posen and the hospital for tests, which all proved negative. We never learned what caused her illness, but as a precaution the surgeon removed her appendix to avoid a recurrence at a time when it might take her life.

The episode confirmed my decision to return with the children to Posen, where we could access competent medical care and would not be at the mercy of erratic train schedules. While Irmgard continued her convalescence, I returned to Hazelthal to complete the moving arrangements. I left a few of our possessions for Waldemar to bring to Posen whenever convenient, but took with me our maid from Hazelthal, Nina.

The experiment of living in Hazelthal had proved worth trying, and the arrangement offered many favorable points. But during our six months there, Posen was bombed only twice, and neither time too seriously. The risk seemed insufficient to warrant such remoteness from medical care. Besides, Hans' doctor had hinted that he might soon allow Hans to come home to live, with the stipulation of a return once a week for control.

One person seemed especially happy to see us back in Posen again our loyal and willing servant Michaline. And when the day finally came for me to bring Hans home, Michaline was as excited as any of us. She helped me pack a civilian suit and overcoat for him in a suitcase. It made an extremely heavy load, so I took Nina with me to help carry.

Smiles wreathed Michaline's face when she bid us farewell as we left. She knew that when next I walked through that door, "the master" would accompany me.

CHAPTER 32

Hans Comes Home

October - December, 1944

In the end, Hans reached home long before we did. He arrived in a little automobile owned and driven by Georg Donner, his paraplegic roommate who left the hospital under terms similar to Hans', and at the same time.

I learned of it only after Nina and I had reached Pudewitz and made the long walk to the hospital, dragging our heavy load. Nearing our destination, we saw a tiny vehicle approaching us at a speed greater than advisable on those cobblestone streets.

As the car passed us, a head and hand poked out of the little window and I recognized Hans' wide grin. He waved and shouted, "See you in Posen." I also recognized his companion, and noticed as they flashed by that both wore uniforms. Evidently, Hans had not needed civilian clothes after all. Our effort in carrying all that weight for all that distance had come to nothing.

We set the suitcase down with sighs that were half exhaustion and half exasperation, and rested. At least we had two hours to make the 15-minute walk back to the station and catch the westbound train for Posen.

"Why didn't they stop and take that heavy suitcase with them?" I thought out loud, forgetting my companion. Nina suggested that perhaps the car lacked room to carry more than two men and their crutches. Her explanation seemed probable, but still I felt indignation and anger. How unlike Hans to be so inconsiderate. Had the Army and all his dreadful experiences changed him? My rancor and fury grew during our return trip to the railroad station and with every step of the long, tiring walk home Posen. I trudged on, hungry and exhausted.

With just a few steps more to go, all of a sudden I knew I did not want to go home. As a matter of fact, I did not want to ever go home again. I sent my maid dragging our burden alone as best she could, with the message that I still had an errand to do, while I dropped down on a bench in the park-like square across from our home and fought with myself.

I resolved to settle my internal battle right then, that day, knowing that more than my exhaustion and anger over the afternoon's affair needed quelling. I faced a much larger, much harder issue than that, one I had refused to confront earlier.

With Hans' return, I knew that a normal conjugal life with my husband would resume. Such wonderful, tender moments had formed the basis of a marriage as satisfying and beautiful as any wife could experience, and I loved my Hans with all my heart.

But all my life, I had cringed at contact with anything, anyone, not physically perfect, not physically whole. I remembered saying to him when he left for his Army life, "Darling, come back to us, no matter how. We need your spirit. " I had said that despite my aversion for physical imperfection, assuming I would cope with that if and when the time came. Maybe I believed it never would—but it had. I could not face it, I told myself, and yet I must!

As I sat crying, passersby took notice but did nothing. In those war times, a sobbing woman on the streets was no unusual sight. Finally, the streetlights turned on as night fell. Chilled through in spite of my seal-lined coat, I still sat. Across the street I saw the lights of my home, and I looked at them and then away again repeatedly. In that home Hans waited all unsuspecting and thinking only of his wonderful wife, when she wasn't so wonderful at all.

I knew but one solution. To face anything, one began by doing just that. So, I finally got up and walked home. My husband, if he noticed my tear-stained face, assumed I wept for joy, and that was good. Never, never, never should he ever feel rejected for the maiming he suffered in the service of his country. I would conquer my aversion.

November and December remained dark and dismal—not unusual in that part of the world. We tried to keep the lack of sunshine from disturbing our equilibrium by creating our own internal glow, but that became increasingly hard to do. Gaiety required peace of mind, good friends, good food and wine along with a bit of song. We suffered no shortage of friends and song, but the scarcity of food became urgent.

Daily life turned into a scavenger hunt for any and every extra edible, down to primitive barley and blood sausage and even horse meat and cats—the latter far more acceptable when labeled rabbit. Coal for cooking also was in desperately short supply.

One could, of course, stay in bed to conserve heat, but who dared? It took alertness and preparedness to answer the ever- more-numerous alarms that sounded day and night. Yet no bombs fell and rumors circulated—correctly, it appeared—that ammunition supplies were being dropped once again and stored in hideouts in the countryside. For friend or foe, we knew not, but probably for foe. That disturbing assumption, added to the too- apparent deterioration of every aspect of life, was inconceivably frightening.

As Christmas neared, our coal supply dwindled so noticeably that we used but a handful of briketts a day—a few in the parlor kachel-ofen, which kept us warm if we huddled together, and some for the simplest cooking in the kitchen. Once in a while we heated bath water on the coal stove in the kitchen. When poured into an ice cold tub in an ice cold room, the water cooled quickly, necessitating a brief plunge. Like in the Old West, one tubful served the entire family.

In spite of all privation, we stayed healthy. Hans visited his business acquaintances at the bank and the remains of the Treuhandstelle, and kept stimulated. He really made a handsome sight, my tall, lanky Panzer-funker (tank telegrapher), as he swung down the street on his crutches wearing his black uniform and cocky hat. People stopped to watch him and probably hoped with me that his crutches would not slide out from under him on the icy pavements.

During the holidays Hans received an unexpected visit from two men in Panzer uniform. Michaline ushered them in and, after a moment of hesitation, the strangers and Hans gave out glad cries of greeting. Hans quickly rose and stood supported on his crutches, and I too greeted them, assuming rightly that they were comrades of Hans' from the Russian front.

With a few hours to spare in Posen, they had remembered that Hans lived there and had decided to look him up. They brought news of interest to Hans. But first, their visit called for a snack and a bottle of champagne, with toasts and well wishes all around.

Hans' friends knew that he had been wounded, but were completely unaware of the resulting complications.

"Now you are at home with your loved ones again and need not return to the front," said one, while they both wondered in their minds and hearts what lay ahead for themselves.

"You were lucky even then, Hans, and we, too," said one buddy. "Just after you fell, Paul and I took two badly worn-out jeeps back of the lines for repairs, with orders to return after the work was finished. During our absence, a German-speaking Russian, impersonating a high ranking German officer and carrying falsified orders from Berlin, took command of our division and led it into captivity.

"This sort of thing happens more and more. The front looks terrible, and we think you and your family should not stay here in the East. In fact, we urge you to leave. No one wants to believe us, and we risk court martial to tell the truth. Worst of all, after 10 days of furlough, we must go right back into that inferno."

In spite of the boisterous laughing and the hearty handshaking when time came for their leave-taking, grimness edged the humor. Once more events forcefully had showed us the handwriting on the wall. Our luck had held in the past, but would it survive the terrible menace we still faced? What must we do? And where should we go? Berlin seemed an awful alternative.

Christmas and New Year found us still undecided, living in our Posener home and observing the holidays in the company of a few good friends, with some of the spirit. Our supply of champagne still remained, since I had used little during Hans' absence.

We put on a festive front for the children, who remained uninhibited and gay. But once they retired to their beds, we sobered down with trusted friends to renewed discussions of what we knew of the various fronts—including the news brought by Hans' two comrades.

As they had predicted, the Russian front came nearer day by day, with the Polish plains affording no obstacle. The Nazis issued hopeful-sounding reports, but we concluded those amounted to no more than unfounded statements of optimism by the Propaganda Ministerium. But why the lies? To build up hope? Prevent panic? Why did Hitler seem to want to keep us there?

We refused to believe their claims that "very special weapons nearing perfection will rescue us yet." Sitting nearer the front than those in Berlin, we thought we also were closer to the right judgment. Our forebodings told us we were in a last calm before the fury. For the millionth time, we asked ourselves, what shall we do? Where shall we go to survive? And what, if anything, can we save besides our lives?

CHAPTER 33

We Flee Approaching Russian Tanks

January 1945

In the next days, pandemonium swept Posen. Everyone talked only about plans for leaving. Some lacked a place to go, and officials refused to grant a departure permit to anyone who lacked a definite destination and a real place to stay.

Frantically, these unfortunate ones begged those with destinations to take them along. They tried to line up any possible type of transportation—horse carts, carriages, even straw-covered flat boards drawn by horses or oxen. Yet few actually left the city; most seemed too nervous, much too agitated to make up their minds.

We too, felt uncertain about our next step, but began making the necessary preparations. Hans phoned the headmaster of Bob's school and explained cautiously that we might leave Posen (one did not spread rumors). If the school disbanded, Hans said, Bob was not to be sent back to Posen but to our home in Berlin. The headmaster said he understood. Hans then decided to return to the hospital to try for an official dismissal.

In the meantime, forewarned that Posener children soon might be evacuated, I waited in line with mothers of other large families for an official permit to leave the city. After four hours, I secured the precious permit and dashed for the bank.

On arriving, I looked on in astonishment and then dismay as I saw a double line several blocks long leading to the doors of the bank.

"I'll never make it," I groaned aloud. "A run on the bank—why did I not foresee this?" I continued my conversation with myself: "There's a way around everything, they say. Move quickly, young lady, move quickly."

The sight of a guard at a rear door gave me an idea. That door led directly to the office of the manager, a man who had been a guest on occasion in our home. But he knew Hans far better than he knew me. Would he remember me? And even if so, he might think me presumptuous to ask his help. But Hans' absence left me no other choice.

The guard announced me to Herr Behrendt. "Guten Tag, Frau Bohle, what can I do for you today?" he asked politely.

"Hans is still in the hospital, but I expect him back today or tomorrow. He asked me to withdraw RM 3,000 of the RM 25,000 on deposit in our account. You know that we may have to leave Posen."

Herr Behrendt looked at me gravely. "I do not mind telling you that our reserves here in Posen are limited. In light of that long line waiting outside, RM 3,000 for one family is a large sum. Yet I concede your right to ask for that much. If you will please return through this back door in one hour, I shall try to give you what you asked."

I returned home through streets filled to the brim with refugees. For days, caravans of vehicles drawn by horses or oxen had arrived in Posen from further east. Everywhere animals stood unharnessed and blanketed, with feed bags over their noses. People moved about dressed in every conceivable type of clothing for warmth—long, heavy coats, mitts, far caps, mufflers, boots and even cut-up carpet or blankets wrapped around their feet. They set up primitive cooking paraphernalia (hibachis) to heat a bit to eat, and kept the tiny fires burning through the night.

The big city square at the entrance to the railroad station was packed with people waiting for trains. Most of them came from Lodz, near the Russian border. They stood or sat on suitcases, filled knapsacks or any old sack. Women and children, the old and infirm, prepared to spend the snowy night under open skies.

At our apartment, thank God, I found my husband waiting for me. The doctor had kept Hans for five days, and then allowed him only a three day leave of absence to take us to Berlin.

"But don't worry, Cherie. I'll wager that in three days, the hospital will be in the process of evacuation. I have no intention of returning, and in this confusion, not one soul will notice."

Horst came to tell us he planned to leave the next day. Eva and their children would follow by horse and straw-filled wagon, thereby rescuing some of their possessions.

"I can get you a horse and wagon, too, Hans. Do you want it?" he asked.

"No sir," Hans answered emphatically. "I want a faster way. We shall try the station and train tonight."

"You'll never make it; you'll never get through that jostling mob, not even to the entry—let alone to the ticket office," Horst replied.

Hans looked to me for confirmation.

"I'm afraid Horst is right, especially with luggage," I answered. "But of course if you wish, we shall try, without luggage—or maybe with just one suitcase?"

An hour later I returned to the bank and luckily received my RM 3,000. Now we had a permit and some money. Home again, I packed a suitcase and Horst hired a Pole to take it to the station, who promised to wait for us there.

* * *

Then Horst, Hans von Papen and Waldemar Steinecker arrived. Two days earlier, Waldemar had sent Barbara, his daughter and Mrs. Armsberger from Hazelthal by horse and wagon with as many of their possessions as they could manage, and some of ours. They had not yet arrived, and Waldemar was very nervous.

In the midst of all the tumult and confusion, the air raid alarm sounded. We hardly took notice, our senses were so numbed. But later we learned that the mob outside the train station—the man supposedly guarding our things among them—had run for cover and left all their belongings unprotected on the pavement. Once again, no bombs fell, but when the people emerged from shelters after the all-clear, all the luggage, including our suitcase, had disappeared.

Trains left infrequently and at irregular times for Berlin, each packed to more than capacity. Yet there was no diminishing the crowd that gathered and waited. We remained at home, out of the crush, while Horst, Hans von Papen and Waldemar debated what to do. Then Horst proposed a possible solution to our dilemma.

"You can take my little Fiat Topolino, if you can get it fixed and find some gasoline," he said.

"And I know a mechanic," volunteered Georg Donner, who also had come to call.

To this, Hans von Papen piped up with an offer. "If you can make it go, park it in front of your house in the morning and I'll siphon five gallons of gasoline into it from my truck."

Gratefully, Hans bade them to join us in a modest repast, and then he, Horst and Georg Donner started out on the difficult job of finding the mechanic and some parts. This proved very trying for Hans, so slow and handicapped compared with his once quick, dynamic movements. After almost a year in hospitals and in bed, he lacked stamina and grew fatigued much more easily than he would admit or wished to show. But he pressed on, balancing on one leg and crutches, determined to make this plan work since it seemed about the only one left to us. Long past nightfall the men worked, but by morning they had accomplished their aim and the little vehicle stood outside our door.

"It runs, but we could not repair the faulty starter," Hans

explained. "If the motor dies, the car must be pushed manually to get the engine going again.

"I'll take on that job," I promised, but Hans thought if the need arose, we would find someone along the road to help us. He visualized the road to Berlin as already crowded.

The congestion in the Posen streets seemed greater than the day before, if possible, and the conglomeration hardly left room to move between vehicles. Horses and oxen stood everywhere and in all directions. Edible animals had joined the throng, and the trampled snow was thick with their defecation. People stood stamping and beating their arms around their bodies for warmth, with hardly a forward movement.

Hans was anxious. "Cherie, let's pack now so we're ready when Hans von Papen comes by with the gasoline, if he can get through at all."

He stood downstairs alongside the little four-wheeled "hopeful," leaning heavily on his crutches and keeping watch for the promised, precious, indispensable gasoline. We did not for one moment speak of what would happen if our plan misfired, or if somewhere along the way we stalled and couldn't continue. We did not dare to think of anything but a successful journey.

I packed two knapsacks, which we strapped onto the front fenders. Next we piled quilts and blankets in the empty space back of the only two seats, to create a place for Irmgard cramped, of course, but the only choice. She would hold our baby, lying snug in a long white sheepskin coat zipped up to his chin, while Dieter sat on my lap. Hans somehow would drive with just one leg.

"Children," I called, "Come. We must get ready to go to Berlin."

They considered it a lark when I undressed them and then dressed them again in three layers of underwear and more than one of everything, until they wore so many clothes they could hardly move.

With the little remaining coal, Michaline roasted a rabbit—a gift from someone. She wanted us to stay and eat, but we told her we had to reach Berlin before nightfall. Hans gave her money, bade her to take good care of everything and said we would return in five days. He told her this to give her reason to fight for our possessions if looters appeared. We hoped that within those five days we might find some way to rescue some of the more valuable items.

We also asked Michaline what she would do if the Russians came.

"Go barfuss to Apolonitze," to live with her sister, she said in her halting German. Hans knew she meant to say she would go "by foot" to her sister, not "barefoot," as she actually had said. Correcting her, he added gently, "German language, hard language." She grinned sheepishly.

What did the Poles think of the fleeing Germans, knowing that the next siege might destroy Posen? The attitude of Horst's maid was typical. When he offered to take her into Germany with his family, she declined.

"Poland ruled once before by Russians. I work, nothing happen. Then come Germans. I work, nothing happen. Now come Russians again. I work some more. Nothing happen so long I work," she explained. But how long could Michaline, already more than 70 years of age, stand up under the Russians' kind of work?

Hans von Papen arrived as promised, with five gallons of siphoned gasoline that he poured into the tank of our little borrowed car. Then with the promise that we would meet again—somehow, somewhere, some day—we bade each other an emotional farewell.

It proved no easy task to get out of Posen as we threaded our way slowly through the dismal multitude of people, animals and vehicles. Once on the open road, however, we were amazed to find no traffic. Occasionally during the cold drive we passed lone sentries. They carried radios, binoculars and guns and wore white uniforms that gave protective camouflage amidst the five- foot snowdrifts.

Always they called to us, "How far the Russians?" Our answer, "Eighteen kilometers east of Posen," left them speechless, and we were equally dumbfounded by their lack of information.

We did not stop to talk, but pushed on through the thick ice and snow until finally we reached the eastern outskirts of Berlin. As we prepared to cross the whole city from east to west rim, we prayed, "God be with us. Help us find our way through this tortured and twisted city and reach our home without an air raid."

As darkness descended, the five occupants of our little Topolino stood at the entry of our home and surprised our tenant, Mr. Schuetzendorf, with a request for admittance. Although he had known this might happen, he seemed reluctant to accept the reality. Despite his unwillingness, however, he could not refuse to take us in. Moreover, he no doubt realized that if we were among the first to leave Posen, refugees from that city soon would overrun Berlin.

Mrs. Schuetzendorf came to the door to find out what kept her husband. When she heard, she invited us in and graciously conducted us to the three rooms on the third floor, as our lease stipulated should just such an emergency arise. She also turned over to us the second bath, on the second floor, ignoring her husband's complaint that doing so encroached on their privacy. We agreed not to impose on their hospitality and to keep to ourselves in every way possible.

Cooking facilities? The kitchen could accommodate only one family, they insisted. They made an exception, however, for the baby's food, which their maid would prepare. For the rest of us, Mr. Schuetzendorf suggested a "good enough little eating place down about one-half mile on the Heerstrasse."

He chose to ignore how hard the walking would be for Hans, and immediately I realized how quickly fate could transform one from a respected citizen to an unwanted refugee. Clearly, he and his wife, living in a nice warm home most comfortably, wanted to keep us from the kitchen to avoid revealing the extent of the peacetime asylum they enjoyed in the very middle of a wartime inferno.

In the three bedrooms on the third floor we found only three beds remaining. Old, mediocre mattresses took the place of the beautiful new ones we had left earlier. With no bed linens available, we resigned ourselves to getting along with the one blanket apiece we had brought with us. Thanks to Michaline's foresight, the baby would sleep comfortable and warm in the long zipped-up sheepskin coat.

We also felt grateful that the whole house was heated although we could not stop wondering how Mr. Schuetzendorf managed to finagle enough coal, since we knew how much it took. But why bedevil ourselves with questions, since we could not answer them anyway? Instead, we used some of our remaining gasoline to drive to the small cafe on the Heerstrasse. Later that night, we each rolled up in a blanket on top of an unmade bed for the first time in our lives.

* * *

The following morning we all awoke a little surprised to find ourselves in Berlin. It also was the first of many mornings in the several years to come that my first thoughts upon awakening were to wish I need not.

Quickly dressing, I went down to the first floor and found the baby's food ready. Irmgard and Dieter then walked with me to the cafe and helped me carry breakfast back for Hans. Later that morning Hans drove to the Spandau Police to register for food cards. When he returned, we crossed the street to see our dear next door neighbors, Franisch and Wally Grubert.

Still recovering from a heart attack, Franisch joined us in their parlor despite the physical strain our visit imposed on him. From the very beginning, he had viewed Germany's war prospects pessimistically. Now, our reports from the East seemed to confirm his assessment.

"I told you long ago that our Air Force is a farce—no support at all. No fault of theirs, you understand, but a result of poor judgment on the part of those political fools who think they know everything best and will not listen to the military. Believe me, I know something about it," he insisted.

He paused to catch his breath, tremendously excited, and that was not good for him. His next words tumbled out of his mouth like mush, almost incoherently: "We are on the edge of the end, and it will be terrible."

We all sat stunned. In my lap I held socks I had intended to mend, but his words left me so overwrought I could not even thread my needle. Thoughts about the end of the Reich and what that would entail for us, the hopelessness and suffering we all would have to face, seemed more than I could bear.

Worse yet was my anxiety concerning Bob's whereabouts. A severe pain knifed through my chest at the thought of him, alone and unprotected, and I feared my heart would break. In the utter silence I heard someone sobbing and was startled to realize that I was the one who wept.

Wally broke the mood. She gasped, jumped up and ran for the window.

"Look who is coming down the street," she exclaimed excitedly, heading quickly for the door. The rest of us watched from the window as our son Bob shuffled slowly down the street, bedraggled and exhausted and weighed down by a heavy suitcase.

For a brief second I stood rooted in place, weak and sick with relief, then with Hans and the children I rushed to join Wally at the door. Seeing everyone standing in the Grubert's entrance, Bob walked right over to their house and set down his luggage in the hall. The poor boy allowed the hugs and emotion, but just stood there eyeing us silently, too worn out to take part in our joy at seeing him again.

Wally quickly warmed some soup and cut a slice of bread for him, and after Bob had eaten, he quietly told us his story. As expected, the school had closed. But instead of sending Bob to Berlin, as promised, the headmaster had sent him back to Posen, directly into the line of fire.

Bob had reached Posen at 2 o'clock the prior afternoon and had gone directly to our apartment. Michaline told him we had left for Berlin and added that he could stay, since she expected us back in five days. Instead, Bob had decided to join us in Berlin. He asked Michaline for money, which she claimed she did not have, but the janitor willingly lent him RM10.

Keenly aware of the tumult in the streets, Bob had started quickly for the railroad station. On arriving, he had encountered a milling crowd so thick that it took the greatest of effort to worm his way to the station entrance and, with further tenacity, to the ticket office. Fare in hand, he had slithered through the mob to a waiting train and crawled into the corner of the back platform. There he had seated himself on his suitcase and made himself small and inconspicuous.

"So many people crowded in and stood in front of me, no one noticed me," Bob said. "I stayed quiet all evening and all night, a long, long time. My train left Posen at 4 o'clock yesterday afternoon and did not reach Berlin until 10 o'clock this morning."

He suddenly became emotional as he continued his tale.

"Oh, Mother, oh, Dad, it was horrible. The children cried, people became ill, some fainted and they could not move in the packed car. Standing people even filled the toilet rooms. And the freezing cold! My hunger made me begin to feel sick, too, with all that smell.

"One lady said her baby was dead, then she laughed like a crazy one, opened the window and threw it out into the snow." His audience gasped, and he stared at us with sad, sad eyes but did not cry. Maybe he had already, but we did not ask him.

"I'm glad I found you," Bob continued. "In Berlin, all I could remember was that we lived in Pichelsdorf, but by asking the streetcar conductor and recalling certain landmarks, I made it."

Hans put his arm around his son's shoulders. "Bob, we are so proud of you, so very proud of your resourcefulness," he said.

At those words, Bob looked up into his father's face and smiled. I am sure he had not realized our frantic concern for his welfare, since he took his own actions as a matter of course. How lucky that he had refused to believe we would return to Posen. With the family reunited again, I vowed to keep it that way.

Each subsequent day brought visits from Posener friends. They came and sat with us on the unmade beds in the third floor rooms, very quietly discussing the present and speculating on the future.

One visitor carried a message from Herr Behrendt of the Posener Bank. Despite his efforts to bring us more of our money, all of the bank's remaining funds and valuable papers had been transferred to a bank in Leipzig. The knowledge that we could count on no more money from the Posener bank caused my heart to flutter and my imagination to run wild. What method of transfer was used, and how much of the valuables really reached Leipzig?

During the first three days after our arrival in Berlin, one of Hans former colleagues at the Treuhandstelle decided to return to Posen in a borrowed truck, hoping to rescue some of his belongings. He offered to bring back some of our things, too, if he got through. But his try failed; Russian tanks had ringed Posen. It was rumored they were near Berlin as well.

Charlotte Kleeberg came to see us, too. She and Walter also had returned to Berlin with their two children and were staying temporarily in her mother's home. Charlotte thought our baby seemed not well and took him home with her, so Walter could examine the child.

Air raids haunted the city day and night during the 10 days we remained in Berlin. At these times, instead of retreating to our own basement, we joined the Grubert's on a trek to a bombed-out factory basement shelter, a ruin in the middle of a Russian prisoner camp not far from the Heerstrasse. The roof of the factory remained intact. On the floor, benches on either side of a central aisle provided a sitting area, but water filled the aisle itself to a depth of nine inches. Someone had piled bricks in the water and laid boards across them to keep our feet dry. Little light penetrated the dim cellar, and whoever happened to sit near the entrance kept watch.

During our frequent trips to the shelter, we renewed acquaintances with many former neighbors and friends. Some had lost husbands and fathers, and we encountered personal tragedy everywhere.

One morning near 5:30 a.m., Mr. Schuetzendorf awakened us with an alarming report of Russian tanks within 15 kilometers of the city. Hans did not seem anxious about this, but we rose anyway and prepared for the day. Hans believed that since American troops already had penetrated east of Berlin, they would take the city themselves and not leave it to the Russians. He felt that the tanks seen approaching the city were just a solitary group and not part of a long range tactic.

"Hans," I said, "I do not care if you are right or wrong. I will not stay in this city to find out. We must leave and go west—somewhere west. Let us get the baby and talk it over with the Kleeberg."

"We'll get the baby, but it's not necessary to discuss this with Walter and Charlotte," Hans responded. "If you feel that strongly about it, we'll go."

A telephone call for Hans interrupted our discussion, and he took to the stairs. After a few words, he called to me.

"Cherie, please come down. It's my brother, Walter, and we must make a decision." I took the phone and greeted Walter calmly, but he did not respond in kind.

"My God, my God, how glad I am you have left Posen!" he shouted into the phone. "What do you plan to do now?"

"So far, we only know we will not stay here, but we're not sure where we will go."

"You must come to us," he said, all excited. "I am stationed in a military hospital in Stralsund on the Baltic Sea. My commander says to tell you we can put you up here—food and lodging. Please come and we will take care of you."

In response to my question, he continued. "Am I a patient? No! I entertain the patients and officers. Yes, I'm in uniform." This news caught both Hans and me by surprise.

Walter already had outlined his proposal to Hans, who wanted my reaction. I told Walter we would consider it very carefully and phone him back shortly.

As Hans and I began discussing Walter's idea, we got out a map to pinpoint his location and found that it lay directly north of Berlin. If Russian armies advanced on a broad front, we would find ourselves no better off there than in Berlin. Too bad, we concluded, since at first it had seemed like an enticing offer.

"Hans, here's a new thought," I said. "I'd like to phone Aunt Bertha in Hamburg. I feel like going to the edge of the continent, somewhere I can jump off if necessary, rather than fall into the embrace of victorious, woman-hungry warriors. We also must think of Irmgard. I think I'd like to go to Hamburg."

Thereupon, we phoned Aunt Bertha in Hamburg, and she responded as if expecting our call. With no hesitation at all, she offered us her parlor. "We have only two unoccupied beds left and the rest of you must sleep on the floor, but you will have a roof and a place to cook." I relayed the message to Hans, who nodded his assent.

"Thank you," I told her. "We will come day after tomorrow."

CHAPTER 34

Our Final Farewell to Berlin

February, 1945

With our decision made, we felt much better and even a little excited. Leaving Bob and Irmgard at home, we took Dieter with us to the Kleebergs to get the baby and tell them our plans.

When we arrived, we found Horst von Valtier there, too, in a terrible state of excitement. His family had left Posen eight days earlier in a horse-drawn wagon, and still had not reached Berlin. Horst sent out scouts along all roads radiating from the city, but they failed to turn up any trace of Eva and the children.

Almost out of his mind with fear, Horst talked, cried and paced the floor. He knew, as did we, of other missing friends and acquaintances. Some, like Horst's own brother, seemed to have just disappeared from the face of the earth and never were heard of again. The thought of their fates was terrible, so how could we offer Horst any realistic hope? But we could—and did—show him our sympathy and support by remaining and waiting with him.

Several times the telephone rang and each time Horst jumped up, expecting news. His disappointment, and ours, when it turned out otherwise seemed almost more than we could bear. Horst's imagination tortured him as he visualized his beautiful Eva and their four lovely children in the most awful of circumstances.

Charlotte could not sit and watch this drama without offering help, so she busied herself in the kitchen warming herb tea, then serving us all. Other wifely tasks offered distraction, too. Walter left the house repeatedly on unexplained errands, probably for the same reason. We only knew one thing for sure: news would have to come pretty soon if... well, never mind the "if."

Once more the phone rang, and again Horst jumped for the receiver. This time he heard one of his men on the other end, with good news: they had located Horst's family! Horst left on the run almost before his man could give directions. We knew nothing of their condition, but rejoiced that within hours they all would be together again and safe with Walter and Charlotte, two people with the biggest hearts and kindest hands we ever had known.

After Horst left, we told our hosts of our plan to leave for Hamburg, and Hans offered Walter the little Topolino. "I'll leave it in front of the railroad station—assuming our gas holds out for that long a ride," he said. Hans thought that as a doctor, Walter might gain legal access to some gasoline.

As we talked with these good friends, we recognized a parting of the ways. Walter had received orders directing him to report to a hospital in the southwest reaches of Germany, and his family planned to accompany him. We, on the other hand, were bound northwest. Promising to somehow find each other again some day, we said "God keep you and yours" with tears and great sadness in our hearts. We felt sorrowful to leave them yet were frantic to get away.

Riding home, we saw no other civilian cars on the streets, only military vehicles. Yet no one stopped us for questioning, and we assumed that Hans' uniform and the general nervousness of all Berliners provided our best protection against the usually- observant traffic officers.

Our first order of business the following day was to exchange our food cards for a permit to leave the city—which we needed to buy railroad tickets to Hamburg. As head of the household, Hans insisted on handling this task himself, even though it involved an arduous and hazardous trip into the heart of Berlin. I wanted desperately to accompany him, but he resented too much help, so I let him go and tried to restrain my fears.

Hans set out early in the morning on crutches, rather than by car, to conserve our few remaining drops of gasoline for the possible trip to the railroad station the next day. First he walked to the streetcar stop several blocks away on the Heerstrasse, then later transferred to the S-Bahn, an elevated train.

From the minute he walked out the door, I began worrying. I knew that many wide steps, covered by ice and snow and unprotected by railings, led to the S-Bahn platform. People ran around hysterically, in such a state of excitement they hardly realized what they did. They could so easily knock Hans over, I feared, and in those days everyone seemed to look out only for his own skin.

The S-Bahn trains, too, posed dangers of their own. The electrically-controlled doors opened and closed rapidly, barely allowing time for people to leave or enter. And what if an air raid warning sounded? Where would Hans go, and how would I find him if something happened to him?

Hans' tiring and wide-ranging mission kept him away the entire morning and into the afternoon, and I died a thousand deaths waiting for his return. Finally, however, he walked in the door, triumphant, with the permit secured and our railroad tickets already purchased. Noting his well-deserved pride at his accomplishments, I kept my fears and worries to myself.

That evening we told Mr. Schuetzendorf, our landlord, that we would leave in the morning. He then confessed that his family, too, would depart the next day for the Island of Sylt, while he and the maid "held the fort" at home. He added that he planned to send some household articles by special messenger, and offered to include anything of ours if that would assist us. All we could think of was our blankets, and he agreed to include them in the shipment.

One last time before we left, Berlin offered the spectacle of an air raid. At 10 p.m. that night, as we prepared to turn out the lights, the alarm sounded. We rose and dragged sleepy children, an exhausted baby and our luggage through thick snow to the shelter. There we sat with friends and neighbors, while plane after plane flew over our heads to drop their terror on the more populated sections of the city.

Not until after 3 a.m. the next morning did the seemingly-unending chain of bombers head back toward their point of origin. Exhausted, we trudged home again, wondering how we would wake the children again in three hours to make ready for the attempt to reach Hamburg.

Morning came much too soon, and we rose to make final preparations to leave. Mrs. Schuetzendorf and child departed by chauffeured limousine, which left little doubt in our minds of her husband's status as a most influential Nazi—especially so if his family could take refuge on the Isle of Sylt.

Seeing a physically perfect man "wield the magic wand" might have filled our hearts with envy, since Hans had to shoulder a knapsack and pick his way with one leg and crutches through the ice and snow. But Hans did not covet the luck of others. "We must be happy, because everything will turn out all right," he insisted. "Let us keep faith."

The little Topolino lacked room for all of us, so Bob and Irmgard said they would take the street car and S-Bahn and meet us at the train station. In normal times we never would have consented to such an arrangement. But Bob knew the way, so once more we resigned ourselves to the risk and prayed.

As we prepared to leave, Wally came out in dressing gown and coat, stepping gingerly through the deep, white snow that still fell. In her hand she held a pot of hot ersatz coffee, a cupful for each of us.

"You are abandoning all your wonderful possessions," she cried, in tears to see us go. "You should stay here with us and fight for them."

Although we understood her feelings, we did not share them. For us, our lives and those of our children took precedence over any material belongings, and we based all our moves on that belief.

We embraced in tears. A deep emotion filled us as we exchanged Auf Wiedersehens and thanked each other for the love and friendship grown so precious between us. How much I wanted to take them along, but they felt "chained" to their homestead. As we drove away, I looked back sadly at our dear friend, realizing that most likely we would never see her or Franisch again.

Our route took us through the tortured and tumbled ruins of a once-great city. Debris lay everywhere and we detoured often from one street to another as we tried to find our way through the half-light of an early wintry morning. How would Bob and Irmgard find us, Hans and I both wondered in our hearts. Our anxiety grew to panic when they did not appear when we expected. But then, oh how grateful we were when they finally reached us, our two plucky youngsters, miraculously and without any show of concern.

We left the little car at the station, as agreed with Dr. Kleeberg. Hans strapped one knapsack on his shoulders while I took the other and the baby, wrapped in my sheepskin coat. Bob and Irmgard each grasped one of Dieter's hands, and we set off together.

Entering the dismal station, we found the platform designated "trains to Hamburg." Already a huge mob waited. But when people saw our group—four children, one a babe in arms, and the father a one-legged warrior on crutches—they unfailingly offered help, even if only a suggestion.

One kind soul told us a train soon would back up to the platform. "If you stand here," he said, pointing out a particular spot, "the doors to the last coach will open right in front of you." We thanked him and stood where he suggested.

The train did finally back in, but stopped a full coach-length away from us. The huge mob lunged forward toward the doors while we stood staring, already believing our cause lost.

"We must try," Hans urged, and moved forward.

We succeeded in pushing into the midst of the crowd, then

could advance no further. Wondering what to do, we just stood, looking up at the train windows high above us. Irmgard, in sudden panic, sat down on the pavement and sobbed hysterically. That would never do. The crowd would trample her. I spoke harshly, fearing that sympathy would not penetrate her consciousness in time. Bravely, she stood and straightened her little shoulders and looked at us with trust in her eyes. If we refused to succumb to fear, so too would she—but courage did not come easily.

"Cherie, look up," Hans gasped. I did, and saw Bob looking down upon us from a coach window. We had not even missed him. He had crossed the tracks and managed to climb up on the coach from the other side.

Next to him stood a sailor. Bob reached down with both his arms and I held our toddler up to him, but he could not reach down far enough. I begged the sailor's help, and, when he understood my request, he assisted. He took Hans Bernhard from my arms and handed him to Bob, who disappeared into the coach and then returned immediately.

I took my cue and hoisted Dieter, and again the sailor lent assistance, this time enthusiastically. Irmgard went next, followed by the knapsacks. They all were in!

"We must join them somehow," Hans said, threading his way forward. We got as far as the door, but there people already hung from the last step, making further advancement utterly hopeless. So we struggled back to the window, where Bob still looked down. Despairingly, Hans called out instructions to Bob.

"We will follow as soon as we have the slightest chance. You must depend on the Red Cross at the station. They will locate Uncle Gustav, who will be there awaiting us."

Bob nodded and said he knew what to do, and we believed our son, only 13 but already so grown up and capable.

The crowd still surrounded us, and of course many heard our frantic conversation. Suddenly, two tall men in SS uniforms approached us. Without a word, they grabbed me, each an arm and a leg, and swung me feet-first through the window far above. I landed atop luggage piled in the gangway and fell headlong to the floor, but rose in time to see Hans land in much the same way, followed by his crutches.

My heart fairly burst with happiness as we tumbled this way and that over knapsacks and blanket rolls to the entrance of the compartment where our children waited.

We all were in! Hans and I found room to sit, not too comfortably but better than standing. The children sat on the baggage that covered the floor. A miracle—another to add to our imposing list since the beginning of the war.

At last the train moved forward. Would the trip turn out well, I wondered? Or would strafers come to destroy us? And if so, what should we do? Hans and I knew that in such cases trains usually stopped and many passengers fled to hide underneath the train or in whatever shelter the landscape afforded. But since many who ran lost their lives, I doubted the prudence of that course. In my own mind, I thought it better to just duck between piles of luggage and hope for the best.

Once we left the outskirts of Berlin I could not help but observe how much open land surrounded us—no forests for cover. At a steady pace, we would reach Hamburg in three hours. Instead, however, we moved, then stopped and waited before moving once more. Again and again, and always.

The hours began to stretch out—two, three, four and more, and I only could guess how much distance we had covered. Finally, we saw ruined houses more frequently, and I knew Hamburg lay somewhere nearby.

Another hour passed during which we saw nothing but ruins, much more extensive than in Berlin. Or perhaps we just noticed them more, with nothing else to do.

The children peered through the large train window and called astonishing scenes to our affection. As we passed one destroyed building, we saw a bathtub suspended in space five floors up, held in place by a single pipe.

"People will have to be awfully careful when they use that

bathroom," Irmgard observed, laughing to ease her own misgivings. Other sights also caught our eyes—a couch hanging by a nail, a huge mirror left unharmed on a wall, a child's broken doll on a window sash, a pail, a sock, rags of curtains billowing in the breeze, a lamp, a bed, mattresses, a stove.

We saw not one single intact house during the whole last hour's ride to the station in Hamburg. Here a chimney, there another, a whole wall torn, facades and rubble, rubble. rubble.

The sight of all those ruins shook my confidence, and I badly needed reassurance that I had not used poor judgment and listened to the wrong voice. I had insisted on coming to Hamburg, not Hans. I bore full responsibility. And it was too late to turn back.

CHAPTER 35

A Refuge with Family in Hamburg

February 1945

Once we arrived in Hamburg, it took us some time, with Hans on crutches and all the other passengers, to leave the train. Finally, however, all six of us stood on the platform, glancing around. A graying gentleman stepped up to Hans Uncle Gustav.

"Well, Hans, you caught me unawares, you've lost so much weight," he said. "I confess I would not have recognized you if I had not known you were coming. I'm surely glad you made it. I've waited for hours and worried that perhaps you encountered strafers."

He stopped, greeted the rest of us and then repeated, "I'm mighty glad you arrived and all is well. Come, Aunt Bertha will be anxious, too. Where is your baggage?"

"Blankets underway and otherwise just these two dufflebags," Hans laughed, making a joke out of our misfortune. "Doesn't seem like much, does it, but we have four trunks full stored in the Black Forest. We will send for them now that we're here."

Uncle Gustav returned his laugh, but it contained the irony that accompanied the next remark. "I see you still have some optimism left. Well, you can try."

We took another train from the center of town to the suburb

of Rahlstedt, one of the parts of Hamburg farthest removed from the center of the once-great metropolis. From the station we walked 10 minutes to Uncle Gustav's home. Once there, the welcoming arms of Aunt Bertha enfolded us. Aunt Emma, the mouse-like widowed sister of Uncle Gustav who had lived with them since the war began, also greeted us. Her complexion reminded me of a porcelain doll.

Aunt Bertha's manner chided gently while poking fun at the same time. "My dear children," she said, eyes sparkling, "We are together now and will finish the war in good company. I am sure you all are both hungry and exhausted.

"Come, here is your room. It is the parlor, but who needs one now? For a social room, we will use the dining room. Put your things in there; you can freshen up in this bathroom and then we will eat."

"Is a refugee office established yet in Rahlstedt?" Hans asked. Aunt Bertha nodded affirmatively.

"But remember," she warned, "you are among the first to arrive from the East. Our authorities have so much to worry about right here, I fear they will not yet be oriented concerning the Warthegau."

We ate, and related in detail all that had happened since Posen. Gustav and Bertha shook their heads gravely. As we talked, two visitors arrived—first their son's wife, Ilse, and then their daughter, Anni, a war widow. Ilse told us her husband was a soldier on the eastern front and she was terribly worried. She and Anni left after a short stay, as alarm time neared. But no alarm came that night, thank God! We slept.

With only two beds available, the rest of us lay on blankets piled on the carpeted floor. I recalled my complaints in Berlin about sleeping on beds without sheets. Now we slept without a mattress. But already that seemed unimportant. Only survival mattered.

Once more morning dawned in a new place, with new worries and duties. Our primary worry came from above. Hamburg, our hosts told us, experienced alarm every day, not necessarily to bear the burden of destruction upon itself, but because sometimes whole chains of bombers just passed over, or flew nearby en route to other targets. That still sent the entire population of the city to the shelters.

The first duties we faced were registering with the police and obtaining our food cards. Hans undertook those tasks right after breakfast while the children (except the baby, now 18 months,) and I explored the shopping area of Rahlstedt with Aunt Bertha. She offered valuable, practical suggestions for us.

Aunt Emma tended Hans Bernard while we were gone; he had gone down for a napping. While she watched him, she also prepared vegetables and what meat they had ready to cook if the electricity came on.

"With gas no longer available, we cook on an electric hot plate," she explained. "Yes, it's true; during the day electricity is available only during an air raid, when they turn on the power for the sirens. It's not meant for our convenience, but we take advantage."

When I asked how such a tiny plate could cook the food thoroughly, Aunt Emma grinned impishly.

"It doesn't," she admitted, "but it gets good and hot. Then we pack the pot in old newspapers and put down pillows tightly around it. We leave it that way for several hours and, when we re ready to eat, the food is usually edible and warm."

Looking around the shops at the very limited items on display, I saw that Hans would not relish his food for quite a while to come. He would add no fat to his sparsely covered bones from that despised fare—rutabaga, turnips and cabbage. And even those were available only in very small amounts per person.

Potatoes were scarce, fruits almost nonexistent and long queues of people stood before each shop. Aunt Bertha looked at me sympathetically, understanding my dismay at this new hardship to which she was an old hand. I realized then how much our family had been spared with our various moves since the beginning of the war.

"Bob and Irmgard, you can help your mother and dad," Aunt Bertha suggested to the children. They turned to her eagerly, anxious to be of service. "You can stand in line each day while Mother does her work at home. Then one of you can leave the line as your turn draws near and come home to get Mother or Daddy, who will relieve you and make the purchases."

This proposal excited the children, and they looked forward eagerly to doing their part. I knew that soon they would grow to hate the boring waiting, but still they would do it.

Then Bob's face clouded over. "But what if the alarm sounds?" he asked.

"You leave the line and run home, only five minutes away, so that we can go to the shelter together. We keep food and supplies packed ready to leave, and your family will do likewise." The children nodded, understanding.

As we talked, Hans joined us. "We are registered," he said, taking the food cards from his pocket. Aunt Bertha asked for them and, separating them, suggested that Hans get them stamped by the various proprietors.

"Only a soldier on crutches and in uniform has precedence over a whole long line of waiting, tired, harassed mothers and housewives. Only he can enter the shop first."

Since he was not buying at the moment, the idea of making use of such a privilege seemed less repugnant to Hans than it otherwise might, and he obtained the necessary stamps quickly.

"Then tomorrow we can buy, can't we, Aunt Bertha, and make up to you what you are sharing with us today!" I said, and she smiled her assent.

We prepared to return home together, enjoying the bright, unusually warm day. For the first time in weeks we felt the sun's rays on our faces, and this brought a welcome bit of cheer. Then the sound of the sirens dashed our high spirits. Destruction loomed once again.

"Come, children, let's go," Hans said, turning toward home. He set an unbelievable pace, keeping the children running to match him. They laughed at the sight of his swinging long strides on his fabulous French-type crutches. Aunt Bertha and I followed as quickly as we could.

"Is he still always that cheerful, my dear?"

"Yes, Aunt Bertha, never failing."

"Grossartig (Wonderful)," she sighed.

I looked at her. She, too, was marvelous, no sign of fear, only courage, duty and kindness also never failing.

At home, we found Aunt Emma, true to expectation, with a stew pot on the hot plate. Uncle Gustav hunched over the radio. He informed us that a great mass of planes was headed in our direction.

The prior evening Uncle Gustav had told us that as soon as the sirens sounded, all Hamburg tuned in to a given station on their radios for information about the number, whereabouts and direction of enemy planes. This allowed one to decide whether to risk staying at home or go to an air raid shelter.

Based on what he heard, Uncle Gustav advised us to take the children and Aunt Bertha to a shelter nearby. He and Aunt Emma would stay home, and retreat at the last minute to their basement if necessary. We followed his suggestion. Hans and I took knapsacks on our backs and I took the baby in my arms. Aunt Bertha carried her own belongings, and the three eldest children kept together.

At the shelter entrance, Aunt Bertha greeted a number of friends and neighbors and introduced us as relatives and refugees from the Warthegau. Then we sat, silent and tense, on wooden planks to await our fate. This bunker was not soundproof so each ear strained to hear the possible drone of a plane or planes, or the whistling of descending bombs.

The children—even the baby—remained calm, quiet and very good throughout their forced inactivity. With much time to think, I wondered how the war would end and how much longer it would continue. I reflected, too, on the monumental changes in my life. I felt exhausted with no loyal Michaline or Klaerle to help me anymore—and no likelihood of such help for a long while. I had to rely on Bob, Irmgard and Hans.

Already Irmgard played the role of a sweet little mother to the baby and a wonderful companion for Dieter, and Bob had proven his ingenuity in the face of danger. Hans, so used to servants and softened by his hospital experience, offered his help in any way I could use it, with no loss of his dignity. Somehow we would make out, I knew.

But what would we do after the war, I wondered? Hans and I both believed that immigrating to America represented our best chance for a normal life, and that goal kept our hopes alive. First, of course, we needed our documents. And they, along with everything of value we still owned, lay in trunks stored in the basement of Klaerle's aunt in the Black Forest. We must send for them immediately, I concluded.

I leaned toward Hans and whispered this thought into his ear. He nodded, and I saw by his expression that he agreed. "This day yet," Hans whispered back to me, again nodding his assent.

As the hours flitted by, the children grew hungry and thirsty, and I gave them the last of the Leibnitz Keks (cookies) we had brought from Posen. The treats provided a momentary diversion but did little to stave off their hunger.

After watching me for some time, a lady sitting nearby broke the silence. "Isn't it awfully heavy to carry the baby in that sheepskin coat, especially with a knapsack on your back?" she asked.

"Yes, it is heavy. Thank you for your concern. But really, we are lucky to have this coat.

"I am sure you are," she answered. "But I have a better idea. I shall send my daughter's baby buggy over to you later. You may keep it for as long as you can use it. I won't need it again—my husband gave his life for his country and I'll have no more babies." She sat dry-eyed, sad but resolute.

True to her word, the baby carriage arrived after the raid. She included a note explaining that she had acquired two sheets at the Bezugscheinstelle (distribution center) the day before on special request and wanted me to accept one as a gift. What wonderful generosity! Only someone who knew how reluctantly the government dispersed sheets could realize how badly she probably needed them herself. Yet she gave me one.

After less than a day in Uncle Gustav's home, we realized that he resented his wife's impulsive and generous invitation for us to join them. He walked around grumbling, in bad humor, but Aunt Bertha appeared not to notice.

"Why can't Hans get his own coal for heating?" he asked irritably. That seemed a reasonable suggestion, so Hans made application and received a supply, which he added to Uncle Gustav's coal pile.

But Uncle Gustav remained unhappy. "The wood needs splitting," he noted one day. "Why can't Bob grab an axe?"

Bob looked up at Uncle Gustav, and I saw fear in his eyes— probably more of Uncle Gustav than the job of splitting firewood. He glanced at his father and me, but he said nothing.

"Uncle Gustav, if you will please show Bob how to use an axe, and remember that he has never used one before, I'm sure he will do his best," I said.

I regretted that we seemed to get on Uncle Gustav's nerves. In light of the strain that Hamburgers had borne for so long, plus the added stress of having six new people suddenly invade his home, Uncle Gustav's reaction seemed understandable. Then, too, Aunt Bertha said he suffered from high blood pressure and was of a naturally grumpy disposition. For her part, she took everything in stride and remained her sunny self day after day the same.

News delivered by the postman later in the week cast a shadow over the entire household, however. One letter came from Aunt Bertha's daughter, Liselotte, who lived in Kassel with her husband and five very small children. The other was for us, from Horst von Valtier.

Quite suddenly Aunt Bertha laid her letter down on the table. "Ruth, why are you gasping? What in the world is the matter?"

"Horrible, horrible," I said, shaking my head and squeezing

my eyes shut, trying to obliterate the picture that lingered in my mind. Looking up at her finally, I explained.

"Aunt Bertha, you recall what I told you about Horst and Eva, and the Steineckers from Hazelthal? This letter comes from Horst. Thank God he and his family were reunited safely. For the moment they remain in Berlin with the Kleebergs. But listen to what Horst writes about Waldemar and Barbara."

"As you already know, Barbara and daughter, with Mrs. Armsberger, left Hazelthal by horse and wagon two days before you and Hans left Posen. Waldemar had gone to their Berlin home to await them, but changed his plans and returned to Hazelthal to blow up his factory. He barely escaped with his life as the Russians moved in.

"Back in Berlin, he went to your home in Pichelsdorf and found you had left. Then he came to us. Had anyone heard from his family? No! We sat down and mapped out every possible route from Hazelthal to Berlin, as well as possible detours.

"One possibility brought terror to our hearts. She might have followed the Elbe River to Dresden and been there during the annihilation of that city and surroundings. According to the reports we heard, for three days the enemy literally rained hell-fire. Bombs fell not only on the city but directly into the hundreds of thousands of refugees camped in the open on the Elbe River, a goodly distance out from the city.

"The longer he thought about it, the more convinced Waldemar became that they had gone to Dresden, where friends might have taken them in. Waldemar traveled to Dresden and returned without them, after for three days unsuccessfully searching for them among the thousands of charred bodies. He is frantic, half-demented and inconsolable."

Blinded by tears, I could read no further. I felt sick. What torture and anguish for Waldemar until he knew his family's fate! Were they part of the horrible mass annihilation on the river banks? Or if still alive, did they lie sick or maimed somewhere, needing him desperately?

But Aunt Bertha offered a comforting idea. "Maybe it is good that he did not find them. Maybe that means they still are alive somewhere, allowing for a possible reunion. And if not, he must accept, just as you have accepted, as hard as that is. We are a fatalistic people, my dear. We can only do what we think is right, and then must accept the results and make the best of whatever happens."

"Does that theory keep you so cheerful, Aunt Bertha? Is that why you offered so generously to let us come live with you?"

"I did not know I had a theory," she answered. "But perhaps I do, and if so, it will work once more. Liselotte's letter says she is ill and alone with her five small ones. The Army took Heinrich, my son-in-law. With you here, perhaps you will take my place and let me go to her and care for her. My poor daughter needs me very badly."

"Of course, Aunt Bertha, of course. We will care for Uncle Gustav and Aunt Bertha—at least as much as they allow us."

She smiled sweetly. "I knew you would. I'll tell Uncle Gustav; he may not like it, but he will not object. I will leave tomorrow."

* * *

The happenings of our days soon became repetitious. Feverishly, we used each minute in daily chores—mending clothes, securing and preparing food and caring for the children's and our own physical needs. When the daily alarms sounded, we listened anxiously to radio reports, then often rushed to the air raid shelter. There we sat and endured the wait—sometimes short, sometimes long—as we wondered about our fate. Back home again, we tried to rest or sleep, sometimes in bed, often on the floor.

One night we endured a long, horribly widespread raid. Splinters flew hard and far, and a great fire lighted the heavens brilliantly. Fortunately, the flames failed to reach Rahlstedt, so we remained unharmed.

The next morning, while standing in line to do my marketing, I overheard someone say that a stable housing hundreds of thoroughbred horses had burned to the ground.

When a listener asked what had happened to the horses, the speaker said they all had suffered severe burns and were shot. The horsemeat would go on sale at 5 a.m. the following morning in Hamburg, in a tiny wooden shack, the only building still standing amid a mountain of ruins for miles around. Each customer could buy eight times their normal meat allotment.

I resolved to see for myself. We were receiving an allotment of one quarter-pound of meat per person per week—the equivalent perhaps of one pork chop. By comparison, two pounds per person seemed an unheard-of luxury! True, Hans would never eat horsemeat. He told me once that its sweet taste sickened him. But I decided I would buy it anyhow, and attempt to disguise it by marinating.

After inquiring cautiously of Aunt Emma how I might reach my desired destination, I took the first train the next morning from Rahlstedt—at 5:30 a.m. Half an hour later I found myself climbing and stumbling over mountains of rubble. Many others preceded me, and I just followed.

At the shack, many bundled-up women already stood in a long line, and I took my place in it. No one spoke, not the whole two hours I waited in the cold, damp, dark, windy dawn. The terrain looked eerie, like pictures of the moon.

At last my turn came and I entered the small barn-like structure. In exchange for my coupons I received a huge package of meat, but with no choice of cuts. The clerk just weighed and wrapped the meat and put it in my hands, and I left.

My success left me elated, feeling like a runner who had won a competitive race. The next day, Sunday, we enjoyed a fine dinner.

Hans accepted my explanation that cows had suffocated during the air raid, and he enjoyed the sauerbraten I prepared. Only Aunt Emma knew my little secret.

I returned each Saturday for eight wonderful weeks, and we all enjoyed the tender, flavorful meat. Even Uncle Gustav praised my cooking. Eventually, however, the supply of horsemeat ran out, forcing us to return to our starvation diet—with real beef not so tender. (Hans questioned why, and I decided that someday he would know, but not then.) We didn't much like it, but following Aunt Bertha1s philosophy, we did the best we could and accepted whatever came.

When I thought of the children with no school, however, I wondered if we really were doing our best for them. The younger ones seemed happy and content. But Bob was restless, ill at ease and definitely most fearful of our host. Except when Bob helped split firewood, Uncle Gustav just did not want to see him around. The poor boy needed something to do, to get away.

Hans and I wondered if perhaps Bob should return to his school in the country. Despite our reluctance even to consider letting him leave, we talked to him about it. He exhibited no enthusiasm either for leaving or staying, and we knew his apathy covered up a deep unhappiness. We hated to see him go, but would it help him?

Of course, we did not know whether school had resumed or not. "I will write to find out," Hans said, "and if so, we will discuss it with him again."

While we waited to hear, other matters occupied our attention. During Aunt Bertha's absence of several weeks, I had done very little for Uncle Gustav and Aunt Emma. She kept house and tended her brother very well, making me dispensable. This gave Hans the thought that we should try to find a living space for ourselves alone somewhere. Not much was available, and we lacked furniture of our own. But Hans applied anyway, hoping our status as refugees might help.

Although nothing turned up immediately, Hans kept active

interest going by visiting the housing authorities frequently. And waiting offered one advantage, since Uncle Gustav had all of our coal. Better to stay with him until spring arrived and we no longer needed fuel for heating.

Aunt Bertha wrote to us about her little family, which kept her mighty busy. We surmised from her letters that she would love to bring her dear ones to Hamburg. But there were reasons, she wrote, why she could not. I wondered if she would come if we left for other housing, or if the increased frequency of the nightly air raids in Hamburg influenced her thinking. I knew from first-hand experience of the hardship for children snatched out of their sleep night after night.

* * *

In our family, baby Hans Bernhard showed the most effects from the alarms. He seemed unusually irritable and broke out in a rash of dime-size welts that oozed pus. They called for bandages—which we could not find—and medical advice—equally hard to obtain. Fortunately, we sat next to a nurse one day in the air raid shelter, and she told us what troubled our child.

"That little one is suffering from malnutrition,' she said. "You must find some apples somewhere. He needs fruit for vitamins. And, of course, he reinfects himself because you cannot boil his clothes. Then, too, our soap does little good. After all, 90 percent pumice does not provide sufficient cleansing properties."

But where could I get apples or other fruit? Go into the country to small villages and beg for them? In times like those, people made it their business to help wherever they saw a need, and word somehow got around. Often it meant following nothing but a rumor, like the one Aunt Emma heard about farmers in a little town an hour's train ride north of Hamburg, with apples for sale.

Every day, she heard, women from Hamburg traveled to the little village in Schleswig-Holstein, between Elmshorn and Itzehoe, out in the flatlands that at sea level reached up into Denmark.

They returned with knapsacks full of apples, up to 30 pounds per buyer.

It seemed worth a try, so Bob and I set out very early one morning, each with a knapsack. We arrived finally at the designated railroad station. Dozens of women, also carrying knapsacks, trekked resolutely along the one country road that stretched east through endless bogs on either side. No town lay in sight—only a row of trees on the eastern horizon.

"I guess we just follow the leader, Bob, wouldn't you say?"

He laughed his assent and we both started out. But neither Bob nor I could match the pace these women set, and soon found ourselves "bringing up the rear."

When we finally reached the outskirts of the little village, we turned at left angle into a single street stretching far to the north and bordered on both sides by a single row of farmhouses. We stopped and observed as the women who reached the houses before us knocked at the doors and asked to buy apples. To our dismay, door after door closed on them without a sale. How then could we hope to follow and succeed? Well, after coming all that way, we were determined to try.

"You take one side and I'll take the other," I instructed Bob.

However, just like those in front of us, we only heard "No, no, no." Discouraged, most of the other women soon turned back toward the train station. A final house stood on the street. Suddenly a woman emerged from it with a bulging knapsack. Bob and I exchanged knowing glances and rushed to the door. At my knock, a young peasant woman answered, and I asked to see the farmer.

"He's gone to a party and won't return for hours," she said in broken German. "And besides, we have no apples."

"The lady who just left your house bought apples from you," I said. "I will sit here and wait for the farmer. I am not asking for charity —I will pay your price."

Although my reply astonished her, the girl admitted us, then left. Bob and I sat to rest, while she watched us from the next room. Once satisfied that we meant what we said, she returned with the farmer.

"We do have apples, and pears, too. What will you give besides money for them?"

"Besides money?" I said, clearly surprised and puzzled. "What would you suggest?"

"Well, shall we say a silk scarf and a pair of silk stockings for my Russian maid?"

Those unheard-of items were not available under any circumstances, unless rescued from among one's own personal possessions. I found his request preposterous as well as impossible and bristled at the thought that he would benefit a Russian girl at the expense of a female countryman—which he no doubt supposed I was.

Thus, without compunction and with equal calmness, I responded, "Why, of course. May I send them?"

"Certainly," the farmer said, and the Russian lass beamed.

They filled one knapsack with 30 pounds of apples, and the other with 20 pounds of pears. I paid his price and much more, for I knew I could not supply the silk scarf or stockings. Then we started out on the long trek of four kilometers or more back to the station.

Alone on the road with Bob, I thought for the first time about the train schedule back to Hamburg. My watch showed nearly 2 o'clock as we reached the edge of town and approached open country. Suddenly, an alarm sounded. Already tired and hungry—we'd each eaten only a slice of bread and an apple all day—we faced further delay.

"Mother, can we rest?"

"Yes. By rights we should take cover, but no flyer will waste his bombs on our poor little twosome in the middle of bog land, so let us just rest and then plug onward."

After the bombers flew over, we continued on our way, stopping frequently. When we got to within 200 yards of the station, we saw our train approaching across the flatland. We stumbled the last few steps as fast as our numb limbs allowed and, near exhaustion, climbed the platform with just one small minute to spare. Out of breath and completely limp, we dropped our burdens on empty benches next to our seats.

"We're in, we made it," Bob gasped.

The train pulled out, but then side-railed and waited. And waited. The conductor came around to collect tickets and explained that an air raid over Hamburg was causing our delay.

"Just so long as they don't strafe us," Bob said. He watched the skies intently. I also noticed him glancing at a row of trees along the west side of the train.

"What are you thinking, Bob?"

"Only that if we're strafed, we could run quickly into the trees and wait."

"With or without the fruit?"

"We'd have to take it along, I guess. If we left it here, the fruit would disappear. But it's really heavy."

"That's right, Bob. Why not just believe in our own immunity and stay here, even if we are scared."

Bob's eyes lit up as he smiled. "It's easier to be brave when you're not alone."

The afternoon wore on with no more droning engines from the sky. With nothing to do and no way to change our situation, we just waited. Then at last the train rolled forward again. An hour later, with no further interruptions, we screeched into the station in Hamburg as the all-clear sounded.

We hurried to the gate for the train to Rahlstedt, but needlessly. While we waited, we observed a lone Allied plane swoop down over the station, so low we saw the pilot's face clearly. Dumbfounded, we expected him to open fire. But he just smiled, then pulled up sharply and disappeared into the gathering heavy clouds from which he first appeared.

Another hour and we sat around the table at home, eating a warm meal at last. The whole family shared the excitement of our successful day. Apples and pears! When in my life had simple fruit created such a furor? Aunt Emma washed some of the apples carefully and passed them around.

Baby Hans Bernhard wanted one and ate with an eagerness and concentration that amused us all. After one apple, he wanted more, then still more. He took one after the other until Hans feared they might make him ill. But they did not. Almost immediately his skin showed signs of improvement, and it all but cleared within a week. Each time I looked at him I felt glad we had fought for those apples. As our supply dwindled I began to wonder where to find some more.

Daily Hans walked to the train station and sat near the baggage depot, hoping for the arrival of our trunks from the Black Forest. After many disappointments, he returned home jubilant one day.

"One of our trunks came, and a delivery man will bring it here soon," he explained happily.

What a wonderful surprise! For the first time in four weeks, we could change from the ski togs and heavy boots we had worn when we left Berlin.

After the first trunk, we anticipated the arrival of the remaining three. Within 10 days they all appeared, one after the other, and we hardly could believe our good fortune.

The trunks contained some of our nicest apparel, at least four complete changes for everyone, including overcoats and shoes. I also had packed valuable bed and table linens, arguing with myself at the time that I could make them over into underwear or summer clothing if necessary. But I forgot thread and needles and a scissors, which no longer were purchasable. As for the valuable documents—passports, birth and marriage certificates, etc.— they proved priceless in the months to come.

We unpacked in the cellar, took out only what we needed and could use upstairs, then locked the trunks and left them in the basement. The change of clothes gave all of our spirits an indescribable lift, and even seemed to improve our relationship with

Uncle Gustav—for all except Bob. The contrast between their personalities seemed too great to bridge.

Uncle Gustav was a good man, but stolid and heavy of spirit, lacking spark or ambition. Before retiring, he had held a county assessor's job and done as little as possible. The rest of his time he had spent taking long walks or dreaming dark dreams. He entered conversation only to offer negative views. On the subject of politics, his wrath poured forth loud and clear against the German regime, against the English, the French, the Russians and, yes, the Americans. He insisted that the millennium, the end of the world, had come.

Aunt Bertha was his one big prize, and after winning her he had aimed no higher. She came from a family well-known and respected in "the Yunkers," the north and northeast reaches of Germany, and had known wealth and much better living than he ever provided. What led her to marry such an unenterprising man? In his earlier years he apparently had charm, when he cared to exude it, along with extraordinary good looks.

They had raised three beautiful children: Liselotte, whom Aunt Bertha was tending; Anni, a hospital laboratory technician and a war widow; and Hans-Adolph, an orthodontist stationed on the eastern front. By running a little tobacco shop of her own, Aunt Bertha had helped put their children through excellent schools and saw all of them married. Hans-Adolph's wife and children lived in Rahlstedt and visited us, or we them, as often as possible.

We never understood what aspect of Bob's still-forming personality antagonized Uncle Gustav so severely. But a strong antipathy existed, and after all, it was Uncle Gustav's home.

So, when a letter arrived from Bob's school saying he could return, we packed his knapsack and together Hans, Bob and I set out for a small railroad station in Hamburg reachable only by that city's S-Bahn.

* * *

Hamburg seemed crowded on that Saturday afternoon, and we stood together on the S-Bahn platform waiting for the train to arrive. Despite the warm, spring-like weather, we noted the general nervousness of the people around us. Thus far that day no alarms had sounded—an encouraging sign. But at no time could one escape completely from the fear and anticipation of violence and death. It was a gnawing feeling which persisted at the center of one's solar plexus; like holding one's breath; like the tautness of nerves and muscles as a runner crouched in the blocks, waiting for the click of the starter.

Those feelings hit me strongly as a train stopped and its doors yawned open. Suddenly, an alarm sounded and the whole crowd on the platform made one rush for the open train doors, sweeping Bob along with them. It no longer mattered whether they were waiting for that train or not; they knew, as did we, that the train would leave immediately and travel non-stop to the farthest end of the city, supposedly assured of greater safety there.

As for Hans and myself, the tide swept us aside. We could only call to Bob, "Find a bunker at the end of line, we will come for you." The doors closed and the train pulled out, forcing our poor young lad once again to take responsibility for his own survival with no help from his parents.

Stunned, we stood in place a few seconds, pained by the sense of loneliness he must feel. Then Hans said, "He's a smart boy, he'll be all right, and we'll find him later. Come, we must find a shelter—no time to lose."

Hans and I made our way slowly down the precarious steps of the platform. Spotting the entrance to a subway station nearby, we joined a growing crowd headed in that direction and continued with them through the station and down onto the confusion of tracks leading to the platform underground. A single dim light from above helped us avoid tripping over the maze of steel rails.

We mingled with the crowd that stood frightened and tense,

quiet, waiting and thinking. Many heads bowed in silent prayer, and we joined them, asking for safety for us and our family. We prayed that no bomb would strike this station—or any other on the line, knowing that the pressure of such an explosion would kill us all, no matter where we stood.

As the minutes ticked away into hours, we grew terribly fatigued—especially Hans, who stood on crutches, with no other support. Only fear and hope gave us the necessary endurance to continue. Finally, a stir, a murmur moved through the crowd. Someone thought the "all clear" had sounded. Then we heard it, too.

Slowly the great, silent crowd thinned as people picked their way across the many, many tracks. One almost could feel the heavy burden they shed, as if in awe of life restored. Once we stood in the open again, saved, our thoughts returned immediately to our loved ones, especially Bob.

Thanks to Hans' quick observation, we knew the destination of Bob's train. Once more we climbed the steps to the S-Bahn station and eventually caught a train for the end station of the line on which Bob had traveled.

We spied our son immediately on arriving, sitting calmly on a bench and talking to a lovely young lady none other than Anni, the youngest daughter of Aunt Bertha and Uncle Gustav! They had spotted each other in a nearby air raid shelter and had endured an extremely heavy shelling together.

"I work in the hospital laboratory right across the street, and I live close by, so I wind up in that shelter almost every day," Anni said. "Wasn't it great that we recognized each other, after meeting only once before on the first night of your arrival?

"And now, since we all seem a little weak from our experiences, I think we need something to eat, don't you, Bob? All of you come with me to my apartment for a snack?"

Bob hesitated, knowing he could waste little time if he were to leave town yet that day. Seeing this reaction, Hans addressed him.

"Bob, we can accept Anni's invitation. I understand your hesitation, but don't worry. Your mother and I talked it over on our way to get you. We decided to find rooms of our own and keep you at home with us."

Happily, Hans and I noted the relief that swept across Bob's face at this news. We explained to Anni that by leaving her mother's home, we would make way for Liselotte and her children, should they wish to come. Anni thought our decision a good one.

We soon arrived at her apartment, a few simple rooms on the third floor just a stone's throw from the laboratory. Anni heated some soup and we sat, talked and ate, dipping little pieces of coarse bread into the warm broth. Anni said that she was lonely since the death of her husband in battle, so she worked long hours and remained on constant call to help her forget her sorrow. But, she added, she liked her work.

It was late when we left to catch the train that evening for Rahlstedt. Anni walked with us to the S-Bahn station, so we would not lose our way. The train stood ready to leave, already so packed full of people that we saw no chance of getting on, not even onto the open-air platforms on either end of the coaches.

If the train had left on schedule, we would not have been on board. But it stood there a very long time, at least an hour, and we took advantage of the delay to worm our way into the crowd onto the open platform at the very end of the train.

Much later that evening we arrived home to a rousing welcome from our family, who had spent the afternoon in the cellar, worried about us. They were especially glad that we had brought Bob back with us— even Uncle Gustav. We told him of our decision to move to our own rooms, and he wondered how we would manage without any furniture or household items. But he voiced neither pessimism nor optimism, and made every effort to show his better nature.

CHAPTER 36

An Improvised Home in Rahlstedt

April 1945

As a first step in moving forward with our plans, Hans visited the housing officials the next morning to put a bit more pressure on them. It worked: they offered a choice of two places to live. They also allowed more than 2,000 Marks as a small prepayment against a possible reparation settlement for our losses in Posen and Berlin.

The morning's final good news came at the military headquarters for disabled soldiers. After examining Hans, the doctor fitted him for an artificial limb. He returned home elated by his accomplishments, although exhausted from his exertions.

The children thought it grand that he stayed home so much of the day. Above all they loved to go for walks with him. That afternoon we all walked together to inspect the two possible rentals, both located in Rahlstedt.

One was with a doctor's family in a three-story villa with garden. They offered a large room on the second floor and a smaller one on the third. This arrangement sounded impractical, but we decided to investigate before deciding.

The house stood back quite far from the street, and we entered from the garden. "This is nice," the young folks concluded immediately. Hans and I thought so, too, and secretly we hoped we would like what we saw inside.

The doctor's wife answered our ring. She had the appearance of a fine, proud North German woman. Her eyes twinkled at the children as she led us around, showing the room on the second floor first. She offered to furnish it with three beds of her own, which still would leave a huge space for a guest.

Upstairs, off a small hall, we found a very small room with a slanted roof. It could accommodate a double decker bed and still leave a little space for play. After some pleading, we also gained another small room across the hall – which secured the small hall for us. Hans immediately had seen the potential to convert it into a kitchen, observing that the chimney flue ascended through its walls.

He told the doctor's wife that we liked the arrangement, and asked to rent the rooms. We would solve the problem of cooking either by purchasing a hot plate (if we could find one) or buying a makeshift wood-burning stove and making a break-through to the chimney, if permitted. The children, ecstatic about the garden, asked if they could play there.

"Yes, but you must help me keep it nice. Come, I'll show you," the doctor's wife said. She led them through a thicket at the side of the house and into a lovely Oriental garden. It contained a slow-running brook, a tiny but sturdy and usable bridge, and darling life-size ceramic animals and birds. Our youngsters ooh'd and aah'd, their eyes sparkling. They giggled and laughed and utterly charmed the lady watching them, until she finally looked up at Hans and me and said, "They'll be all right. You may rent the rooms and occupy them as soon as you wish. Do you own any furnishings at all?"

"None,' Hans said, "but we will manage somehow. We always do."

Nothing, but absolutely nothing, could spoil the happiness of our children. Not since their stay in the Black Forest had anything so wonderful happened to them. They remarked over and over about that garden, and what fun if Daddy found some double-deckers, and "the lady is nice."

Each child reacted in his or her own unique way. Bob showed his joy only through his brilliantly lit-up eyes. Irmgard bubbled over with all the things she wanted to do, like cutting out paper doll clothes. Of course, she would need paper and scissors, which we did not own. But her brave little heart told her she would find some, somewhere.

Dieter giggled, his eyes lit up like Bob's, his emotions overflowing. Baby Hans Bernhard observed them all and, anxious to participate in their joy, fell into their moods as he saw them. I felt very fortunate for such beautiful, well-mannered children, clean and helpful as well as understanding. They were our gold mine, our priceless treasure. We might lose everything else, but as long as we had them, we were rich.

* * *

With a home secured, we confronted the problem of obtaining needed furnishings—the double deck bed, of course, but also pots, pans, dishes, knives, forks, a kitchen table and chairs, cupboards, wardrobes, commodes and cooking facilities. Impulsively, we had concluded our rental agreement before checking on availability of what we needed. Our boundless optimism, our ever-recurring and unquestioning belief in ourselves had gotten us into a myriad of tight spots before, and we found ourselves in another.

Hans, fired with new enthusiasm, decided to look around in the stores of Rahlstedt's shopping area, while I took the children home.

Our cheerful shopper returned later that afternoon. "Guess what? I found two metal double-deckers with mattress pads, and put down a deposit to secure them until I can obtain a coupon for them tomorrow." I had not dared hope for news this good, and the children made no effort to temper their excitement about his purchase and their new home.

From the children's happy chatter, Uncle Gustav and Aunt Emma learned what we still needed to set up housekeeping. Thereupon, wheels of intrigue started working, and word spread from mouth to mouth. Soon items began arriving—a pot, a pan, a cup, a plate, a table, a chair, and another and another, each from a different donor. Their kindness overwhelmed us.

A quick survey revealed that we still needed only knives, forks and spoons and a cook stove. But nowhere in all Rahlstedt could we unearth such treasures. We knew of a few shops in Hamburg, but would they offer what we needed? We would visit and see, which inevitably meant braving another whopping air raid.

Our mission there a few days later entailed long walks from one shop to the next, since taxis no longer ran and other transportation was seldom and erratic, unless one could use the S- Bahn. As we reached the middle of the long bridge over the Binnen Alster, a broad river thoroughfare through the city, an alarm sounded! What unfortunate timing—turning back would net us no more than going on. Even though Hans lengthened his swing on his crutches as much as possible, he could not keep up with people on two sound legs. In no time at all, we stood alone on the street.

Strong winds blew often in Hamburg, but that day we faced a gale. Twelve minutes passed very quickly against such odds, and we both realized that we would never make it across the bridge before hell-fire broke loose. And even when we reached the other side, we still would have to locate a shelter with room to accommodate us.

Without realizing, in that minute we embraced Aunt Bertha's fatalistic philosophy. Hans turned his face to me, smiling, making every effort. I returned his smile, reassuring him that we were doing the best we could. We remained calm—not unafraid, not resigned, just fatalistic. We would have to accept whatever happened, but we did not believe in our own destruction.

What are the workings of the supernatural, the perfect timing of the secret call for help? How does one unlock, lay out and examine the structure of faith? We stood alone, but already we were not, and the answer to our secret call arrived. Hearing a soft whir to my right, I turned to see a car stop beside us. An air raid warden and his helper packed us into the back seat and sped us to the entry of an underground shelter.

In seconds we entered and walked down a circular ramp, past one crowded room after another. On the third level down, we found empty concrete benches, and sat. Thick reinforced concrete formed the shelter walls, and it sat scarcely 50 feet from the edge of the Binnen Alster. I assumed our location lay well below the water line of the river. If a bomb detonated in the nearby Alster, would the concussion shatter the walls around us? I abhorred the thought that we might drown in a confined cell without the least chance of fighting for our lives, and oh, how I hated the realization that the door at street level was closed and sealed tightly.

Better to risk injury out in the open than to suffer this lack of freedom. But I kept my thoughts and fears to myself and so did Hans. He sat silently, his face seemingly complacent and showing no fear. Perhaps he thought how much better off he was here than with the fleeing, disintegrating armies on the eastern front. Ones thoughts compounded at a time like that, in the quiet room, since no one talked.

The raid eventually ended, like all the others, with just a bit more heaped-up destruction. We left the shelter along with the other survivors, exhausted by the ordeal and suffering emotional letdown from the pent-up anxious moments.

Although we wanted to turn and head straight for home, Hans and I continued on our unfinished mission. We made inquiries as we left the shelter, and someone directed us to a nearby store that might carry the items we sought. There we found knives, forks and spoons—black and made of iron—and large wooden cooking spoons, but no stove.

What should we do about cooking? The proprietor offered a suggestion, possibly our only hope. Build one of bricks taken from any ruin, he said. Plausible? Yes! And the ruins across the street from our new home just might provide the answer. We would try!

Hans and I resolved to move into our new rooms without delay and confer with the doctor and his janitor about building a cook stove. At home that evening, we found Bob immensely intrigued with the idea. He hardly could wait until we could obtain the doctor's consent to break through the wall to the chimney. He made a list of all the necessary materials—bricks, a thick sheet of iron to cover the top and a stove pipe with an elbow to connect the pipe and flue to the chimney.

We proposed our idea, and the doctor's janitor embraced the idea enthusiastically. "I really know how it should be done," he said. "If Bob will bring me the bricks and dig up some clay, we'll have it ready for topping and drying by tonight."

The doctor and his wife generously consented to the project, and we began a diligent search for materials. The next door ruin indeed yielded up the bricks, iron plate, stovepipe and clay. But then our enthusiastic workmen encountered a hitch: they just could not find an elbow, real or makeshift, not in the next-door ruin nor any other in the area.

Undaunted, our head of household and provider once more showed his winning smile at the Bezugscheinstelle and then with the necessary coupon in hand he tried the scores of stores in town. Finally, after much searching, he unearthed a used elbow and purchased it, thus assuring the successful completion of our cook stove. We couldn't wait to finish the installation and give it a try.

During the two days of construction, we took our meals with Aunt Emma and Uncle Gustav. He made no mention of our coal supply, and with no need to heat the house any longer, we said nothing, either. Instead we applied for and received a permit allowing us to fell two trees in a pine forest some two miles away.

But how could we cut them down, get them home and chop or saw them into wood? And who could do all this work? Surely, not a one-legged man up so short a time from a year of lying in hospitals. Hans helped in other ways, including cooking, which he performed excellently. But this task seemed beyond his capabilities. Bob and I would do the work, but with what tools?

The janitor became our angel. He knew all along what confronted us and saved us the embarrassment of requesting the use of his wheelbarrow and axe by offering them.

At first the project seemed fun. As the weather warmed and spring advanced, we enjoyed our time outside. Bob and I located and chopped down two wonderful, tall trees in the forest. After filling the wheelbarrow with dried pine needles from the forest floor, we laid the heavy trees across the two-wheeled cart. It took the efforts of both of us to get them home—one holding the trees in place and the other sometimes pushing, sometimes pulling. We changed positions often to relieve the strain. Our struggles over the two miles of uneven roads caused us quite a little grief; but eventually we arrived triumphant, if weary and worn out.

Bob and the janitor sawed the trees into logs, helping each other and making separate piles. Then Bob axed them down to size for use in our oven. However, our troubles did not end there; we needed a match to light the fire and paper to keep the spark. Most families, ours among them, used their meager supply of old newspapers in the toilet room or for baby diapers. The pine needles provided a suitable substitute, but the green logs required coaxing and constant attention.

All these difficulties made the first hot meal cooked on our own homemade stove seem quite a triumph. We all sat at our donated table, using four donated chairs and the lower bed of one double decker. The table lacked a tablecloth and our dishes did not match. The meal consisted only of buttermilk soup with cream of wheat and one bit of cooked salt pork per person, along with a slice of bread for each mighty simple fare, and not much of it.

Still, we felt like kings, monarchs of our own realm, exultant and united, and happier than at any previous time in our lives. Even the horrible, ugly black iron flatware could not restrain our high spirits. We grimaced and then we laughed. What could we do but put up with the way the iron ran black on contact with the hot, creamy white soup?

In the past, we would have been very reluctant to let the children sleep so far away from us. However, with all four together, one always could report any trouble. Since they seldom needed us in the night, the distance between us and them created no major problem. And at the first sound of a siren, we flew upstairs to fetch them.

Night after night the bombers came, almost always before midnight. Hans and I never earnestly laid ourselves to rest until after the raids ended. Mostly we stretched out fully clothed on our beds, with shoes kicked off and with hats, coats and knapsacks next to the bed, ready to grab.

Poor groggy youngsters! They responded to our soft low call, Bob and Irmgard taking care of themselves. Dieter I dressed. He helped me quietly and sweetly, but then unless I watched him carefully while I finished up with the baby, he undressed himself again and crawled back into bed.

We allowed ourselves five minutes to get ready and leave, with a walk of five more minutes to the shelter. That gave us two minutes before the fireworks began. The English planes came by night; the Americans arrived by day.

The lead plane dropped flares, sparkling bursts of brilliant light that looked for all the world like Christmas trees—which we called them. Despite their beauty, they fulfilled the horrible function of lighting up the targets for the bombers that followed. It seemed to us that they came a little closer to us each night, as if combing the city by areas. One almost could predict when our turn would come to perhaps find ourselves buried under a mass of rubble amidst the hell-fire. The fascinatingly beautiful yet frightful spectacle mesmerized us to stone.

Our time nearly arrived one night as we visited in the home of Aunt Bertha's son, Hans-Adolph. His back yard contained a concrete shelter, built by his father-in-law, only a hundred feet from the back door. With protection so near at hand, we felt no real sense of urgency when the alarm siren sounded. Then, too, the radio station had reported that the planes would bypass Hamburg.

The first planes did fly over us. Then they turned tail and, together with those that followed, hit us from all sides. No flares lit up any military objectives. Clearly, they meant the bombs for us, the people.

The enemy trick worked to perfection, surprising us inside the house. Could we still reach the shelter, or should we risk it? If the bombs fell nearby, we would fare much better inside the three-foot-thick shelter made of steel-reinforced concrete, with an outside and an inside door.

We thought to take advantage of a momentary lull, and hurried out. But the ear-splitting crackle of flack caught us halfway. Great flashes of light burst in the skies, lighting up the black night. Funny, wasn't it, that I should notice the twinkle of the bright, bright stars high up in the black, black sky in the middle of this terrorizing performance?

Nature also took part in the fury. The wind increased to tremendous velocity and drove red hot metal splinters, big as fists, through the air. They flew past out heads, past our bodies, as we hurried. That 100-foot journey seemed an eternity of hell from which we emerged absolutely unnerved, but miraculously unharmed, unpunctuated.

We remained strangely quiet until the doors bolted us safely inside, but our ordeal left me trembling so hard I could not sit down.

"That was a c-c-close one,'1 I ventured, trying for bravery. The children found humor and comfort in the message.

"Your teeth are ch-chattering, Mother," Irmgard said, then she laughed and laughed, and the others too. But her laughter tapered off to sobs as she slid from the bench to the cold cement floor and put her head down in her arms.

Life weighed so heavily on my poor little girl, I thought sadly. Our circumstances called upon her to bear a heavy load, to do more than her share, for a nine-year-old child. She provided exemplary constant love and care of baby and Dieter—in the house and the garden, hour after hour, day after day—while her parents and Brother Bob attended to their duties. Like all of us, she lived with constant rousing from sleep, a lack of proper food, and the fear of violence and the unknown. Yet with the exception of a few little feminine cries for help, her little-girl need for protection, she always remained cheerful, happy, resourceful and anxious to make her contribution to the family welfare.

One day a new and unanticipated need arose, one that Hans and I determined to tend to without any outside help, if we could. A secret visitor arrived—Hans' brother, Walter. He came to us very ill, his dark eyes wide with fear. We quietly folded him in our arms and put him to bed in our room, hoping no one had seen him.

Just a few months earlier, he had offered us sanctuary at the hospital in Stralsund. How fortunate that we had declined, we realized in retrospect. Our refusal had awakened Walter to the possibility that the Russians might overrun the facility. He took his concerns to the commanding officer, who acknowledged the legitimacy of Walter's fears but had delayed issuing an order to evacuate the wounded until the prior week—nearly too late.

Finally, the commander told Walter to go, to save himself and offered him a bicycle. Walter set out to find us, with practically no food or water. He traveled in short stretches, sometimes walking his bike by night, listening all the while for whatever rumors he could pick up and watching for any indication of enemy troops.

Walter used all his strength and ingenuity to keep himself free of a prisoner-of-war camp and to avoid being shot on sight. Finally, he arrived in the huge rubble heap called Hamburg, knowing only that we lived in the suburb of Rahlstedt.

By lucky coincidence, he ran into me on the street one day while I shopped. I looked up and saw him standing there in his sailor's uniform. In a voice filled with awe, he said, "That I should find you, Ruth," and asked where I lived.

I took him home and quietly we entered our second-floor room, where a third bed stood unused. Removing his uniform and handing it to Hans, Walter sank onto the nice, soft bed. With a long sigh, he fell asleep.

Hans and I sat down to think, since the situation called for most discrete handling. We did not know if Walter had been dismissed officially or only told to run for his life. We suspected the latter, in which case he would be expected, ill or not, to report to German Military Headquarters for reassignment. Musical talent? No matter. They would send him headlong into a new front, caring only that he possessed the courage and ability to use a weapon. And even if Walter escaped death in battle, he might soon wind up in a prisoner of war camp.

Another alternative presented itself. If no one had observed him entering our house in uniform, then no one need know he ever had worn one. Hans could offer a civilian suit, since he still wore his uniform, and we could bury Walter's military garb.

Unsure of the right course, we decided to wait until Walter awoke and discuss it further with him. But even that path presented complications. After sleeping for several hours, Walter awoke incoherent, with a burning fever. His breath came in gasps past his hollow cheeks and his eyes stared wildly. In short, he looked ghastly. We needed medical help desperately, and thought immediately of our landlord, a doctor. But how much could we tell him?

It stood to reason that eventually he would learn of Walter's presence. Still, questions plagued us. On the one occasion when we had met, the doctor had worn a uniform, seemingly with some of the insignia missing. What, if anything did that mean? And why was he at home—wounds, perhaps? What sentiments did he harbor toward the present regime? After several hours of mulling the issues, we tired of thinking and sought inspiration.

Hans finally rose and left the room, returning moments later with the doctor, who greeted me quietly and gravely and then turned to examine Walter.

"Lucky he got this far," he said. "He has pneumonia."

In a few short, reserved sentences quietly spoken, he outlined a recommended course of care. He also indicated that he no longer practiced medicine actively. After agreeing to do what he could, he insisted that no one else know. Very good, I thought, I've got a secret and you've got a secret. That should help insure confidentiality on both sides. We thanked him and he departed, saying he would look in on Walter occasionally.

And so he did, unannounced and with a nod of "yes" or "no" as his casual examination suggested. He left medication on a table nearby. We never could have filled a prescription anyhow. We wondered about this highly irregular procedure but accepted his help gratefully.

Next came the problem of how to feed Walter. Without an official military dismissal, he could not obtain food cards. But how could we draw on our own meager supplies, and thus deny the children of badly-needed nourishment?

Hans' comment: "Remember, Cherie, others have sacrificed for us, so now it is our turn. Besides, all is not lost. I'll find a way somehow. My black uniform with the cocky cap, a confident smile, my one leg and crutches, that should do it."

Whatever would we do without his ever-happy spirits, his sustained optimism since his return to life and to us? He left and, sure enough, returned with food cards "for my very sick brother who just arrived in Hamburg from the East."

He needed say nothing more, for by then refugees were pouring into the city in great numbers, most with no kind of certified identification. The clerks in charge of the welfare of these poor people simply accepted the refugees' claims as truth. Hans' story rang with credibility and indeed was descriptively correct other than the omission of the uniform. And once Walter obtained those first coveted food cards, replacements followed monthly, as a matter of routine.

We told the children that Uncle Walter had come to visit and was very ill. We asked them not to mention his presence, especially while standing in line at the food shops, and they kept their counsel diligently.

The first week of Walter's illness proved very trying for us all.

The alarm sirens meant nothing for him since he could not leave his bed. Each time, one of us stayed with him. Little by little, however, his health returned, and soon he insisted on staying home by himself during alarms.

Our fuel supply gave out several times during the subsequent days and weeks, but we dared not try for a new permit for more trees. A close examination of our existing permit revealed that the date seemed blurred. With a little additional "help," that part of the document wore through completely.

Courage born of desperation led Bob and me to take our altered permit with us to the rapidly-shrinking forest for two more trees, and then two more, and ever more. Despite the frequency of our trips, we only encountered an inspector on one occasion. Even that proved a farce. Apparently understanding everyone's need, the man merely admonished all who could hear his loud voice that he did not wish to catch any of us without a permit. Then, without examining anyone, he tramped noisily out of the woods.

* * *

The Russians drew closer to the city from the east day by day; the English and Americans (the latter more from the southeast) approached from the other side. We could hear the guns in the distance coming ever-closer, and spent more time inside air raid shelters than out. One day, an immense raid coming via the Zuydersee in Holland and destined for Berlin passed so close to Hamburg that it kept us trapped in the shelter for 10 anxious hours. More than 2,000 bombers passed over our heads, approaching in groups at regular intervals. So many planes filled the air that the leaders already had returned home while the final raiders still flew eastward toward their target.

Poor Berlin! How glad we felt for our escape. I doubted that my sanity would have survived such continued bombardment. And how much better in Rahlstedt for the children, I thought, grateful that none of the bombs were meant for us as the planes flew back to their home base.

A rumor persisted that the mayor of Hamburg might surrender the city to the English rather than risk capture by the Russians. Most of the citizens seemed decidedly in sympathy with that idea. The rumor gained credibility when city officials distributed extra food and suggested that recipients store it against the possibility of a temporary disruption to further distribution.

That could only mean one thing: curfew. We all would become prisoners in our own homes until the conqueror determined that law and order prevailed. But not even that seemed bad news to us. We preferred almost anything to the daily hail of bombs. No one stripped off his or her clothes to sleep any more, nor even removed shoes. We all slept fully dressed, slumped across beds, almost too weary to move.

For Hans, getting to the shelter brought added pain and inconvenience once he began wearing his new artificial leg. At first it hurt him, and he moved awkwardly and slowly on it. Not long after he put it on for the first time, an alarm sounded. Undeterred, he refused to remove it.

His senseless self-discipline—or stubbornness as I saw it—infuriated me, perhaps because of my fears. "Biegen order brechen (Bend or break)," Germans often said, and it certainly applied in his case. He intended to walk on that leg or literally die in the attempt.

I sent the children on ahead, realizing Hans never would reach the shelter in time and I would not leave him. The sun shone brightly in the deathly still air as we made our way to the shelter.

"Can you hurry a bit?" I urged excitedly, as tiny silver specks appeared high up in the sky. The bombers flew directly overhead, and their bombs were falling toward us like silver pellets in a glass of water. "We'll never reach the shelter before they strike," I cried.

"Let them come, they won't hit us." With icy nerve, he stopped and looked up for a moment. "The wind is taking them down on an angle, and they won't hit us. Come, Cherie, stop fretting." I saw that he was right, but still felt terrified.

In the next days we received an extra allocation of food—100 pounds each of cabbage and turnips, some salt pork instead of normal meat rations, some extra bread that seemed baked mostly from sawdust, and either a double ration of milk or four times our regular amount of buttermilk (adults received only skim milk).

Bob, our good helper, trekked all this home with the aid of the janitor's wheelbarrow. Our deprivations left him awfully thin. Sometimes his hunger pangs gave his voice a querulous tone when he begged for just a little more bread and butter. But he quietly accepted my answer that I had none to give. His resignation fairly broke my heart.

As a growing lad, he needed the nourishment to handle the heavy work we asked of him. Sometimes on Saturdays he rode a borrowed bicycle or took a train into the country carrying an empty knapsack. He always returned with something—five or ten pounds of potatoes, maybe a pint of milk or an egg or two. Bob described for us the generosity of the farmers he met.

"They always say, 'Come in, lad, and have a glass of milk, you look so thin. Is it as bad as all that in the city?' Guess I'm lucky I'm so thin; otherwise I'd never get that extra glass of milk, or the potatoes, either," he said, his eyes lighting up and a smile on his face.

No doubt he needed more visible sympathy from his parents, but we hesitated to coddle him or the others for fear of undermining the strength and courage they needed so desperately. Our struggle for survival allowed for no letdown, and Hans and I suspected that the real test still might lie ahead of us. Therefore, we showed a harder, less loving side of our natures to our children than we really felt. We expected them to measure up, and they unquestionably did, with no moping or shirking of duty.

Amid all the difficulties of daily life, we still made ample time for fun and joshing and celebrated every conceivable occasion without waiting for birthdays or holidays. Extra food, a day without an air raid, even Uncle Walter's first day at the dinner table, all brought forth rejoicing.

For one event, Hans arranged something extra-special. First, he gathered the children after dinner. "Tomorrow is Mother's birthday," he reminded them, and together they planned an evening of entertainment.

Early the next morning I made my way to the kitchen to begin breakfast, only to find the children up and bustling, their beds made and Bob hard at work trying to start the stove. They did not try to conceal the motive for this unusual behavior, but came to me one and all, offering hugs and kisses for a "Happy Birthday."

All day they remained their usual well-behaved selves as they played in the garden, enjoying the warm sunshine. A conspicuous absence of enemy bombers allowed us all to enjoy an afternoon treat of thin cocoa. That evening, supper over and the dishes done, the children begged permission to play a game before bed, to which we consented.

A few minutes later, Bob came downstairs and said that Irmgard needed me. "Go back up to her, Bob, and I'll be along in a minute," I said. Hans, who knew the reason behind Irmgard's request, said he would come, too, and we hurried upstairs.

When we reached the little hall leading to their room, to my surprise I found chairs set out for us, facing a blanket strung from the bed to the wall. Bob stood at attention in front of the blanket. In his best announcer's voice, he intoned:

"Tickets not needed for tonight's performance of 'The Dance of the Snowflakes,' from 'Peterchen's Mondfahrt (Peter's Ride to the Moon), as learned by Irmgard Bohle in the Royal Theater of Posen." As they began, Walter joined us and took a seat behind Hans and me. This was meat for his love of the artistic and the imaginative.

Ceremoniously, Bob lifted the blanket, and there in the middle of the "stage" sat baby Hans Bernhard, his hands outstretched over crossed legs, his little head and eyes lifted to the stars. He sat as still as a statue and wore a sweet little improvised pixie cap.

Irmgard and Dieter then joined him, wearing costumes arranged from clothing in our trunks. They danced to a tune Irmgard learned at the School of Ballet for the Koenigliche Hoftheater in Posen, where she indeed had played the role of a "snowflake" in one dance and a little "star" in another of the very excellent Christmas presentations of "Peter's Ride to the Moon."

She had taught Dieter well, and they gave a serious and complete rendition. They enjoyed their performance immensely, and I felt touched to tears. What priceless wonders Hans and I had brought into this sad, sad world.

We clapped loud and long in appreciation. When they took their bows, Walter congratulated them. "That was so beautiful, and you worked so hard at it, we must see it again tomorrow night, and I will accompany you on my harmonica."

It was time for hugs and kisses and great big "thank-yous" and then off to bed. For all of us it had been a perfect day.

CHAPTER 37

An End to Hitler and the War!

May 1945

It could have been the end of an unusually quiet and uneventful day, but for the shock we received upon tuning in our radio that evening. Walter pricked up his ears and opened his eyes wide in astonishment.

"Hans, are you listening? I wonder what it means."

Coming over the air waves were strains of Bruckner's solemn Seventh Symphony, certainly the foreboding of a special report of tragedy.

Then came the roll of military drums, followed by the voice of the announcer of the Hamburg radio station, who told the German people that the Fuebrer, Adolph Hitler, was dead. He had died in his operational headquarters in the Reichs Chancellery, fighting to his last breath against Bolshevism, the announcer said. Named as Hitler's successor: Grand Admiral Doenitz.

Admiral Doenitz now came to the microphone and talked to the people. We sat stunned. Coup after coup had been organized and tried against the life of Hitler in the belief that by removing his influence, Germany would be saved. The plotters had talked less of loyalty than of how to rescue their "Fatherland." But they were afraid, for it was uncanny how Hitler had managed to frustrate every try. Sometimes the plans were aborted even before the attempt. People had begun to believe that the Fuehrer was invulnerable.

With Hitler gone, all that was over. Although Doenitz tried to sound strong, no alternative remained but the war's bitter end, which marked the end of the Reich. Surely lesser fanatics would realize that it meant surrender for Germany, but even that brought relief—at least for those of us in the West, believing that our fates would rest in the hands of the English and the Americans.

But what about those poor people, those many civilians and soldiers, who would fall into the hands of the Russians? This prospect horrified all Germany. Its mere mention brought to mind horrible visions of torture, rape and pillage almost beyond the stretch of our imaginations, worse than anything except perhaps what had been described to us by an undiscovered observer of the annihilation of ghetto inhabitants in the East many months earlier.

My thoughts ran rampant. Then suddenly I was aware of silence in the room. Admiral Doenitz had stopped talking, and the radio had signed off.

A knock sounded at the door, and the doctor asked if he might come in. He was alone. This was the first time he had made an effort at more than a nod of acknowledgment, even after his unofficial care of Walter, who met the doctor's appraising glance with a heartfelt handshake and "Thank you" for the help given during his illness. Above all, Walter wanted the doctor to know of his gratitude that his presence in the house had not been reported to the police or military.

It occurred to me, and maybe to Hans and Walter also, that the doctor had not felt it necessary as long as Walter was ill. Was it his purpose to tell us he no longer could hide the fact? Walter was well, and the city still had not surrendered.

The doctor sat down on the one remaining empty chair.

"As you have heard, our Fuehrer is dead," he began. "Doenitz cannot carry on for long. I predict Germany will surrender within the next few days. As far as you are concerned," he addressed Walter, "I have not known of your presence and now I doubt whether it will make any difference. May I suggest you stay off the streets until the status of Hamburg becomes known?

"As for you, Mr. Bohle," he said, turning to Hans, "I assume you, too, obtained your dismissal from the Army; if not, in your condition it should not be hard to get, and I suggest you do so. I regret that I no longer have any status with the military to enable me to help you."

He stopped and stared down at his uniform, and with an offhand gesture continued. "My uniform suggests that I should, but you see, I am stripped of my stripes. I am, or was, a professional military doctor. It so happened my superior was not. He was a doctor drafted into the service. Rank is not always dealt fairly. Mine remained subordinate because I was suspected of Party disloyalty.

"I admit I had no use for the Party. I was a doctor first, a German second, and outside of that, just tried to keep my own counsel. Unfortunately, there were incidents, even in the handling of patients, when I could not comply with Party requirements, such as reporting the disloyal mutterings of a wounded soldier — or not reporting a sick sailor in one's own home."

He smiled, with a knowing glance at Walter.

"And so, although doctors were not too plentiful in the field, I was dismissed. I was lucky! Some of my associates did not fare so well. It has been a terrible time for me, to be idle in the face of so much need. But now, soon, things will be different maybe—now my time has come again."

The doctor paused, then resumed with a question for Hans. "What do you think will be the next move in the chess game, after our surrender?"

"I'm not sure," Hans said. "But I know what I wish it would be, and so do many others. Are you perhaps thinking the same thing?"

"I don't know." The doctor seemed to study what he wanted

to say next. Silence filled the room, but neither Hans nor Walter spoke.

"I don't know," he repeated slowly. "Maybe. Many German soldiers now will enter American and English prisoner- of-war camps. Unfortunately, many also will be imprisoned in Russian camps. And for them, there will be no help, unless.. well, unless. . . ." he paused. "Unless the Americans and the English—the Allies—enlist our soldiers in a turnabout against Russia, to free them and the Russian people, too, of Communism.

"After all, how different is Communism from Fascism? If the one was so dangerous that it needed to be destroyed, the other is equally so. Although I am sure the German soldier is tired, sick and tired of war, he knows the ropes of Eastern warfare. And I believe his fear of the Russian Bear overrunning his country would make him a most willing collaborator.

"The time for such action is now, or almost. But will they? Will the West realize that this should be their move? I cannot sleep at night for wondering and hoping. If they do not, I believe some day we all will be sorry."

A long pause followed this unusual suggestion. We all were busy with our thoughts. Our visitor looked up at us with the question in his eyes, and when he saw no answer in ours, he said, "Well, enough for tonight. We can talk about it again sometime later, maybe after the next few days, if you wish."

He arose and bowed to us. "Gute Nacht, Meine Herrn, Gute Nacht, Frau Bohle," and left the room.

Hans and Walter had risen with him and Hans saw him to the door. He was gone.

Walter took up and played on the doctor's suggestion. "What do you think of the doctor's hopes? I never thought of that, but is it such a bad idea? Do you think the West's military authorities have thought of it? And if so, would they actually gather up our men and our experience and go against Russia? Right now, at this time? I don't believe it! I have no such hope left."

Walter paused, and then with a brooding look asked a question. "I wonder how he died." Of course we knew immediately that he referred to the Fuehrer.

* * *

Early the next morning and all through the next days, we watched the papers carefully and left our radios on as much as possible. We dared not miss any call-up of extra rations. The end of the war could be only a matter of days. Our larders showed that we could exist meagerly for a week.

Not so our supply of fuel, so Bob and I took daily trips to the forest, evening after evening, as much for the twigs and dried needles as for the logs. One night total darkness surprised us before we had completely felled our tree. Returning eagerly the next morning was a lost cause. It was gone.

Air raids continued unpredictably but did not last as long and seemed less organized. That was demonstrated when a single bomb fell over the railroad station in Rahlstedt, flinging us out of our beds one night with no previous warning.

We could hear the guns as all three fronts drew nearer. Speech among the people became freer. They talked openly about what the mayor would do with the city. The citizens admired and respected him greatly and without exception believed he would choose whatever method of surrender he felt would be kindest to the people. None of this "Fight unto death!"

A suspenseful week passed before the news of Germany's complete surrender was assured, and the once-free city of Hamburg (one of the Hansiatic free cities) was given without further bloodshed into the hands of the English.

The fighting war truly was over. No more fires would fall from the skies, but we were apprehensive about what further hardships were in store for us.

The first edict announced by radio decreed that all inhabitants of Hamburg must stay behind doors, windows and curtains for the next three days, the house arrest to end at midnight of the third day unless the release was rescinded. We were given to understand that it would depend on our conduct. Any revolutionary activity, any rioting, would find quick retaliation. Any individuals found on the street would be shot. The city in total would pay.

Just minutes before curfew enforcement, Bob and I returned from our last wood-chopping expedition in the forest, exhausted. Time after time, during the next days, we looked through the curtains at the street. Not a soul was in sight. Never had a huge city been so quiet. It was so strange, it was unbelievably eerie, that silent city in the dreamy half-sunlight.

There was nothing to do, nowhere to go, no business to transact, no commerce, no telephone to ring, no communication with anyone outside the home, no outside chores, no shopping, no trains, no cars, no planes, no movement of any kind. Yet behind all the windows, behind all the doors and walls, thousands of eyes, hearts and minds—yes, a whole great city—waited. And if there was no sign of life by night, no lights, no sound, there was once again undisturbed sleep.

By midnight of the third day, no reversal of orders had been issued. The next day we would be free to leave our homes, free to circulate—but as we pleased?

CHAPTER 38

Living Under Allied Occupation

May-June 1945

The three long days and nights of curfew provided much time for reflection and a flood of questions came to mind. How would life change, once we could move about freely once more? And what about food? Would we receive the same rations as before? Less? More? Week after week, without fail? Regarding work, how would we earn a living?

We also wondered how the new military government would rule. The local German authorities had provided Hamburg and its suburbs with wise leadership. Would the conquerors allow them to help effect a smooth transfer of power? Or would the Allies choose instead a course of spiteful retaliation, hard and unreasoning and radical? We suspected that for the answer we just would have to wait.

Distribution of food resumed when the curfew ended, but our enforced idleness continued for many days. To break the routine, I decided to visit Hamburg proper and see for myself the damage inflicted by the weeks of intense bombing since our last visit.

"Hans, I said, "I just must see how Hamburg looks now—how many people remain alive. Want to come, too?"

He laughed. "Go, Cherie, and see. You'll find plenty of survivors. I don't want to go, but you can tell me all about it."

I knew his leg hurt him, so I urged no further. On my own, I tramped in exhilaration from one end of the Aister to the other, past the Rathaus, the famous old church nearby, mingling with and watching the people. With no air raid to fear, they promenaded up and down the streets, as in peacetime on Sundays or a holiday, leisurely and aimlessly and wonderingly.

"Hans, dear, you have no idea how many people survived!" I exclaimed excitedly on my return, to his amusement. I attempted to tell him all I had seen, and although I held his attention to some degree, I also felt his restiveness. Lacking a purpose for too long, he desperately needed something to do.

As for Walter, the absence of a piano left him like a fish without a pond, with no outlet for his emotions and his anxious fingers.

"Patience—yes, I know it's necessary, but I find it very difficult," he confessed, speaking freely with Hans and me in English. The fate of his musical possessions in Leipzig, which had fallen into Russian hands, weighed heavily on his mind.

"I wonder if I ever again will see my concert grand piano," he worried aloud. "And all my music, a veritable library of irreplaceable first and only editions, hundreds of works with full orchestra scores. If lost, they are gone forever."

That was his life. He paced, anxious and troubled, finding no peace. Nor would he, he realized, until he took action to rescue his treasures. But how?

We marveled at the children's inventiveness at filling their hours. They wanted to take a walk and look for English soldiers, to see what kind of uniforms they wore. We often strolled with them through the streets of Rahlstedt. One day, we met Uncle Gustav, out walking with his cane, and people with whom we had shared the air-raid shelter night after night. They acknowledged us politely but made no effort at conversation, since group gatherings for discussion were forbidden by threat of arrest.

One morning a huge column of German soldiers, now prisoners, marched past the front of the house as I watched from behind my window. Their disheveled uniforms bore no insignia of rank as they straggled along, drooping shoulders revealing their exhaustion and discouragement. With downcast eyes, they glanced about furtively, hurt pride still wishing to disavow the shame of defeat as they headed for a prison camp. But for chance and coincidence, Walter and Hans might have marched with them.

A few good nights' sleep put us all in a somewhat better frame of mind. Nevertheless, persistent problems plagued us: Walter's piano and his music; Hans' restiveness and his desire to find useful activity once again; and our desire, Hans' and mine, to repatriate to the United States as soon as possible.

Since the English had taken Hamburg, we wondered how to find American authorities who might assist us. Hans suggested I visit English Military Government Headquarters in Hamburg, where someone might direct me to the proper authorities. I knew this made sense, but still shied from meeting those military personnel in their new role as conquerors. How much easier if Americans had taken the city, I thought to myself!

Also, despite the tremendous urgency of our situation, I needed a little time to adjust my thinking. All these new orders assaulted my feelings as an individualist. I rebelled at the restrictions placed on the populace. My name, age and nationality were posted on the front door along with all the others living in the house.

Yet perhaps the posting of my country of origin might prove beneficial if observed. Once more it might provide protection for me and my family, as I believed it had all through the years in Poland. I still clung to an unshakable conviction that as an American citizen I was invulnerable. It was a magic word!

But what good would my U.S. citizenship do for me if I was caught in possession of my Belgian Browning revolver? The victorious Allies had ordered all Germans to surrender their weapons, but I did not feel myself German. As a resident, did the requirement apply to me? The thought was overwhelmingly repugnant— or was it only my unwillingness to conform? I thought carefully about the matter, not wanting my family to suffer for my lack of good judgment. I knew I must be prudent, not stubborn.

A placard appeared on the entry door to the city hall, and its words offered hope. If it meant what it said, we could expect understanding, wisdom and feeling in the coming difficult adjustment period. It said: "To the German People: We have come, not as conquerors, but as liberators, to free you from the tyranny of Nazism. (signed) General Eisenhower."

Throughout history, people have been "freed" from one ruler only to suffer abuse at the hands of another "liberator." Hitler, too, offered freedom from the wrong of the Treaty of Versailles—with his ideology of Nazism. That new proclamation declared freedom for the German people from the terror of Hitler's regime. But freed to what? How could one clearly fathom the meaning of the statement amid the confusion and weariness that prevailed? The people could not yet feel themselves free. They only could wonder if they had become captives of another.

Perhaps, I hoped, under careful administration, the inherent obedience of the German people could be turned to loyalty and allegiance to an imposed democracy until they understood and could establish such a system themselves. I hoped with all my heart that the compassion revealed in the words of that placard reflected the true feelings of the new men in charge. I believed that it would—maybe not always, but largely. In time, all could, would be well again.

These thoughts raced through my mind as, one sunny morning, I rode to Hamburg in search of an answer to my own personal problems. A visit to the English Military Government Headquarters, if I could locate it, might do the trick provided I found the man with the information.

* * *

But once in Hamburg, I grew disconcerted by the steady stream of soldiers who raced here and there, on foot and in the many jeeps. Which building, among the many, housed the right person for me to talk to? No use to hurry aimlessly from one place to another. Better to walk slowly and watch carefully, feeling my way. Finally I stopped at the Park Hotel. Was that it? I showed the guards my U.S. passport and they admitted me but left me to wander from room to room, over four or five floors. Since I was American, not English, no one felt like talking to me—but also no one threw me out.

It seemed aimless, that wandering around—and it was just that. What should I do? Just leave again, as leisurely as I had walked in, and go home knowing nothing?

"Hey there, little lady, what ah you doing heah?" said a voice right behind me.

I whirled to face a high-ranking British officer, approached him and explained my mission, showing him my identification.

"American, eh?"

He stood a moment in thought. "Wouldn't the Swiss mediate for American interests at this time? You might inquire; they, too, are in Hamburg, and you will find them. . . ."

He paused and fingered his thin mustache delicately. "Just a moment, I shall make inquiry."

Disappearing into a room off the hall, he returned in a moment with a slip of paper on which was written the address. To my proffered thanks, he responded, "Quite all right, quite all right."

A lead at last, and not too far away, I guessed. But I had walked a great deal already that day, just picking my way that far. On the near-starvation rations we received, I lacked the energy for anything beyond the long walk back to the train station. I decided to return home and start anew the next day at the Swiss consulate.

The menfolk at home applauded my progress and urged me on toward the next day. Walter offered to accompany me, hoping someone might help him find a way to get to Leipzig, where he could try to rescue his belongings.

"Why Leipzig, Walter, not Munich?" I questioned.

Walter stared at me, aghast. "Haven't I told you about the offer I received several years ago from the Leipzig Conservatory?"

"No, we knew nothing of it, but good for you—that's quite an advancement," Hans replied. "But what now? Leipzig is in the Russian Zone, not very promising. Do you think you can get in and out again with your valuable possessions?" he asked, worried.

"I'll have to take that chance," Walter answered. His bravery exceeded mine. "Something would have to be worth my life to make me venture into Russian-occupied territory," I said.

"You've said it exactly; it is my life," Walter commented. "It is my life."

The next day Walter and I visited the Swiss consulate and began what eventually became a year of standing in line. A young lady official made very short work of me.

"You should have taken our offer to send you back to the U.S.A. at the beginning of the war. Now you are no longer an American citizen," she said, and started to walk away.

At her words I felt the pain of heart spasm. But if she believed she could finish with me that easily, she soon learned otherwise. Perhaps she mistook my shyness for a lack of tenacity. Speaking up for myself took me double the effort required of a natural extrovert. But I had not been sustained by my belief in my American citizenship all through the war years only to allow a disinterested Swiss employee to cast me aside with one short clipped sentence and a wave of the hand.

I followed her. "What offer to go to the U.S.A.?" I asked.

"You and your two children were offered repatriation," she said. This came as news to me, and all of a sudden I did not believe her. She stopped to look at me, to see my response to this devastating information.

" . . . and if so, madam, do you believe for one minute that I would have left my husband, my oldest son and my baby here to fend for themselves? Americans are not that cowardly. We may fear trouble, but we do not run away from it."

I stopped, trembling. Once again my life hung in the balance and I was sure I had finished myself with my outburst. But my tormentor seemed to enjoy the repartee.

"Well, then, why don't you get a permit to go to Bremen, where the American Military Government can help you contact your state department."

Now, that was a good suggestion, and probably the only one she could give. It told me exactly what I wanted to know, namely that the Swiss no longer held American foreign records. I could accomplish nothing there and I resolved to go to Bremen.

Walter also failed to find help at the consulate, and I had been "dressed down." By then we were fatigued and emotionally drained. I decided we would spend the following day at home recovering from our ordeal. One day more or less would make little difference for our next move. Besides, I needed to find a way to Bremen. Other than the suburban connection from Rahlstedt to Hamburg, no passenger or freight trains ran between the major cities.

* * *

During our many months in Hamburg, we had received no visits from any of our friends. Our only outside contacts were with Uncle Gustav and his family, whom we saw at intervals after we moved to our own rooms. Aunt Bertha was home again. Her daughter Liselotte was well again and had remained alone in Kassel with her five children to await her husband's return from the front.

I met Aunt Bertha by accident one day as I shopped, and we stopped to talk. Almost her first words were that she missed us. "And if I had been at home, you never would have needed to leave," she said sadly.

I tried to reassure her, to tell her that we left in part to make room for Liselotte and the grandchildren

"They did not want to come," she answered. Then, brightening, she asked, "But do you know who is home?"

After a moment's thought, I said, "Your son, Hans-Adolph?" Smiling, Aunt Bertha refused to say. "Go see for yourself" she insisted.

On the basis of my assumption, that evening Hans and I paid

a visit to Aunt Bertha's daughter-in-law, Ilse. For the first time since we had moved to Hamburg, we spent a social hour without fear of an air raid.

Ilse was not alone: we found her sitting in the parlor with her husband. We last had seen Hans-Adolph several years earlier, and he had personified the typical North German—lean, blond, blue-eyed, well-groomed; with an arresting vibrancy; serious, yet full of quick wit. But that evening, he greeted us without surprise or enthusiasm. Clearly he was very tired, and his wit took on an edge of irony.

He rose and walked toward us, dressed in civilian clothes. The glass of wine in his hand reminded us that Ilse had seemed to enjoy a surplus of food and drink all through the war. We never knew whether she drew from an unusually large stockpile or whether her wealth afforded extra privileges. Perhaps she had possessed the dexterity to manipulate the black market, or maybe she just had tapped her pre-war sources. That night again, the wine and refreshments were not abundant but very good.

We talked, enjoying a social occasion. Hans-Adolph said he had "hurried home" to reclaim his practice, which had been in the hands of an elder physician for the duration of the war. He worried that the substitute physician, having lost all equipment of his own, might attempt to ignore their agreement.

The words "hurried home" sounded simple enough when mentioned in that casual manner. But later, after the wine loosened his tongue, he lost his reticence to fill in what the statement really implied. Ilse, I noticed, just sat with a gleam in her eye and watched him, clearly pleased about something—and soon we understood. She admired spunk and courage, and loved Hans-Adolph for "cheating the Russians out of one more dead man, or one more German prisoner."

Hans-Adolph, on the plains of Russia, had recognized his own fatal position in time to remedy it—but not without his heart fairly bursting in horror and fear. In the final stages of the war, he had seen men all around him torn to bits by Russian guns. Legs, arms, heads and torsos flew through the air in all directions, he said, and the horror literally turned him to stone. Then he ceased to think and simply ran, ran for his life. Fortunately, he headed north toward the Baltic Sea. Arriving at the shore, he maneuvered himself into what was, he believed, the last ship out. He had not known its exact destination—Germany, or perhaps Denmark or even some other unknown goal. He only knew that it sailed away from the carnage.

Hans-Adolph never told us where the ship finally landed. And we knew, without any further comment from him, of the intelligence, nerve and strength, required for him to get past the checkpoints and the prisoner camps and make it home again. He arrived tired and hungry, but miraculously with hardly a physical scratch.

But it was left to the future to reveal in his emotional nature the cracks which that and other nightmarish experiences on the eastern front had produced. They had made him hard, very hard. For that he was not to be blamed. One could only preserve one's sanity with the weapons at hand.

Hugo Frohne, our banker friend, visited us one day. He was back at work again in Hamburg, his pre-war home. It was good to see him, and he thought our set-up unique. Of course, we expressed mutual congratulations on surviving until then—which led inevitably to a serious discussion of "what next?"

Have I not said repeatedly that each time we faced a problem, an answer came from somewhere, as though an unseen hand guided our destinies? This time Mr. Frohne served as our deus ex machina.

"My wife is visiting friends, the Grobiens, in a suburb of Bremen called Lesum," he explained. "Why don't you, Ruth, obtain a travel permit and go to the autobahn. You'll find it somewhere in the Hamburg harbor area. From there you could beg a ride to Bremen. All sorts of vehicles are traveling these days. From Bremen, you could reach Lesum easily. Mrs. Grobien is a lovely and gracious lady who would help you, I am sure."

He made it all sound so easy. Consequently, one morning soon thereafter, Walter and I took the suburban train to Hamburg. Although we arrived early at the office for travel permits, we still found a waiting line already "a few days long." That meant coming day after day without guarantee of any special place in the line despite hours of waiting the previous day.

My impatient nature rejected that idea immediately. But how could I convince those already in line that I deserved special treatment? Turning to Walter, I said loudly in good American English, "They said for me to come forward immediately today so we can get this thing underway."

Walter remained silent and waited, but those around us understood enough of my statement to automatically clear a way for me to enter and move forward. I feel, in retrospect, very much like apologizing for my deception to all those patiently waiting, equally anxious people.

But at least my needs were minimal and quickly filled, and I did not deter them for long. In a matter of less than 30 minutes I obtained my permit for Bremen. Walter, however, needed a permit issued by someone in a special department of the British Military Government, and that meant a personal interview at another office a long walk away.

We stopped en route to eat the bit of lunch we had brought along and longed for a cup of good hot coffee. Even ersatz or water would do. But with neither available, we did not dwell on our longings. Anxious to try our luck, we pushed forward hopefully.

Poor Walter was repulsed at every turn. We soon found that only I could gain entrance and speak for him, but even my evident nationality and American English failed to impress those English officers. They disdained him, and me as well, for doing the inquiring for him.

Yet how could I hesitate to help Walter, a musician with no taint of politics in his life, no act unworthy of himself, his creator or his fellow man. I knew I must aid him, and continued on from room to room, building to building, with the same request—but with no success, hearing only "sorry," always "sorry."

By 5 o'clock, only one officer remained unvisited—the chief of them all, Colonel Mathers. Looking through his glass door, we saw a distinguished-looking, white-haired gentleman seated behind the desk.

Although thoroughly disheartened, Walter agreed not to concede defeat without tapping all sources. We approached a very beautiful girl sitting outside the colonel's office and explained our problem to her. She listened, then bade us wait while she spoke to the officer. Dared we hope? She returned and announced, "The colonel will see you both."

Rising to greet us, he offered us seats, then carefully and quietly drew from us our reason for needing his assistance. With a show of interest tempered by caution, he asked about Walter's career—where he had taught and played, what he had done during the war, and about his plans for the future.

My brother-in-law was a finely-chiseled personality, cultured and sensitive; kind with a quiet simplicity, a thorough gentleman and, above all, a truly great musician. For the first time that afternoon, he and I received the respect and understanding due us.

Walter answered the colonel's questions fully, describing himself his positions on the teaching staffs at the conservatories in Munich and Leipzig, his concerts in Europe and his world tours with renowned artists. At last the colonel looked at the clock.

"I will do what I can for you which, unfortunately, is not much. You will have your letter assuring you of safe travel to the border of the Russian zone and back. But at the border you must go on alone and unprotected. Have you the courage?"

"Oh, yes, I do, I must; it is my life. Thank you so much for even this much help, and for wanting to help."

The secretary then took the colonel's dictation while we waited. When we finally left him, our hearts overflowed with gratitude, not only for the precious letter but also for the restoration of our self-respect. Now we each had the "go" sign for an adventure. We wished we could continue together, to lend each other additional support. But our missions lay in opposite directions, and each would push on alone.

CHAPTER 39

The Journey to Bremen

June 1945

I was not just a little frightened at what I was about to undertake. Silly, actually. Normally, Bremen was only two hours distant by rail from Hamburg. But the times were not normal.

My instructions said go the harbor and "catch" the autobahn. Where it was I had not the faintest idea. The harbor area was immense, one of the main ports, with all its branches, of Northern Europe. It was logical, of course, to take the suburban train from Rahlstedt to Hamburg proper and then ask my way along.

What should I wear, and take along? A black and white suit? Yes. A hat? No—impractical, and besides, I had none. A white silk scarf would do, and that I had. A raincoat? Yes, and one change of everything. Also documents.

But why was I fiddling over a choice of clothing? I was wasting time. Subconsciously, I am sure, I was hoping my dawdling about would cause me to miss my train to Hamburg. I didn't want to go and then, I did. Really, I had to.

Perhaps my disordered feelings did not show. We ate breakfast. No one had much to say, nothing was different, yet it seemed to me that Walter sighed an unwonted number of times. He was troubled, his emotional level high, like mine.

Walter left first that morning, and a little later, Hans and I kissed each other farewell. His confidence in me was unbounded, he said. The children clamored for a hug. With a promise to somehow, if possible, get word to them of my well-being, I closed the door behind me.

I was on my way and, even with the stalling, I could not avoid catching the suburban train to Hamburg. Really, what was the sense of a suitcase? What an encumbrance. But I could not make up my mind not to take it.

It was a nice day, no rain, hazy sunshine, not too cold. All the way to Hamburg I wondered where I would find the autobahn to Bremen. But why was that so hard? It was only a matter of once more overcoming my eternal shyness, and asking the people around me, time and again.

In the station in Hamburg I asked, and out on the street, again and again, adding and subtracting the various descriptions. A few streetcars still were running, and at one stop I talked to the conductor while others boarded.

"You can take this car and transfer onto number six going west, then on to the end of the line; that ought to do it," he said.

I boarded and paid my fare, but wasn't satisfied. The conductor had not sounded too sure, and so I determined to remain on the back platform and continue talking about it with other riders. Some did not know, others did not care, but one person thought the conductor had been right.

He was. And long before reaching the terminal of the second tram, I learned that from there on it was a two-mile jaunt to the point of goal, the bridge. All that took much time, and I was both impatient and apprehensive. The conductor called out none of the stops, but it was quite evident when finally we reached the end of the line since everyone left the tram.

The scene was sort of country-like, with trees, the river, and a road on which a long black limousine waited. I hesitated, viewing my surroundings. I had no desire for that tiring, time-consuming two-mile trek, especially with luggage. For whom was the man in the black car waiting? Three women who had left the streetcar with me were negotiating with him. No doubt they, too, were trying to avoid the hike. Or was that all?

I walked over and listened. It was evident that the man wanted riders, ostensibly for money, maybe for other reasons. He had room for one more, and I decided to join them—at least for the next two miles. We paid him, climbed in and quickly were on our way.

In what seemed like no time at all we approached a controlled checkpoint at a bridge over the Were River. I expected the driver to stop and let me out, but he saw at a glance that the military police already had their hands full examining the many cars ahead of us. He gave just a hint of slowing to a stop, a mere suggestion of intent, then swiftly continued over the bridge on his way, unhindered.

"Was that not the checkpoint to the Bremen route?" I asked.

"Yes," he answered. Already we were on the far side of the bridge.

"Please let me out," I begged.

He did, and then quietly and quickly sped on his way. I wondered where he was going. For what point of destination were the other women bound? I had not even asked. Why not? Maybe he would have taken me all the way to Bremen. But I had an instinctive mistrust of him.

Of one thing I felt sure, and on that would have been willing to place a bet. He had crossed the river and avoided control far easier than he had deemed possible. Pure luck! Maybe he was a Nazi official, or even a fleeing SS man. I wondered.

While mulling those thoughts over in my mind, I recrossed the bridge back to the checkpoint from where I hoped to obtain a ride to Bremen. Many people already had congregated there, all begging rides. They dashed from car to car as the military police stopped each vehicle and checked credentials. I followed suit, ignoring a new 'no fraternizing" law. It forbade military personnel to talk to me, a civilian, but was there any reason why I should not tell the soldiers on duty what I wanted? I needed no answer from them, only their cooperation.

Amazingly, many cars were bound for little towns, but none seemed to be going to Bremen. How tiring to flit from car to car, only to find more disappointments and dashed hopes. The hours passed, noon came and went, the guards changed again and again, and still no car was bound for Bremen.

A group of us wanting Bremen finally had gathered. About 4 p.m. a huge truck piled high with large sacks of something—maybe potatoes—pulled up and stopped. The cry came from one of the group: "Bremen!"

Turning, I dashed for the truck and, asking no further questions, started to climb aboard, but it was too high. Several men already were on top, and only one man remained to climb up after me. Seeing my inability to make the grade, and noting the impatience of the driver, he made little ceremony of the method of his help. By the time he followed lithely, the truck already was in motion out and across the bridge.

I had begun to believe I would need to return home and go through the whole aggravating routine again the next day, but there we were, way up on the top of a truck. There were five of us, four men (two of them German soldiers) and one lone female, me.

I assumed we would take the autobahn, since that was the quickest and best road. But when we came to a crossing, our driver turned off onto a secondary road. How consternating! We were on our way to somewhere, but was it really to Bremen? From where we sat, the driver was inaccessible for questioning. We would have to go where he took us.

In addition to watching the landscape apprehensively, I observed my fellow passengers more closely. The two robust men were not in uniform. The other two were infantry men, pale, thin and suffering. The noise of the truck left no chance of conversation and, had I questioned them, they would likely have offered no explanation. Their freedom probably was dependent on silence.

Maybe the soldiers were hungry. In my bag were two sandwiches. I had had no time, nor any inclination for lunch and since I still was not hungry, I offered one to each. Surprised, they accepted quickly. From somewhere, I figured, I would get more for myself.

After about 30 minutes, our truck approached a little town; we were halted on the outskirts by a constable. With him stood at least a dozen people who climbed aboard immediately. We heard the driver scolding and fussing, but the constable remained firm. They need a ride. Take them as far as you can," he commanded.

"If they could walk this far from East Prussia, they could manage the rest of the way," our driver complained, in a very bad mood.

"Go 'long with you," admonished the policeman, seeing that all were set safely for the ride. The truck driver ground his gears sharply into first, then second and once more we were moving.

It was still light when the truck, after another good stretch of driving, pulled up at the side of the road. Again we were at the very edge of a small town. "Rothenburg," said the sign.

Jumping down, the driver called, "Far as we go." Immediately, he turned and walked toward the town, leaving his passengers no chance for argument.

Almost all had descended and assembled in a group by the time I slid over the last sack to the ground. If that was as far as we were going, that was where we would have to spend the night.

My ears picked up talk of some who suggested sleeping out under one of the many haystacks that stood in the open fields. That was not for me. I turned and followed the driver into town, on the long street that evidently ran through the commercial zone.

* * *

In a short time shops came into sight on both sides of the street—a cafe, a konditorei, and others of general description, with living quarters in between. To overcome a sudden weakness which most probably was just the need for food, I entered the first cafe. It was dark inside, but I discerned that it was filled with soldiers. English troops!

"This is off-limits to you, lady," I heard someone say.
"Sorry. Then please tell me where I can get some food."
"Not a place in town for civilians," the speaker replied.
"And military government headquarters, where do I find them?"
"Two blocks down and across the street. Sorry, lady."

If the town was completely off-limits to civilians, where would I find food and a bed for the night? I saw lights still on in the military government headquarters when I reached it, and asked for a ride.

"Perhaps a jeep might be going to Bremen?"

"We will gladly accommodate you tomorrow morning, but no one will be going that way any more tonight."

Then to the urgent question of where I would sleep for the night. For a solution, it was suggested I hunt up the officer of the day. "He lives in a villa two miles out of town, one mile west and one mile north on the main road. You cannot miss it; there 5 a tiny guardhouse at the entrance."

With no choice but to follow that suggestion, I headed in the indicated direction, stopping frequently to ask if I was proceeding correctly. Despite the "no fraternizing" law, my good American English startled those I met and usually loosened their tongues, and I received the help I needed.

I arrived finally at my destination, dragged out and scared. The villa stood far back in a beautiful fenced-in garden. A British soldier stepped out of the guardhouse and demanded my credentials. Taking my U.S. passport and my travel pass, my only identification, he disappeared into the house.

Fully 10 minutes later, he returned and bade me enter. By then I was so frightened by my own courage that I almost succumbed to a strong impulse to run away. Instead, I followed my guide and entered the house.

"The officer of the day is away for supper and has been called," a guard told me at the door. "Please come in, and if you wish to freshen up a bit, take the steps to the second floor. By the time you finish, he will return."

I followed a military guide up the stairs and into a bedroom. There he introduced me to two tall, immediately likable, refined young English officers. They quickly placed at my disposal soap—real soap—a linen towel and running warm water.

"This is almost something to get sentimental about," I said, looking down at the precious bar. "I haven't seen real soap in years."

They both smiled, suddenly very alive and happy.

"We haven't seen an English or an American woman in almost that long," said one as the other nodded. "Now we can write home and tell them we received a lady visitor today. The stuff we write about gets pretty boring, you know."

At that point I was summoned down to the parlor, to meet the officer of the day. He seemed most pleasant and greeted me so kindly that I was relieved of my fears.

"Have you eaten today?" he asked.

"Breakfast, but nothing since."

"Well, then, join us in the dining room, won't you?"

"Us" turned out to be all of the English officers in the house, at least a dozen of them, handsome, well-groomed, some young, some closer to 30. Cheese and cold cut meats sat on the table, along with white bread—real white bread—and real butter, real tea, wine and cigarettes. I hung back a bit at first, but when they all gathered around and offered me dish after dish.

My excitement and the cigarettes made me slightly sick. I was also filled with apprehension. Their treatment was deft and delicate, but the questions came thick and fast. I answered everything truthfully, and even told them my husband was a German—a Kraut. They seemed unimpressed by that one way or the other.

* * *

But night had come and the problem of a place for me to sleep remained unresolved. I had to be "brought under," so they said. At last the officer of the day said, "I will drive you to Bremen," and ordered his jeep brought around.

I saw no complication in his offer, assuming that he just enjoyed the companionship of a woman and the peculiarity of the circumstance. So I accepted gratefully. I would have enjoyed the "jolly good company" of the officers for another hour, but it already was 8 p.m., so we set out on our way to Bremen.

We left, and I wondered how to convey my thanks to my host for his goodness. But I was promptly startled to find that he already had thought of a way. He suggested we stop for a stroll and a rest in the forest nearby on our way.

Maybe I should have anticipated something like that, but I had not. And even if I had understood him, I could not respond. I was not an adventuress, only an over-sheltered, scared wife and mother forced on a somewhat hazardous mission and in no mood for bestowing favors.

I assured him gently that I needed no rest and that I did not want to take any more advantage of his time and kindness than necessary. Groping in my mind for ways to shift his thoughts in another direction, I decided that conversation might prove more effective than silence. And the safest subject probably would enlighten me, too—his home and family in England.

Once more, as we neared Bremen, he questioned me about stopping. Again I pretended to misread his meaning, and he considerately dropped the subject.

How glad I was when we suddenly entered Bremen and stopped in front of the brightly lit American military government headquarters on the Contrescarpe.

"This is as far as I can take you," my companion said, turning me over to the German policeman on guard.

"My God, my God, what can I do with a woman at this time of night?" exclaimed my newly-appointed custodian. "In a few minutes it will be 10 p.m. and curfew. The prisons are full and lousy."

I turned and thanked my English officer most sincerely, who then drove off into the night. The policeman, unwilling to assume any responsibility for me, ordered me into the military government headquarters building to await the officer of the day, Major Haguewood. The American officer soon appeared, dismissed the guard and offered me a chair in his office, also a cigarette. Dared I refuse?

"This is my identification," I said, handing him my passport. He thumbed through it and then, handing it back, asked what he could do for me.

"Somewhere, there must be someone I can talk to who will tell me how I can get myself and family back to the U.S.A.," I said. "Four of us are American citizens, but my husband and eldest son are not." I proceeded to explain about the law of 1934, which allowed children born abroad of one or both U.S. citizens the privilege of applying for U.S. citizenship, which we had done and received. Our eldest was born before this law took effect.

We spoke of my reasons for living abroad, of Hans' excellent coal and oil experience and holdings, and how Hans had managed to evade Nazi Party membership. I also explained how Hans' independent attitudes, along with my American citizenship, was used against him and led to his induction into the service despite his age and four children.

Then I mentioned my brother, no doubt somewhere in the service of the American military, and how I would appreciate help in finding him. Last but also important, I admitted that I still possessed a revolver, a Belgian Browning, and wondered what to do with it.

The major noted all those things, plus my brother's name and address. By then, I was beginning to shake with fatigue. A look at my watch told me it was 1 a.m.

Still one more subject was vital to the major: where was I bound, and where would I stay until morning? I explained that my destination was the home of a family by name of Grobien, in Bremen Lesum, relatives of friends of mine. "The lady is American, her husband German, although born and raised in South America."

And as to where I would spend the rest of the night?

"Please, sir, if you will just give me something to read and a chair in the entry, I will be still as a mouse and leave in the morning."

"Can't do that. I cannot allow you or anyone to remain alone here. Come with me. I have an idea."

I followed the major out the back door, over long paths, and through garden gates until we came to another house, brilliantly illuminated. Up the steps to the first floor, we entered a lovely parlor occupied by five or six lounging U.S. Army officers. The officers' club!

"Ah-ho, what have we here?" asked one of them. They all stood and were introduced.

"The lady has no place to stay for the night, and I thought I could double up with one of you fellows and let her use my room," the major suggested. I saw nods all around.

A way had been found, but first, wouldn't I please sit down and talk to them a while? Certainly! And so the same questioning and answering began again. They listened with interest and curiosity. who could blame them? As for me, the answers remained the same, the goal unchanged.

It was 3 a.m. when the major finally took me to his room and showed me the connecting bath with its extra entry from the outside, which he said he would use to enter for shaving in the morning. I should be neither surprised nor frightened to hear him. With that, he left.

Locking my door, I closed the one to the bath and threw myself fully clothed onto the bed. I was afraid to let myself drift off since I did not want to oversleep and embarrass the major by my presence at dawn. Then, too, after the long, tense day I just could not relax. I lay there thinking, backward and forward.

The major entered the bathroom at 7 a.m. and left again. Immediately thereafter I "freshened up" and prepared to open the door to leave when I heard the major's voice from the other side. Evidently speaking to the maid, who wanted to enter and straighten his room, he proclaimed roughly, "Stay out of there, will you; I've got a woman in there."

Opening the door, I looked into the face of a startled maid and an open scowl on the mien of my benefactor. Did his generosity of the previous night seem folly to him in the light of morning? Gruff and short, he told me where I might get breakfast. Then for a moment he softened, returning to a suggestion made during the conference with the officers the night before. I was to ask Hans to come to Bremen and work for the military government in coal and oil liaison, which they needed badly. Did I need money? No! Just help, friends and understanding.

"I will find your brother, and you bring me the gun for safe-keeping," he said. With that, he dismissed me matter-of-factly.

In search of breakfast, I followed his directions and found the place, but without a written order I was turned down unceremoniously. My next move yielded better results. A lone gentleman on a deserted street told me that neither bakeries nor cafes would open until much later, but that another two blocks would find me on the direct route to Lesum. I walked to that street, stood on a corner and waited, wondering if I would be able to hitch a ride.

In the distance I saw a span of two horses with the driver sitting high up. The horses pulled a huge flatbed, with people sitting all around the edge, their feet dangling.

"Fahren sie nach Lesum (Going to Lesum)?" I called before the driver reached me.

"Ja, ja," he shouted back, grinning. He slowed a bit but did not stop. His passengers, some men, some women and some soldiers, overheard. As the vehicle was passing me, someone called out (in German, of course), "Quick, throw us your suitcase and jump aboard."

Quite without thinking whether I possessed the strength, I swung my suitcase and someone caught it. In the interim, the vehicle had passed me, and I had to run to catch it. But I did and was pulled aboard by some of the riders. That strenuous business made my heart pound furiously, but again I was headed on my way.

Thanking my fellow passengers as soon as I regained my breath, I settled next to a young woman and, like the rest of them, let my feet dangle over the edge of the board.

"How far to Lesum?" I asked.

"Twelve kilometers, and we must cross the Weser River before we get there. At the river is a very strict checkpoint, where they search for SS runaways." The young woman who spoke looked me sharply in the eye as she volunteered the information. No doubt she meant her glance as a warning, both to me and to the young German soldier on my right, to make sure our credentials were in hand, and in order.

When finally we approached the river, the horses slowed to a walk and my neighboring soldier jumped from the truck and disappeared. That provided explanation enough. As for myself, the inspection caused no trouble, but even so, such moments always brought apprehension.

In Lesum, the driver stopped to let me off. I paid him five RM and thanked him, and then the whole informal "equipage" moved onward. What next? I was nearing the end of my quest. Although I knew the name of the lady whom I sought, I lacked an address, knowing only that the house and gardens sat on a hill bordering the Weser River.

"Ought to be easy," I muttered to myself. "Everyone is registered with the police. I wonder where to find the Gendarmerie?"

An old man walked toward me, and I asked him. "Oh, up this street and down the next, then just ask again." But even when I finally arrived and stated my goal, the answer was far from satisfactory.

"We have lost all records of Lesum," said the official in charge. "The police station and courthouse burned to cinders in an air raid and nothing, absolutely nothing, was saved. The name is not familiar to me," he added.

The police officer asked around, but to no avail, then suggested I go to the welfare department or the Red Cross. There a woman said she thought I wanted the big white house at the end of the narrow path to the river road. She went into considerable detail describing how to locate it, and I soon found out how important it was to follow her explicit directions.

My way took me through multiple streets to a narrow path bordering a forest stand. It continued on so long through an isolated section, making such strange turns, that I stopped and re-read my instructions.

Finally, however, I saw a big white house through the trees. That must be it, I thought. By then I really had nervous flutterings in my stomach.

A lady answered my ring of the doorbell. "Frau Grobien?" I asked. "Yawohl," she answered.

I told her my name and our mutual friend Hugo Frohne, on whose suggestion I had come in search of the American consulate. Mrs. Grobien immediately asked me in and took me to her lovely parlor, where we sat and talked for another quarter-hour. She inquired about my trip and then offered me a place in her home for as long as I liked and needed.

"I'll set up a cot for you here in the parlor; you can help me," she said. "Then we1ll go to the basement for something to eat."

"My home is filled, three stories of it, with homeless people," she explained. "My children and I live in the basement. Only one area, the master bedroom suite on the second floor, stands empty. That I reserve for when my soldier husband comes home again. I dare not think in terms of 'if;' only 'when,' and so far I have received no notice to the contrary." She was determined and commented with finality, turning on the smile in her face. "And you, my dear, as soon as you have eaten, must sleep off your exhaustion. Then we will formulate plans."

CHAPTER 40

An Adventurous Return to Hamburg

July 1945

The sun was just beginning to cast shadows when I awoke and dressed hastily to join Mrs. Grobien's family for the evening meal. Of her four children, all but her eldest son were at home. Her daughter and two younger sons greeted me, as did Mrs. Frohne. They knew of my adventures from Mrs. Grobien, so they asked no more but accepted me promptly in a friendly and casual manner as one of the family.

I shared a modest meal as their guest. Afterwards, the children cleared the table and did the dishes together. They took this little chore as a matter of course, and kept up a lively conversation all the while, dotting it with light banter that I found thoroughly refreshing.

Mrs. Grobien excused the dimness of the light in the room and through the halls, saying they had few reserves of light bulbs and candles and could not obtain replacements. Besides, they were lucky to have electricity at all.

Any day, I was told, train traffic would resume between the suburbs and Bremen. With no automobiles permissible to ordinary civilians, and no train or bus transportation, walking provided the only remaining way of reaching a destination. I, for one, lacked dedication to acquiring the skill of a sprinter, and surely not to the tune of 25 to 30 miles a day. Yet I faced a return to Bremen in the next few days because my mission remained unfinished. Therefore, I once more would have to overcome my aversion to begging for a ride from drivers of military government vehicles and perhaps try to convince some driver that "fraternizing" did not appeal to an American woman.

I waited in Lesum for one more day, resting and hoping with the others. But when Friday morning arrived and the trains still were not running, I decided to wait no longer. I needed to see the major; he must have no chance to forget his offer of work for Hans, and to that end I needed travel permits for both of us.

My day became beset with obstacles. Once on the main thoroughfare from Lesum to Bremen I quickly discovered a checkpoint where all cars stopped. One by one I approached the drivers of jeeps, trucks or whatever moved. Practically all were American Military Government personnel. My American English caught their attention, and they at least listened to my request, but the non-fraternization edict apparently kept them from giving me a ride. Eventually, however, a driver came along with the courage to take me along.

Once in Bremen, I found my way on foot to the headquarters building. But there again my trials continued, as I encountered a large crowd waiting for admittance. For someone less inhibited, it might have simply been a challenge. However, for me to push through the crowd and use my American identification to gain quicker entry was a trial, every time.

I felt timid and frightened as I entered the "sanctuary for the second time and waited while the major's secretary announced me. Major Haguewood received me, visibly surprised.

"I thought you would be over the seven hills by now," he said.

"I told you my destination, and that is exactly where I went," I responded.

"I begin to see. And what may I do for you today?"

"Please, Major Haguewood, I need travel permits for Hans

and myself. I want to go to Hamburg and get Hans so he can work for you."

"Well, I begin to like this," the major said. "Sit down, sit down, while I phone my buddies."

He did call, and then left me while he joined them for a brief conference.

"No doubt you realize that your husband's record as a possible Nazi will be checked?" the major asked on returning.

"Yes, I realize that but it is quite all right."

"It's your funeral if there's a problem," he said, with a shake of his head.

The major asked me to return at 1:30 p.m. for the completed permits. The request meant no lunch, more standing in line and nowhere to wait until then. Obviously, officers failed to recognize the discomforts such instructions entailed—or perhaps they just simply didn't care. And when no permits were ready at 1:30 as promised, I concluded that they again were testing my truthfulness and the strength of my purpose. I waited, and in time received, but by then it was almost 4 p.m.

Again I faced the need of a ride, and the humiliation of getting many refusals. Some of the soldiers were anything but kind, yet I always managed to find someone who would help.

Arrived in Lesum once more, I related my tiny bit of progress to my new friends, and they were delighted. We discussed ways and means of returning to Hamburg, since my travel permit did nothing to provide a mode of transport. I had suspected that would be true, so while waiting for the permits I had struck up conversations with passersby, hoping for guidance. Most responded pleasantly enough but offered no enlightenment.

One person, however, had insisted that the trains from Lesum to Bremen would start rolling again at 6 p.m. that evening. He had added that freight trains once again were running between Bremen and Hamburg, and that one would leave from the freight yard in Hanover at 10 p.m. that night. It seemed an extremely hazardous undertaking for a woman traveling alone, but if there was no other way, so be it. I would go, but please, God, be with me, I prayed. Maybe others, too, would try for that same ride.

With that knowledge, I asked Mrs. Grobien for advice. "What would you say if I left right now to catch the expected train to Hanover, and then try to find the freight train going to Hamburg?"

During my day and a half in her home, I had become impressed with this woman's charm, nobility of spirit, and yes, her bravery, too. She had taken me into her home on the basis of a mutual friendship and fed me from her own meager allotment of food, supplemented by homegrown vegetables from her garden. It took all her strength and ingenuity to provide for her family and the homeless ones under her roof. All the while she hid her deep anxiety for the welfare of her soldier husband, whose whereabouts and status still were unknown, to spare her children worry and concern.

With her characteristic strength she viewed the prospects of my adventure, believing in my ability to handle the difficulties before me. I felt it! So we looked steadily into each other's eyes, squared our chins and straightened our shoulders as we bade each other farewell and "Good luck."

"Bring your husband," she called as I walked away. I turned and nodded. How could I thank her enough for all she had done? Our life in Bremen was just beginning.

Many people already stood waiting at the station in Lesum, which was encouraging. I spoke to several, and each had heard that a train would arrive at about 7 o'clock that evening. The adage "follow the rumors" had led to some interesting complications during the war years, but often to good results as well. Rumors all seemed to contain at least a vestige of truth. And so it happened again. At close to 7 p.m., a locomotive approached slowly, pulling three coaches. With the station closed, no one held tickets, so we just climbed into the nearest coach, expecting that a conductor would find us later.

The coach I entered had only one vacant seat, next to a handsome young man at the window. I stopped and asked if the seat was free.

"Bitte, bitte," he answered, with such a warm, clean smile that I felt drawn to speak to him—or perhaps I just needed someone to listen. As soon as I sat down, I burst out with "Well, here I go again," and told him of my plans for the night. He responded with equal excitement. "It's no good, your plan, it's no good. To roundabout, too many... well, never mind, you just cannot do it."

"Then what can I do?" I answered, questioningly.

"Stay in Bremen overnight and try the military government motor pool in the morning."

"Great idea, but where do I stay in Bremen?"

"I don't know, but I suggest urgently that you switch plans."

"Thanks, I believe I will. Perhaps I could sit all night in the railroad station. I did notice it was deserted just a few days ago and maybe still is. That's eerie."

"Better than a railroad freight yard at midnight," he responded. I nodded.

Time flew, and soon the train approached Bremen, leaving me with no time to further contemplate a decision. I left the train as my seatmate had suggested. Once outside, I found myself lost in thought as I wandered down a lonely street in the gathering twilight, pausing in front of a display window filled with dusty travel brochures.

A lady passed, evidently a citizen of Bremen who recognized me as a transient. I felt a bit embarrassed that she saw me loitering casually on the street at that time of evening. She stopped and turned to me.

You looking for a place to sleep?"

"Yes; I know of none."

"Almost the only possibility is the little hotel about a block and a half straight ahead," she said, pointing down the street. "Try it."

"Thank you, I will," I said and headed for the destination she indicated. I found it easily, and it was still open. I walked up a short flight of stairs through the entry and into a small lobby. The proprietor was there but he looked past me indifferently. Maybe he suspected any lone woman at that hour.

"Have you a single room for me?" I asked.

"No ma'am!" Silence.

An idea came to me. Fingering through my purse, I pulled out my American passport and held it up to him.

"And now do you have a room for me?"

"Yes, ma'am," he said, obviously a bit intimidated, but without changing his tone. "Follow me."

We walked up four flights, entering a single room with a narrow, broken window, only partly glassed. The outer walls stood intact, but the top half of the wall to an adjoining toilet was mostly missing. The room contained an unmade bed, rumpled and soiled from the use of many former occupants, and a chair. The proprietor demanded payment in advance, and I requested a call at 6 a.m. Fortunately, I did not depend on it, because it never came.

He left, and I examined my surroundings more carefully. My scrutiny revealed a horrible room, but at least it got me off the streets. Better that than a jail cell for missing curfew.

Standing on tiptoes gave me a full view of the lavatory over the damaged wall, similar to the public rest rooms for men in Paris. Refusing to sleep in the filthy bed linens, I pulled them off; turned the mattress and spread my raincoat over as much of it as it would cover. Then I lay down fully clothed.

Before long I fell into semi-consciousness, but was fully awake again at the first sounds from the street. My watch had stopped, but the number of people out and about suggested that curfew had ended and I guessed it was nearly 7 a.m. Quickly I rose and left.

* * *

I was getting used to asking my way around and soon found the military government motor pool. The place already buzzed with activity, but what surprised me was the large number of people asking for rides to places of every description. Once again the odds seemed against me, since few trucks traveled as far as Hamburg.

In the normal routine for acquiring a ride, a group headed for a given destination gathered together and then made a formal request to the officer inside. I tried my hand at organizing a group and seemed to be making some progress when, just at noon, someone called out my name. I rushed into the office.

"Mrs. Bohle, if you go to this address, a small truck carrying two passengers will leave for Hamburg at 2 p.m., and it will take you."

The clerk behind the counter gave me a note with a name and address. It was noon when I reached there and a lady answered my ring. In response to my inquiry, she said, "Yes, my husband is going to Hamburg at 2 p.m.; at least I hope so. His driver is very tired and must sleep first. Will you come in and wait?"

She ushered me into the parlor, furnished only with one chair, nothing more. Then she left me in the company of an enormous German police dog, shutting the door to the rest of the apartment. Considering that the room was bare, why did I need the guard? He lay quietly, head on forepaws, his great eyes watching me intently. Oh, yes, I was thoroughly familiar with the uses and habits of police dogs. and so for the next two hours I did not move, not even a finger.

At 2:30 p.m., a gentleman entered. "Please come," he said. "My chauffeur is rested and we still can make the trip."

I followed him down to the garage where a small, enclosed, black half-ton truck stood waiting, with room for two in the front seat. He asked me to crawl inside the rear and sit on the floor. A tiny window behind the driver allowed me to observe our progress and make sure we were headed in the right direction.

The ride passed uneventfully until we neared the bridge crossing the harbor in Hamburg. A lone soldier stood signaling for a ride, and we stopped. He climbed in back with me and the chauffeur locked the truck again. Although I felt apprehensive at the change, the soldier took no notice of me. We were just two pieces of cargo.

One glance told me that his thoughts were focused on the checkpoint on the far side of the bridge. I worried, too, but for a different reason. Whether or not the military police knew we were inside, we moved on without inspection.

In downtown Hamburg we came to a final stop. I paid the driver and asked whether by chance he would be returning to Bremen.

"We will be here until noon Tuesday," he answered, whereupon I made arrangements then and there for Hans and myself to return with them. We agreed to meet at that very spot. Then they left me and I hurried to catch the S-Bahn for the hour-long ride to Rahlstedt, followed by a 30-minute walk home. I had not eaten for more than 36 hours, and only sheer willpower kept me going.

It was nearly Saturday night; although I had been gone only since Tuesday morning, it felt like a lifetime. In all those days I had hardly thought of my family, my mind too loaded with problems and decisions. Excitement filled me at the thought of seeing them again, and at their surprise over my news.

How wonderful to feel their loving arms around me once more, to hear the happiness in their voices and see it on their faces. Home is a magic word, when it represents so much love. They hovered over me, anxious to show their pleasure at my safe return.

I told them at the supper table of my travels and what I had done. The serious side of my venture I waited to discuss privately with Hans later.

When I told Hans about my trip home and my arrangement to take him back with me, he agreed, despite his misgivings about leaving the children alone to take care of themselves. We knew that they could and realized they probably would enjoy the challenge.

Hans said that Irmgard and Bob had clipped the ration coupons and done all the shopping in my absence, and he had done the cooking. With Dieter's help, Irmgard had bathed, clothed and fed Hans Bernhard. Bob had gathered wood from the forest for the cook stove. So in reality, they had kept house for their daddy and reveled in it.

Our only concern was for their health and well-being, and for that we no doubt could call on the willingness of the doctor in the house. Together, then, Hans and I visited him and his wife. With a twinkle in their eyes, they agreed readily to assist our plucky youngsters if asked. We left them the address of Mr. and Mrs. Grobien in Lesum, where they could reach us if necessary. They had noticed Walter's absence and were interested in our plans.

As a family, we spent a happy weekend at home. I felt the need of the quiet security and relaxation after the previous week of excitement.

All too soon, Tuesday arrived. We bade our children a very fond farewell and left, allowing plenty of time to meet our contact.

Both Hans and I felt twinges of sadness—a far cry from the exuberance with which our children accepted our trust in their ability to play "mama and papa" and keep house. No trace of doubt or fear occupied their minds, and they could hardly wait to take over. Irmgard, only ten years, provided the leadership, and the others were willing collaborators.

Not one word of complaint came from Hans as he endured the tortuous pain of walking to the S-Bahn. I, too, kept silent about the ordeal of dragging our heavy baggage. We pressed on because we needed to grasp the opportunity for a ride to Bremen, and we arrived at the designated meeting spot with perfect timing.

"Lucky for you that you arrived first," said our chauffeur. "We would not have waited."

Again, as before, neither the driver nor his passenger said anything more—nor did we. We assumed that they were on a legitimate mission, since they held permits from the military government motor pool. Nevertheless, when the doors to the truck closed and locked, it gave us an oppressive jolt. Occasionally the riding grew rough, forcing us to brace ourselves with outspread hands, but the time passed more rapidly since Hans was with me.

When we arrived in Bremen, Hans bargained with our drivers to take us on to Lesum. Reluctantly they complied, but took us only to the town center, where they left us to walk the rest of the way. By 5 p.m., we stood at Mr. and Mrs. Grobien's doorstep.

She met us at the door, beaming.

"I knew you'd make it somehow, but this is record time. Welcome, Mr. Bohle, your room is ready and waiting."

We entered and stammered "Thanks," the best we could, too moved by the munificence of her hospitality. I noticed a new air about her, too, a new vivaciousness as she laughed and talked with Hans about the difficulties of present-day travel. She seemed so changed, almost glowing. Surely our arrival had hardly made the smile on her face so shining. I followed them both as they led the way to a new room, set up for us and equipped with two beds and a half-bath.

"After you freshen up a bit, I'll have a surprise for you, she said. And with that she left us. The house seemed very quiet as we walked through the halls to the second floor. Was she alone that day? I wondered.

Fifteen minutes later, Mrs. Grobien tiptoed toward us.

"This way," she said, and we followed her to a huge room at the end of the corridor with windows, doors and a balcony all facing the long slope of grass and trees down to the Weser River. That was the first impression. Then I noticed a king-size bed standing against the far wall. Mrs. Grobien led us over to it and, bending down, kissed the man who lay there.

"This is my husband, Mr. Grobien, who just reached home this morning," she said proudly. "God be praised for his safe return."

The man in the bed was no doubt a returned warrior. From what field of baffle, or of what rank, he never spoke. Nor did we ask. He lay still, too weary to rise even to a sitting position in acknowledgment of the introduction. His fine features, elegant small movements and the expression of his face typified more the slender easy grace of the Spanish Grandee than a German military man.

We exchanged a few pleasantries and expressed our happiness at his safe return. Then, as he wearied, we made haste to leave.

"That was the reason for her glow," I said aloud as we made our way down to the familiar kitchen, but of course Hans could not appreciate the transformation.

In a few more days Mr. Grobien recovered fully from his exhaustion and joined us at meals.

* * *

On a rainy Wednesday morning, Hans and I began our new venture by "bumming" a ride to Bremen. It still was difficult to get someone to stop and take us, but persistence was rewarded. At last we stood before the guard on the Contrescarpe, holding up our special permits in hopes of seeing Major Haguewood.

The exchange of measured glances between the major and Hans, when they finally met, was frightening. I had never told the major about Hans' injury, which he took in at a cool quick glance. One look at Hans' face told me he felt like a slave on the block for the first time.

Again I suspected that the major had assumed I would not return, and yet there I stood with Hans, as promised. He seemed finally to realize that he would have to cope with us.

Major Haguewood ushered Hans into the office of Major Borland, leaving me to sit outside and hope. The result of that interview was a questionnaire to be filled in by both of us. It dealt solely with citizenship and relationship, if any, to the Nazi Party. Once we had completed the form, the security division would process it, and the outcome of their investigation would determine the question of employment.

For the next two weeks we endured an endless wait while we stayed with the Grobien family, who shared our hopes and anxieties. Then came good news—Hans had received assurance of employment! However, with the starting date unsettled—it might be any day—Hans had to remain in Bremen.

We both felt that I should return to the children, at least for awhile, since postal service to Hamburg had not resumed and we both needed assurance that our young folk were well. I prepared to leave, promising to return within a week if possible.

The Grobiens and Hans bade me farewell with reassurances that I would be able to return safely. If only I shared their confidence, I thought, instead of always being sick inside with fear. At least my fear did not show to them. But Hans knew, I felt certain, although he pretended not to, which gave me strength and reassurance. After all, I scolded myself, anyone could accomplish what I did anyone but me, frightened, pampered me.

Once again I secured a travel permit and checked in at the motor pool in Bremen to inquire about a ride to Hamburg. As I stood waiting, a man behind me tapped my shoulder.

'Pardon me, madam. I overheard your request for a ride to Hamburg. I am an employee of American Express Hamburg, and am anxious for passengers. I have a truck with lots of room. If I can find at least six passengers, I will go."

We agreed on a price, and I said I would wait at the desk for him to find five more passengers, unless I got a better offer in the meantime. He seemed nervous and ill at ease, and that made me uncomfortable as well. But maybe all was legitimate, and at any rate I might have to take a chance, despite the strong aversion I felt toward him, instinctively.

An hour passed, and nothing more favorable came along. My American Express man returned with the news that he had found seven others who wished to go to Hamburg, and they were waiting outside near his truck. I resigned myself to travel with him and followed him outside to what seemed more like a moving van than a truck. Fortunately, I was given the chance to ride up front.

He asked to see our travel permits, but instead of returning them, kept them in his possession. That would enable him to present them all together at checkpoints and speed us through the inspection process, he said. I preferred to hold my own documents, but I agreed.

We boarded and began our journey, but the truck headed in a direction away from, not toward, Hamburg. When I questioned the route, he just smiled quietly and said he was picking up a bit of furniture at the edge of town before leaving for Hamburg. Devious, I thought. Clearly he was being paid both for the transport of the goods and by his passengers. He should have told us that earlier.

His "bit" of furniture turned into a sizable shipment, and loading it on the truck delayed us for more than a full hour. But then he did turn toward Hamburg, and the ride was smooth and good. Shortly before reaching our destination, he turned to me and asked if I planned to return to Bremen. If so, might I want to lease my apartment in Hamburg to him? I answered evasively, since we still were unsure of our plans. But I also left open the possibility in his mind. As long as he still held my travel permit, diplomacy was better.

* * *

"Mother, Mother, Mother!" squealed four happy youngsters upon my arrival. The three youngest rushed forward, arms outstretched for a hug and a kiss. Although equally thrilled, Bob hung back a bit, showing his enthusiasm only through the shine of those big blue eyes in his quiet face.

In years past I would have brought each of them a gift after so long an absence. I no longer even thought of such niceties, nor seemingly did they. Quickly they took me on an inspection tour and, indeed, I found everything not only commendable, but remarkable. The children had bought each day's rations and either used or stored them. The kitchen was spotless and the baby's clothes were washed, smoothed and put away. Firewood stood cut, stacked and ready for use. How proud my little Trojans made me.

The doctor and his wife heard the furor and came to see, meeting us in the halls with kindly questioning faces.

"Everything is proceeding well," I said.

"Here, too," they countered. "You truly have wonderful children."

I looked proudly upon my little brood. They are worth every effort, I thought, with a grateful heart. God willing, we will get them a future, a chance in life.

I spent a week at home, then decided to return to Bremen "to see how Daddy is doing," leaving the children with extra money. Once more they were on their own.

At the station my usual method of questioning anyone and everyone led me to a freight train, scheduled to leave at 5 p.m. Soon I found myself entering along with many other men and women, young and old—a car usually occupied by hogs.

Once again rumor served me well the train pulled out at about 5 o'clock that evening, as predicted, in the direction of Bremen. My fellow passengers sat silently as we moved forward. Some smoked cigarettes filled with weeds—stinking stuff, but they said it calmed their nerves.

Lovely scenery bounded the tracks. I succumbed for a while to the desire to sit in the open doorway and let my feet dangle. But as we crossed a river, one of my boots nearly became caught between the bridge trestle and the freight car, and I realized how close I had come to being dragged off my perch and thrown into the river. From then on I sat in retreat, in a corner, and brooded. With all my heart I hoped we really were headed for Bremen, but I could not be sure. My watch said 7 p.m., and it still was light—normal for that northern clime, but still I grew anxious. Would we arrive before the 10 p.m. curfew?

Finally, we seemed to approach a city. The train stopped in open fields, then started again, screeching to a halt on a siding that ran parallel to the city but far, far from it. For the first time, I realized we would not necessarily roll into a railroad station. Where were we?

I saw the outline of buildings, some tall, on the horizon. But nothing cued me in to our location. And evidently the train was going no further. The other occupants seemed resolved to staying where they were for the night, but I decided to cross the fields and head toward the tallest building in the distance. I saw no obstacles between me and it. I needed to orient myself so that the curfew would not catch me on the street. I hurried across the weed covered empty land toward the closest of the buildings.

Suddenly it became clear that I approached, or perhaps already had entered, the grounds of a prison. Ahead of me a big wall towered, topped with barbed wire. For a moment I felt dismayed, but soon I discovered a tall iron gate that I could see through. How often Hans had reminded me that "with the need comes the solution." My heart lifted.

A guard saw me and approached the gate. His mien of disapproval gave way to understanding as I explained how I had gotten there and where I wanted to go. Without speaking, he brought out a great ring of keys from under his coat and opened the gate. He then led the way as we walked to another gate, which he also opened and motioned me through. I found myself standing on the road between Bremen and Lesum. It was not quite 8 p.m. and twilight. The signs on the road said, "Lesum 9 kilometers." That meant I must manage more than one kilometer every 15 minutes to make it under a roof on time.

I set out with an urgency, walking and running in turn, timing myself exactly and hoping to gain a little to allow for fatigue and growing darkness. To save time I could make a short cut along the top of a ridge bordering the river. It might be dark by then, although the dark, lonely road, used mostly by occupation troops out for a "stroll," most assuredly was not without hazard, either.

Postponing my decision regarding the shortcut, I kept up a running gait for the next 105 minutes. When finally I reached the river, 15 minutes remained before curfew. By the river route, I could make it to the Grobien house in 10 minutes. Going through town required 20. Those 10 minutes could mean a curfew violation, and jail. With no real choice, I plunged into my last lap with the greatest possible speed and determination—along the river road shortcut.

My heart beat like a triphammer and my eyes followed every shadow. It was just light enough for me to recognize what I thought was the back gate of the Grobien estate—at least I hoped so. To reach the house, I had to leave the open road and run down through about 100 yards of lowland, full of very tall grass and brush.

"Don't think, just do it," I said to myself, but my fearful nature responded, "You are tempting good fortune by being here." My reasoning side answered back, "I can't help it, and anyway now I am in it, I must finish! I got myself into it, now I must get myself out."

I reached the high gate and struggled to reach the lock; it gave way. Slipping through, I locked it again, viewed my surroundings to make sure, and then smiled with gladness. Home! It was 10 o'clock, and dark.

* * *

A dim light still shone in the kitchen.

"May I come in?" I called when I found the door to the garden ajar.

The adults in the household jumped from their seats and rushed to the door.

"Du Grosser Gott!" Mrs. Grobien exclaimed, folding me into her arms. Her husband followed right behind, with a big, happy smile, while Hans came to me in no less record time.

"Nein, so was (Can you believe it)! Setze Dich und trinke mit uns einen echten Kaffee (Sit down and drink some real coffee with us)," said the lady of the house, releasing me to Hans' embrace. We proceeded toward the table, where I fell more than sat on one of the benches. Hans took my wraps and then came to sit with his arm around me. He was so relieved, he said. They had just talked about my possible whereabouts, each a little more worried than they cared to admit.

"Did you walk from Bremen?" Mr. Grobien asked: I nodded assent.

Mrs. Grobien set a cup in front of me and I drank. "Real coffee?" I gasped. "What a treat. Who has been working the black market? Gosh, this is great." I sipped again and they all beamed with pleasure at my appreciation—but no one offered an explanation.

"Are you feeling all right?" Mrs. Grobien asked.

"Yes, I'm fine now."

"Anything to eat today?"

"Kind of you to ask. Yes, a few sandwiches this afternoon."

My hostess ignored the answer and soon set a little offering on the table. Hans hovered about as I ate, visibly relieved and happy to know my whereabouts. Then, since they all seemed anxious for news, I told them of my trip and how proud I was of the children. Before the clock struck midnight in our dimly lit basement kitchen, we all agreed that most of us, in peacetime, use only a very small portion of our full potential. Perhaps it was not all bad to have seemingly-impossible tasks thrust upon us, at least some of the time, to reveal to us our capabilities.

I, too, waited anxiously for news. Hans supplied it later in the privacy of our room within the circle of his warm, strong arms. The news was good. He was definitely an employee of the American military government. They wanted me, too, within a week! The military government housing office would assist us in finding lodging, and a jeep would drive to Hamburg to collect the children and our few newly acquired possessions. It all sounded great, but the "how" of the many details overwhelmed me. Yet, enough for one day. Tomorrow might solve itself.

The task ahead of us was not simple. Even though I had become accustomed to walking some 10 miles a day, for Hans to accomplish this would bring much pain. First the walk to Lesum, then the wait and fight for a ride to Bremen, followed by the awkward climb-aboard whatever vehicle we found for the ride to the military government housing office. Later, no doubt, would come another walk to the prospective home, the subsequent inspection and a return walk to the housing office. After that, if all arrangements worked out, yet another walk to the transportation office to arrange the time and day for our move from Hamburg to Bremen.

I shuddered! Hans would walk his stump sore, rub it raw, and it would take days to heal—and then only if he could stay off it. That seemed hardly the way to prove himself effective for a job that would require his full energy every single day.

But what right did we have to complain? For the time being, Hans belonged to the vanquished and I with him. We must hide our pain and show our willingness to cooperate, to help ourselves and our children in any was we could.

The next several days passed just as I had mapped them out in my mind. At the housing office, they offered us a choice of two homes; the nearest was a half-hour walk from the Contrescarpe. We went there first.

The house was lovely, with both the second and third floors available. Furniture filled the second floor to the brim, while the third, which consisted of bedrooms, contained only two beds. The children once more would use our double-deckers, but we would need a bed for baby Hans Bernhard. The whole house lacked heat and electricity, like all others in the area.

In a tiny kitchen under a peak roof stood a small coal stove which we and two other guests in the house would share. We would need to come to an agreement concerning hours needed and who would furnish the coal. Still, it really was a good house that offered all we could ask for, and more.

At the housing office we received excellent news coal and electricity for the entire house would be available to us as soon as we moved in. Hans and I took it.

Next we visited the transportation division to arrange our move from Hamburg. We were told an Army truck would arrive in Hamburg four days from then at about noon and would bring the family and any possessions we had.

No question about it! When we explained that we really should go to Hamburg to help the children, who otherwise would not know what to do, they supplied us with travel permits but coolly ignored every plea for help with getting there. Evidently they expected us to solve that problem alone. We considered reaching out for the influence of Major Haguewood, but he already had done so much for us, we could not ask for more. It was our problem.

Hans and I were extremely tired by the time we returned to Lesum. Our accomplishments made us happy, but we were also apprehensive of the future. What therapy, then, to enter the Grobien home, with its atmosphere of sanguinity, its faith in the future, its trust in Divine help. Not just fatalists, the Grobiens were believers.

It helped a great deal the next day that the sun shone bright and cheerful, since we had decided to try the new train from Bremen to Rothenburg (Weser), where we hoped that the British Military Government would consent to take us to Hamburg by jeep. Our travel permits said, "U.S. Military Government would appreciate assistance to two Americans to reach Hamburg."

Rothenburg! The town where, about a month earlier, the officer of the day had driven me to Bremen so graciously and kindly. He had my gratitude, and yet that day I hoped we would not meet. Perhaps it was because our travel permits, listing us as two Americans, were not quite correct at least, yet.

Arriving for the second time in that small town, we managed a ride with no difficulty. But Hans and I had hardly boarded a truck and it had just begun to move forward when the side door of the military government transportation center burst open. My erstwhile benefactor hurried out. He stopped, hand thrust upward questioningly, as he recognized me. But we were already on our way.

At home in Hamburg, the doctor and his wife were dismayed when they saw both of us returning, fearing the collapse of our whole plan. when we explained the truth, they rejoiced with us. The children liked living in their lovely home, but seemed ready and willing to tackle any and all new adventures, especially one that included the prospect of a ride in an Army truck.

We packed and prepared for the arrival of the jeep and bid farewell to family members and friends. The truck arrived on time on the appointed day, driven by two American soldiers who were not very friendly, but no matter. As we drove through the streets of Hamburg, we bade it and our fine stay there good-bye. A new phase of our lives was about to begin. Like pilots of our own little ship, we were headed for a harbor not yet in sight.

* * *

Before nightfall, our few belongings sat in their new place in our Bremen home and we all were "in business"—except baby Hans Bernhard. Until we found something better, he would sleep on the floor wrapped in my great sheepskin coat. That minor imperfection was remedied a few months later when a friend among the military government officers visited our home. Seeing where the baby slept, he arranged for a bed to be made and delivered. His generous act typified our experience during the year we spent among those wonderful American men, and our memories bring us great happiness.

Because of my ability to speak, read and write German, Major Haguewood asked me to find someone to care for the children so I, too, could work for the military government. We thought of Hans' cousin, Ursula, in Essen, who maybe had nothing to do and might help us. We got word to her, and she came.

The arrangement worked wonderfully for all of us. I found myself employed in the office of Major Haguewood, translating and making reports. His offices were located in the German police building. Hans worked under Major Borland, as a liaison to fuel distribution, out of the Contrescarpe. To spare Hans' strength, the major provided him with a car, an old and rickety one but reliable enough and very much appreciated. We shared it most of the time, to and from work.

CHAPTER 41

A Message from Home

July-September 1945

Hans had been anxious to do something meaningful, and he threw himself into his work. Aside from his extreme leanness, he looked and acted more like the real Hans than he had for a long time.

As for me, I felt nervous, excited, dazed and scared. I wanted desperately to prove my worth, and yet not even a simple letter emerged from my typewriter those first two days without fumbled erasures. Major Haguewood observed, but said nothing. An exacting master, he expected better. I strained to please him and things improved. His least sign of appreciation encouraged and delighted me.

Months passed with no talk about my family's desires and ambitions and the possibility of contacting my folks especially my brother George, whom I knew must serve in the U.S. military somewhere. I had thought the major understood how all-encompassing was our goal of repatriating eventually. As time passed, however, I began to wonder if he remembered, or still understood its importance to us.

Meanwhile, every day brought some new excitement in that office. More than once a German of seeming importance walked into our citadel, only to find himself discovered as a Nazi offender. He would then be hauled off to the adjacent prison, while the major crossed off another name on his list of sought-after criminals. New and undisclosed documents arrived steadily, needing translation. Also, the major's report of daily events kept me busy.

* * *

One day a special letter arrived from the United States along with the stack of official mail. Addressed to the major personally, it bore the Seal of the Golden Eagle from the Pentagon. I was in his office when the major opened the envelope, read a letter inside and then handed a smaller envelope to me. In a voice gruff with emotion he said, "Go sit in the corner and read."

I examined the envelope. "From the desk of General Clay, The Pentagon, Washington, D.C.," the return address read.

"It must be from my brother, George.. .Can it be?" I asked.

"I've read mine, so I know," he answered. "I told you, go into the corner over there and read yours."

He had not forgotten, bless him. He had found my brother; he had forgotten nothing. My eyes moistened as I turned away from him and sought the corner. The envelope was not sealed; of course not, it would not be. It had to be censored. A check fell out as my unsuspecting hands fumbled with the thin sheets. Addressed to "Dear Sis and All of You," the message read:

> "We are overcome with relief and jubilant with happiness, you can guess, especially when I tell you that in five years we have had only two Red Cross messages. We knew nothing of Hans' war experiences, nothing of your new baby; in fact, we doubted very much that you were alive. Mother and Dad have grown old and gray with worry, and now they can think of nothing over and beyond a possible reunion with you...."

A reunion with them? That's what we wanted, too. I glanced up at the major, but he scribbled away busily on something. I wondered if he already had read my letter. But of course he had. The letter continued:

> "Major Haguewood says you and Hans and the children want to come to the United States, and we want you to do just that. We will do all in our power to help you. Contact with you directly is still impossible, but it will come. In the meantime I will keep in touch with the major. The check? Can you use it? Maybe by now you will even need it. All of us back here send all our love.
>
> Your brother, George."

I squeezed shut my eyes and held my breath. The room was quiet, the pen scratching had stopped. Unsure of my emotions, I jumped up and hurried to the door, but from behind me the gruff voice sounded again.

"C'mon now, c'mon. Come back here and sit down. I want to read something to you," the major insisted. So I choked back tears of gratitude as I walked back to the chair opposite him at his desk. He flashed a knowing smile.

"Your brother wants to know what you need, okay? This is what I just wrote to him: 'Warm clothing of every description, used or new, for Ruth; Hans; boy, 13; daughter, 10; boys, 5 and 2. Shoes, socks, stockings, hand soap, laundry soap, scissors, thread, darning stuff, needles, pins, shoe polish and laces, toothpaste. You name it, they need it. Food will be supplied from here.' Now, then, can you think of anything else?"

But I could not, and would not have said so if I could; I was too overcome. Were I more impetuous, and he not so anxious to appear nonchalant, I would have hugged him. But true to our natures, we remained two formal people, suppressing emotions.

"By the way, how is the food situation?" he wanted to know.

Well, yes, the food situation. In a word, poor; in fact, worrisome. We lived on the same inadequate rations as all civilians, with no complaining. Yet for growing children the diet was hardly adequate. Hans and I took our noonday meal in the displaced persons mess hall, at no cost to us in coupons or money. During the last few weeks their generous menu had given way to a steady daily diet of lima bean soup—not always too savory but still hot and filling. And the coupons we saved by eating there meant that much more for the children.

My general description of our daily diet did not satisfy the major, who insisted on an exact list of what our weekly coupons bought us. When he heard the result, he exploded in fury, absolutely enraged, by what he learned.

"You should have told me that the children were starving," he accused.

Once more the hard outer shell of his emotional center fractured, showing the soft, good heart inside. I guessed also that it appealed to him to demonstrate the scope of his authority. This thought renewed my speculation about his civilian occupation, and whether it afforded him an opportunity to use all his pent-up energy.

"If in the next week you do not receive additional supplies, let me know, and that's an order," he commanded.

The hard shell knit shut again, and I knew myself dismissed.

Back at my desk, I reread the message I hardly could believe. Such good news and a check, too. I wanted to sing for joy, to spread my happiness. What would Hans say when he heard? He always had been firm in his faith. When I thought of him and the children, and how glad they would be, my lurking skepticism gave way to an overwhelming eagerness for the day to end.

* * *

Promptly at 5 p.m. I hurried out into the autumnal air and across the pretty wooded area that separated the police building from the Contrescarpe. Hans, it seemed, was finishing late that afternoon, so I sat in our borrowed car and waited.

For the umpteenth time, I drew out of my purse the letter

from George and read it. So much had come with his message "All of us over here send love," it said. He also offered food and clothing, friends and hope—hope, above all, for the children. Their future was what mattered: the chance to grow up and be educated in America.

"Why don't I rate even a glance or a smile tonight?" Hans' voice interrupted my thoughts, and I looked up into his smiling face. I had not even noticed his shadow as he approached, and I jerked to surprised attention.

"Oh, Hans, I'm sorry. I was so engrossed in this letter. I have so much to tell you.

He laughed, opened the door and sat down behind the wheel.

"What's on that sheet of paper that is more important than I am?" he inquired.

"Here, read!" I shot back at him, watching his face as he did so.

"Great, great, GREAT!" A glad smile gradually stretched across his face. "Cherie, this is simply wonderful." We both could not resist an impetuous hug and kiss before he primed the motor and put our car into motion. As we drove, I told him about Major Haguewood's promise of supplementary food. We both hoped it would arrive without delay.

As usual, Ursula and the children, their happy faces shining, met us at the door of our home. Hans and I had just enough time to get ready before dinner was announced. Ursula tried to make a good hot meal each evening of necessity just a casserole, and terribly improvised. That night as I ate, I thought of the promised extra food and could not resist telling Ursula and the children.

But when a week and then two passed with no delivery, my hopes began to falter. They need not have. Major Haguewood remembered and asked one day if extra food had arrived. When I said no, he chided me for not mentioning it sooner, then made inquiries. That cleared the air. By noon that same day, a Red Cross package arrived at our home. An expectant group greeted Hans and I that evening, hardly able to wait for the opening celebration to begin.

The major really should have shared in this little scene of anticipation, and then in the uncovering of the various treasures we found inside the package—powdered milk, instant coffee, cube sugar, sweet butter, butter cookies, chocolate. By the time we unpacked everything, little Hans Bernhard had climbed up on the table in his stocking feet. In sheer joy, he bent over the treats and danced around them. Both he and Dieter became almost sick with "overjoy."

I tried to convey our thanks to the major the following day by describing the excitement the package caused, but our benefactor waved it aside. He still was not satisfied.

"How the hell do seven people exist with only one Red Cross package a month? You need more than that, and I shall see that you get it."

When Hans and I saw how excited the children became over the food packages, we were glad we had decided not to mention our letter from Uncle George. "It would be too much for them," Hans suggested wisely. "Let's wait until things move forward and become more certain."

Still, the prospect of repatriation became a frequent topic of conversation between us, and with Ursula, after the children were in bed. We also reminisced about happy days gone by there was nothing else to do, with no records to listen to or reading material to divert our minds. Sometimes we just sat and brooded. Such a long and hazardous road still lay ahead, and we lacked a clear vision of how to accomplish our goal.

Because we identified with people not quite belonging in Germany—or at least I did—we watched with particular interest the military government's plans for repatriating occupants of the displaced persons camps to their homelands. These included people who had been brought into Germany to serve as forced labor after German military forces conquered their countries—Dutch, Danes,

Belgians, Czechs and Poles. Each week, trainloads of them left Bremen for their original homes.

Everyone seemed happy to leave, all except the Poles, who wanted to stay and put up tremendous resistance to being deported. No one assumed they had acquired a sudden love for Germany, but rather that they were reluctant to return to a country ruled by Russia. Determinedly, they remained in their already-established camps on the outskirts of the city, if they had the option, causing not a little concern for the U.S. military police entrusted with maintaining law and order.

Frequently at night Polish refugees left their camps and for shooting and raiding parties through the countryside. They sometimes destroyed farmhouses and cattle and burned wheat fields—after first torturing or even slaughtering the German farmers, families and helpers they encountered.

Those were abhorrent atrocities, especially when farmers and the food they produced were of utmost importance to the restoration of public health and maintaining regulated food distribution. Military government police tried their best to control the terrorists, but anticipating their next moves proved difficult. Food warehouses and storage places became next in line for destruction.

Eventually, something induced the Poles to lessen their violence. Maybe the trials of apprehended perpetrators served as a warning. Some of those still at large left the county; a few others assimilated into the population.

With the dismantling of the labor camps, where many foreigners had been herded, the term "displaced persons" came to symbolize a wide collection of people unsure of their future. The main gathering point for observing this group was the so-called displaced persons mess hall, run by the military government, the only place where the new group came together. Unlike the noisy, happy throng that had already been returned home, these sad, unhappy people were not going anywhere.

Displaced in the real sense of the word, these refugees of many nationalities had found themselves, for a variety of reasons, caught in Germany during the war. With the conflict over, they still could find no way out because no consulate from their country existed in Germany to intercede for them.

Almost totally without money or friends, and with no legal support, they always seemed cheerless and sullen. Hans and I always felt that if we could hear their stories, maybe we could help. But their understandable distrust of everyone made it difficult to win their confidence. Each day we joined their long line for the handout of ever-thinner bean soup at mess time, advancing step by step, like so many beggars. The demoralizing process hardly created the setting for shared confidences.

After awhile, we had seen a number of them often enough to exchange greetings. Gradually, a few lost their wariness. As they opened up, we learned the depth of their distresses, the basis for their feelings of dismay and hopelessness. Many were the victims of marriages to Germans. Some had come from countries too insignificant to warrant immediate renewed diplomatic relations with Germany. Moves through other countries would have to be arranged so that they could finally return home.

One day we met a very lovely Brazilian woman, the widow of a German soldier; also a young, very emotional Hungarian widow. Neither had any further ties to Germany, but could not manage to leave. A Latin-American woman whose husband was missing poured out her dilemma to us. "What if he is alive, sustained only by the hope of finding me again? What if he then learns I have left him and his country?" she told me one day. "How long should I wait, and on what shall I subsist?" With no answers to her questions, she lived with constant worry.

A middle-aged Panamanian woman who overheard our conversation with the Latina said her case was similar. She told us that a distant relative had willed her a beautiful estate in East Prussia, with both forest and grazing land and a large manor with servants' quarters, on the stipulation that she reside on the property for two years. She had lived there for only a year and a half when the war broke out. Rather than lose her inheritance with only six months remaining, she had decided to stay—foregoing a chance early on to return to Panama. At war's end, her inheritance had fallen into Russian control. She could not communicate with her homeland and saw no likelihood that a consular service for Panama would open in Germany anytime soon. And in the long, long meantime?

Then one day we learned why the beautiful young French women we saw often in the mess line always seemed so terribly sad. Torn between love, duty and self-preservation, she aroused our compassion in fullest measure. She had married a young and promising German officer. The unfortunate young man had come home from the front so maimed that she could hardly speak of it. The doctor had informed her he would remain hospitalized for the rest of his life. "How can I stay with him, but how can I leave him?" she sighed.

Always, after trying to lift the spirits of those most unhappy people, Hans and I somehow felt extremely fortunate. Of course, we, too, still faced many problems, not the least of which was the question of how the State Department would classify Hans and Bob, the two non-Americans in our family, when it came to the decision of repatriation.

Until that time, we had let no circumstance separate our family into two groups and we were determined not to let it happen. We all needed each other. The subject was painful to us yet always just below the surface of our consciousness.

Except with Ursula, we avoided discussion of our plans. Now and again she forced us to talk about the future, and we really owed it to her to do just that. Since we planned to leave one day, what did the future offer her then? She argued against our desire to leave.

"I find it sad," she said. "If our crippled country loses all its useful thinking people, with no hope for the future from growing youngsters such as yours, how will she ever rise again?" Over and over explained that we were not running away, that this was no new desire for us.

"Many times in my business life I became so disgruntled by

the illogical, unfair, small-minded, over-organized bureaucracy that I wanted to leave," Hans explained. "But instead, I stayed. Later, during the war, I decided that I had been wrong, and that if I lived to ever see the cessation of arms, I would take my family to the United States. I have not, nor will I ever, change my mind, no matter how hard the new beginning may prove to be."

Of course, we knew that Ursula argued from the standpoint of all young Germans who must remain behind. They felt closed in, restricted by the many limitations on their capabilities and ambitions. They also assumed that present day conditions would remain permanent. Both Hans and I tried to convince her that the rehabilitation processes were proceeding well. Wanting desperately to believe us, Ursula clung with all her might to the comfort our words brought her.

Many new faces appeared as new officers relieved those whose tour of service was finished or who were returning to the United States for a furlough. I always found it disconcerting. We had placed our hopes and faith, our destiny, in the hands of these good men. What would we do without them? We felt a great sense of loss at each departure, although we need not have, since many of the newcomers proved equally encouraging and helpful.

I arrived at the office early one bright crisp day. Major Haguewood apparently had come in even earlier, because no one knew he was there until the door of his office opened quite suddenly. He stood in the doorway, aloof and stern, looking directly into my upturned, surprised face.

"Come in here. I want you to meet someone."

With pad and pencil, as I usually did, I entered the large, well-furnished office and seated myself next to him at his desk, awaiting the orders of the day. Facing us in a large leather chair sat a tall, "no monkey business" officer, Captain Chuck Huston, to whom I was introduced immediately. The major broke the speculative stillness that followed, that quick evaluation process that comes into play with first contact.

"Mrs. Bohle does those God-damn reports that have to go out

every day—those dry, dull documents that describe the events of our day which, if we were allowed to depict the actual happenings with the attendant excitement, would paint the liveliest pictures and unfold most revealing and interesting situations.

"But no, they must be understated, without color, terribly plain and factual. Only with a fertile imagination can one understand how stunting this kind of reporting can be. I'm glad she's doing them, not me."

Turning to me, he continued. "Captain Huston has some questions he wants to ask you. Okay, Chuck," he added, "Shoot."

That sounded ominous.

"Mrs. Bohle," the captain began, shifting suddenly to the edge of his overstuffed chair, "I have just arrived from the United States. Before leaving, I corresponded for a while with Major Haguewood here."

The captain spoke very rapidly, mumbling his words so badly that it took my strictest attention to catch what he said. Despite his lack of articulation, his tone conveyed military authoritativeness.

"Major Haguewood informed me of a good deal of your background, and it interested me that your original home was in the vicinity of Chicago. Mine was in Flosmoor, Ill. Does that mean anything to you?"

"No, sir, nothing," I apologized.

"Think again—a few people live there who know you."

Astonished, I tried hard to think who they might be. But despite my usually good memory, I could no longer relate back to events before my marriage. My girlhood was gone, and I sat facing a blank wall.

"Don't let it worry you," he counseled, smiling, discerning the blank agony on my face. "Does the name Nancy mean anything to you?"

"Nancy," I repeated slowly. "No, the name means absolutely nothing to me."

"I think it does. Was your grandfather a Baptist minister and organizer?"

"Yes."

"Did you ever sing in a chorus formed by members of the various churches he organized?"

"Yes," I answered, wonderingly.

"And did you know the son of the minister of one of those churches, one who also sang in that chorus, named Stracke?"

"Why, yes," I recalled hesitantly. "I knew a Bob Stracke, but. . . ."

"Did you also know a Claire Wolf who sang in this same chorus, and later married this Bob?"

My memory began to return, but vaguely. "Yes, dimly, I remember I knew them both.

"Well, sir," the captain addressed us both, "They are Mrs. Huston's and my neighbors, and I took the liberty of telling them about the Bohles. You should have heard the excitement. Claire jumped up and ran to the phone and called Mrs. Bohle's mother and father in Oak Park, and together they cried over the phone. 'It's Mr. and Mrs. Kuechler's lost daughter,' she said, puffing down the receiver, as tears coursed down her cheeks."

That was just what mine were threatening to do, but the major put a stop to any "sob stuff."

"You've had enough for today. Dismissed! Anyhow, you've got one more friend," he added, as I thanked the captain for telling me and for his proffered friendship.

The ways of God are truly wonderful, I thought, again at my desk. And they really were.

By his own suggestion, Captain Huston relieved the major of some of the responsibility he had assumed voluntarily concerning our family, and I was allowed to begin a correspondence, although not directly, with Mrs. Huston and her neighbors, Claire and Bob Stracke. They, like my parents and my brother George, gathered clothing for our family from their own supplies and those of their friends. These they sent to Captain Huston, and in turn he gave them to us. Unfailingly kind, he constantly searched for opportunities to assist us, anywhere and everywhere.

Captain Huston also soon found his original hatred for Germans replaced by an attitude of understanding and compassion. He left the hate where it belonged—with the defeated Nazi regime. Instead, he brought Christian charity, loving kindness and hope. He encouraged our complete confidence, and knowing that he listened with understanding and belief we gave it freely. He came into our home, saw how we lived and learned our motives and reactions. Since his visits always were spontaneous, his judgments were pure and that was very valuable to us as well as to him.

CHAPTER 42

Searching for Lost Loves

October 1945

Captain Huston was the first and, for some time, the only guest in our home in Bremen. Eventually, however, we enjoyed visits from many old friends who eventually learned of our new location. Some, like us, became part of a tremendous mass movement in Germany, as reunited families sought a safe place to relocate and resume their lives. Others were pieces of families, homeless women and children who had lost their homes to bombing or had fled advancing troops. They now wandered from city to city, taking refuge in the railroad station for a few days, being fed at refugee kitchens. Then they moved on, not by choice but because each city provided the wanderers with three days' food and shelter, no more!

Some of the lonely drifters were returning soldiers, searching for lost loved ones. Lists posted in all railroad stations recorded the name, arrival and departure date and intended next destination of anyone who had been there. Soldiers scoured those lists looking for clues to the whereabouts of their families. If no departure date was listed, that person still remained in that city. Since all who found a place were obliged to register with the police to obtain food cards, many reunions resulted.

Poignant scenes in railroad stations were witnessed in those days. Most touching were the gatherings of women whenever posted arrival schedules showed trains coming in from the East, possibly carrying released prisoners of war from Russia. One hardly could bear to watch the sad, silent faces of the waiting women. When a train pulled in, they thronged the opening doors and scanned the faces of the returnees, hoping for a glimpse of the one they loved and for whom they longed. Occasionally a gasp of recognition was followed by a happy reunion, as two hearts pressed together in a long and tearful embrace. But for the most part the silent, sad, weeping women once again turned away unassuaged.

We had been part of this moving mass that milled about in Germany. Many of our friends and relatives were unaware of our location, however, and had to search fruitlessly in Berlin and Hamburg before tracing us to Bremen.

* * *

The first of our acquaintances to make that round was Hans Schwarz, a very likable young man who once had been Hans' private secretary in Mannheim. His father had been an old and trusted employee of Father Bohle, in charge of the fleet of company cars, and had chauffeured Hans and me to our honeymoon spot in the Black Forest. We last had seen the senior Schwarz the day before war broke out with Poland, as Hans and I had returned from a stay with his mother at a spa in South Germany.

One night when Hans and I returned home from work, we found Mr. Schwarz waiting. Since Bremen had no hotel rooms available, we invited him to stay with us.

Our guest, still in uniform, told us that he had been dismissed two weeks earlier from a prisoner of war camp near the Danish border. Since then, he had traveled about in Northern Germany, searching for his wife, whom he had not seen in almost two years. He knew she had lost an expected baby during that time, but knew nothing of her current whereabouts. Did we know anything?

His greatest fear was that she might have remained in the Russian zone and that he might never find her again. His fears were not without foundation. He needed reassurance, and together we argued that a woman of her intelligence and ingenuity would not stay in the Russian zone. But where could she have gone? What was logical was not always possible. Still, the logical presented clues worth following.

For two days he enjoyed the quiet of our home and the intimacy of our family, and our conversations gave him hope. When he left, he did so with renewed confidence and vigor. We promised to keep his wife with us if she came to Bremen during his absence, and he vowed to return.

Up from the Black Forest came a message from Georg Donner, the hospital-room buddy who had been dismissed with Hans. Georg said he was "rotting away" in a little nondescript town. Despite the prostheses he wore, one on each leg, he was alive and breathing and longing to be of some service to someone. Hans told military government of Georg's experience as a dairyman and vouched for his integrity, and he was brought north and put to work.

In the course of the next few weeks Guenther Brink turned up briefly, no longer in uniform. Hugo Frolme also came to visit, deeply involved in the banking business of Hamburg once more. Lottchen Krumeich, the Potsdamer doctor's wife, sent a message telling us that after a long search she had learned that her husband still was being held in a prisoner of war camp in Schleswig-Holstein. The clever doctor soon thereafter managed an escape by hiding in a laundry truck. He and his wife settled eventually in Dusseldorf and he became one of the prominent practicing physicians in that city.

Then word came from Hans Schwarz. After endless, heartbreaking searching, he had finally located his wife in the Russian zone, but alive. She had written him many letters trying to find him and had deposited them in a postbox that had never been opened. They had finally been reunited.

But the strangest experience of all was a visit from one of Horst von Valtier's brothers, who, dressed as an old and tottering grandmother, had escaped the Russian zone and cleared the checkpoints because of his ragged "get-up."

We answered our doorbell very early one morning and found him standing there, teeth chattering from fright, dazed and incoherent.

"Are you alone?" he whispered. "Are you being watched? Is it all right to come up?"

His questions went on and on and his furtive glances and wild, excited eyes took in every motion as we coaxed him up the stairs. He was thin, hungry and tired, and both physically and emotionally exhausted.

It took several days for us to get him quieted sufficiently for any semblance of a story to emerge. He refused to move from the house or change into any of Hans' clothes, until finally Hans convinced him that in Bremen his disguise would attract more attention than a normal suit. When at last he felt like talking, he told us how he barely had escaped the clutches of the Russian military police.

"I was living with Eva, Horst and the children," he said. "We had left Berlin together some time earlier, traveling by horse and wagon in the direction of Thueringen (middle Germany) in search of a place to anchor. Terribly tired of the cold and snowy roads, with never a proper place to sleep, we wandered accidentally into Russian occupied territory.

"A day or two later, Horst spied a factory at the top of a hill— a toy factory. It was for sale, with a home connected to it. The factory appealed to him as something he would like to own. Without once considering that it sat in the Russian zone, he bought it and we stayed.

"Impetuous Horst had become enamored with the idea. Because the Russians seemed friendly during the transaction, he naively assumed that all animosities between vanquished and conqueror had been cast aside. I doubted that supposition, but stayed with them anyway.

"One day more than six months ago, two armed soldiers arrived at the house and led Horst away. They put him in a Russian concentration camp, where he sat cold and hungry, wasting away. His toy factory had done too well and Horst had not been discreet—in fact, he had been boastful about how well it was doing. The Russians decided that if the factory prospered for him, it could do as well for them. They dispossessed Horst and the family without remuneration."

The picture Horst's brother painted was not a pleasant one but unfortunately all-to-realistic. Apparently, Horst had been true to the racy, emotional, temperamental, good-hearted, lively man we knew him to be, so willing to forget animosities and expect the same in return. We urged our guest on with his story.

"Even in the months before Horst's imprisonment, we all were keenly aware of constant spying, day and night. After he was taken away, we became jumpy, our nerves frayed to the breaking point. Mine are completely snapped.

"Last week I saw two soldiers carrying rifles making their way up the hill to the house. I knew they were coming for me. I ran out the back entrance and kept on running, miles and miles, to a railroad junction. It had been rumored that elderly people were allowed to proceed into the West zone. I was pale, emaciated and unkempt, and along the way acquired the garb of an old lady as a disguise.

"I almost fainted with fear when guards asked for my identification papers. I just acted like I didn't know what they were talking about. Luckily, they took me for demented and ill and pushed me into a waiting freight train.

We kept Horst's brother for several weeks. From him we learned that Dr. Walter Kleeberg and his wife Charlotte had settled in a small town near Lake Constance, in South Germany.

During the weeks of his stay with us, Mr. von Valtier ate, slept and brooded. Finally one day, saying he felt better, he announced his intention to return to help Eva and the children, if they were also at home, in any way he could, at least until Horst was freed.

After all that could happen at any time, since no reason ever was given for his confinement.

He left that day, in clothing that Hans provided, and we never saw him again or heard what befell him. Years later, we learned from other sources that Horst had been freed not long after his brother left us. He and his family then had left Thueringen, abandoning any hope for the toy factory and settled in Hamburg, broken in body and spirit. Dr. Kleeberg had traveled to Hamburg to offer medical assistance, but Horst had refused any help. He was remote and ill and died soon thereafter.

Another returnee from the Russian zone—Hans's brother, Walter—surprised us prior to Thanksgiving. Although exhausted, he exulted over the rescue of his music and his grand piano, too, which he had stored with friends. When we asked how he had managed that feat, he rolled his eyes to the ceiling. "You can't imagine," he answered enough to tell us that his experiences were indescribable. He would tell us when he had the strength and felt like it.

Walter had returned to Hamburg to find us gone, but managed to track us to Bremen. We made arrangements to have his piano delivered to our living room. Little by little, he opened up. We also enjoyed the pleasure of hearing the great music of the masters once again in our home, played by skilled hands.

Newly found friends among the military government officers began to gather at our home for evening recitals, some of them bringing lady friends. All of those women had known personal tragedy, and the lovely music often brought tears. But that did not deter their desire for music. On the contrary, everyone craved the lovely sounds, and soon Walter was entertaining officially, joined by remnants of the Bremen Orchestra—those still alive who had managed to rescue their instruments. Old schools or hall basements were rented with improvised stages, unheated. Civilians and military government officials and personnel all gathered together with many listeners bringing blankets in which to wrap themselves as the cold weather set in.

Those performances were at once very wonderful and very sad. Besides the officers, the majority of the audience were widowed women and old men whose great need for music brought them long distances on foot, at much discomfort. Perhaps those few hours brought them solace or forgetfulness. Each seemed sunk in his or her own little purgatory. No exchange of conversation followed the concerts. As I glanced about at such gatherings, I realized the depth of despair among the German people and sank myself into the blackest of moods. But I could not stay down for long. When forced to face reality, I admitted that we had come a long way in a very short time. We still had far to go, and the future seemed far from certain. But Hans and I worked in warm offices and our family lived in heated rooms and now had food, coal for cooking, electricity, clean fresh water and restored sanitation.

* * *

Music provided a daily respite, but relaxation from tensions came in other forms as well. Now and again our very special friends the Meentzens offered us a weekend with them at their hunting lodge in the lovely Luneburger Heide (Heatherland). Bombs had damaged their home in Bremen during the war, and they were lucky to have such a refuge.

The Meentzens had adjusted quickly to rural life and had exchanged their formal clothes for an apron and rolled-up sleeves. They kept chickens for eggs and goats for milk and depended on the heather game wardens for their meat—rabbits and wild boar. The meats they preserved by smoking, marinating, salting or making sausage; fruits and vegetables were canned or bottled.

Hans and I found the hours of relaxation we spent with these friends most refreshing. We returned from each visit renewed, with eyes that noted the steadily-improving conditions, not only in our personal lives but in our total surroundings.

Indeed, we could be very proud of our small role in the military governments huge accomplishments. It had brought into being more and better freight train service and had improved control of farming communities, the fisheries and dairies too, offering more output of food for all the people. Germans were returning to work, serving and earning, although rigid screening to identify former Nazis continued unabated.

Water mains worked once more, bridges reappeared and produce delivery trucks were repaired and returned to service. Coal moved in carloads from the Ruhr to the cities, first for the factories but soon, we hoped, to fuel home fires before the intense cold set in. Clothing and housing still were in short supply, and people resigned themselves to endure one more uncomfortable winter—hoping it would be the last.

Much more, even then, remained to be accomplished. Endless mountains of rubble still stood, also facades and partial ruins. Rats infested the debris left along the River Weser banks by the huge spring flood, creating widespread fears of a possible plague. The entire population of the city received free inoculations as a preventive measure.

Ruins also lay next to our own living quarters, so we insisted that the children leave the house only when attended—thus forbidding them the joys of a game of "hide and seek" just where it would have been most inviting.

Yet another type of plague kept military government officers and the military police busy day and night. With the arrival of coveted American cigarettes and real, honest coffee, black marketing flourished. The milling populace in and about the railroad station provided ideal camouflage for illicit trading.

Occasionally when I had time, especially in the afternoon, I entered the prison courtroom to listen to the trials. Translations from German to English or Polish to English and back again took longer than the legal proceedings themselves, but those in charge exercised great care in the interests of justice, sometimes reversing guilty sentences if the facts warranted.

However, "justice" took on a different shape in everyday office encounters. Nuances of language or subtleties of thought often got lost in imperfect translations—or sometimes were overlooked deliberately. Lamentable hardships sometimes resulted, pointing out the importance of understanding the other man's language.

CHAPTER 43

Charges Against Hans

November - December 1945

As the year advanced, Hans' work became less routine. He was required to visit other portions of West Germany to find, if possible, besides all else, persons of ability who spoke English and might like to come to Bremen to work in the American military government. At such times, I walked instead of rode to work, and back again in the evening.

But one day when Hans should have been back and at work during the day, he was not waiting for me in the evening. It had snowed, and the streets were slippery for walking, but of course, with no choice, I started on my way.

It was all but dark when I passed the garage where Captain Huston kept his car. He was just putting it up for the night when we saw each other.

"Hello, there, Ruth," he called.

"Good evening, Chuck," I answered.

Perceptive as always, he inquired, "Why are you walking?"

I told him. "Hans evidently has not been to work and I am worried about what it could mean." Swiftly he returned his car to the street.

"Jump in, we will ride home and see."

Captain Huston was a dynamic personality. Hardly was a decision made when he began with the solution to the problem, no wait, no fuss. Nor did he spare himself trouble in any way.

"Ruth," he said as we rolled along, "As you know, all messages to your brother in Washington, D.C. are given to me to read and censor."

He glanced at me to see what? Shock or approval? I waited.

"In one of them, you say you hope that Bob and Irmgard can soon attend school again. Why are they not now doing so?"

"Bless you, Chuck, the answer is the same for all civilians. We have not been able to discover a source for leather soling for their shoes. But some day we will, and then they will return to school, such as it is."

"What do you mean by 'such as it is'?"

"Well for one thing, the only classroom available for Bob is in a four-story building. His class meets on the fourth floor. One wall of the building is completely missing from the roof down to the street; it is cold, windy and exposed up there. All work is done from memory. They have no blackboard, no desk, paper or pencil, and I think maybe he is less likely to catch cold at home. The only regret I have is that he misses the hot lunch which is served the children by the Swedish Red Cross."

Our arrival home cut short the questions and answers. Hans must have seen us arriving, for he met us at the door. He was smiling, but his smile was sick.

"I heard that you did not go to work today, and so I brought Ruth home. Are you okay?"

I watched Hans lead the way to the parlor. He walked all right. Could it be that the nerve pains in his stump plagued him again with the changeable weather? Chuck and I followed him.

"No, I am not ill, at least not physically, but I am sick," Hans answered as we took chairs on either side of him. "And I feel thoroughly crushed by what has happened."

He was quiet again, sitting with bowed head, fighting for composure.

"Chuck," he addressed the captain with a voice terribly constrained, "My boss called me into his office this morning and told me that someone has submitted a report to headquarters saying that he had it on best authority that I had been a Nazi. Lt. Leonard told me that he was awfully sorry, but the colonel had asked him to lay me off until I could clear myself of this accusation.

"This means that I cannot work for the military government, nor anyone else for now. A Party member and a liar that's what it make me. I do not know of anyone here who could know me well enough to point me out for such an accusation, nor can I understand why anyone would want to. Please, Chuck, believe me at least until I can prove it, that I have been neither one.

"I told my lieutenant the same thing, and he believes me, but in what a hell of a fix does that place me and my family until I can show the fallacy of such a denunciation."

"Hans, I believe you, too," Captain Huston said. "Has any way been suggested for you to go about getting such a clearance?"

"Yes, I know on what the charge is based. It was said that as a combat soldier I was a member of a tank regiment named 'The Feldherrnhalle,' composed solely of SS men. It is true that this regiment was, in the very beginning of the war, composed of SS men; but long before I became a part of it, the SS detail had been 'rubbed out' completely. The name, however, was kept as the regiment had once been famous.

"You must believe me that all those in it with me were simple recruits. I became a corporal only after I was wounded. And as a recruit, I was a plain wireless operator in an open tank. I must clear myself, or we can never think of entering into any negotiation with the United States consulate or State Department for visas to the United States, and all of our hopes of returning there will be dashed. All our efforts will have been in vain."

Captain Huston consoled him with, "Well, so far the United States consulate has not arrived, and so you have time."

That was true, and maybe lucky, but the pain I felt for Hans and for all of us was sharp and cutting. Captain Huston then told Hans that he would "stand by him" unless and until his accuser could prove beyond the shadow of a doubt that his statement was right. Then he asked what Hans proposed to do.

"Just this," he answered, "I will write a complete resume of my life, since 1927, showing where I have been and what I have done, and I will supplement this with sworn affidavits by people who also have been no Party member, and who either have worked for me or employed me, or just know me and my sentiments. It is a matter of time and the ability in all of this turmoil, to find these people, who are in some cases relocated."

"And in the meantime?" asked Chuck.

"In the meantime, unfortunately, I sit idle."

* * *

The captain left us alone then, to pick up our shattered hopes and find a way to put them together again. Hans began that night his long resume, starting with his journey to the United States in 1927. He wrote long into the night and before morning already had drafted the letters that had to be sent.

Captain Huston, too, had not been slow. By noon the following day, he had contacted the various officers of military government with whom Hans worked and discovered the name of the man responsible for the shocking charges. He came to me, asking if I knew the man.

I had never heard of him. Neither had Hans. Since neither of us had ever met the accuser, what could be the motive for his denunciation? Chuck thought it bore investigation, but he said nothing more. Days went by with no new turn in events, while Hans' boss strove in vain to find someone who could fill Hans' place in the affairs of his particular department.

Then came a message that provided the first ray of light to lift our spirits. Unable to find anyone as knowledgeable about oil and coal who also spoke both German and English, Hans's superior had made a formal request to the colonel for his reinstatement until the truth of the accusation made against him was proved. The colonel had agreed and Hans went back to work.

More days and weeks went by while we waited for letters and certified statements in our favor from qualified sources. Hans' accuser had been unable to bring any proof for his statements. The officers with whom we worked continued to be friends. Brother George wrote happy and encouraging letters, although he knew nothing of our newest trials.

A little of the approaching Yuletide spirit reached our troubled hearts as happy children and music filled our home. Captain Huston had managed to find leather for shoe soles, and Bob and Irmgard were in school. Mrs. Huston had sent clothing from the United States. Her husband had guessed at the sizes and come very close to right in everything.

Both Hans and I made a brave effort at cheerfulness. We were so grateful for all the tasks that confronted us daily. We also were on the alert for the frequent rumors that came every now and then, saying what we must do and where we must go to register, in order to be ready when the consulate finally arrived. We complied with all of them for fear of slipping up on a single technicality, but most were false.

One such rumor was that all displaced persons and Americans were to register in Polish camps. Another rumor had it that all Americans were to be sent to a camp in the middle of Germany—somewhere—there to be processed for repatriation. The rumors continued, making nervous wrecks out of us, for fear that something else in addition to the charges against Hans might destroy our possible chance of returning to America.

The rumor about a camp "somewhere in Central Germany" for processing all Americans nearly cost us more than peace of mind. Captain Huston had used military government wires to investigate and was reprimanded by a higher official for doing so. He also was ordered to fire me. Fortunately, the captain considered this directive the result of a temporary bad mood, not reason.

He therefore fired and rehired me all in the same breath, and we continued our work together as usual.

Christmas came and with it a number of lovely parties, sponsored by military government officers. The ice and snow on the ground and the few lighted trees also did much to generate a holiday spirit.

Major Haguewood went home on leave, another took his place, offices and personnel continued changing, and new warm friendships developed. It was a great time, really, and we never would forget it—or those wonderful American officers who propped us up with their constant words of encouragement.

CHAPTER 44

Vindication and Reinstatement

January - March, 1946

The day came when Hans had received and assembled enough certified data to substantiate his resume and his position, and he turned it in for examination. But again the time spent in that process was so "forever" that we feared no proper clearance would come before the consulate arrived.

I voiced my concern to Captain Huston one morning. On those wintry days the morning light came late and it still was dark when the working hours began. That morning, Captain Huston stood outside the commissary near where we sometimes stopped for breakfast.

"Chuck, I can hardly take the strain any longer. Is there no way of hurrying this thing?" I asked.

His philosophy. "You know as well as I do, Ruth, that it often depends on the kind of a day it is, how well a person feels, little things that govern the mood of the person making some of our decisions. In a matter that means so much to you, can't you believe it is better to let him take his time?"

I thought it awful that decisions of such import should be decided by mood rather than by justice, but I agreed with the captain from my own experience. He was right, and our waiting had its reward.

Hans' report was given full consideration, but the motives of the accuser also were studied. It was found that he, the accuser, had sought out just anyone, that time Hans, to denounce, for the purpose of elevating himself as a "loyal" American. It was explained to us that he had changed his loyalties often, depending on which country he anticipated would be the victor in the war.

Originally a German, he had acquired U.S. citizenship while in the United States. But when it seemed that Hitler would rule the world, he had returned to Germany and proclaimed himself a loyal German, only to quickly undergo renewed metamorphosis, back to American, when it became plain that Germany would lose.

And for that, all the pain, the anguish, the sleepless nights, nerves worn to a frazzle, stomachs too sick to eat? Yet from us he needed to fear no reprisal. We were only too happy to be cleared. That foolish man would reap what he had sown through another source.

It was almost as if the American consulate had waited for Hans' clearance, since shortly thereafter its impending arrival was announced officially. It was real, right in Bremen. People who, like ourselves, felt that they had a claim, arrived from far and wide to present their cases. We did likewise. Again, it was very exciting.

As we expected, no immediate decisions were made. We would be called for interviews as soon as their investigation had progressed far enough, and that interlude could be long. It was long, but Hans and I had learned the value of patience in waiting—provided, of course, one could remain steadfastly aware of the ultimate goal.

Our daily routine helped us fill the time gap until the day of our interview finally arrived. My citizenship and that of three of our children definitely was affirmed as American, and because the major percentage of our family of six was American in nationality, the two remaining members, Bob and Hans, also would be granted the privilege of passage to the United States. They would enter as aliens, of course.

First, however, we would need sponsors, and be able to show

we could cover both steamship and rail fare in American money. Health, ability to work and loyalty were important items in their final consideration. The resume that Hans had been forced to make with all its substantiating affidavits was deemed as positive. Brother George immediately offered his sponsorship of Bob and Hans and the necessary funds to the steamship line and the railroad company for our journey to Chicago.

* * *

As the possibility of reaching the United States once more loomed greater, our minds began to plan ahead. We thought much about what we could and would do to earn our living over there. The concern we felt in that direction was noted and stressed by those in charge of our repatriation, as over and over the admonition was expressed, to Hans in particular: "I hope you know what you're doing. A German will have no easy time getting a job. The sentiment will be against you and our returning men will get first choice."

Hans' answer inevitably was that if it had been possible to have lived through the problems of the last seven years, he could at least try to lick one more. He had not the slightest doubt, nor did I, that with the desire and the stamina to tackle any difficulty that came our way, we would succeed.

With our return to the United States seemingly about certain, the military government asked Hans to make one more trip for them, again to Mannheim and surrounding cities.

Lieutenant Leonard suggested I accompany Hans, and asked if there was anyone we would especially like to say good-bye to, and of course Hans said his mother. But that would double the length of the trip, which we hardly expected them to agree to, mainly because they would be unable to guarantee fuel for us in the French zone.

However, they did agree since Hans felt sure he could draw on his own former resources in the Black Forest, and in South Germany in general, for the necessary additional gasoline. The possibility of making the total trip was therefore contingent upon receiving the required documents, mainly passage into the French zone. Those then would have to be approved by delegates of both the British and French sectors.

Hans was excited about our trip, and so was I, but I knew this trip would be more than a little difficult. Such a journey would require, under prevailing conditions, at least two weeks. Even with papers, in duplicate, triplicate or more, the crossing of the various zones would not be without its hazards. Didn't we hear rumors almost daily of people just like us having their papers removed forcibly and then being held as hostages in the French zone?

Hans thought we would find no difficulty in crossing from Bremen enclave to the British and then back to the American zone. But he conceded that the checkpoints, guarded in the French zone primarily by Moroccan troops, with their scanty regard for certified passes and women, could give us some trouble. However, we had chanced so many things, should we not try just one more?

Captain Huston finally put an end to my indecision. "It looks to me as though Hans has made up his mind to go all the way," he said. "You'd better go along, Ruth. Hans just might need you. I'll look in on the children often enough to know they are not in need."

With that he handed me what he termed was his contribution to the comfort of the trip, some very personal hygienic articles that his wonderful wife and our newly-found friend Claire had had the foresight to send, realizing how much they would be appreciated.

CHAPTER 45

A Hazardous Trip and Poignant Farewells

May - June, 1946

Hans and I were ready to leave early one morning, our car filled with enough Red Cross packages to feed us lightly for 12 days. We also carried with us five certified copies of every necessary document, tucked into our shoes, hats, miffs, pockets and purses. And we had stashed Jerry cans filled with gasoline in the back of the car, sufficient to get us to South Germany.

On that parting, our hearts were heavy at the thought of leaving the children and Cousin Ursula, and we noted with surprise and misgivings that they shared our mood. We saw no tears, but it was apparent that as our young folks were growing up and aware of problems; their spirits were troubled more easily than even a year earlier.

We knew that they would be well cared for, however, and that they would get along fine. I forced away my own tears and, to dispel the gloom, busied myself with examining a map. So many detours were to be accounted for because of rebuilding. They would cost time and consume fuel, so we had to be careful.

All day we rode and by six that evening we arrived in darkness at the first checkpoint, the entrance from the British to the second

American zone. We dreaded that stop, our first try at changing zones. Even though confident that our papers were in order, we knew that Chuck Huston had spoken correctly when he said much would depend on the mood of the men at the time of decision.

We drove up. A searchlight played across our faces. Three young soldiers stood guard. One took our passes and examined them while the other two circled the car, shining flashlights on the piled-up rear seats. Quickly one of them turned back and, without waiting for the examining officer to complete his perusal of our documents, declared loudly that our car was loaded with forbidden goods. Gruffly, he ordered us out of the car. At that point I held out my most recent American passport.

"Hold on," said the first guard to the second. "The lady is an American from my home town. Where did you go to school?'1 he asked.

"Tuley High, and then on to Oberlin. And you?"

"I went to Northwestern.. Oh, Evanston," I broke in.

"Boy!" he exclaimed. "Someone from home and not in uniform. Where'd you live?"

"Oak Park," I answered.

"Huh, whaddya know. Gee, it's a small world, but great, isn't it?" Then, turning to his impatient buddy, he said, "Let her alone. Their credentials are absolutely okay."

He turned back to me. "Are you returning this way? When are you leaving for the States?" But we did not know, so he waved us on with a final "Good luck."

In all that time Hans spoke not one word, and suddenly I realized Captain Huston's wisdom when he had suggested, "You'd better go along, Ruth, Hans might need you."

On into the night we drove. Our progress was slow, uncertain and hazardous, and when we reached Kassel we decided to pull up somewhere seemingly protected. Next to the city hall was an empty lot. We eased up against a tall, bare wall, needing to eat something and to try to sleep.

After quieting the motor and dimming the lights, we felt uneasy in the dark stillness. Unwilling to turn on the interior lights for fear of attracting unwanted attention, we fumbled in the dark for our boxes of cheese, butter and crackers.

"Oh, skip it. Maybe the moon will come up—or something," Hans said. He was hungry but more tired than apprehensive. We settled for sleep, but every tiny, insignificant stir outside drew our attention. Time passed all too slowly, with sighs and changing positions.

About midnight, the absolute silence was splintered abruptly by wild and intense shooting nearby. It stopped and started again many times during the rest of the night, but came no closer—for which we were mighty glad!

Once during the early morning hours, a German police guard, possibly for the city hall, circled our car. After frightening us out of our half-sleep, he walked off again silently.

By 4 a.m. we sat wide awake, stiff, half-frozen and very hungry. With the use of a flashlight we rummaged until we found the Red Cross packages. Our meal was no gourmet delight—the butter was rancid—and we both fussed, but we ate. We wished fervently for a cup of good hot coffee, or even cold water. But what use wishing? For the moment none was available.

* * *

At the first streak of dawn we set out again, glad to be moving and to see our surroundings once more. The road was ours alone for a long while, and around 7 a.m. we saw landmarks that told us we were approaching Mannheim.

The autobahn widened and elevated about 25 feet above a wide portion of cleared land edged on both sides by a forest. Coming up behind us we saw a rarity—another civilian car.

"It's going lickety-split, a whole lot faster than our 'putt- putt' can make it," I said. A man sat stiffly at the wheel and two women clad in black occupied the rear seat. Middle aged, or maybe older, I judged, but they zoomed by so fast I could not be sure. A jeep passed us and moved up behind them, and in a few more minutes they both disappeared from view. Once more we were alone.

But what was that? Ahead of us on the flat land edging the wooded area we saw a car lying on its top. A man stood next to it who, as we approached, appeared to be trying to light a cigarette, but his hands shook so hard he could not. On the ground next to the car lay two still forms, both women, dressed in black.

"Hans," I said breathlessly, "That is the civilian car that passed us not 20 minutes ago. Has all of this happened in that short time?"

We stopped and Hans called to the man. "What has happened? Can we help?"

"Sideswiped," he answered. "And no, you cannot help, thanks. My women are dead."

At that moment a military ambulance bore down on the scene from the direction of Mannheim. It stopped and two young men in uniform pulled out a stretcher. Since help had arrived, we left. But we were puzzled. Everything seemed too pat, too made to order. Who had notified the ambulance attendants? Why did they not ask any questions as they proceeded quickly and matter-of-factly about their business?

"Hans, if that car really was sideswiped, why weren't we the victims, not they?" He did not answer, but the incident stayed with us all day and in fact never left our minds the whole journey through.

"Oh, Hans," I wailed, "I need a cup of steaming hot coffee, or any kind of soup, or something, don't you?"

With a warm smile he told me, "Yes, my love, soon. It's not yet seven o'clock. Paul and Lise Lawrenz settled somewhere around here after military occupation took over their home. Let's go see them. I am sure they will have a cup of hot coffee for us—ersatz, I mean. If I remember correctly, the address is 169 Muhause Strasse. Anyway, let's try"

We found their house with little difficulty and only minutes later drew up in front. It took me but a second to check the list of occupants posted in the entry; then I returned to the car.

"According to the names listed, they live up on the fourth floor. I wonder if they will forgive us for coming so early and unannounced. But they always were early risers," I recalled.

We locked our rickety-faithful car as best we could and entered the building. Those spiral steps were a chore for Hans with his artificial leg. The first three flights were easy, however, compared with the task that confronted us on the fourth floor. The house had been damaged by bombs, and the fourth staircase hung in space supported only by the railing that hung still clinging to the narrow side of the spiral.

If the Lawrenzs really lived up on the fourth floor, they must use those stairs, we reasoned. As much as I dreaded that final stretch, I couldn't be bested by a couple one generation older than we. When I expressed this thought, Hans laughed, saying that I had read his mind.

"Want to go first, and see if they really are there?" he suggested. This seemed a good idea, and anyway the stairs could not support two at once. I climbed up and found that the Lawrenzs were, indeed, at home and awake. Hans followed me, and the effort was well worth it. Tears and warm embraces were followed by a bubbling over with experiences, finally sobering down to speculation on how life would continue.

Over the coveted cup of hot ersatz coffee, we recalled their daughter Rosmarie's wedding. Rosmarie returned after her imprisonment in the Czech concentration camp, and resumed her work as a professional infant's nurse. Constance, their youngest daughter, had remained at home and now constantly fought illness caused by privation and malnutrition. Still, they demonstrated a kind of resilience we found heartening.

We then told them of our hopes to make our home in the United States, and our belief that soon we would leave. They understood our decision but wondered with dread how Hans' mother would react to the parting.

When we left, tears filled their eyes. But they soon turned to tears of laughter as they watched us, especially Hans maneuvering back down the trapeze-like steps to the third floor.

* * *

By 9 a.m. exactly we stood on the steps of the military government offices in Mannheim. Hans left me for an indefinite time, just as I expected he would. And I had time to think. The sun shone weakly and the wind was not exactly cold but it had the sharpness of spring. Traffic moved at varied paces—streetcars moderately, dog carts slowly and orderly, and jeeps swiftly and adroitly as they wound in and out.

These conveyances represented still diametrically opposed worlds. Would Germany eventually absorb the American influence, brought mainly through the military forces, or would it hold fast to the old and established traditions and customs?

I envisioned the past, the Germany as I had learned to know it. When I tried to rule out of my consciousness the fact of politics. I had to admit that much of life in this land had been most beautiful. Before the war, the pace of living had been serene and unhurried, and culture—music, art and drama—had abounded even in the smallest towns. Travel had been tempting and indulged in across neighboring borders. It all was so near. Vacations with skiing in the Alps in winter, relaxation on the shores of the Baltic or North Sea in summer, within reach and inexpensive.

As a young household in Mannheim, we had hunting, paddling and berry-picking in the forest of the Odenwald. Later, in Berlin, our sailboat had offered diversion and pleasure. Servants relieved any strain in the care of the children or household with occasional guests. One had not necessarily needed to be rich to enjoy all that. It was close at hand and there for the asking in whatever style one could afford, from the very simplest to the most elegant. It had been a wonderful way of life.

During the war years, I had hardly contemplated the question of whether such a good life ever would return—we were too busy trying to keep alive. And the chaos, disorder, fear and confusion still prevalent prevented thoughts of serenity or vacations. Maybe some day again we would have them, but for now it was good to be needed, busy and useful.

Our car door opened. Hans finally was back. "Through for now; more on the return trip," he said, smiling. "Now, I'm hungry!"

It took an effort to pull myself out of my reflective mood, but while Hans threaded our way through the city traffic I turned and foraged for food in the boxes on our rear seat. There were crackers, rancid butter and cheese—the same as the night before. Also powdered egg, powdered cream, a few lumps of sugar, a bit of chocolate, and some instant coffee. Now how could I turn those ingredients into a gourmet's delight? Oh, yes, I recalled, we had one small can of corned beef. But then . . . maybe I had better not touch that yet. We might need it to trade, for a special inducement if we had trouble with the car.

"What do you have there? I'm starved," Hans said.

"Oh, my dear, a rare treat of crispy salt-laden shortbread called crackers, covered with a light yellow spread of the same rancid flavor unique to the high Himalayas, often used in the prayer lamps of Tibet, only that in this case the origin is cow, not yak. Covering this is a deeper yellow substance of slightly thicker consistency, which smacks of Wisconsin wintering and premature aging. With a lump of sugar and an imaginary glass of champagne, here, sir, is your lunch.

Hans joined in this bit of nonsense; he ate my cheese crackers and declared that the lunch met my promised standard of perfection. It was delightful. Bah!

Once out of the city, we made excellent time despite the many winding roads and the narrow streets of the small towns we hurried through. Somewhere along the way we crossed into the French zone without going through a checkpoint.

Shortly before sundown we made our final stop of the day at a gas station just outside of Freudenstadt, in the Black Forest. The owner stood near his pumps. He looked us over casually for a minute, and then a tiny gleam of recognition lit his eyes.

"Gruess Gott, Herr Bohle, Gruess Gott, Frau Bohle," he said excitedly as he came to stand beside our car.

"Gruess Gott, Herr Bentler," Hans answered, as he climbed out of the car.

Our old friend smiled slowly. "I was surprised to see a civilian car pull in and hoped it would not belong to French military government personnel. What a pleasant surprise to find it's you instead. Wie geht es, un was gibt's neues (How are you and what's new)?"

Before answering those questions that involved so much, Hans asked Mr. Bentler if he could sell us any gasoline. Motioning Hans to follow, our friend walked to the pumps and then to the workshop behind them. Noticing Hans' limp, he asked about it and they stopped while Hans explained. They kept their voices subdued, and soon I gave up trying to hear their conversation.

Eight long years had passed since I last had seen Mr. Bentler at a full day's entertainment by Hans' firm for the associated retail dealers all over Germany. Mrs. Bentler had been there, too.

The program for the day had been an excursion for about 60 people, a boat ride starting at Heidelberg and traveling through the many locks on the romantic Neckar River, passing between densely-wooded, beautiful hills. Caterers had brought food on board at each of the various stops. The lovely entertainment had been highlighted on our return by a spectacular display of fireworks after dark and very special illumination of the Castle at Heidelberg, seen from the boat in the middle of the river. Then dinner and dance at the Europaische Hof until midnight.

Looking over to where the men stood talking together, I marveled at how little Mr. Bentler had changed in the intervening years.

Wasn't Hans going to get gasoline? Both men, still engrossed, walked back toward the car. As Hans climbed in, Mr. Bentler looked in toward me. "Good night," he said quietly. "We will see each other again in the morning."

We drove off! "Hans, is there no gasoline available?"

My question startled him back from wherever his mind had wandered. "Oh, yes, yes, of course. Tomorrow. For now I just found out a good place to spend the night and the directions for getting there. I don't mind saying I'd love a good sleep. You, too, Cherie?"

Yes, me too, I thought to myself. But why did he dismiss the subject of gasoline so quickly? Would obtaining some be so difficult? I wondered at the secrecy of the two men, but I did not ask. I could wait.

* * *

Hans took a narrow street up a steep hill, driving through a lovely forest of tall pines. Up and up we went, meeting no one, seeing no houses until we reached the very top. Isolated in this gorgeous woodland stood a typical Black Forest hotel. A small clearing in the trees provided a spectacular view of a village far, far below.

A slim, dark-haired, olive-complexioned gentleman walked outside to greet us as we stopped at the entrance.

"May I introduce myself," he said, shaking Hans' hand and bowing to me. "Mr. Bentler just phoned to tell me you were coming. Welcome to both of you, Mr. and Mrs. Bohle. I am happy to have you. At the moment there are no other guests. I am very much alone and could use a bit of outside stimuli." A valet took our luggage and the car was locked in the garage.

Our host showed us to a beautiful room with a private bath. "Hot water will be available immediately," he said. We could bathe and rest, and then, he asked, would we please be his guests for dinner in his private dining room at 8 o'clock?

After so many years of war, it seemed a fairyland, like old times—heavenly. We bathed, rested and shortly before 8 p.m. we greeted our host in his private parlor. From there we were escorted to the dining room, typically Black Forest, rustic and cozy, with a fire of pine logs in the huge fireplace. The table was set for three and no explanation was made for the absence of a hostess.

Our host was most charming and the dinner of wild pheasant with all the trimmings, accompanied by the appropriate wine, was exquisite. Dessert was followed by mocha and cognacs standing in the parlor. The evening was warm and friendly, so comfortably ceremonious, and we loved it.

Suddenly the perfect evening was shattered by terrible screams and crying emanating from the village below. Voices of terrified women and children reached our ears. We sprang to our feet and rushed to the window, looking questioningly to our host for an explanation.

At first he said nothing. We watched tiny figures far below, recognizable as turbaned troops, chasing the fleeing women around the houses and woodlands. The sounds of terror rose and fell and after a while ended in moans and sobs.

Finally our host spoke, his voice thickened by sadness. "Herr Bentler had so hoped you would be spared this scene. It does not happen every night, but often enough. Our poor women. The war is over, but the men do not return and the terror and horrors continue.

"During their off-duty hours, mercenaries from North Africa rape and pillage unmercifully. Many villagers who have fought back have lost their lives to the brutality and some young women have taken their own.

"Up here, we never have been molested. We are so glad we could offer you rooms, and that you and your wife did not happen to go first to the village. You are not well protected, Mr. Bohle and your wife is pretty. When you leave tomorrow, my dear young friends, please seek the most unused side roads you can find, and God be with you."

That explained Mr. Bentler's eagerness to hustle us up here before anyone noticed us. How sad we felt for the poor women and children in the village below. An urge to help somehow soon replaced the shock of our experience. But how?

In a flash I recalled a similar incident not long before in Bremen, when I had heard screams and crying one night from the backyard of our house. "Please leave her alone; she is just a child, please, oh please," I had heard a mother pleading for her daughter.

Immediately I had called the military police, but my imagination of what must be happening made me so overwrought I could not remember the name of the street on which we lived. At any rate, the screams and crying stopped almost immediately. Perhaps the young soldier's better nature prevailed and he let the girl go, or maybe the M.P.'s had heard the commotion and had come to her rescue.

Trying to keep such events to a minimum kept the military police and our public safety officers busy day and night. In Bremen I had felt relatively safe, but in the Black Forest. . . ? Where occupation troops from North Africa enjoyed free rein. . . ? What could Hans, or even my treasured American citizenship, do for me here if. . . ?

We awoke the next morning rested and reluctant to leave our peaceful haven. As best we could we offered our host our warmest thanks for his hospitality, then drove back down the slope, returning to Mr. Bentler's station for gasoline.

In the interest of a speedy transaction, he exchanged our empty Jerry cans for full ones, not taking time to refill them. His obvious haste to see us on our way made me question our judgment in stopping for gas, and I hoped he would suffer no repercussions. Everyone in the French zone seemed as frightened as our host of the previous night, Mr. Bentler, and now we, too. We thanked Mr. Bentler and bade him good-bye, and as we drove away again we heard "Gott behute sie (God protect you)."

Our luck held, and we avoided any fright or grievance for the remaining miles, except for a flat tire. An audience of poorly clad old men, pipes in hand and mouth, gathered to watch Hans make the change They smiled as they watched Hans struggle awkwardly, and volunteered no assistance. Then one old man, speaking just loudly enough to make sure we heard, expressed a view they all seemed to share. "If he can have the use of a car, he also can change its tire. I'm not helping even if he does have only one leg."

* * *

We reached Allensbach in early afternoon. The little southern town was taking its cue from the snow-covered Alps just across the lake; the streets were covered with snow. It took several false starts to finally find Mother Bohle's rooms. For weeks she had been the guest of a friend, but not wanting to impose further, she had taken two rooms in a larger apartment which she shared with her sister, Betty. Her letters had told us of other tenants in the building among whom she had found wonderful friends.

We stood, finally, in the hall of that building, facing three doors. One of them no doubt was Mother Bohle's, but which? No names disclosed who lived there. "Let's try this one, shall we?" Hans knocked, and a second later his Aunt Betty stood in the doorway.

"There you are at last. I'm so glad to see you!" she said, embracing Hans. Then she called, "Klarchen," and Mother Bohle came quickly.

"Na, da seid Ihr (Well, there you are),"—her typical greeting. "Come in, come in, don't leave the door open any longer than necessary. It's cold enough in here already.

"We've been so worried," she continued. "We hear so many stories, yet we cannot know whether there is truth in them. Sit down for just a moment so I can tell you what you must do."

She then explained that they had no room for us there. Aunt Betty already slept on a couch in the kitchen, which served them as a dining and living room as well. But Frau Meinach, a good friend, had offered to "double up" her family for a few nights.

We were sworn to secrecy and asked to make ourselves scarce on the streets, so that the French housing authorities would not learn of our presence and force the Meinachs to give up some of their already-limited space.

Happy to comply, we took our suitcases and meager belongings to Frau Meinach. The cheerful, resolute woman showed us our room—clean and simple, but cold. Still, it was the best she could do, and it was much, very much. As we left, she gave us a cake fresh from the oven.

"Take it to your mother," she said. "She wants to give you a welcoming treat for tea this afternoon. I made it because I have more coal, and I wanted to be part of the gift. The ingredients came from your mother and Aunt Betty, who saved their coupons for a whole week.

"That is mother love, my children. But you have earned it. The way down here was not easy, I'm sure, especially for you, Hans Bohle."

Our few days with Mother Bohle passed uneventfully. The two rooms in which she and Aunt Betty lived were cold except when they prepared a meal. Mother spent most of the day sitting with a blanket wrapped around her. She was not too well, so Aunt Betty did the chores.

We talked much of our experiences together before the war, told her about the children and described our work with the military government—at least to the extent it seemed prudent. We said little about our future plans. She knew of them and they distressed her. We met her friends and neighbors, visited the cathedral, and just once drove down to admire moody Lake Constance, with the outline of the Alps rising on the opposite shore.

We heard many stories about the illogical, unpredictable methods of the French rule and "misrule," which seemed to have, as its sole purpose, keeping the German inhabitants of the zone cowed and totally submissive. We wished so much we could help them, but how? All of us knew that in time, maybe much time, things would improve. Meanwhile we could only hope and endure.

The time for us to continue our journey arrived, and the parting became very different from what we had expected. My mother-in-law, a woman of intensely controlled emotion, burst vehemently into tears and sobs. Embracing Hans, she wailed, "And now, my son, you will be going to the homeland of your American wife, and I shall never see you again."

She was tall, but not quite as tall as the man she held in her arms for the last time, he who so recently had been snatched from the grave, only to be taken from her in another way. And it was with tears coursing uncontrollably down her cheeks that we had, finally, to leave her, completely broken up ourselves.

Had she hidden a much deeper love for Hans all those years? Her grief that day seemed genuine and clearly overran her usual in-check nature. I had not until that moment taken into account how alone our departure would leave her. True, we seldom had seen each other in Germany, but we had been there and accessible. With Father Bohle gone, Walter unreceptive and Hans and I and the children about to leave, her world had become pitifully small.

We drove away slowly. Shaken by her sorrow, I felt oblivious to all else. I even forgot my fears. One look at Hans' face told me that his pain was no less.

* * *

And so for awhile I did not notice that the back road we traveled followed a more easterly direction than necessary.

"Where are we going, Hans? Is this the right road for home?"

"Not directly, no, but I had an idea. Maybe we can find the Kleebergs. It cannot be more than an hour out of the way, at most. Of course, all we know is that they live in Ueberlingen, but the town is small. Before we leave Germany, I must know how those wonderful people are, and besides, it will do us both good to be with them even if only for a little while."

A new thought, a new venture. New faces, good faces, wonderful to see and love. That would help dim the agony of our last parting. But oh, then having seen them, our hearts would be sore again. Our new world would be so far away and, for awhile at least, I assumed we would be too poor to travel the long distance back.

"Yes, Hans, I think it's a great idea," I answered enthusiastically. Ever mindful that we could be stopped by military police, we drove carefully along beautiful Lake Constance, with its ever-changing moods. Shortly we arrived in Ueberlingen, a lovely, picturesque little village on the lake, where we discovered a small business center and an old damaged cathedral. After stopping to ask directions, eventually we found the unassuming, simply-equipped office of Dr. Walter Kleeberg.

Although he greeted us warmly, it was apparent that our good friend was tired and on edge. Charlotte was with him. She was his laboratory technician, office girl, bookkeeper and medical records librarian and she, too, looked very tired.

Recovering in a minute from the shock of our unexpected appearance, Charlotte laid aside her work and took us to their home, an outlying rented villa where they lived with their two children and her mother. Through good luck they had been able to buy a few mattresses, quilts a table and a few chairs and some cooking pots and simple dishes. A single light bulb illuminated this 'rich blessing."

The impoverished state in which they lived was not the cause of their distress. Those feelings stemmed from living with uncertainty, day after day, as to how long the village fathers and the French Military Government would allow them to remain and practice there, Charlotte soon explained.

Originally they had come to Ueberlingen because Walter had been ordered to the military hospital there. Their beautiful home in East Berlin had been destroyed, requiring them to begin a new life as refugees. If they were to become forced to leave Ueberlingen, they would be destined to wander from place to place until some town accepted them—a terrifying prospect since they had no certified papers, no permits, no passes.

"How much time can you give us?" Charlotte asked, eagerness in her voice. "Will you stay with us tonight?"

"If you can keep us, we will leave in the morning," Hans said. We made the decision easily, since we really wanted to spend more time in their company, and at that late hour, we could either stay with them or sleep in the car again.

That evening we shared a simple meal with the family, lukewarm for lack of fuel. Then, since it still was light, we walked with them through the apple orchard behind their house. The superb view of the lake with its backdrop of Swiss alpine splendor cleansed us for a little while of the heaviness in our hearts.

Long into the wee hours of the next morning we sat and talked, recalling our last visit together in Berlin, the day prior to our departure for Hamburg. That same day, Horst von Valtier had found his family and brought them to the Kleeberg's home for refuge. A few days later, the Army had transferred Walter to a military hospital in Southwestern Germany.

"Walter and I agreed," Charlotte explained, "to give up the house in Berlin, and that I and the children would follow him to his new station, with any civilian means of transportation we could find. Horst and his family then decided to move south as well and invited us to ride with them in their horse-drawn, straw-filled wagon.

"It certainly was no pleasure ride, nor did we expect it to be. The miserable cold slowed our travel, and our son, only six years old then, developed an ear infection that caused me great concern.

"Then one day, in the middle of nowhere, Horst stopped the wagon and told us to get off and walk. I still cannot fathom his action, so out of character. We were unceremoniously dumped out into the ice and snow with nary a town in sight."

"Impossible," I murmured.

"Yes, that's right," Charlotte continued. "I hardly could believe it either, until I stood there and watched them pull way. We all cried a little, and then started to walk. It took several hours to reach a little town where we sought help."

Charlotte paused in her narrative, and we all concluded that

Horst's nerves must have "cracked." With his high-strung temperament, it seemed the only answer.

"How did you get the proper help?" I wanted to know.

"Perhaps the day's happenings were a blessing in disguise. A kindly doctor in that little village took us in and cared for us. He also telephoned Walter and told him we were safe but that we could not travel for a few weeks until our son was well.

"By the time we finally could resume our trek, Walter had been transferred again, this time to the military hospital here in Ueberlingen, where fortunately we had friends willing to give us a room in their home. With that joyous news, we left the doctor who had befriended us and started for Ueberlingen."

"But what speed could we make in those days, when we depended totally on chance rides we could beg for along the way? By the time the children and I finally reached Ueberlingen, our friends' home was fully occupied and once more we were without lodging. But when the children's welfare is at stake, as you well know, one cannot give up. And, thank God, Walter was here and could help."

"You must have found a way," I said, proud of her. "You still are here and working, and the war is over."

"The shooting is over, but we continue to wage our little war for survival," Charlotte said. "The area became the French zone and...." Pausing, she turned to her husband. "You tell it, Walter."

A well-remembered grin appeared on Walter's face. Life to him was still a game, and he enjoyed the challenge.

"Here in Ueberingen I became a prisoner of war in my own hospital," he said. "By the time I was released, we both had decided we liked the little village and wanted to stay."

"How long were you confined to your hospital?" Hans asked, a question that brought a renewed gleam of mischief to Walter's eyes.

"Prisoner or not, I still was THE doctor in the hospital, and soon I noticed that every time I reported a patient-prisoner very sick or in need of surgery, he was released to his family. I decided that if this was the way it worked, why shouldn't we have a little more surgery around there! So a rash of appendicitis broke out—the reason, of course, poor food. The system worked so well, even when the incision was no more than skin deep and clamped or sewn, that the French Military Government decided to close the hospital as a military facility and discharged the few remaining soldiers. That left me free to tend to the townspeople," he laughed.

I could not resist asking them of their present reactions to Horst. How did they feel about him? We all agreed that our friend's nerves must have given way. Charlotte gave us the answer while Walter stood by with a far-off gaze.

"War does queer things to people," she said. "Why? I don't know. Maybe Horst responded to pressures I know nothing about, but we must forgive and forget. Upon hearing of his imprisonment, we decided to brave the dangers of crossing into the Russian zone to see what we could do for Vera and the children.

"Eva refused to leave their home as long as Horst remained in prison so near, but she allowed us to bring her four children back with us to Ueberlingen. They needed care and rest from the terrible tensions. Living in the French zone still is far freer than under Russian domination. You already know of Horst's release, but do you know that the family moved to Hamburg?"

We had not and promised that we would try to reach Horst and his family there before we departed for the United States, to help if we could.

The next morning, we bade those dear, dear friends "Auf Wiedersehen." Somewhere, somehow, we would meet again.

Hardly were Hans and I out of Ueberlingen when we realized that our car finally was protesting the long journey. The battery soon gave out. So from then on, each time we stopped the car, the motor died. The hilly, unpredictable terrain and narrow, winding roads with filled cows, geese and required many stops, so by the time we reached Mannheim for the final part of Hans' mission, I—who had to push to restart—had "conked out" too.

Fortunately, Hans and Bertha Greinert, friends from our hunting days, invited us to stay with them. They also managed to "locate" a battery we could purchase—for the proper price. That meant a can of meat in addition to money. A day and night were spent in pleasant reminiscence with that couple, who seemed to have escaped the war with no visible scars except badly frayed nerves.

Finally, with a sense of relief, we headed out once more on the last lap of our journey. The transition from zone to zone went smoothly—whether because of practice, a greater show of assurance or simply the mood of the guards, we did not care.

Two weeks away with its multitude of impressions seemed a longer time than it was and our home looked almost strange to us as we drew near. But the welcome was warm and wonderful. Our dear family really had missed us. And oh, how good to listen to the children's happy chatter while we enjoyed a good hot meal and Walter's beautiful music.

Of all the happenings during our absence, one thing stood out in the children's minds—a visit by American soldiers checking for hidden arms. Ursula had told them that ours was an American home, and we had no arms. They had believed her and made friends with the children.

The next day we returned to our offices, back into the warm fellowship of our co-workers. How nice! They, too, had missed us, they said. In fact, Hans' group announced a farewell party which we would enjoy together at the officers' club one of the next days since, as they said, "The time for your departure soon will arrive, and you must take our greetings back to our loved ones in the good old U.S.A."

We certainly hoped our departure time soon would be at hand, but our military government friends did not know of a few remaining snags to be overcome. At home again we had found a summons from the consulate, which I had answered in person.

"There is some misunderstanding," the clerk said. "The steamship company has not received payment for your reservations as yet, and it is time. And there's a new technicality. It seems the State Department has decided that for now, at least, only American citizens will be repatriated. Germans will follow later."

That would send us home in two sections. The one thing we vowed we never would allow was a separation of our family. It brought back all my sickening fears. I knew how easily a family could remain apart, once divided.

The clerk lightened my mood somewhat when she said every effort was being made for clarification. Maybe that ruling did not apply to families, only to individuals, or maybe an exception could be made for us since we were so close to departure.

I thanked the young lady the best I could. Although cold fear possessed me once more, I resolved not to neglect any way that could influence the right outcome. Hurrying to the wireless office, I sent a message flying to my brother. He would take care of the steamship company, I knew. For the rest, we just would have to wait.

At home again I found the children at play. Hans had gone to Hamburg on military government business and we did not expect him before late evening. Walter sat alone in the parlor, restless and in the mood for a chat.

"Ruth," he began as I seated myself at the window, "Do you know that the Passion of St. Matthew will be sung at the cathedral tomorrow afternoon?"

"No, and if I had, I probably would not have thought about it much. Why?" I shuddered involuntarily at the thought of how cold it would be sitting there, listening.

"You know how cold it is in there," Walter continued.

"Yes, I was just thinking about that. Are you going?"

"Yes, but I have another reason for asking. A good friend of mine is singing the soprano solo parts, and I am worried about her. She must come from Hamburg on the train, which also will not be heated. I would have liked to bring her here for a cup of hot coffee, but time does not allow. Are you thinking of going?"

"No, Walter," I answered slowly and reflectively. "I hardly think so. No, I am sure I will not." Yet all the while I felt a sudden urge, such a strong one, to be the one singing the solo parts of the St. Matthew Passion. I knew every word from memory, in English, of course. Oh, well, it was better so. Music still made me sad, and the words might choke in my throat.

"Well, then, may I borrow . . . I say, Ruth, are you listening?" I heard his voice as in the distance. "Yes, yes, go on."

"I was saying, then may I borrow your fur coat for her for a few hours?"

"Why, yes—of course! She may wear my fur coat. You may take it with you when you go to get her from the station, and do bring her back to us for a bite or something hot to drink before she leaves, if she has time."

That seemed to be all my brother-in-law had on his mind at the moment. He walked to the piano bench and seated himself letting his fingers dawdle over the keys in disjointed motifs, his eyes off in distant reflection, his mind most evidently elsewhere.

As for me, I felt like mulling over our problems—especially the new one, the possibility of a family separation. But I did not care to talk about it. Somehow I just refused to believe that things would turn out that way. I could not under any circumstances visualize leaving Germany until we all left together. I wondered just how soon we would learn of the ultimate decision. It could take days, creating seemingly-endless anxious moments. Maybe I should attend the concert at the cathedral after all. Despite the cold and discomfort, I could use the distraction and the uplift.

If Hans noted my restlessness when he returned from his trip that night, he made no mention of it. Nor did I enlighten him as to the cause. He would know soon enough. But I did ask him if he thought he could meet me at the cathedral for the program, suggesting that it might furnish a last opportunity to hear beautiful music there before our departure.

To Walter I mentioned nothing of my change of mind, but left the house the following day with a blanket thrown over my arm. It would be cold, but I would get along. A good stiff 30-minute walk brought me to the cathedral just as Captain Huston approached. Hans was already waiting. In silent understanding we entered together and found room on one of the back pews. Members of the chorus and the soloists moved into place. The performance was about to begin.

What a setting it was. It was the first time since the war's end that the cathedral had been used. If we really were leaving Germany, it would be a memorable occasion—the organ music, the singing, all in the cathedral, drafty and cold because it had been mutilated horribly by war bombs and had not been fully repaired. A huge hole in one wall and the roof left all those within the structure at the mercy of the elements.

Perhaps this near ruin was as much a part of the attraction as the music itself. The cathedral was filled to capacity with German civilians, U.S. military government personnel, U.S. military police, and uniformed soldiers from other nations—probably Holland, Denmark, Czechoslovakia and Poland, although it was sometimes hard to identify the countries as all insignia on the uniforms were removed. I found the scene touching—conquerors and vanquished sitting side by side. For a few hours, forgotten were the animosities as the glorious music reminded them of Gods love for us all and His sacrifice for the salvation of all mankind. Somehow, those of us still alive would all survive the war, and go on.

Although the blanket helped greatly, we all were stiff and shivering when we arose to leave. In the near-dark outside we parted quickly, Captain Huston headed for the officers' mess hall and we for home.

The consulate did its best to help us, and good news arrived. The obstacles which had mounted before us so quickly and so formidably were as swiftly gone. We were told that we all could leave together and should anticipate a sailing date within a week.

With real zest we hastened to make arrangements. So many little things to do, not necessarily for ourselves, like obtaining a travel permit for Ursula to return to her home in another zone; and finding a cook and housekeeper for Walter, our family bachelor, who, now that he had left Mrs. Rumpel and returned to us, needed his total time and energy to pursue his profession.

We also faced the decision of what to take with us, since only the barest necessities were allowed. Then, there were good-byes to say and thanks to express to all those wonderful people whom we loved, who had cheered and helped us along our way.

After so many disappointments and frustrations, dared we believe we actually were leaving, dared we be so open, unafraid and optimistic? Almost always we seemed to be seated on the edge of reversal and always we hoped anxiously that no new developments would undo our happiness and anticipation.

That Saturday we decided to make a quick trip to Hamburg to bid farewell to Uncle Hans and Aunt Bertha and their family. Captain Huston heard of our plan and sent with us his contribution to the celebration—a bottle of brandy purchased at the commissary for himself. Unfortunately, we put it in our suitcase.

On the trip, we encountered a hostile checkpoint officer who spoke only broken English even though he wore an English military uniform. Seldom had we met with unfriendly guards. After examining our papers, he refused to accept our word that we carried no black market items. Searching our luggage, he found the bottle of brandy.

"Ah, ha, what have we here?"

I hastened to explain, but my words did not impress him—or perhaps he did not understand me.

"You have no right to this," he said. "You know what is going to happen to it?"

I waited.

"It is going to fly right down into that river far below us, that's what."

"I believe you," I said, "but it will be empty."

Immediately I regretted my imprudent rebuttal, since it touched upon his real intentions and made him furious. I feared not for myself but for Hans, who stood beside me. The guard rummaged through our suitcases with a vengeance. Fortunately, finding nothing else incriminating, he waved us on—keeping the bottle. What would Captain Huston think about what had happened to his gift? I decided not to tell him.

By Sunday we were at home again and had guests. Waldemar and Barbara Steinecker had dropped in to see us, the same Barbara who had survived the three-day bombing of Dresden that destroyed that city. In anguish, Waldemar had spent days searching for her amid the charred bodies. She had escaped death, but she had suffered near starvation and was not well. Later that day we also saw Guenther Brink again, quite by chance. Restless and not wishing to talk, he said hello and good-bye almost simultaneously.

* * *

Life became ever more exciting. The pressures sometimes felt unbearable, and my nerves seemed at the breaking point. But the days kept passing, and as they slipped by, one by one, the chance of reversal faded with them. Finally we received word. It was Monday, and on Thursday we would sail.

On that beautiful, sunny Monday, Hans left in the early morning hours for Hamburg to complete one final mission. By late morning, we faced a new crisis. A messenger from the consulate arrived at our door saying we were to leave immediately for debarkation camp in Bremen. Anyone not there by 6 p.m. that evening would be left behind, and we would be sailing on Tuesday!

How could Hans possibly make it in time, unless we located and notified him promptly. But how would I find him? How could I let him know? Desperation stirred me into action, and I pursued every idea that came to mind, knowing that my effectiveness would be determined by nightfall.

Captain Huston stopped in to see us at noon. He knew.

"Chuck," I asked, "Why are we leaving two days early?"

"Threat of a seaman's strike, which should begin in two days. If you already are at sea, they cannot refuse to leave the harbor."

I nodded. "Do you think we've done all we can to find Hans?"

"Lieutenant Mansfield has left tracers everywhere to notify Hans for you. They'll find him, I hope, and leave it to Hans, he'll get here. Be ready yourselves with whatever you plan to take along. At 2 p.m. this afternoon, a truck will pick you up and take you to the camp.

"For tonight, I'll round up as many of your military government friends as I can on short notice and we'll come by to see you and say 'Au revoir'!"

"Chuck, how can we ever begin to thank you?"

"Don't," he answered. "It has been a pleasure." Then he ran down the stairs, pausing at the bottom to call back. "Tell Walter and Ursula to join us tonight. I'll come and get them. And by the way, don't worry about them. I'll see that Ursula gets back home and look in on Walter until he finds help."

* * *

It was 10 minutes before the 6 p.m. deadline when Hans pulled into the debarkation camp and jerked to a stop. He had had no time to stop at the motor pool. The military government would have to pick up the car there. The children and I fell upon him in relief, and he was as exhausted as we with anxiety, worry and the tension of haste. For awhile we just sat and unwound, resting quietly on our assigned double-decker bunks, a few of the countless ones set up in the huge hall. There that night several hundred unacquainted men, women and children slept without privacy, hardly aware of one another's presence, so engrossed were each and every one in their personal problems.

Supper was called and we stood silently in line and waited for our plateful. Afterward, the children curled up on their bunks while we moved to the adjoining courtyard to stroll and wait for our promised company.

They came at dusk, Hans' office friends and mine, and so many others on the perimeter of those associations. We formed a wide circle to talk, but already there was almost nothing to say. Only superlatives could express our deepest feelings, and those we could not express. So we talked about loved ones in the United States, where we might settle, and our hopes to meet those wonderful friends again some day.

But darkness came, bringing with it the camp curfew. How difficult to accept that we really were leaving those many friends who in so short a time had become so dear to us. The prior seven years had brought experiences both terrible and wonderful—terrible when it seemed we would lose our lives, and wonderful when a new future opened to us in which total strangers became our mentors and our friends. Soon we would leave them behind. The Americans would follow us some day, some of them soon, but for the moment their missions there were not completed.

With warm handclasps and fervent embraces we promised to keep contact. As for forgetting -- we just never could!

They waved as they walked through the gate of the compound, and again from their cars when they moved slowly away. We waved, too, and stood for awhile looking after them, into the darkness. Then, in thoughtful silence, we turned and walked slowly back into camp. One more night, and then. . . .

CHAPTER 46

The Lady with the Torch

June 1946

We all were eager to be up the next morning. The huge hall in which we had tried to sleep stirred with people quietly packing their few belongings. The children preceded Hans and me to the long breakfast line at the far end of the room, anxious for a warm meal.

We sat on the edges of our bunks to eat, then disposed of the plates and joined another line at the entry where huge, canvas-covered trucks had lined up to take us to the railroad station. Then, riding along, we sat in two single rows opposite each other and watched the ruins of Bremen pass by. What did Hans and the children think? I don't know. As for me, I said oh so bitterly to myself, "Good-bye Germany, I never want to see you again."

Subconsciously, I probably knew that the lump of pain in my chest eventually would go away, that the tears in my eyes would dry. When that day came, I would remember only the good—the much good—from our lives in Germany. Then we could return. For the present, however, I thought only of the ship and the voyage, and wished passionately only for the shores of my own country.

From the trucks we were settled into fourth class cars in a train, moving erratically toward Bremerhaven. The passing countryside and the novelty of our journey intrigued the children. But

Hans and I noticed the chilling damp that came in through the open doors and windows and the uncomfortable wooden seats. The ancient cars bumped along on wheels that we suspected had lost their roundness. However, we were moving, and soon that part of the journey would end.

At last we reached Bremerhaven, the dock and the ship! We stood in a great crowd, waiting to board. But how? Climb the huge ladder, that narrow bit of steel reaching all the way to the first deck and swaying precariously in the terrific wind so far out, next to the open sea?

"Women and children first," said a sailor standing by. Since ours were among the few children present, they were the first to try. Gleefully they accepted the challenge and soon stood standing on the deck above, waiting for us. Beside them stood another sailor, observing the whole procedure.

It was my turn to try the ladder. With a knapsack on my back and one arm encircling Hans Bernard, now almost three-year-old, still wrapped in his sheepskin, his arms around my neck, I climbed the ladder one riser at a time. Making headway only slowly with my heavy load, I began to feel hysteria on that tall, swaying ladder. How high was it—five stories maybe?

Halfway up, I knew I could go no further. I stopped and held on with all my strength. In addition to my burden, heights always made me dizzy and I dared not look down. The watching sailor above understood my plight and in a flash descended to my side with the agility of a monkey. Carefully he took my child from my aching arm and climbed back up. With a determined upward glance, I made it the rest of the way alone. We were escorted immediately to an officer's cabin for six on the main deck. I did not see Han's tortuous climb.

Officers' cabins were few. They were there for the women and soon filled. All men of the nearly 900 passengers, mostly Poles and Jews headed for employment in the garment labor markets, were assigned to sleeping quarters in the hold of the ship. Hans and Bob were sent there too.

Assigned to my care in my cabin with the children were two American girls, 10 and 12 years old. They had been visiting their grandparents in East Prussia when the war broke out and were finally returning to their parents in the United States after spending the entire duration of the war in Germany.

With everyone on board, the ship departed without delay. For our young charges, our children, and especially for Hans and me, the moment brought indescribable emotion, representing as it did the culmination of our dreams and the beginning of new hopes. We stayed together on deck and watched the waves until we heard the call to dinner.

The food was in no way extraordinary, except in quantity. Our children had not seen such abundance in years, and they seemed both astonished and moved. Irmgard, for example, refused an egg offered to her the next morning at breakfast, explaining that if she became accustomed to such goodies, giving them up again would be too difficult.

The first morning out, a rumor swept through the ship that we had run along a mine during the night—an unpleasant thought. But at least we knew that the likelihood of encountering such a hazard would lessen as we progressed to sea.

The vessel on which we sailed was a Liberty ship, a troop transport designed with a too-narrow hull that caused the ship to roll excessively even in relatively calm waters. Most of the passengers suffered from seasickness at some time during the voyage.

Much more frightening was the mutiny of the Cuban help on board. One night several of them went on a rampage, chasing women passengers who ran in terror, screaming for the captain and first officer. I awoke to find a Cuban sailor entering my cabin. Having grown up in a country where one mingled with people of many races and colors, I did not fear him or the other Cubans like the European women did. And so I reacted quite differently. Quickly jumping out of bed, I faced the intruder boldly.

"You get right out of here," I demanded, in English that he recognized and understood.

Stunned, he stared at me, his big eyes bulging in surprise. With one final look of consternation, he turned and fled.

The culprits were apprehended and confined for the remainder of the voyage, but as a safety precaution Hans stayed in our cabin with us at night from then on.

On the day of our arrival at the three-mile limit, landing officials came aboard and summoned the passengers for a final examination of our papers, beginning with U.S. citizens. They found my documents and those of the three younger children in order, and we all returned to the cabin to tell Hans and Bob the good news. Then it was their turn, and I waited with Irmgard, Dieter and Hans Bernhard for that last formality to be completed.

But 30 minutes passed, then 45, and still no Hans or Bob. Where were they? What could have happened? Panic seized me, along with a fear that some error in their documents would separate us after all. I looked out to the forward deck, but saw not a soul. Would a technicality, however slight, send them back to Germany? I paced the floor, unable to believe I could be losing them after all.

At last they stood in the doorway, happy and gay. The examination of their papers had gone off without a hitch, and they had decided to take a final tour of the entire ship together, never dreaming I might worry when they did not return. My surprise soon turned to anger—at them for their lack of consideration. But then I softened; we were almost home.

* * *

The sun shone hot and bright on the afternoon of June 26, 1946, when at last we arrived in New York Harbor. The Statue of Liberty was straight ahead. I went over to the left side of the ship to see her better; Hans and the children went to the right, to await the ship's tie-up.

As the majestic lady moved closer, she seemed taller than our boat, taller than I could ever have imagined her. I was suddenly overcome—emotions that must have been slumbering inside me all those years came tumbling out, and I wept openly. All of a sudden everything America stood for was just ahead. We were free. Our children were free. We would never again be forced into a police state. We were home, at last.

CHAPTER 47

Home Again in Chicago

Our first day in my parents' home left my mind in a haze. I realized that we had achieved the first part of our dreams, the children were safe. That knowledge brought a release from the terrible tension I had borne all the war years. But our struggle for survival was just beginning.

The children had fared better than we through the grueling travel conditions from New York to Chicago by train. Bob, a tall slim lad of 15, responded positively to his grandmother's prodding, stating a vague recollection of having been there before, as a three year old child. For Irmgard, now 11, Dieter, 8, and Hans Bernhard, 3, it was their first meeting with their maternal grandparents. The seven tumultuous years of war had held little time or inclination to talk about unseen grandparents in America, so for the children the impact of the meeting was strong. They realized that at last they had a family of their very own, and their happy faces showed it.

Bob found a seat in the only rocking chair and the others huddled together on the sofa.

"Are you hungry?" my mother asked. The children glanced at each other shyly. "Oh, yes," they said, and we all laughed at the eagerness of their response.

"Could we please have a piece of bread, and something to drink?" Bob asked for them all.

"With maybe some butter and jam, too?" their grandmother suggested. 'And do you like milk?"

She had anticipated their answer, and the children did not have to wait long before Grandmother and Grandfather appeared with several platters stacked high with sandwiches and a great big pitcher of milk. The sandwiches disappeared in no time. They were our first food since the meager meal of the night before.

"Well, those days are over," Grandfather said, followed by his favorite expression, "You can bank on that!" Grandmother explained to the children that they could stay as long as we wanted.

"Come, children, let's go see where you will sleep tonight," she said.

Meanwhile, Hans and my father settled in a corner for a long talk, Hans already disclosing to him our desire for a fresh start. With Hans' stump reacting to rain and cold weather of any kind, we had decided we wanted to go to California. Poor Dad and Mother. That news shattered their hopes of having their children and grandchildren nearby. But perhaps it would not happen. Dad offered to help Hans find work; he was not without influence in the Chicago community.

For awhile I listened to the men but soon was diverted by the happy prattle of the children in the kitchen, helping their grandmother get dinner on the table. She described it as simple fare, but for us it was a feast.

Finally our first day at home came to an end. Everyone settled down quickly—except me. Little Hans Bernhard was nestled close to my side on a narrow cot, and I feared crushing him. Eventually weariness overtook me and I too slept.

The next morning I wakened to find Hans Bernhard in convulsions. My frightened outcry immediately brought Hans, who lifted him high, his hands under his arms. The convulsion ended immediately. One thing was evident, that child needed much quiet and rest.

Sunday came and Mother begged us to accompany her and Father to church. "When we received no word from you for more than two years, everyone in the church said you had not survived. But I defied them. I said you still were alive and you would come to the United States. They said, 'impossible.' My faith in you and God proved them wrong. Today I want to say to them, 'See, here she is, oh ye of little faith.'"

Hans declined. I went, but probably should not have. I was greeted warmly, but I could not tolerate the opulence of the enormous bouquet of expensive, long-stemmed double chrysanthemums in a tall handsome wicker container that stood on the altar. All I could think of and visualize were hungry and homeless children—even those of some of our friends—in the midst of the devastation.

The experience saddened me for the entire day, but there was no use trying to explain. How could anyone understand who had not seen and felt the travesty of a total war?

Something good did come from that visit to church. Mrs. Larson, who during her European travels in 1930 had been a guest at our wedding, now ran the church nursery and kindergarten. She offered to care for Hans Bernhard from morning until night in the church's beautifully equipped nursery at no charge, midday meal (and nap) included. Her generous act was a wonderful show of affection for both Hans and myself, and my parents, too.

In time, relatives came to visit, including my brothers, George and Carl, and I marveled at the wonderful quiet composure of my parents in the midst of so much confusion. Carl proposed to take Irmgard back to St. Louis to stay with his family for awhile. He had a lovely daughter, he said, who would enjoy a playmate. His suggestion offered a welcome temporary solution to the crowded conditions at my parents' house, and Irmgard liked the idea, so we accepted.

The other children needed something to do. During our afternoon strolls, Dieter delighted in watching the heavy traffic on the street nearby. But one day he slipped away from us and attempted to cross the busy thoroughfare. Chicago motorists did not stop for pedestrians, even small ones, and Dieter found himself stranded in the middle of the street with cars whizzing by in both directions. He showed no signs of fright as we tried frantically to figure out how to rescue him.

Our little rascal followed up his adventure that evening by announcing that henceforth he would wash the dishes if we would pay him a nickel. He was eight years old. We agreed, assuming he would quickly lose interest in his scheme. But his enthusiasm remained, and with a smile he extended his hand for pay each day. Bob helped dry the dishes for nothing.

* * *

In the fall Bob attended Oak Park High School. He also took a paper route, at Aunt Cora's suggestion, to help with household expenses. Hans and I never should have agreed to let him try, but our temporary dependency weighed heavily on our minds, since we had not been allowed to bring money or negotiable papers out of Germany.

For several months Bob delivered 200 newspapers each morning before school. Rain or shine, his grandmother and I rose at 4 a.m. to see that he left on time, with a good breakfast and properly dressed. That was crazy, since neither he nor we were in physical condition to maintain that schedule. Bob became ill and for two days lay in a seeming coma, watched by us day and night. Our greatest fear was that he might have polio. But he soon recovered and even insisted on resuming his paper route. We put an end to that. Enough was enough!

Hans, on his own, tried to find work. Hans and I also went looking for an apartment, but with no car at our disposal, we had to use streetcars or the elevated train. So many steps, up and down. For a one-legged amputee, even for me with two, it was exhausting. Winter would bring ice and snow and bitter cold winds. No! That was not for us. We did not belong in that big city.

Aunt Cora offered to give us a down payment on a small house in Maywood, a suburb of Chicago, but without work we could not assume the responsibility. On a visit to Michigan, Uncle Will and Aunt Emma offered us $500 for a car. That was better. We would find a car for that money, if we could go on to California.

And we did find a car, in an alley garage at dusk one evening, in answer to a Daily News ad. The mechanic was inside, working in a dim light on a used car. Hans told him what we were looking for. It turned out to be an evening never to be forgotten. The mechanic noticed Hans slight accent, and his limp, and asked us to stay for a drink and some bread with him at a little table in the corner.

We talked until midnight about the war. He had been a pilot, dropping bombs on our heads, he said, and wanted to know if we had felt bitter against him for having done so. We felt no bitterness, we assured him. Just like Hans, he had been a soldier, responding to his country's call.

At midnight we still had no car. He then told us. He would find a suitable car for $500, put it in tip-top shape and deliver it in two days. We had found a compassionate man. He did that, and a year later, while traveling in California, he found us and stayed with us for about a week. Before he left he tuned our car, put a $100 bill on our kitchen table and quietly disappeared. We never saw him again, that kind and thoughtful man.

* * *

Two famous violins, one of them an Amati, were in our possession when we left Germany. They were a gift from a dear friend, a member of the Mannheimer Symphony Orchestra. He hoped their sale would yield a sizable sum for a new beginning.

Lyon & Healy in downtown Chicago was the place to go with them, but their best offer was $500. No sale. Not knowing where else to turn, we insured the two with Lloyds of London and decided to take them with us.

With the car already in our possession, all we needed to leave for California was money, which we would get somehow. It began with an annuity insurance policy I had left with Mother 16 years earlier. It was in my name and had matured. We used part of the money to buy a few bit of camping equipment and decided it was time to leave, even with such few assets. Seeing our determination to go, Aunt Cora and George came to our rescue. They received a "note of promise," and the promise was kept.

My parents were sad and we hated to leave them, but we were anxious to go. Each member of the family, in turn, warned us about the dangers of such a trip. Cross-country travel was a much different proposition in those days, before interstate highways, air conditioning and motor clubs. What if our car broke down in the desert, miles from help, they asked. We recognized the hazards, but we did not care. We felt compelled to get on with our lives. That meant California, so we prepared to leave.

Perhaps my family also worried about what they would do with our children if something happened to us. But Hans and I had considered such a contingency. We had recently corresponded with two couples from our past, wonderful friends who we knew would care for our children if the need arose.

One of the couples, Fred and Billie Wissenbach, were friends from our Munich days. Fred had studied art and pastored a church there, and we had helped finance their return to the United States. They had settled in Klamath Falls, Oregon. In correspondence they had offered, without hesitation, both a home and work. We declined their invitation reluctantly because of possible snowy winters, but promised to visit them some day.

Instead we were headed for the other couple, Fritz and Anne Laun. Fritz and Hans had known each other in Germany, and had roomed together during Hans stay in Chicago prior to our marriage, when the four of us had spent many happy hours together. They lived in Pasadena, Calif., and had invited us to come stay with them while we got settled. To them we would go, sending for the children once we had a place of our own.

On September 1, 1946, Hans and I loaded our car, said a tearful good-bye to my mother and father and our children, and set out on another trip together—one that would begin the next chapter in the life of our family.

CHAPTER 48

Westward Ho

We headed first to St. Louis, where we spent two days with my brother Carl, his wife Esther and daughter Linda—and, of course, Irmgard. She seemed happy with them and accepted that we were leaving again; she did not ask to go with us.

From St. Louis we headed west on the old Route 66—the primary highway connecting the East and West coasts. We passed through many little towns, considering each as a possible new home—which convinced us we did not like little towns. A middle-sized town in California might do; but our final selection had to be in a warm climate!

We spent one night in Texarcana, Ark., a rough frontier town. The following day found us in Texas, with a new plan, away from Route 66. We had decided to visit Billie Wissenbach's sister, Ruth. She lived in Rogers, Texas, near Waco, with her husband, Hansford Berry.

Rogers, we found, was a cluster of little homes, a tiny town not much more than a stop-over place in the middle of unimportant roads, consisting of a main street and a general store. Hans stopped at the store. Hans told the pleasant lady who greeted us that we were looking for a Mrs. Berry

"I am Mrs. Berry," she replied. As we introduced ourselves as friends of the Wissenbach, her face lit up. "How wonderful of you to stop here. Billie and Fred told us much about you. I hope you can stay. Oh! You must come home with me. We have so much to talk about. I will close the store for the afternoon. Customers needing anything will find me at home. That is not unusual." She grabbed a big steak and other edibles out of the refrigerator and was ready to leave.

Soon we found ourselves at a very nice, well built modern two-story house. Mr. Berry was at home, a rugged gentleman dressed in a cowboy hat and jeans.

Dinner preparation began in the midst of great and animated conversation, revealing interesting things about our hosts. They were ranchers. They owned and operated cotton plantations, vegetable and fruit gardens and a wonderful herd of Hereford cattle. All produce and meat sold in their store was from their ranch. The children's clothing had also been spun, woven and made from their own cotton. Seemingly in the middle of nowhere, the operation was overwhelming, benefiting all the surrounding vicinity. All that we learned from Ruth. Hansford, evidently a man of few words, seemed content to let her carry the conversation while he participated with rapt attention.

Eventually the conversation changed to our relationship with Billie and Fred, and then the war. Later Hansford suggested that Hans and I drive out to see his fabulous herd.

"There's plenty of time," he insisted. "We want you to stay for the night."

We climbed into a jeep, which initially took us swiftly to his cotton fields and then through rough back country roads with trees and small streams crossable only by means of a simply constructed swinging rope bridge, to his cows. We pulled up in front of a fenced-in pasture, where several dozen black and white cows stood grazing. They were beautiful, and he clearly loved them, petting each animal that came to his call.

On our return trip Hansford helped a fellow Texan whose car had slipped off a rope bridge and gotten stuck in the mud. Evidently it was not a new experience. The car was quickly brought back on the road and the owner drove off without a word, but with a wave of thanks and farewell. Obviously, "help" and "goodwill" were the law of the land.

Early the next morning preparing to leave I found Ruth packing a huge bundle of clothes. Handing them to me, she said, "These are for your children." With that she bade us a tearful good-bye, thinking no doubt of the long, lonely journey that still faced us—and the even-harder road of recovery we had mapped out for ourselves. In less than a day we had come to feel as though we had always known each other, and for years thereafter we stayed in touch regularly.

Hansford led us out through a maze of narrow roads, past ranch houses set so far back that they could hardly be seen. We wondered where he was headed, when after an hour's drive, we reached a main artery. Hansford then gave us a quiet farewell, indicating the way in which we should continue our journey. Just a wave of the hand and a fleeting smile was all. It was enough; he was a quiet man.

* * *

Day after day thereafter, we wound our way through lonely, vast Texas—San Angelo, Amarillo, Lubbock. Our route next took us into New Mexico, through Carlsbad, then back into Texas. We were making progress, and each hour we ground up made us more delirious with excitement.

As we neared Tucson, Ariz. the hot, sticky September weather produced a terrific electric storm. Jagged, thick bolts of lightning filled the sky, and torrential rains filled the road. It was frightening, so we turned into a side road that headed uphill, as were other cars, and parked there until the storm ended.

"I see you saved yourselves from the ravages of a flash flood," remarked a passenger in the car next to us. "Luckily, there was a hill here." Hans turned to me and asked if I had known about flash floods? "No," I said, "but we do now."

We liked Tucson the minute we drove into it. The first building we saw was the entrance of a new, small, one-story motel, banked by beautiful desert plants. The tan structure had a brown, low-hanging gable roof and a wide glass entrance. It looked most inviting and strangely cool in the blazing hot sun. The proprietor greeted us pleasantly and showed us to a comfortable room, furnished in desert style—clean and as cool as promised.

We stayed at the tiny motel in Tucson resting and relaxing for several days, realizing again and again the rashness of our decision to cross the burning desert in September without foreknowledge of conditions we would encounter. To avoid making a greater mistake, we informed ourselves with books, pamphlets and discussions about the formidable desert we still had to cross.

Already two weeks had passed since we left Chicago. We still felt positive about California, but a stray magazine in the motel gave us an idea.

"Listen to this,' Hans said on the third day. "'The Bank of Phoenix is looking for partners to share financially in the development of small businesses to aid the city's development program

"If we could sell our violins, there might be something for us. I have business experience. Does that appeal to you?" he asked. Well, why not, I thought. We just need a place of our own to put down roots. Let's go investigate.

We drove north to Phoenix and talked to a bank official. They were looking, however, not for someone ready to work. They wanted a financial partner. Too bad! It might have been nice.

* * *

Again we headed north, toward Flagstaff. The weather continued to favor us as we drove through miles and miles of open, mostly semi-arid land, only occasionally spotting an animal. We had been told that it took 30 acres of such land to feed just one cow.

Eventually the terrain became more rolling, and off in the distance we saw the forerunners of the San Francisco peaks. Late afternoon found us in those hills, shocked at seeing old deserted mining towns, mostly in ruins, still hanging precariously from the mountain sides—rather eerie. Even the narrow road around them was dangerous, narrow and slanting.

Darkness was settling fast and we needed to find a place to sleep. We drove down into the recesses of the valley below, toward Oak Creek Canyon, artists' colony and hideaway. No sign of anyone, anywhere, in that sparsely settled territory. It was dark when we found shelter at a tiny, nondescript inn.

The next morning we began a climb of 7,000 feet to Flagstaff. It was a long day on the road. We arrived in time to buy food for the night. Snow covered the ground at that altitude, and we shivered in the cold, such a sharp contrast to the desert heat. We saw mostly Indians, some in native dress. Their unfriendly manner suggested that few travelers ventured that way.

At a butcher shop, the butcher refused to sell us anything smaller than a full leg of lamb—nothing we could use that night. No warm food for us, but our lodging was warm and adequate.

We awoke anxious to leave. Our food supply was limited—apples, cheese, bread and water. But what should we do with the lamb? We would be back driving through the red-hot desert and it would spoil. Thus we resolved to drive straight through to Pasadena, Calif. by nightfall, to save the lamb.

We eyed each other questioningly, then laughed. Could we do it? Anything to save the lamb and end the long journey, of which we had grown weary. So we pushed on, back into the flat, broiling desert.

The road took us past a fence-guarded desert section where A-bomb tests probably had once been conducted. Vestiges of buildings, no longer occupied, lay bleaching in the terrific heat. We saw a few small settlements, and occasionally a tree or mirage.

We drove at top speed, taking turns at the wheel. With no air conditioning, the heat in the car was nearly unbearable. Occasionally the continual desolation and the heat made us fearful. What would we do if we got lost or the car did not function? Would anyone find us in time? We pushed on across Arizona, through Williams, Seligman and Kingman, then into California and through the Mojave Desert.

We reached Palm Springs at 5 p.m., just as the sun disappeared behind some very high, Rocky Mountains. Their jagged silhouettes looked strange and formidable to us. Always only rocks —so new and strange. Where were the trees?

Continuing westward through San Bernardino, we finally reached our destination in the outskirts of Pasadena. Hans pulled the car to a sharp stop, blew a long breath, looked at me with a big grin and said, "We made it!" A miracle accomplished in one day.

Weary but exuberant, we stood at 8 o'clock that evening in the twilight outside the door of our good friends, Fritz and Anne Laun. When we knocked, the door flew open immediately, as if we were expected, and with a great cry of joy Fritz and Anne engulfed us in their arms.

"We're so glad you are here," said Fritz. "We expected you all last week, and worried that something might have happened to you. It is a very dangerous journey."

Anne wiped her eyes. "Come in, come in," she said. She led us into their parlor, while Fritz brought in our luggage. He then led Hans to our room, while Anne and I went into the kitchen to warm leftovers from their dinner for us. We left unpacking for later except for the now priceless, still well preserved leg of lamb.

Hans and Fritz shared much common ground, particularly their German heritage. The intervening years had done nothing to diminish their longstanding friendship, and they were joyful in being reunited. They laughed and hugged and joked.

"This is wonderful," I said to Anne. "Hans hasn't been this happy in a long time. Bless you for wanting us to come." Anne was excited too, and I saw her again wipe a tear from her eyes. "We need you too," she said quietly.

While we ate, we told them how we had gotten our car, about St. Louis, the Berrys, the little happenings along the way, also of Phoenix.

"And how was the reception in Chicago when you arrived?" they asked. Hans left the explanation to me.

"Exciting and exhausting. A dream come true for my parents," I said. "They wanted us to remain with them in Chicago, but we were fully aware we were really a nuisance and could hardly wait to leave. We are determined to find new lives for ourselves in a warm climate and Chicago's climate is no place for an amputee. I am sure my family is actually relieved that we are solving our own problems, fending for ourselves on our own."

"You are not alone," Fritz said emphatically. "You will make it; we will help. You must stay here with us until you are settled."

* * *

Within two weeks we sold our violins to a Hollywood entertainer at a good price. Then we began to search for housing. We discovered that in Southern California, that was very expensive. Hans also began contacting oil companies he had worked with while in Germany. It was discouraging. He was told he was "overqualified" for a lower-level job and executive positions were, understandably, being reserved for returning GIs.

For the next six weeks, Hans responded to other ads, submitted applications and attended interviews, all negative. So after two months in California we decided to try ranching, inspired by Hansford and Ruth Berry's wonderful example of what could be accomplished.

We found a small ranch about 40 miles from Pasadena in Cucamonga, financially within our means, we thought. Five acres of excellent orange trees and another five equipped to handle several hundred chickens, a small but adequate farmhouse in a picturesque setting. A gentleman farmer was running it. He and his wife were tired of ranching and wanted to go to Hawaii.

We knew nothing about ranching. However we just felt right about it, impulsively buying the property almost on the spot.

A week after we moved in we sent for the children. Two weeks later they arrived on the Santa Fe Chief, having traveled two days and a night together, even little Hans. It was November and hardly four months since our arrival in the U.S. Together as a family at last.

CHAPTER 49

Together in California

Our introduction to our new life as a family in California began with a steady four-day downpour. The children immediately got an introduction to the fact that it was raining, but the chickens needed tending, fair weather or foul. Hans could not be expected to go slipping and sliding on the muddy paths to do chores. All of us began, more carefully, to assess what needed to be done to make our crazy venture a success.

Much about the place was appealing: the roomy little house, well-built, country style and old; the trees and fresh air; Mt. Baldy rising in front of us to 10,400 feet, soon to be crowned by snow; the lack of outside stress; the Santa Fe Super Chief rushing by each day, such fun to watch; a neighborhood school one-half mile away for three of the children and a high school in Ontario for Bob by bus; a hospital within reach; and kind and friendly neighbors nearby. All this was positive, raising our confidence.

But had we assessed correctly the money needed to operate the farm before we would earn a profit? We had bought the barest necessities for the house and warm clothing for the children. The nights were getting chilly and we would soon need heat. We also needed oil for the smudge pots and prepared ourselves for a nightly vigil to make sure our orange crop would not be damaged by frost. Clearly I would have to rely on help from Bob. Maybe with careful, frugal living, we would make it work. There was much to learn.

The children were cheerful, never complaining, accepting another change in their lives like troopers. Fritz and Anne Laun and their son Wilfred came each weekend, always bringing food and sometimes clothing. Christmas arrived, and with the company of our friends it was lovely. Evenings found Hans and I starting to write our memoirs as we remembered them, irrespective of where they stood in the total picture.

In January we harvested some of our oranges. The profits from oranges and poultry were not bad, but they were not enough. One night, we found that we had paid our bills but had hardly enough money to put food in the house. As it happened to us, even throughout the war years, whenever we did not know where to turn next, something wonderful happened. So it was that Wednesday night.

It wasn't the weekend, their usual time, yet there were the Launs, bringing with them a fully cooked pot roast and all the trimmings. "A premonition," they said.

* * *

Hans felt the need to do more than he could at the ranch. He found work as a full-time bookkeeper for the nearby farmers association. That, and the reduced need for heat and other winter expenses as spring arrived, helped the money pot.

As summer approached with warmer temperatures, we began living out-of-doors most of the time. We harvested mulberries and figs from our own trees and ate our meals under a gorgeous tree that bore chestnuts by the bushel. We also acquired a few dogs, two cats, and a family of bantam chickens, all of them sleeping on our covered patio at night.

Just for a change and some fun, the Launs one day persuaded us to go on a picnic in a wild reserve on Mt. Baldy, about a half-hour drive from the ranch. A ranger met us and warned us "no shooting." We found a nice open space, spread our food on a tablecloth on the ground and allowed the children to roam close by.

Our sense of peace was quickly ended when Irmgard came and said, "Come see the nice pussy cat we have found." It was a Bobcat that they had found in a trap that never should have been there. The cat was almost dead.

We admonished the children to remain with us, but of course Bob managed to sidestep the order by showing up a few moments later with the now-dead cat. "I took it out of the trap," he said. What novices we were.

It can be said ranch life was never dull. Now and then Mexicans came from their camp about a mile away to buy whiskey. Sometimes they tried to get into the coops at night to steal chickens or eggs. To help prevent a habit forming in that direction we installed a system of lights that flooded the area with light whenever I pressed a button at my bedside.

One night quite a commotion broke out around the coop and barn. The floodlights revealed an animal being chased by one of our dogs, rushing into the barn. In a flash I was out, slamming the barn door shut to imprison the animal, assuming it was perhaps a coyote or cougar from the neighboring wildlife area.

Hearing noise, our neighbors came with rifles over their shoulders, anxious to be of assistance. Before opening the barn door we peered through a small window. The frightened animal crouched in a corner. No coyote or cougar, just the neighbor's own dog. Our neighbors were embarrassed, but it was really so funny, and in the end we all had a good laugh.

With only one car, I had to take Hans to work in the morning and get him again after dark. One morning I had just recrossed the Santa Fe railroad tracks in a dense fog when the Super Chief whizzed by not more than five feet behind me. I screamed as it passed traveling 90 miles an hour. Paralyzed with fear, I almost killed the motor. I decided not to mention it to Hans.

Two years passed and it was time to assess the future. We weighed our gains and losses, then decided our progress was not enough to make ranching our livelihood. Two winters of monitoring the orchard for potential frost, lighting and refilling smudge pots when needed, cleaning chicken coops, checking the birds for diseases, monitoring their water and food supplies, collecting eggs and preparing them for market, butchering and cleaning chickens and preparing them for delivery, irrigating during the summer, all took its toll on us, even with the children's help. Ranch life had been wonderful, but we were ready to move on.

* * *

During this next phase of our life, Hans became a citizen. He decided to anglicize his name, which when translated, became John. He found a bookkeeping job with a construction company in Ontario, Calif. We sold the ranch and moved into a small rental house on Fourth Street. For John it was convenient and I could take the bus to the community hospital in Upland, where I now worked. The children walked to school. The transition was relatively simple.

With the move came a number of added benefits. With both of us at work, we now had steady income and weekends to spend with our friends, including the Launs who helped us beautify our new home with a coat of paint.

Most important of all, John liked his work. The bookkeeping was routine, leaving much time to study the art of estimating construction projects, which fascinated him. He quickly developed his own skills and before long began to assist the owner of the business with other operations.

We settled into a routine. Everyone was happy except Dieter, who was constantly harassed about his name by schoolmates who called him "Diaper." He begged to have it changed. At his request Dieter soon became Charles, named after the military government officer Charles (Chuck) Huston, who had so generously befriended us in Bremen. Believing that our youngest, Hans Bernhard, might encounter the same problem, we had his name legally changed to

John Bernard. Irmgard kept her name because she liked it, even preferred to have one that was unusual. Those who tried to call her "Irma" were politely but firmly corrected.

Two years passed by quickly. Then suddenly John lost his job to the owner's son, who had decided to join the business. John was not dismayed. He had learned estimating so well that he felt confident he could find another job quickly. And, soon after, he joined a much larger construction firm in San Bernardino, about an hour's drive each way. As the firm grew, so did John—to the point where the firm decided to expand its operations to San Diego and appoint John as their chief estimator and office manager there. It was a wonderful opportunity, but since it was a two-hour drive each way, we got to see John only on weekends.

Even with the advance in his salary and my small income, the looming fact that Bob soon would be ready for college compelled John to take on additional small bookkeeping jobs on Saturdays and Sundays. My work at the hospital never seemed to offer an advancement in pay, although my duties had become heavier, until one day when I let it be known that I had a better offer from the neighboring hospital.

* * *

Time was stretching out into years with John away from us too much. We considered moving to San Diego, but doubted that its slow growth ever would offer the challenges that John sought. Eventually he applied for a job in Los Angeles and was hired quickly by another construction firm. Another move for the family was inevitable—Los Angeles was too far for a daily commute.

Anne Laun came to our rescue again. She had lost Fritz about a year earlier and had become a real estate agent. She found us a charming two-story Spanish home in Pasadena, near schools and only 20 minutes from John's new office. I found work assisting several doctors, specialists whom I had met at the hospital in Upland. We moved and, happily, the children liked their new surroundings. Unfortunately, John's new firm was not sound financially and folded within a year.

Needless to say, John was out looking for new work. One morning his attention was drawn to a tiny, half-inch ad in the Los Angeles Times: "Estimator Wanted." Wondering how big a firm it would be that needed only an unpretentious ad, he responded. It turned out to be the Los Angeles office of a large San Francisco-based construction company, an old and well-established business. His resume was received and discussed, some wondering whether John's experience was enough to handle projects as large as theirs. Then one of them decided. "Let's take him," he said. "He's German, and they know how to work." A three-month try was agreed on and John stayed 12 years.

It was a marvelous opportunity. John had found his niche. He was a natural at his work and loved every minute of it. The atmosphere was harmonious and they trusted his work. He was especially adept at finding ways to cut costs on projects that were over budget. As a consequence, he was soon asked to travel to the Hawaiian Islands to trouble shoot an important project which was having difficulty, and I occasionally got a chance to go along.

Over dinner along the shores, John would tell me some of the problems his firm encountered. One of them—and easy one, he said—concerned a 30-story building, the location so close to the water's edge that pumps would be required to keep out the water at high tide. The distance from floor to ceiling in the lobby of the building was 20 feet. Raising the floor by two feet would surely not be noticeable or spoil the appearance of the building and the pumps could be eliminated or at least would not often be required. Eliminating some of the fancy roof decor, which would only be seen from the distant hills anyway, brought the budget farther back in line. Of course, the required consent of the architect who had created the building design was not always easy to get.

There were other cases, sometimes very stressful, which often brought on terrible nerve pains in John's stump. That was a constant problem, since the pains became so unbearable he couldn't sleep at night and I questioned if he could continue to work. But once the pain subsided, his lips would curl up in a ready smile. "What's over is past," he would say. John's wonderful sense of humor, his forward looking attitude and ever present optimism served him well throughout those many years.

* * *

Much had happened while John was building his new career. We heard from the Midwest only at special occasions, such as my parents' Golden Anniversary and my father's and Aunt Cora's passing. Each time I alone made the trip to Chicago. Aunt Cora had left a legacy to all, including me, which I shared with John. The amount of the check, which we received after a two-year wait, exceeded our expectations and gave us a nice boost.

We changed homes several times, sometimes renting. Our wonderful children went along with all our shifts, sharing our sense of adventure. One after another entered the university and graduated. All brought home their friends, sharing their relationships and experiences with us. All found ways of paying a substantial share of their education.

Now and then calls came asking for advice, a request of help or to share a special event. On more than one occasion we drove Friday night after work until 3 a.m. to Northern California to have breakfast at 8:30 a.m. with them, giving help where needed. We stayed a day and then once more drove through the night to Los Angeles to get back in time for work Monday morning. While such trips were strenuous, we felt a special joy in being able to share the children's successes, trials and tribulations. No call ever went unanswered.

For all of them, the University of California at Berkeley was their alma mater, although our youngest, John, spent his first two years at Cornell. A strong allergic reaction to the many elm trees on campus brought him, too, to Cal.

Eventually they all married and brought us many wonderful grandchildren.

With Aunt Cora's legacy, we found it possible to invest, at a bargain, in a large hilly lot in Pasadena, which we later divided into three portions, selling two for homes and leaving one for us. On that section John built a modest home, fulfilling a life-long dream. It became a great place for our family gatherings and our German visitors.

Saturday breakfasts became famous—the smell of bacon, eggs, hot coffee, cocoa, fresh warm breads and fresh fruit salad, usually laced with cognac, and all of it accompanied by symphonic music, played through our speakers at full volume with John singing along and waving his arms, conducting the music while he cooked.

One year John received three weeks vacation so we could return to Germany for a grand reunion with the many friends who had shared the war years with us. They all had made a splendid comeback from the ravages of war, all but Horst von Valtier, who had never recovered from his two-year imprisonment by the Russians. Once again we visited our old haunts, the hunting grounds in Heidelberg, the ski slopes and the great days of our early marriage.

Events in California the following winter made us decide to leave the hills for safer ground. The smog was thickening constantly, the unusually severe and lengthy rainy season left houses and swimming pools seemingly hanging on a thread on the hills above us. A watchful eye one night quickly diverted a mudslide that easily could have filled the whole house or even moved it off its foundation. Nine days and nights of rain without stop.. would it ever stop?

We decided to sell our now too large home in Pasadena to young people who could take the stress. We found a little "doll house" in Irvine, close to the ocean breeze. Wall papered and painted, small and compact, with indoor Jacuzzi and an outdoor enclosed patio to clean air, it seemed nearly perfect. In back was a long grassy lawn with trees. But it was a long way to work for John.

Another year went by. John was 67 years old and it was time

to retire from the company. During the following months, he took leave of his friends at Swinnerton & Walberg in Los Angeles and established an office at home, notifying builders and architects that he was in business for himself. For the next 12 years, he never was without work nor was he ever left unpaid.

Our family was still a lovely unit. We saw them and our growing number of grandchildren often. The famous breakfasts were still in vogue. Unfortunately, Bob and Barbara and family lived in St. Louis and could be with us only for special events.

As a freelancer, John was able to use his time as he chose, and we returned to a bit of travel, making special trips in and out of the country. Once more it was Hawaii with a drive over the still-hot lava from a recently-erupted volcano, and a peek at the rebuilt harbor in Hilo, hit and destroyed by a great tidal wave from the great Alaskan earthquake a few years earlier. We loved eating at a little restaurant at the base of Diamond Head at sundown, watching a ship disappear over the horizon bound for the United States, the flares and torches lighting up the small beach in front. And last, but not least, feeling the soft, gentle trade winds around our heads. Magnificent!

The Canadian Alps came next and, needless to say, that was a trip one could make more than once and still be entranced. But we also had to see the Panama Canal, one of the wonders of the world, a monument too important and wonderful to give away.

By 1985, at age 78, John was showing signs of progressive weakness. Even though he still enjoyed the work and still was in demand, he gave in to my urging and agreed "it was enough." We began to take afternoon rides in the country, to the sea and various other sites, even stopping for leisurely window-shopping.

Friends noting our habit urged us to visit them on such occasions. They lived in a retirement community in Laguna Hills, not far from us and thought we should see it. We did so and admired their home, and were enchanted by the whole area, its well-kept beauty and the opportunities and advantages it offered. One of the manors, located across from a small creek and surrounded by beautiful trees, was vacant. We went to see it. For some reason known and understood only by himself John sat down at the dining room table and wrote out a check for $2,000 as a down payment, then and there. So we put our wonderful house in Irvine on the market, sold it for a substantial profit and moved into Leisure World.

The home John chose was light and airy, with a living room, dining area, two bedrooms, two baths and a kitchen. The living room and bedrooms overlooked a wonderful ravine that sloped down 50 feet or more to the creek bed. During the rainy season, the creek's usual trickle became a raging river, although the ravine was deep enough to prevent flooding. In the summer the tall trees were filled with leaves that screened other homes from view. Birds, raccoons and other wild animals abounded.

The gated complex contained gardens, tennis courts, swimming pools, facilities for gymnastics and six clubhouses for entertaining. Medical facilities, shopping and churches were right outside the gates. More than 20,000 seniors over the age of 62 lived in the community. Today I realize why, without question, John wanted this change. He already felt his years were numbered and in his thoughtful loving way was thinking of me and my future alone.

Our travels ended shortly after we moved as John's health deteriorated rapidly. Finally on December 3, 1988, after three years of constant pain and suffering, my dear husband, friend and the love of my life, departed for the great beyond.

A memorial service was held in our home on December 18, attended by more than 70 guests—friends, relatives, neighbors and business associates. It was not a mournful occasion, as John was a happy person He would not have had it any other way. What a wonderful party to start a new journey. The special warmth shared by family, friends, neighbors and colleagues during this occasion reflected his approach to life. He would have loved to have been there. I'm sure he was.

As was his wish, John's remains were cremated and his ashes

strewn to the waves of the Pacific Ocean. So, too, will mine when my time comes.

John left behind for all, and especially his family, a legacy of courage, fortitude and love. Years earlier, as a young 10-year-old girl, I had incurred my father's displeasure by finding and reading a marvelous story of the tender love of a man for his lady. I had resolved at that time to find such a love for myself. In John I had found it.

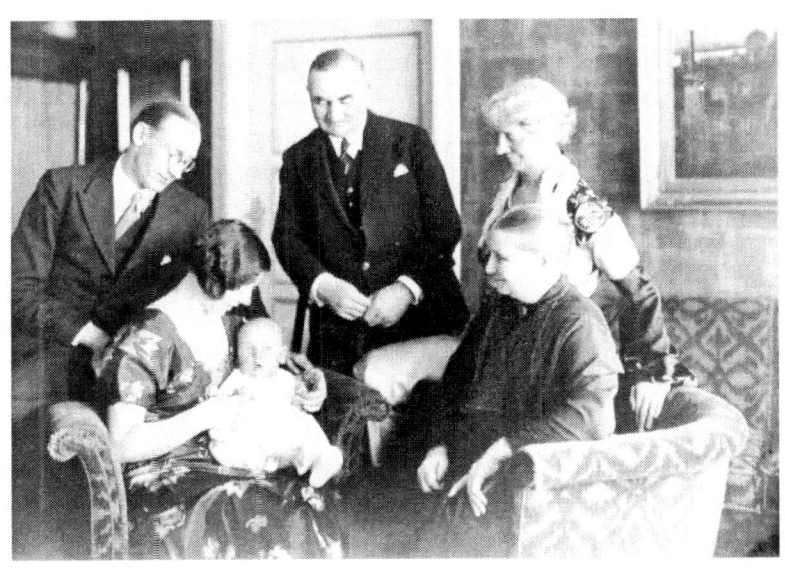